NTR Netsuzou Trap 2

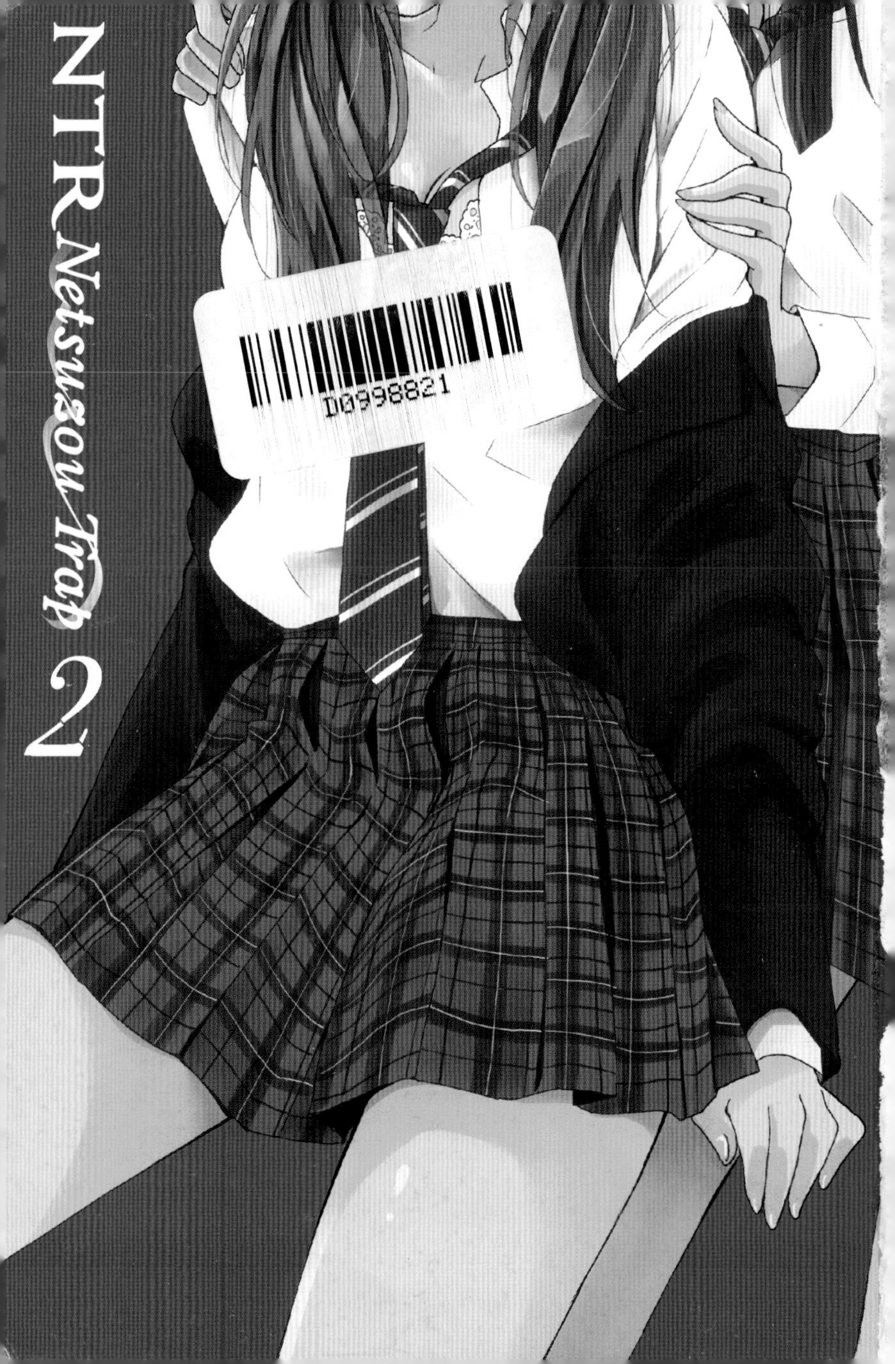

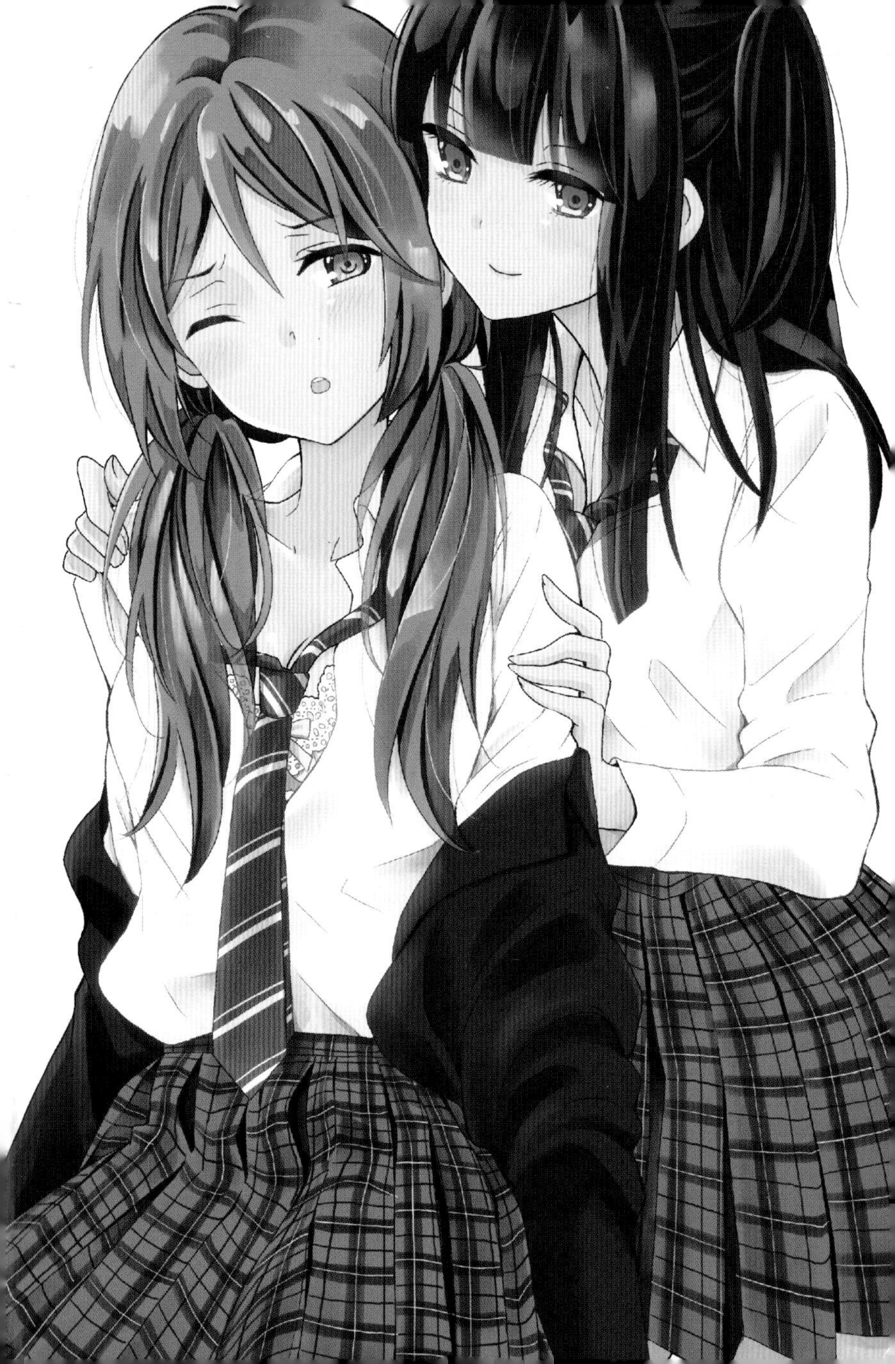

trap 5

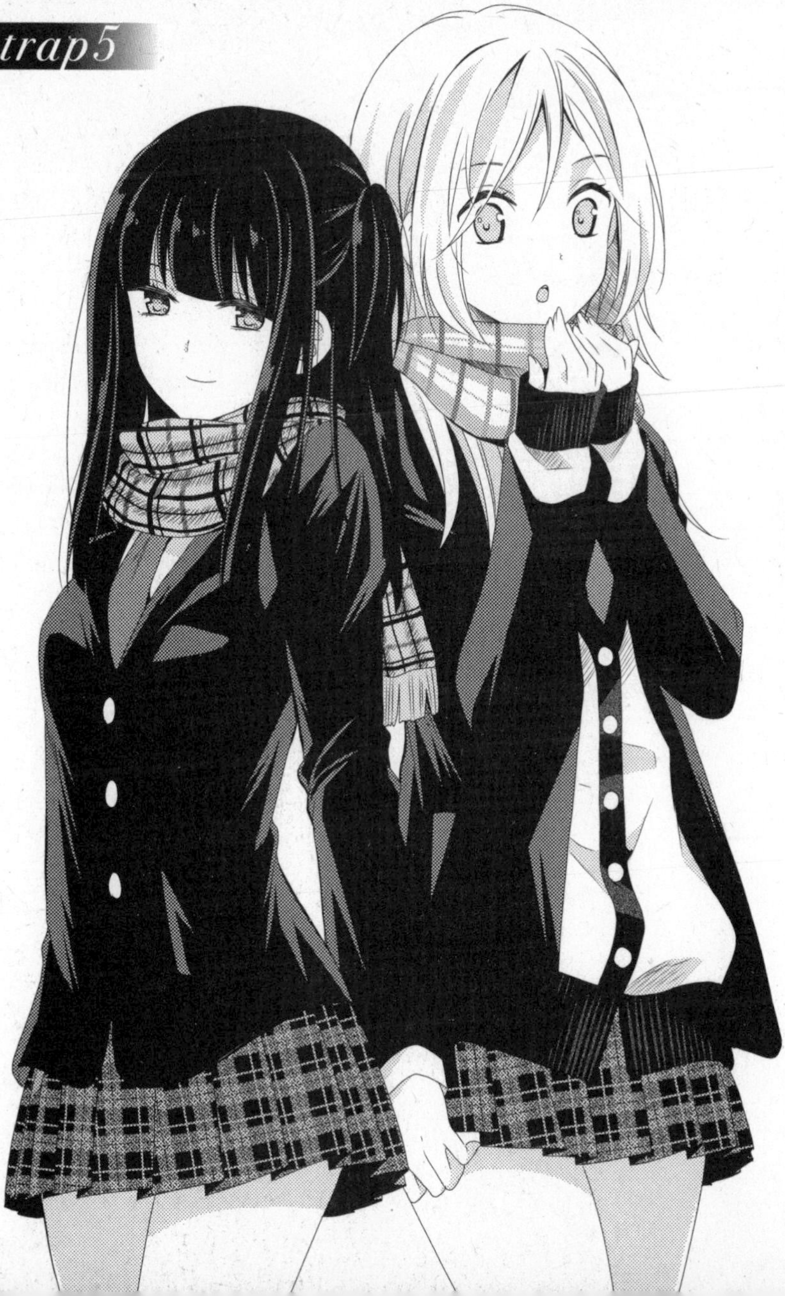

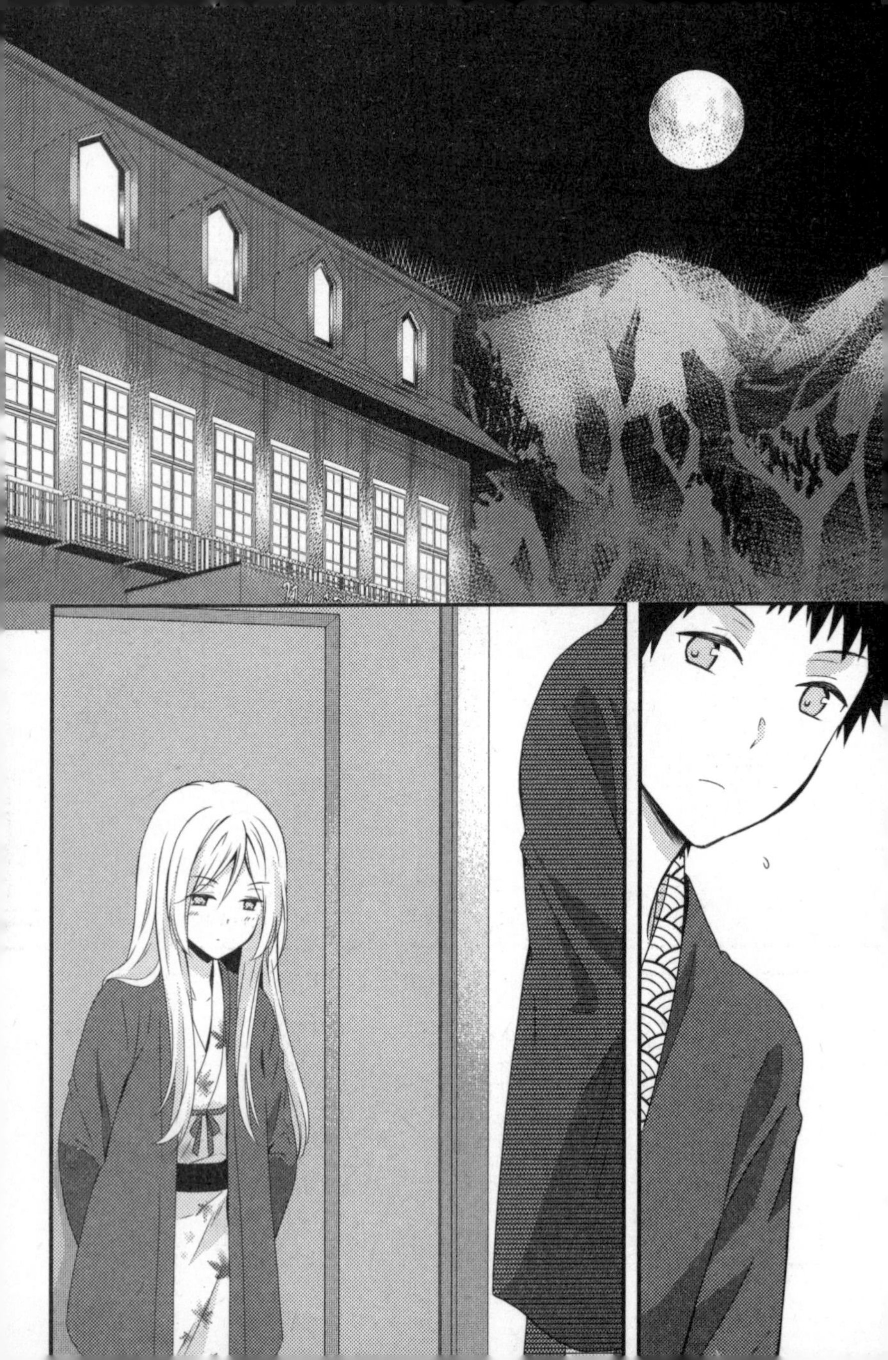

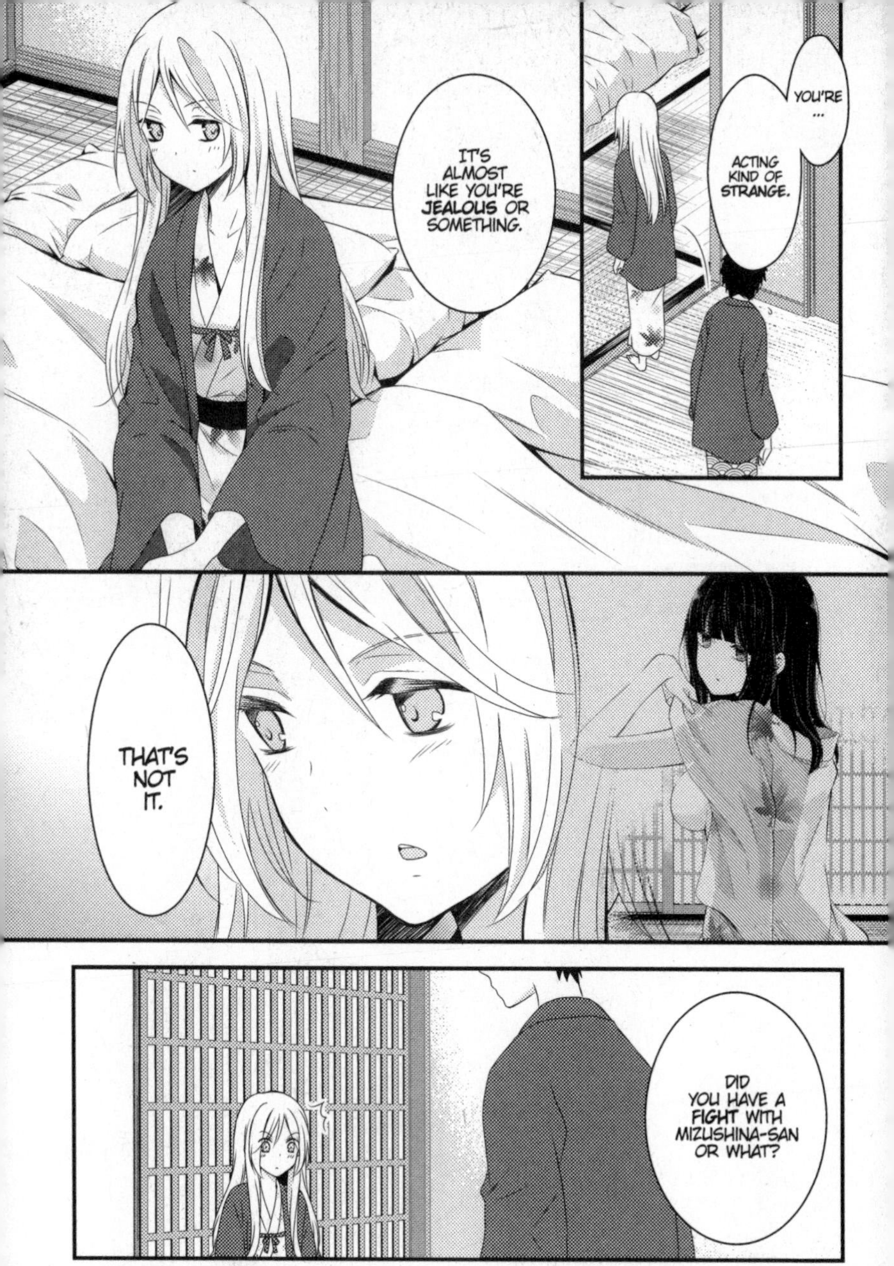
YOU'RE ...
ACTING KIND OF STRANGE.
IT'S ALMOST LIKE YOU'RE JEALOUS OR SOMETHING.
THAT'S NOT IT.
DID YOU HAVE A FIGHT WITH MIZUSHINA-SAN OR WHAT?

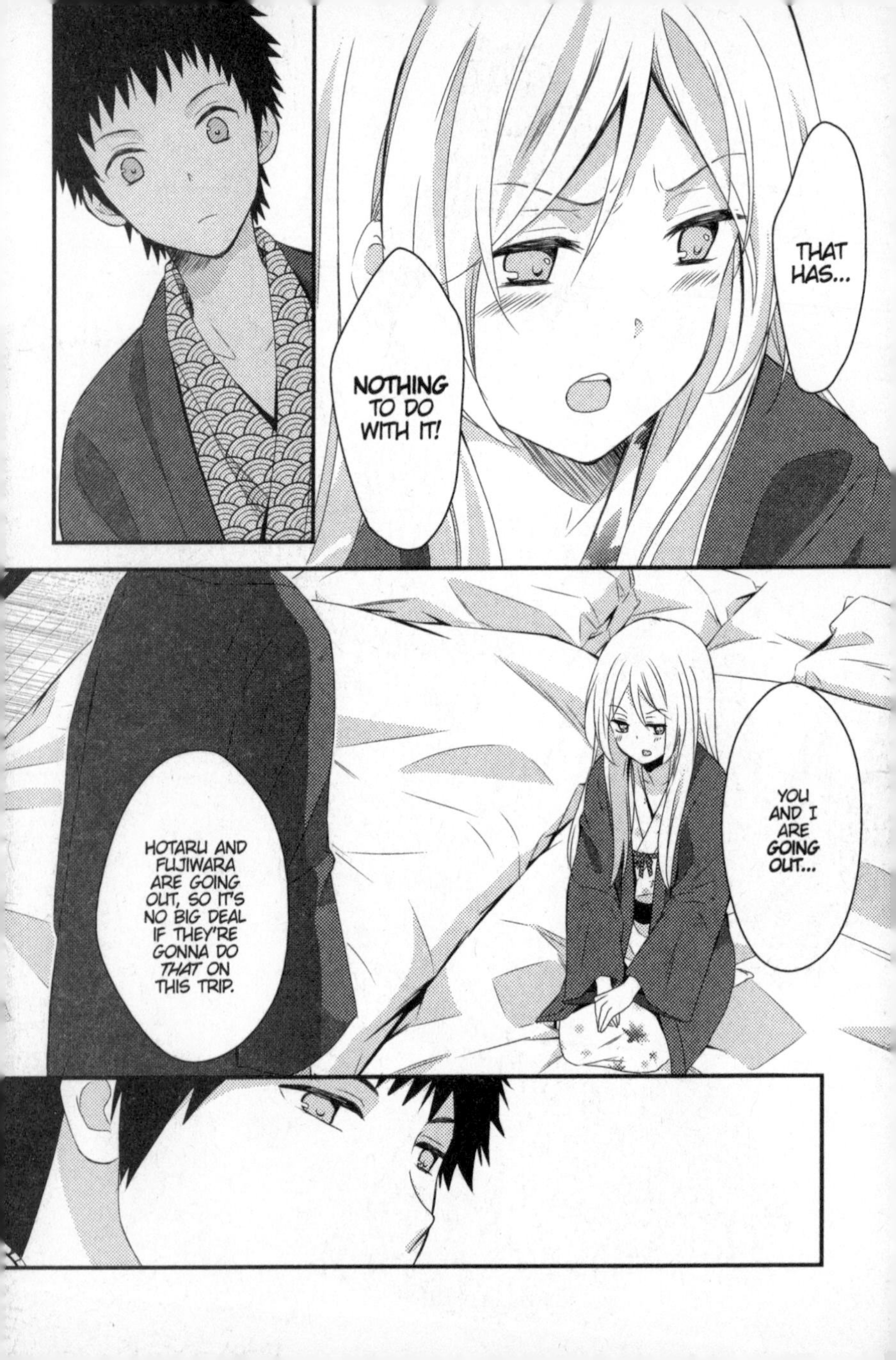
THAT HAS...
NOTHING TO DO WITH IT!
YOU AND I ARE GOING OUT...
HOTARU AND FUJIWARA ARE GOING OUT, SO IT'S NO BIG DEAL IF THEY'RE GONNA DO *THAT* ON THIS TRIP.

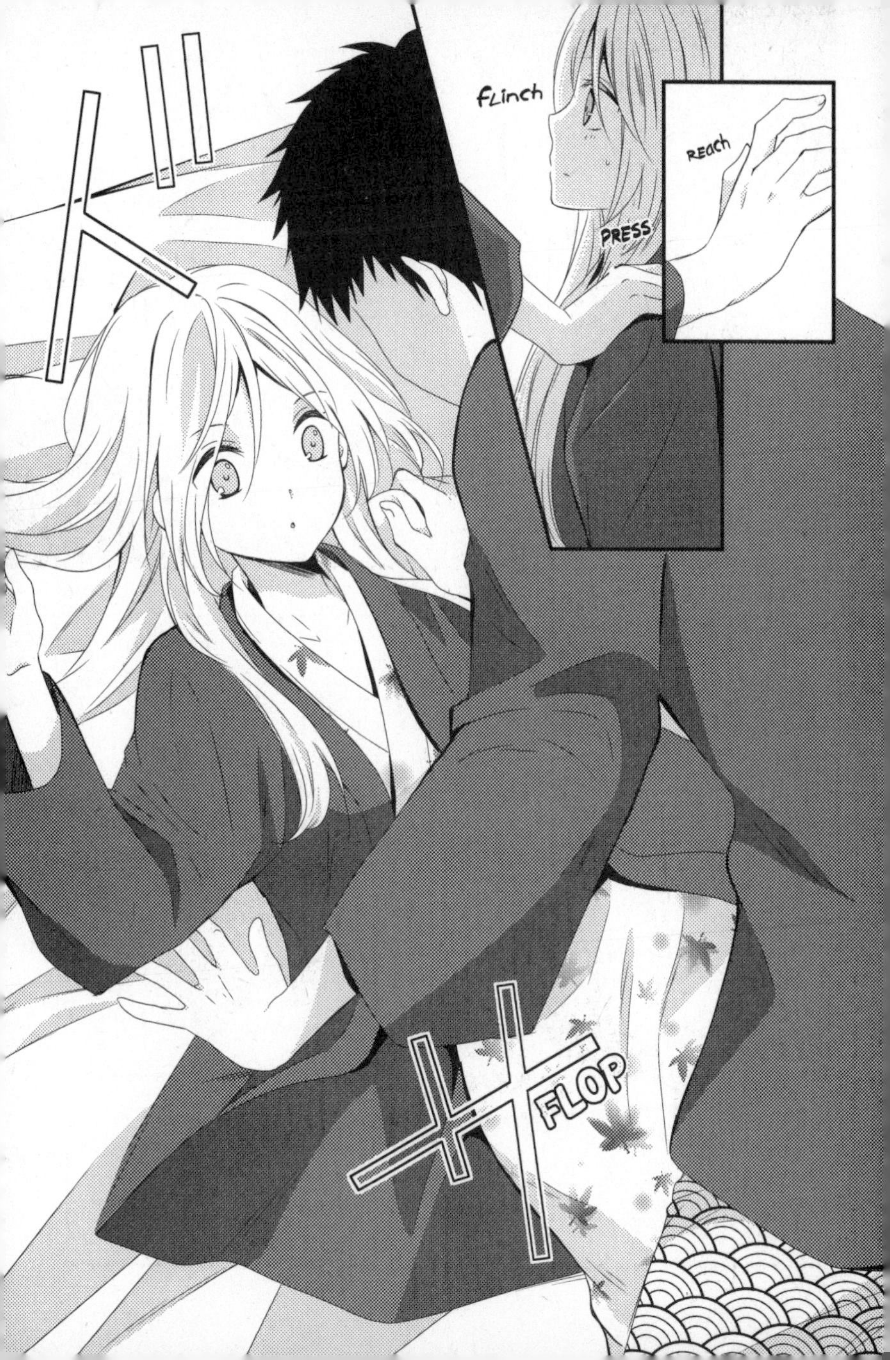
REACH
FLINCH
PRESS
FLOP

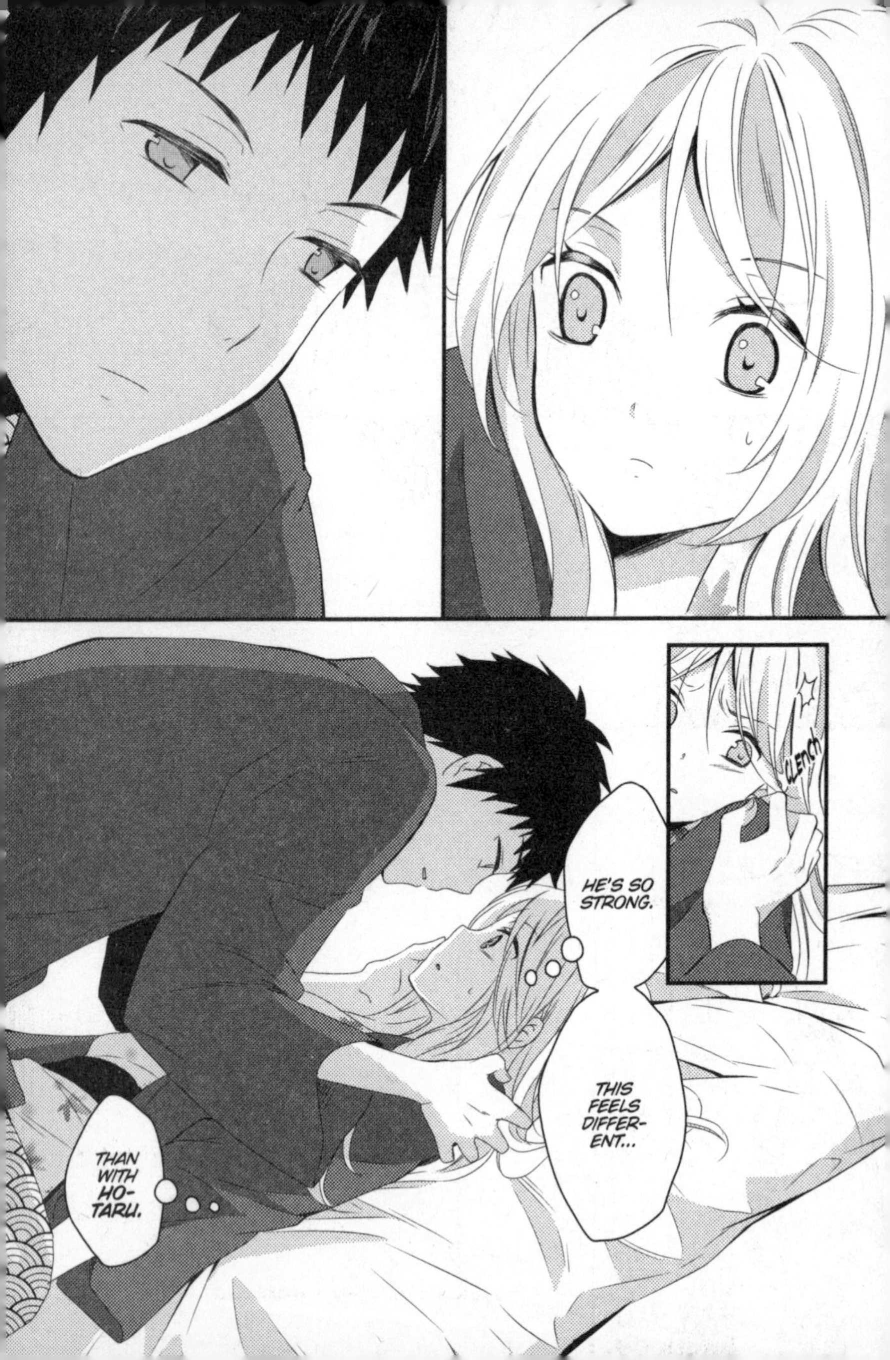
CLEnch
HE'S SO STRONG.
THIS FEELS DIFFERENT...
THAN WITH HOTARU.

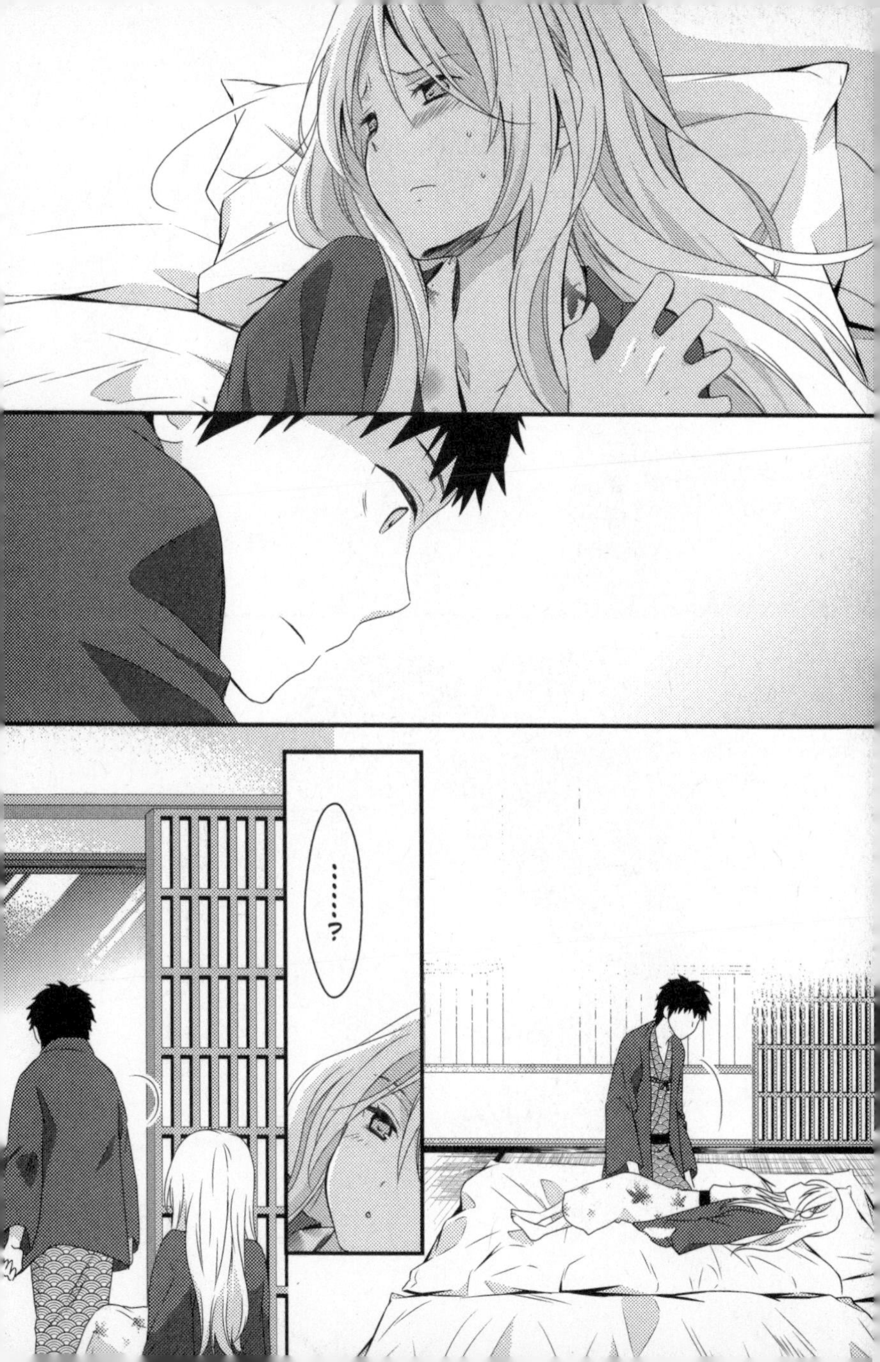
……っ

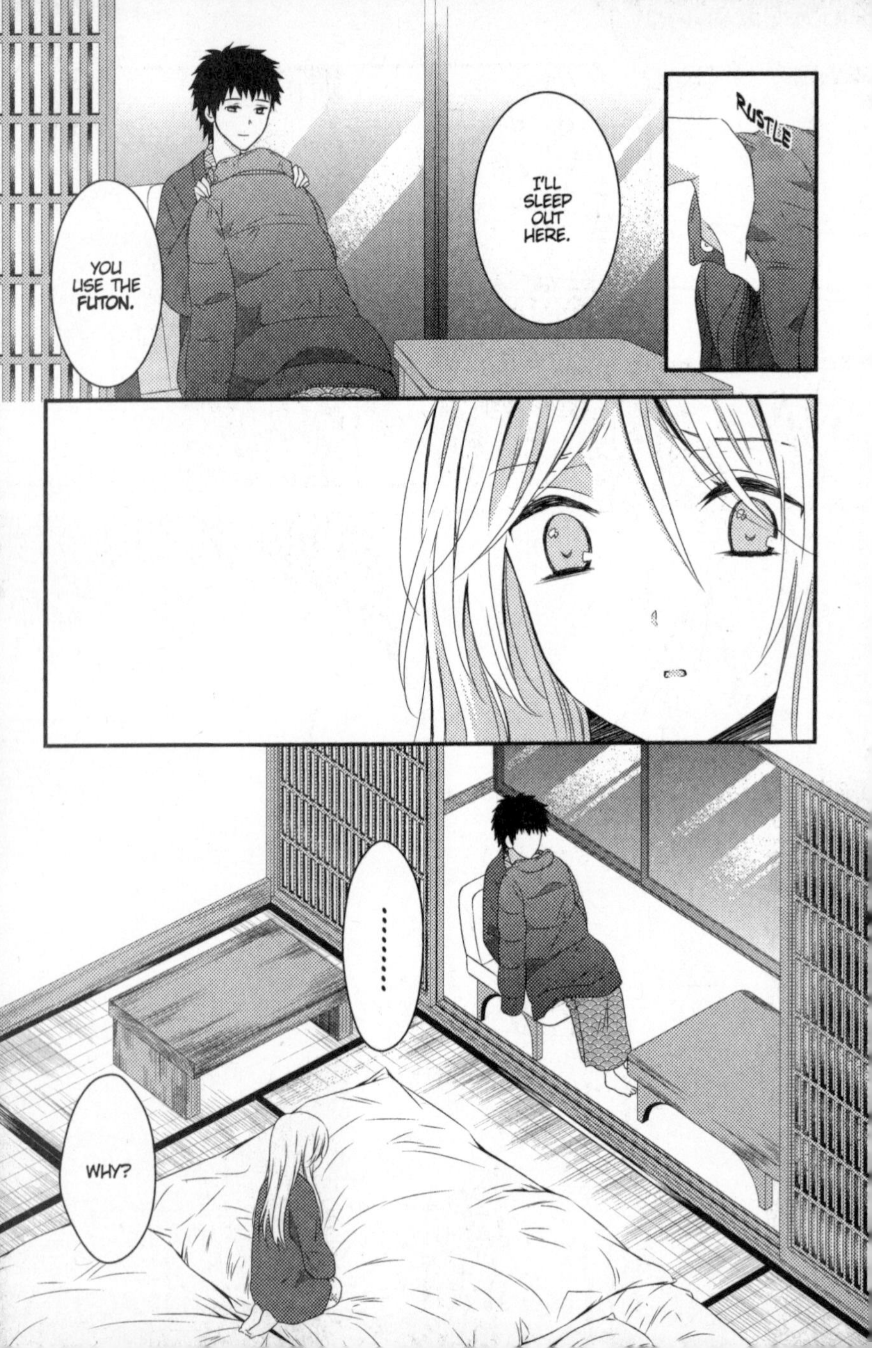
RUSTLE
I'LL SLEEP OUT HERE.
YOU USE THE FUTON.
......
WHY?

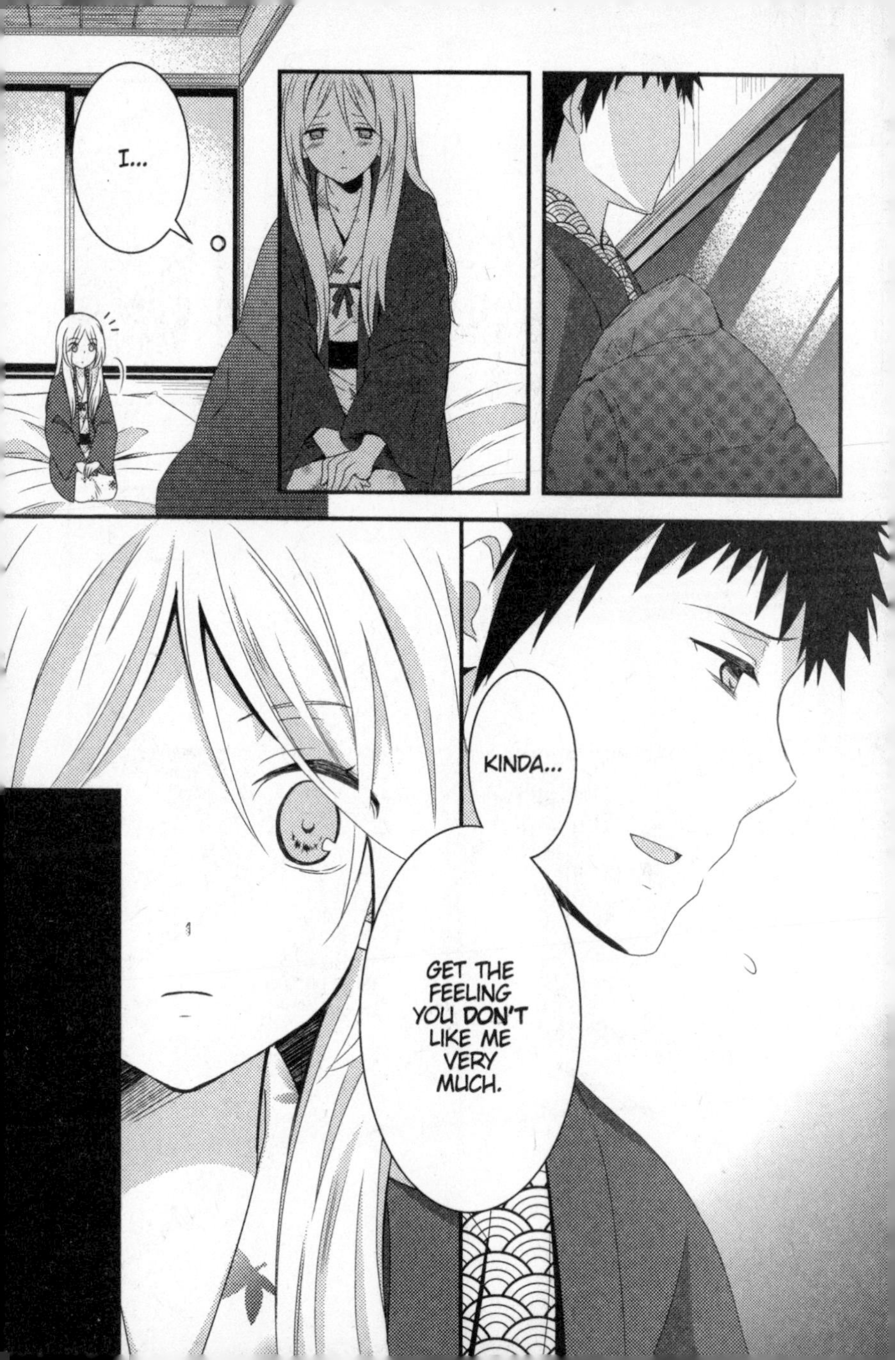
I...
KINDA...
GET THE FEELING YOU DON'T LIKE ME VERY MUCH.

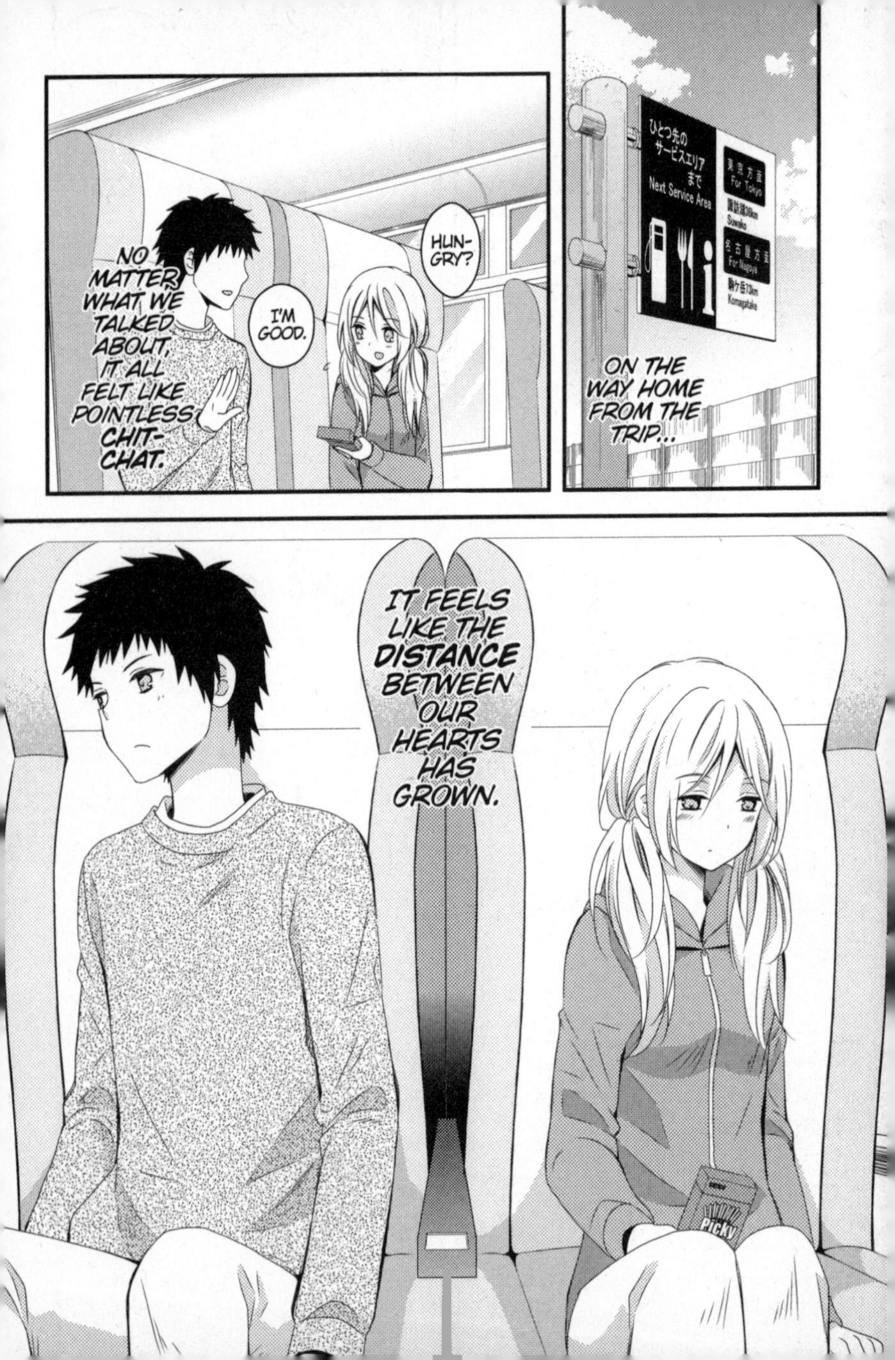
ひとつ先の
サービスエリア
まで
Next Service Area
東京方面
For Tokyo
諏訪湖36km
Suwako
名古屋方面
For Nagoya
駒ケ岳73km
Komagatake
ON THE WAY HOME FROM THE TRIP...
HUN-GRY?
I'M GOOD.
NO MATTER WHAT WE TALKED ABOUT, IT ALL FELT LIKE POINTLESS CHIT-CHAT.
IT FEELS LIKE THE DISTANCE BETWEEN OUR HEARTS HAS GROWN.
Picky

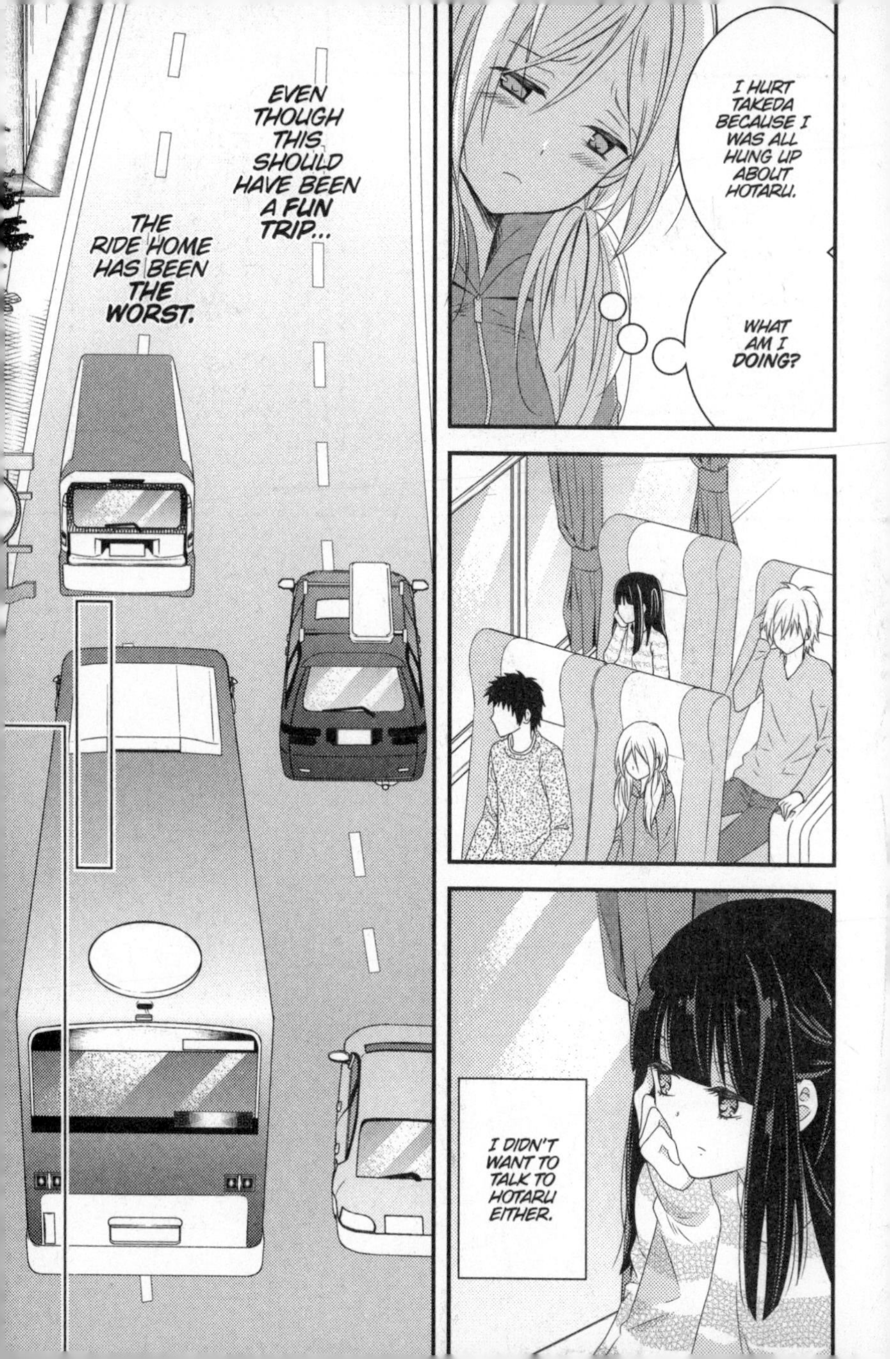
I HURT TAKEDA BECAUSE I WAS ALL HUNG UP ABOUT HOTARU.
WHAT AM I DOING?
I DIDN'T WANT TO TALK TO HOTARU EITHER.
EVEN THOUGH THIS SHOULD HAVE BEEN A FUN TRIP...
THE RIDE HOME HAS BEEN THE WORST.

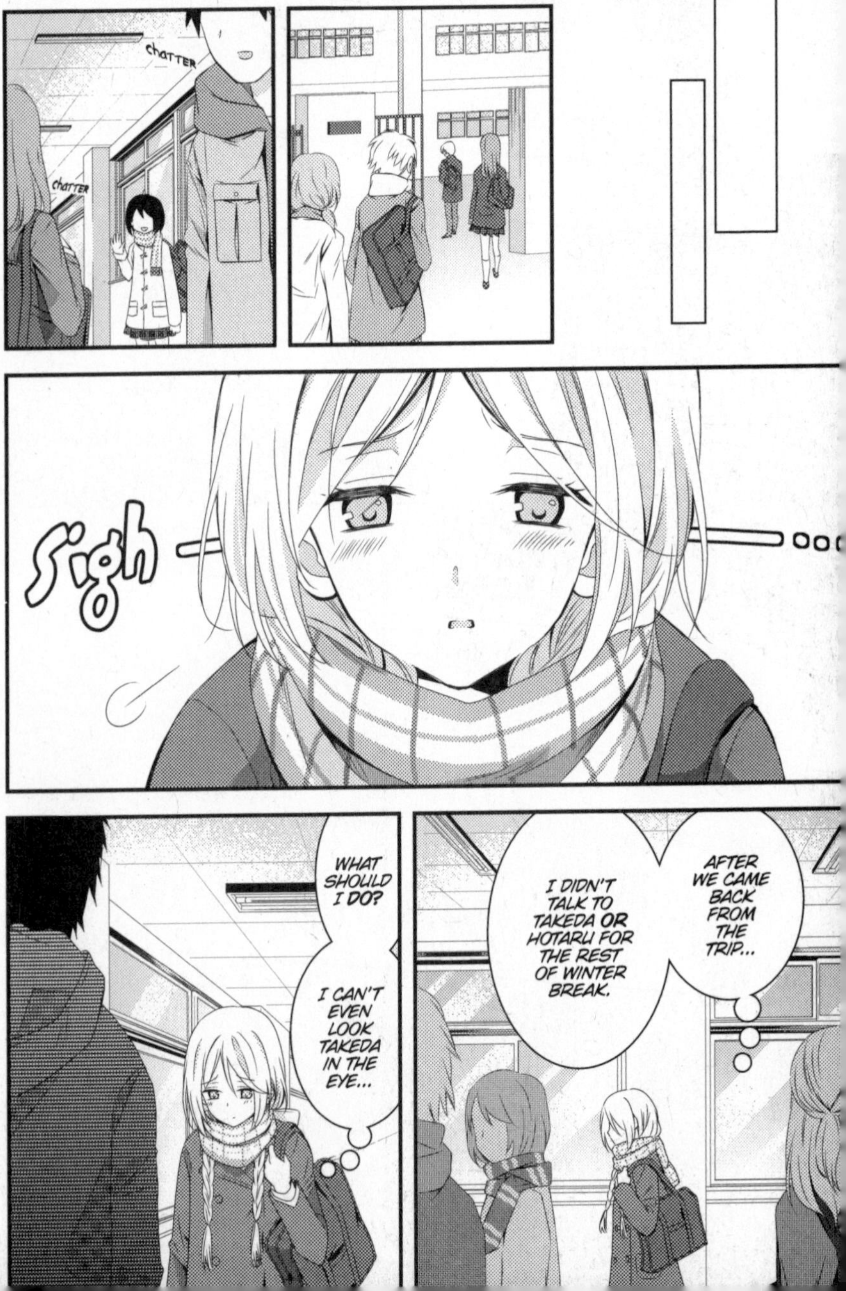
CHATTER
CHATTER
sigh
AFTER WE CAME BACK FROM THE TRIP...
I DIDN'T TALK TO TAKEDA OR HOTARU FOR THE REST OF WINTER BREAK.
WHAT SHOULD I DO?
I CAN'T EVEN LOOK TAKEDA IN THE EYE...

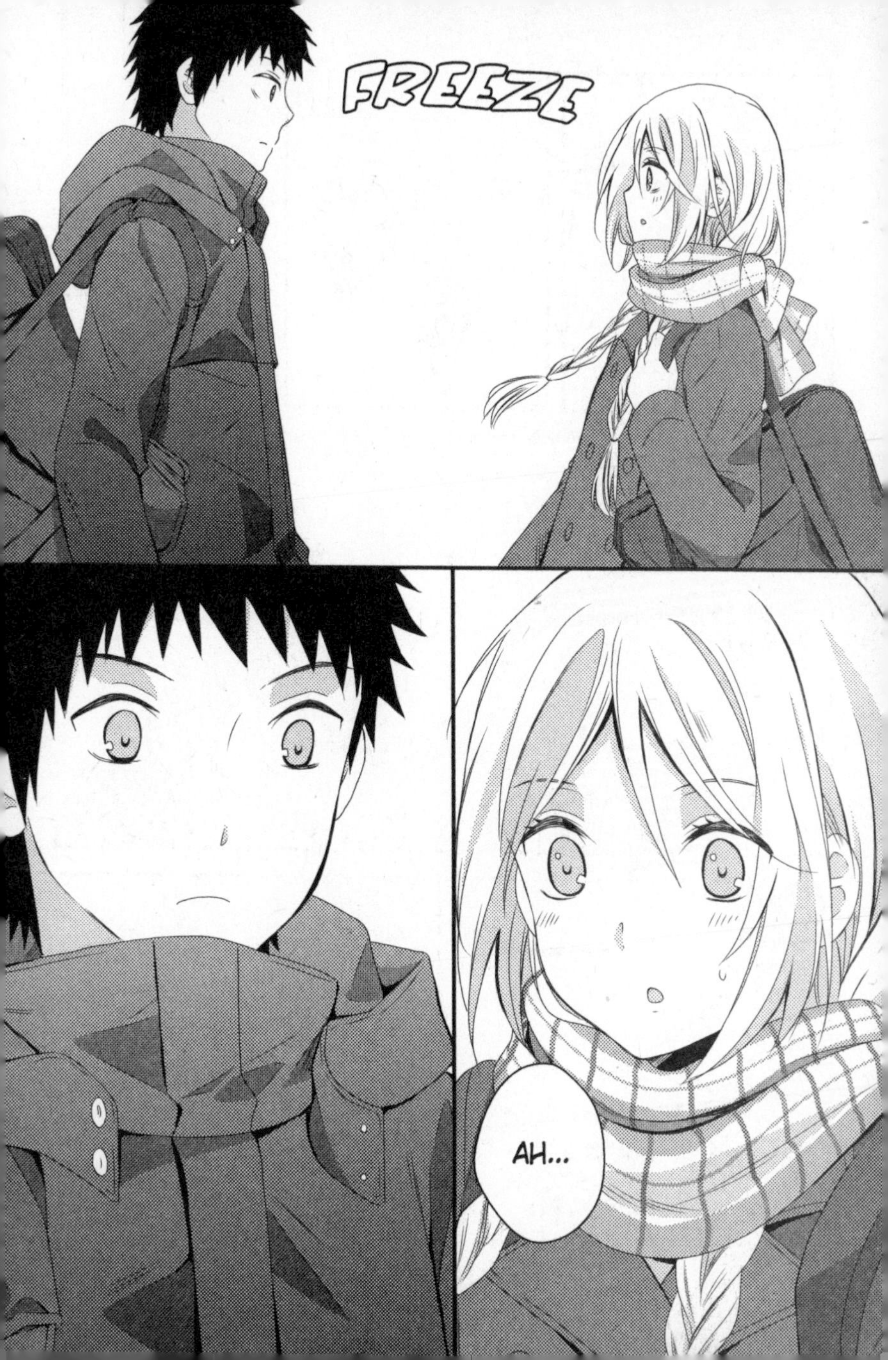
FREEZE
AH...

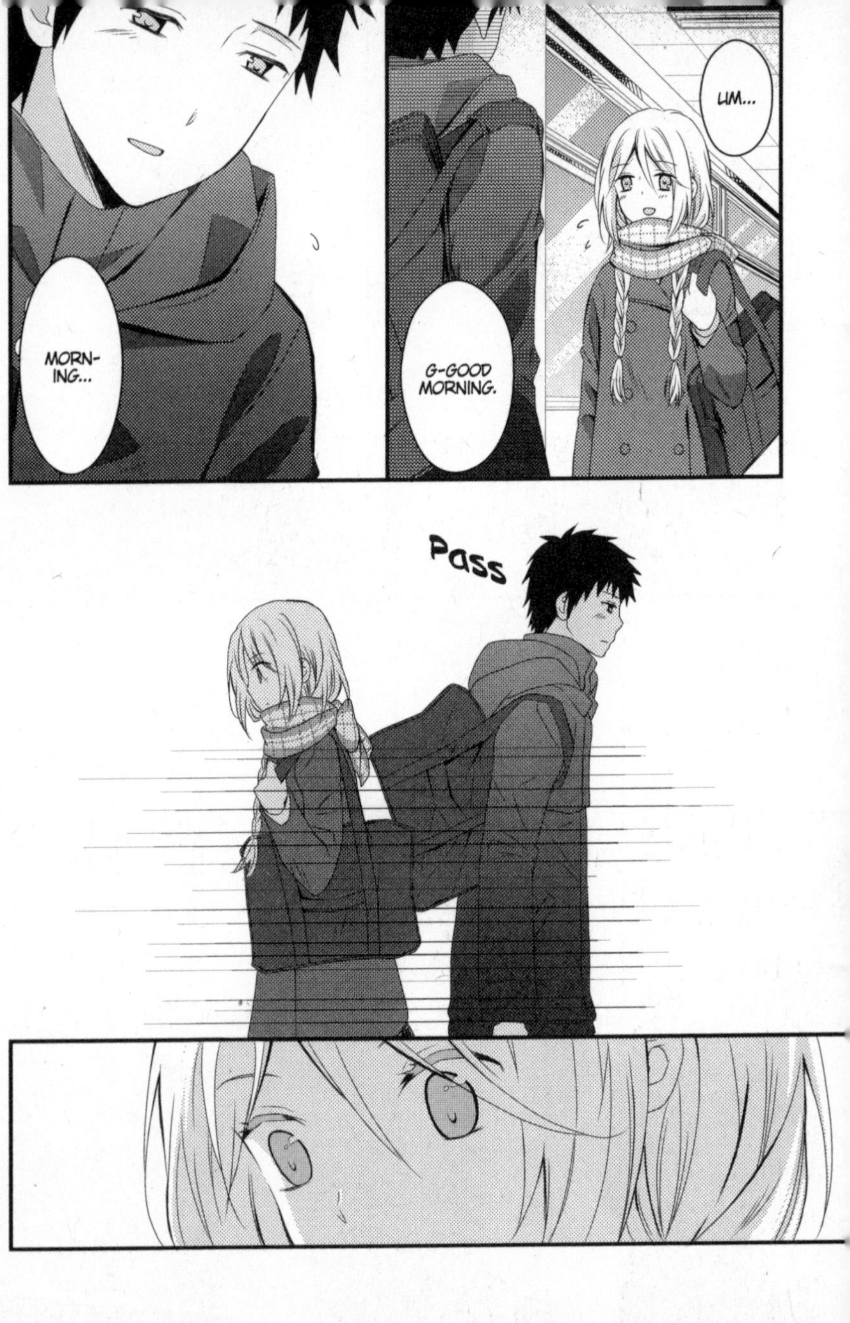
UM...
G-GOOD MORNING.
MORN-ING...
Pass

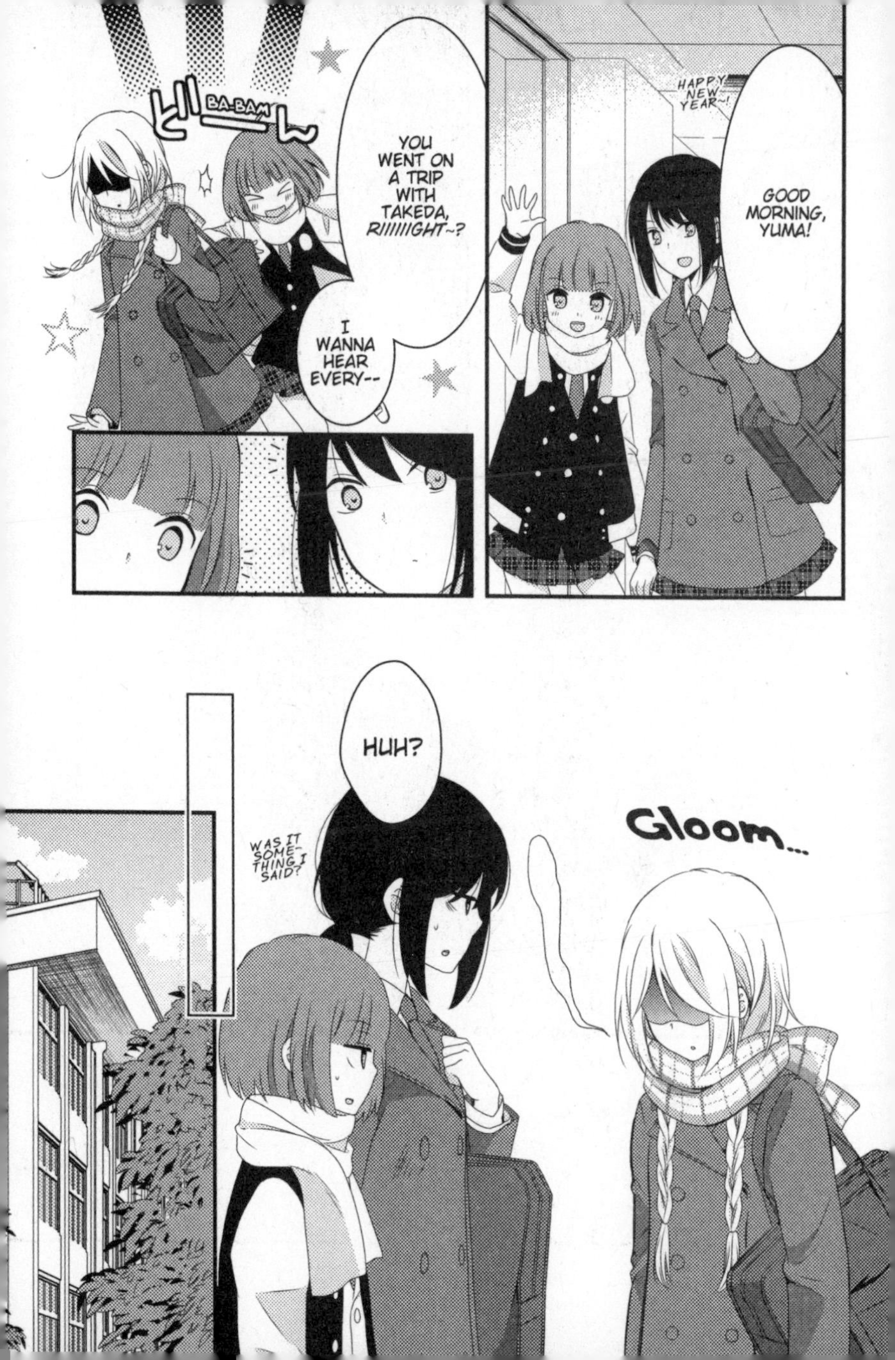
HAPPY NEW YEAR~!
GOOD MORNING, YUMA!
YOU WENT ON A TRIP WITH TAKEDA, RIIIIIIGHT~?
BA-BAM
I WANNA HEAR EVERY--
HUH?
Gloom...
WAS IT SOMETHING I SAID?

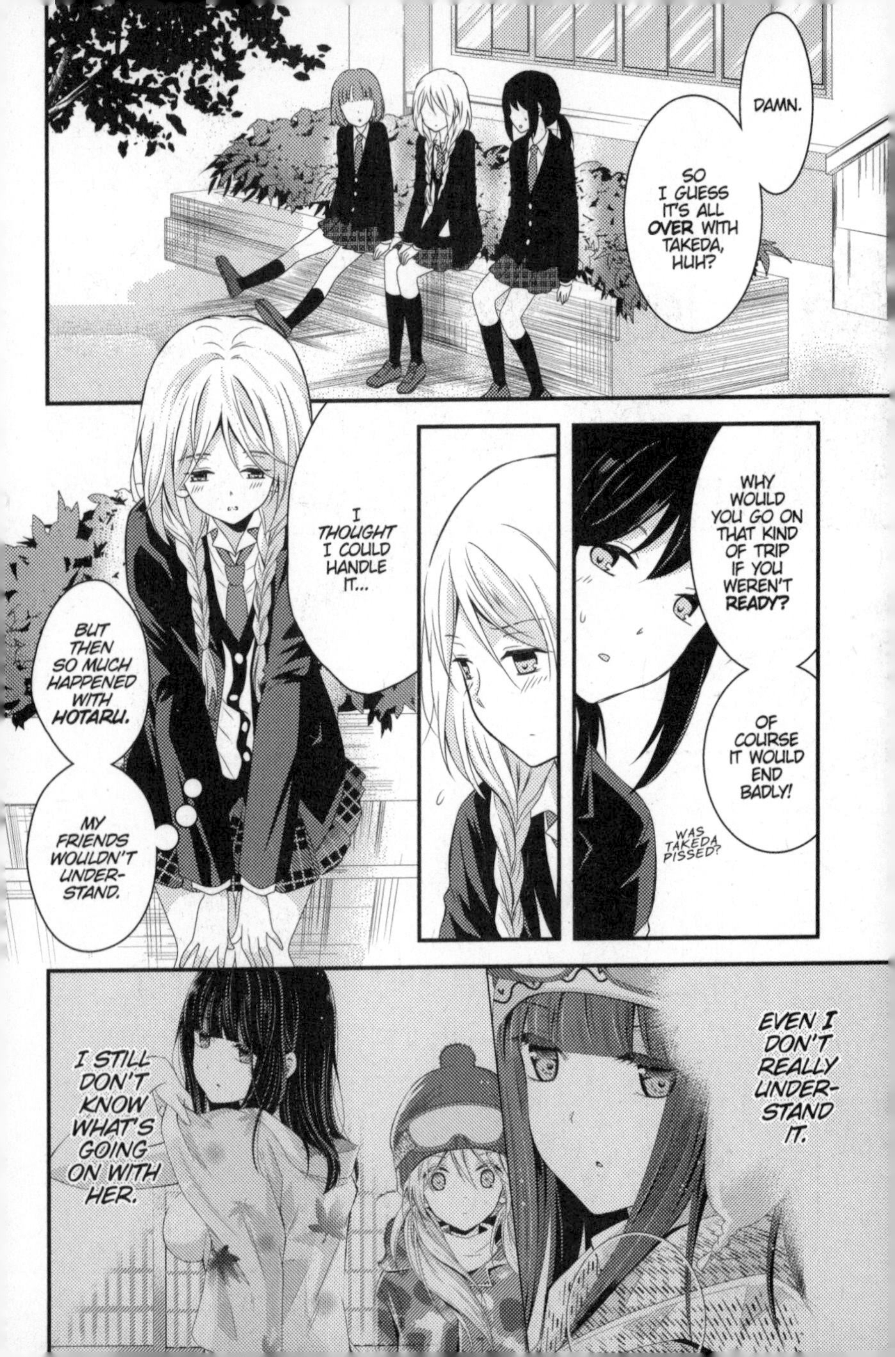
DAMN.
SO I GUESS IT'S ALL OVER WITH TAKEDA, HUH?
WHY WOULD YOU GO ON THAT KIND OF TRIP IF YOU WEREN'T READY?
OF COURSE IT WOULD END BADLY!
WAS TAKEDA PISSED?
I THOUGHT I COULD HANDLE IT...
BUT THEN SO MUCH HAPPENED WITH HOTARU.
MY FRIENDS WOULDN'T UNDER-STAND.
EVEN I DON'T REALLY UNDER-STAND IT.
I STILL DON'T KNOW WHAT'S GOING ON WITH HER.

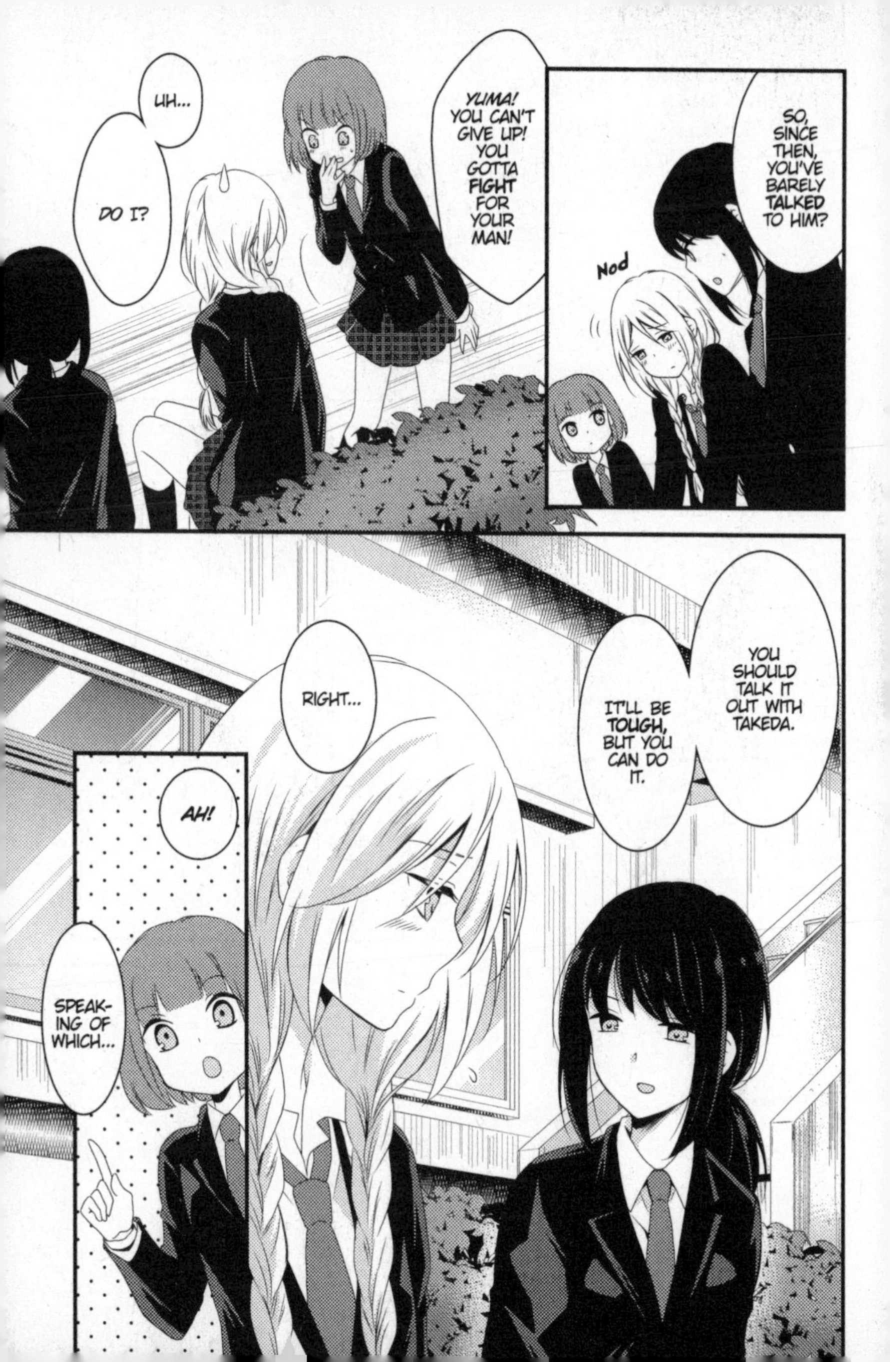
SO, SINCE THEN, YOU'VE BARELY TALKED TO HIM?
Nod
YUMA! YOU CAN'T GIVE UP! YOU GOTTA FIGHT FOR YOUR MAN!
UH...
DO I?
YOU SHOULD TALK IT OUT WITH TAKEDA.
IT'LL BE TOUGH, BUT YOU CAN DO IT.
RIGHT...
AH!
SPEAK-ING OF WHICH...

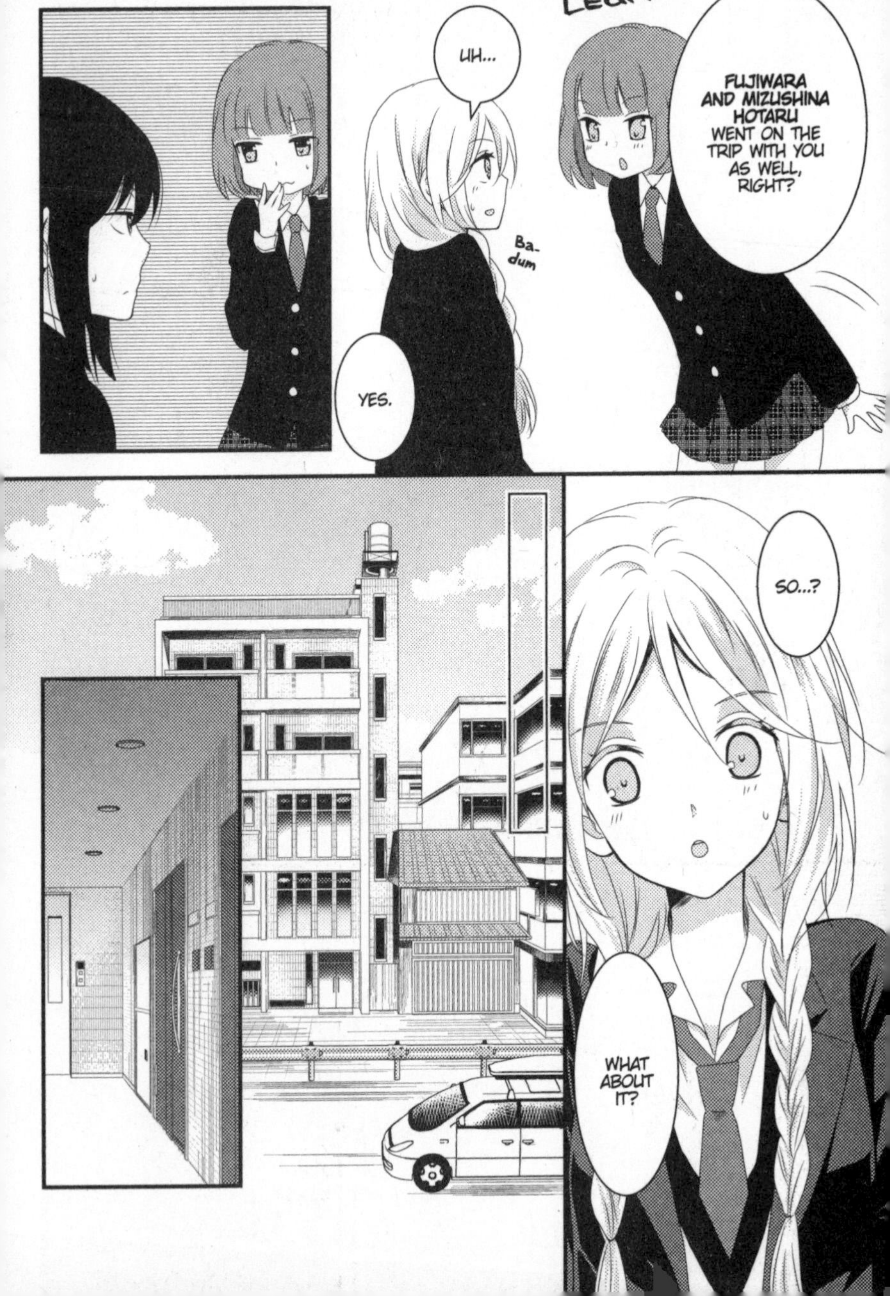
LEan
FUJIWARA AND MIZUSHINA HOTARU WENT ON THE TRIP WITH YOU AS WELL, RIGHT?
UH...
Ba-dum
YES.
SO...?
WHAT ABOUT IT?

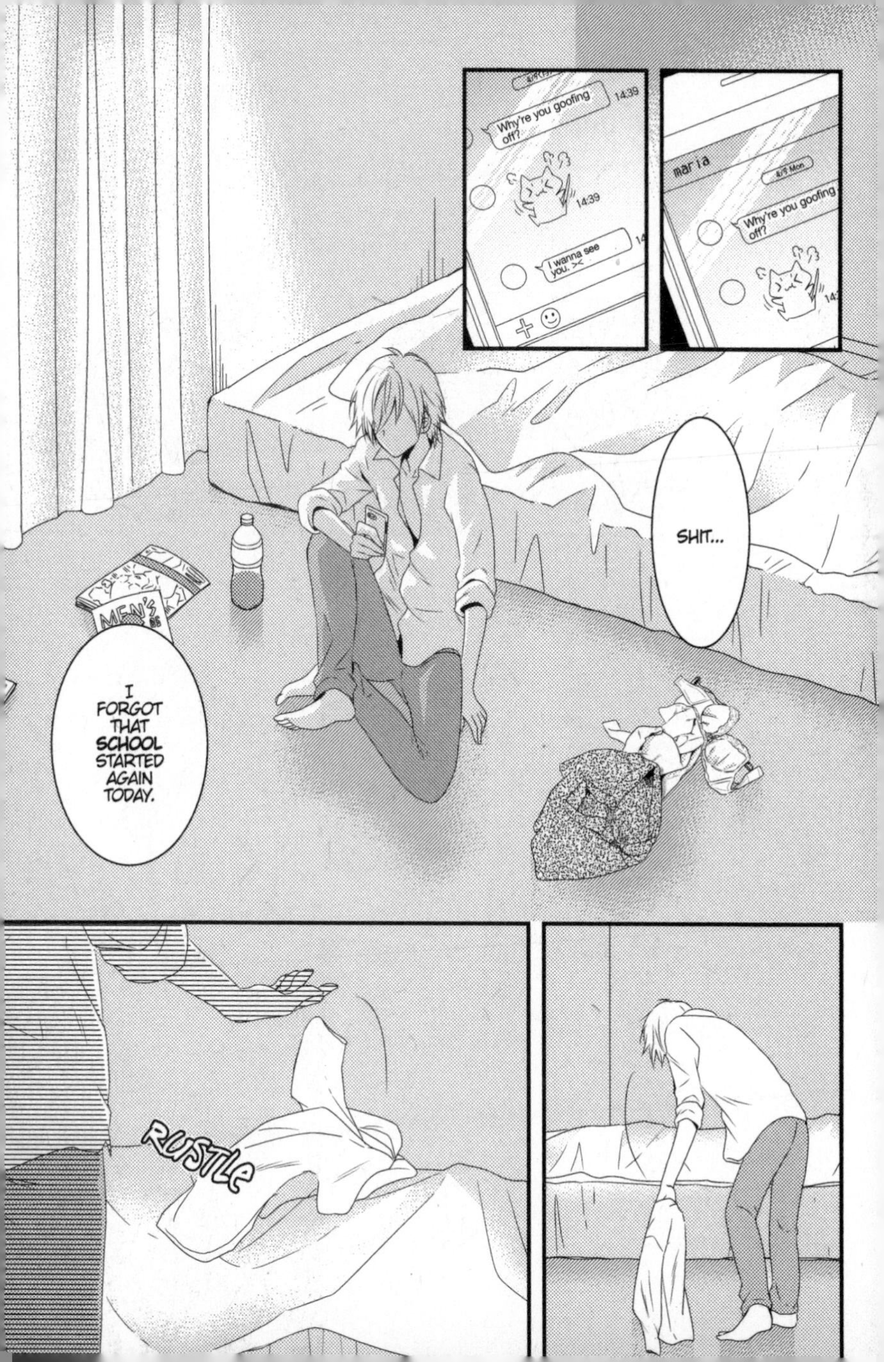
maria
Why're you goofing off?
Why're you goofing off?
14:39
14:39
I wanna see you. ><
SHIT...
MEN'S
I FORGOT THAT SCHOOL STARTED AGAIN TODAY.
RUSTLE

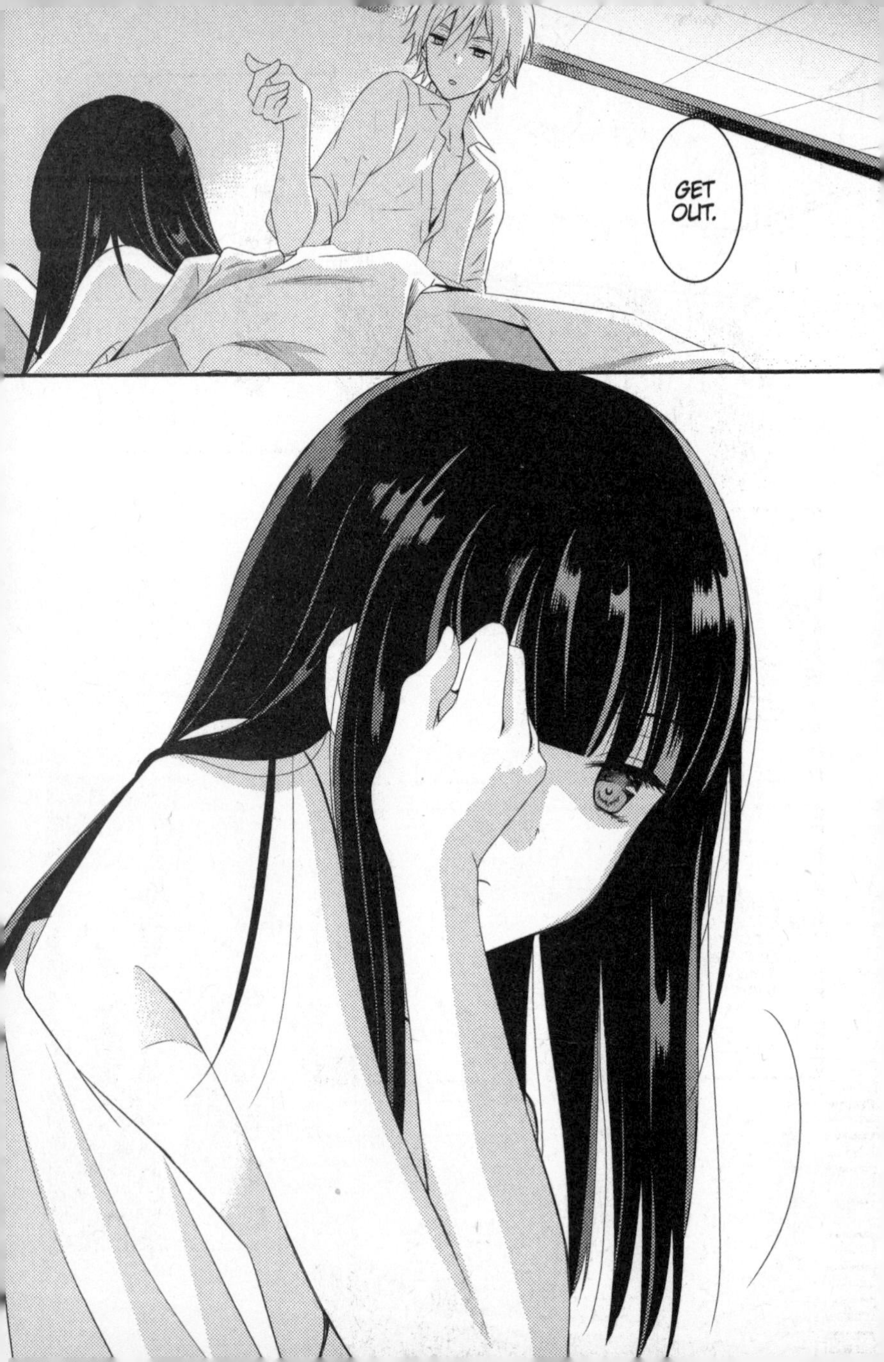
GET OUT.

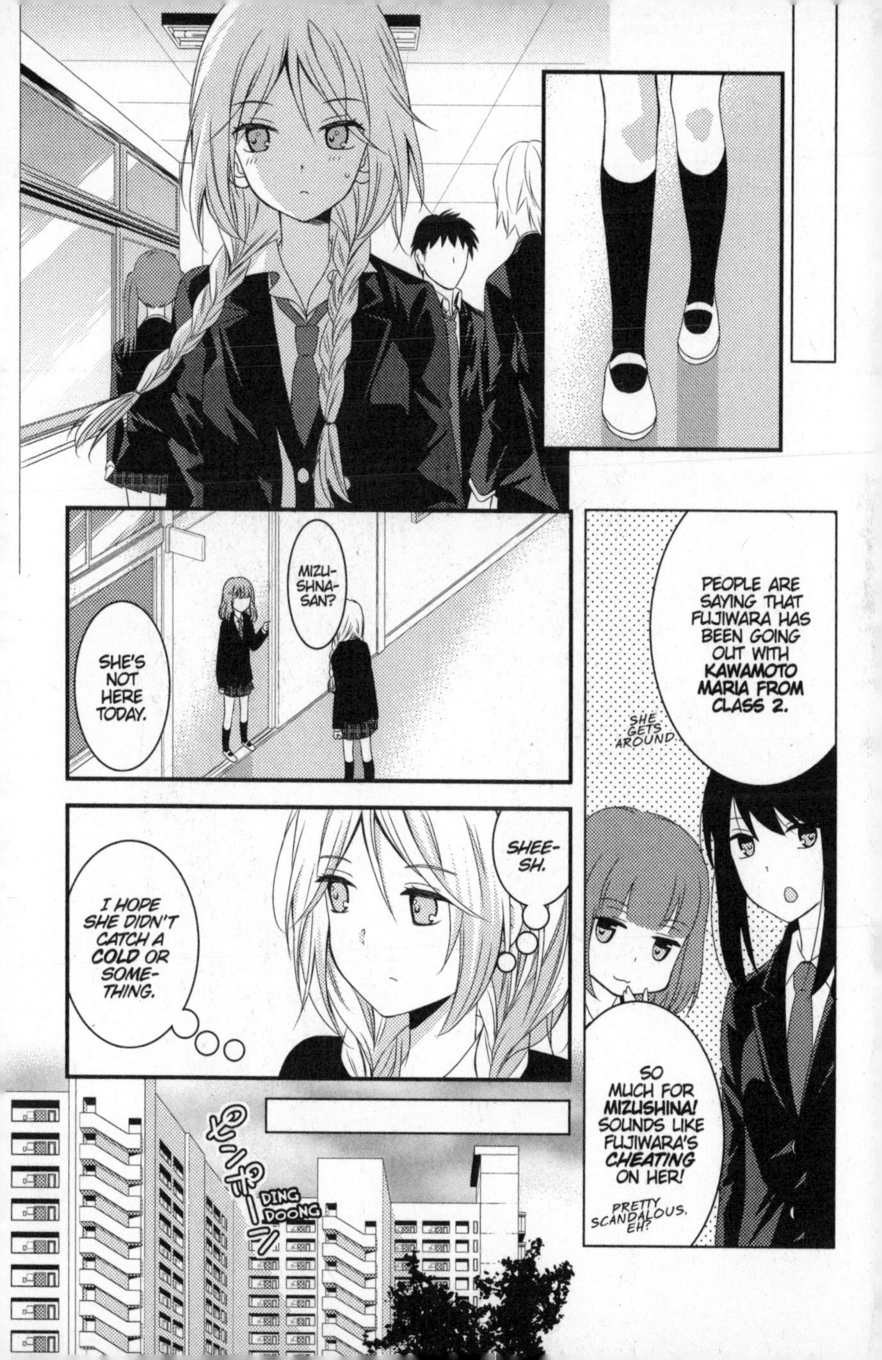
PEOPLE ARE SAYING THAT FUJIWARA HAS BEEN GOING OUT WITH KAWAMOTO MARIA FROM CLASS 2.
SHE GETS AROUND.
SO MUCH FOR MIZUSHINA! SOUNDS LIKE FUJIWARA'S CHEATING ON HER!
PRETTY SCANDALOUS, EH?
MIZU-SHNA-SAN?
SHE'S NOT HERE TODAY.
SHEES-SH.
I HOPE SHE DIDN'T CATCH A COLD OR SOME-THING.
DING DOONG

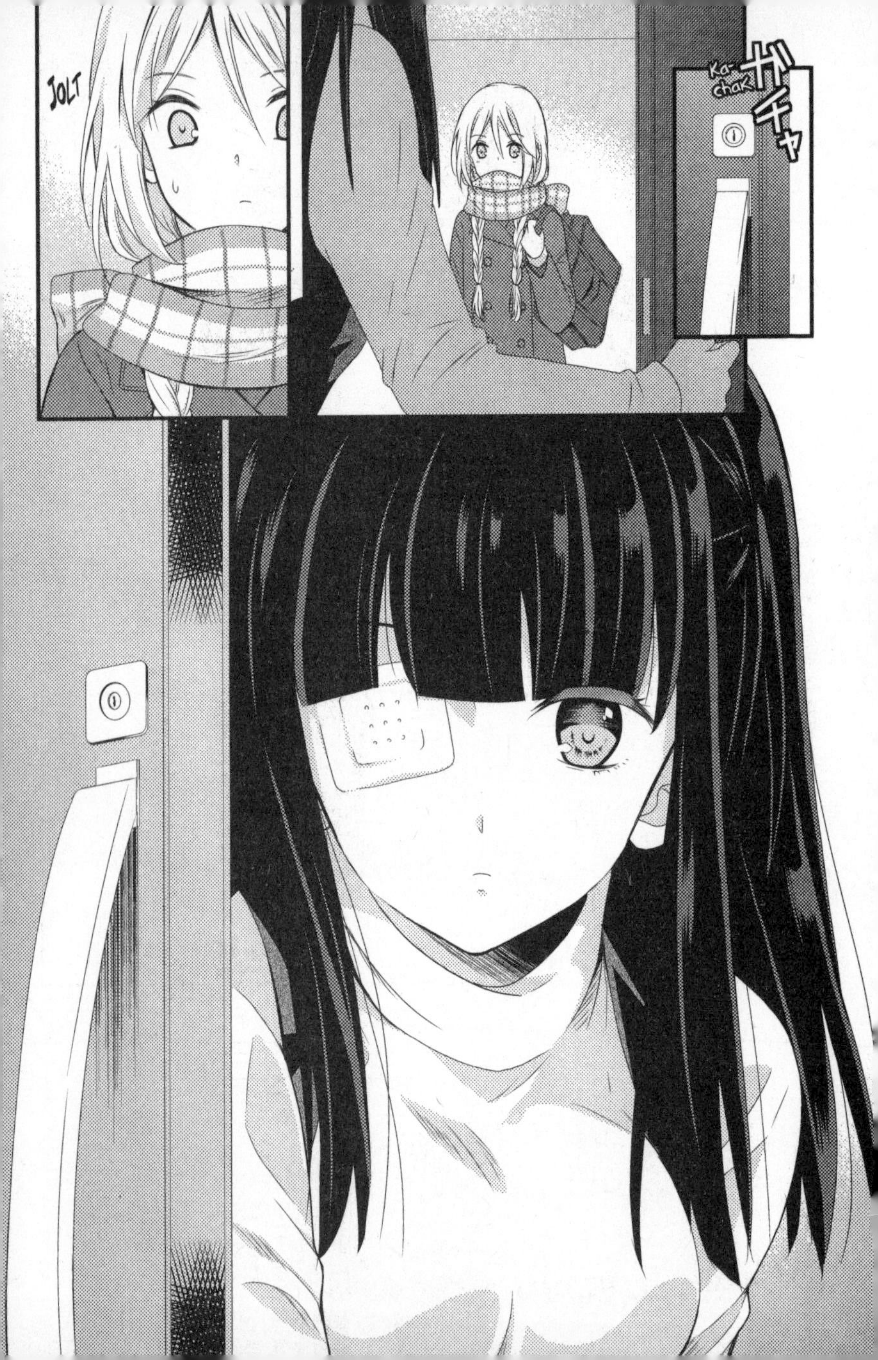
Ka-chak ガチャ
JOLT

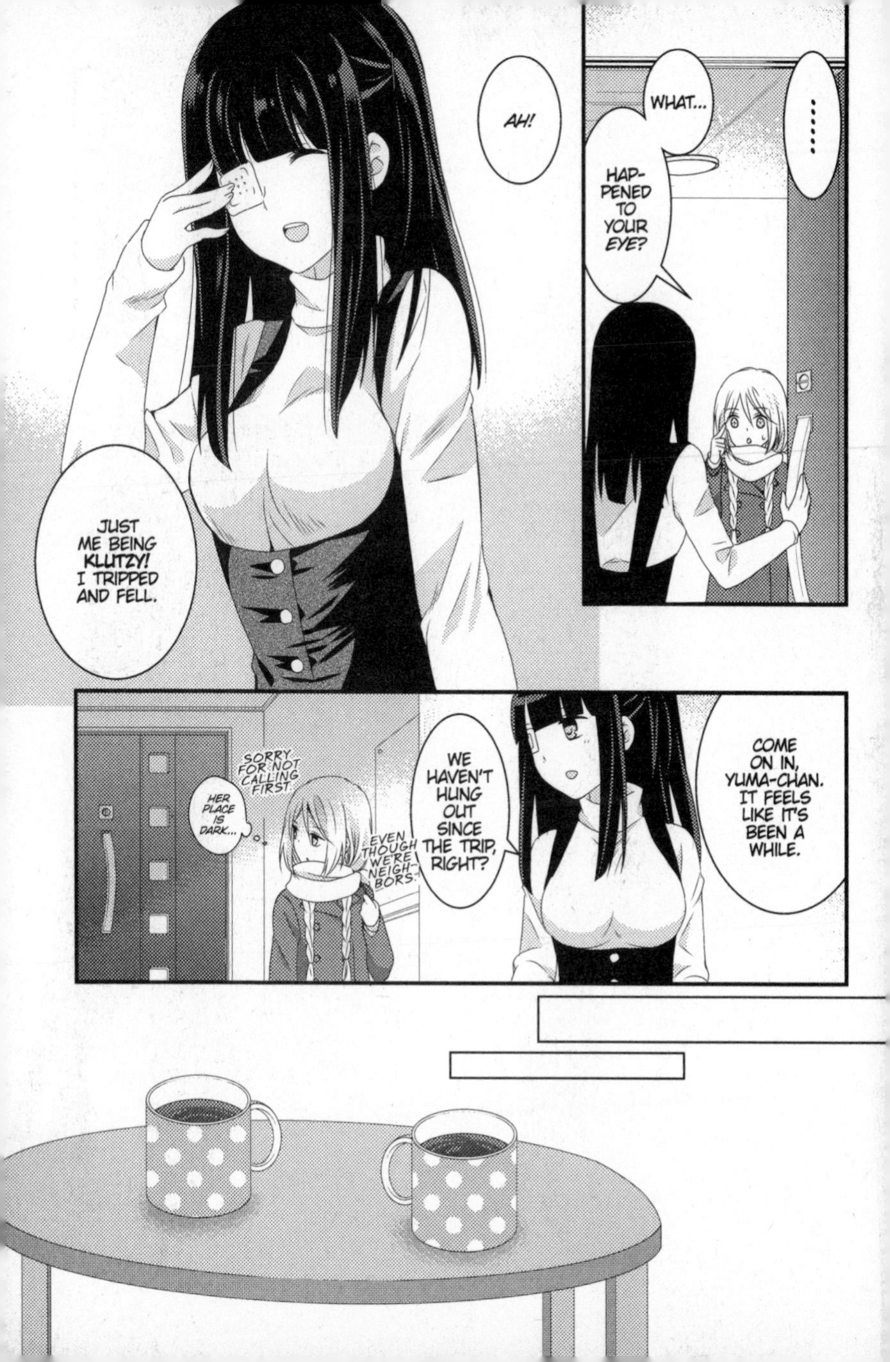
......
WHAT...
HAPPENED TO YOUR EYE?
AH!
JUST ME BEING KLUTZY! I TRIPPED AND FELL.
COME ON IN, YUMA-CHAN. IT FEELS LIKE IT'S BEEN A WHILE.
WE HAVEN'T HUNG OUT SINCE THE TRIP, RIGHT?
SORRY FOR NOT CALLING FIRST
EVEN THOUGH WE'RE NEIGHBORS.
HER PLACE IS DARK...

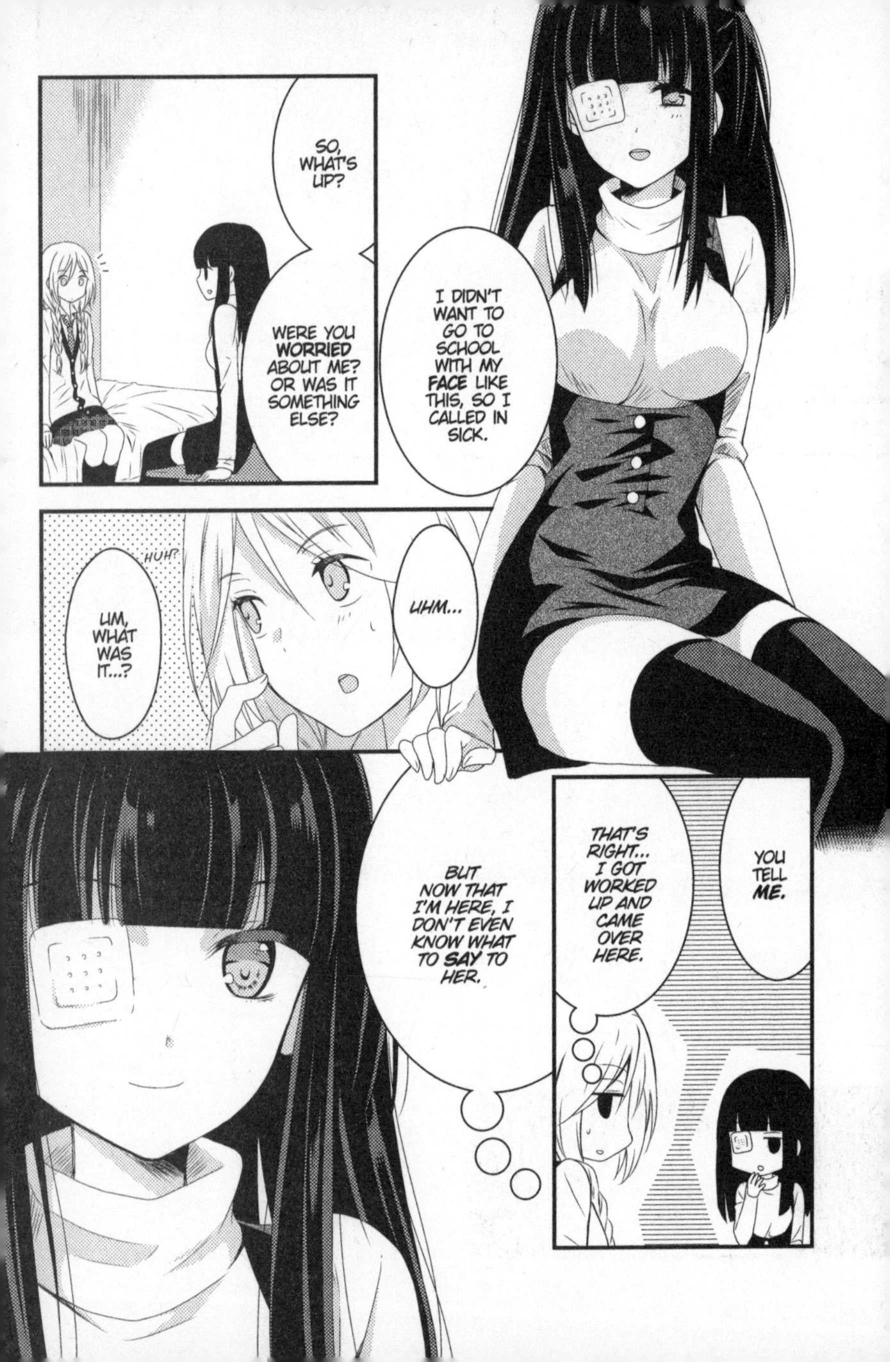
I DIDN'T WANT TO GO TO SCHOOL WITH MY FACE LIKE THIS, SO I CALLED IN SICK.
SO, WHAT'S UP?
WERE YOU WORRIED ABOUT ME? OR WAS IT SOMETHING ELSE?
UHM...
HUH?
UM, WHAT WAS IT...?
YOU TELL ME.
THAT'S RIGHT... I GOT WORKED UP AND CAME OVER HERE.
BUT NOW THAT I'M HERE, I DON'T EVEN KNOW WHAT TO SAY TO HER.

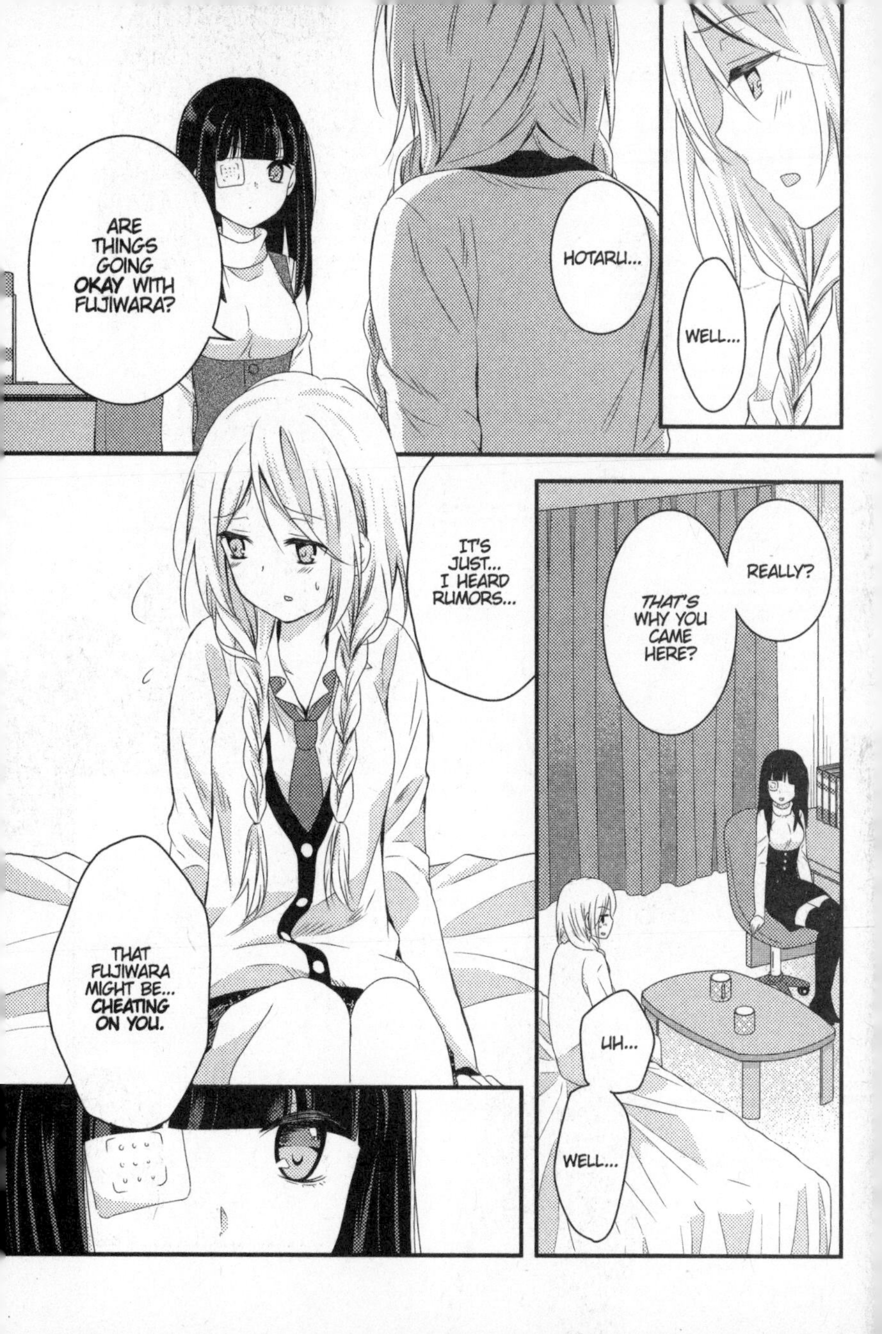
WELL...
HOTARU...
ARE THINGS GOING OKAY WITH FUJIWARA?
REALLY?
THAT'S WHY YOU CAME HERE?
UH...
WELL...
IT'S JUST... I HEARD RUMORS...
THAT FUJIWARA MIGHT BE... CHEATING ON YOU.

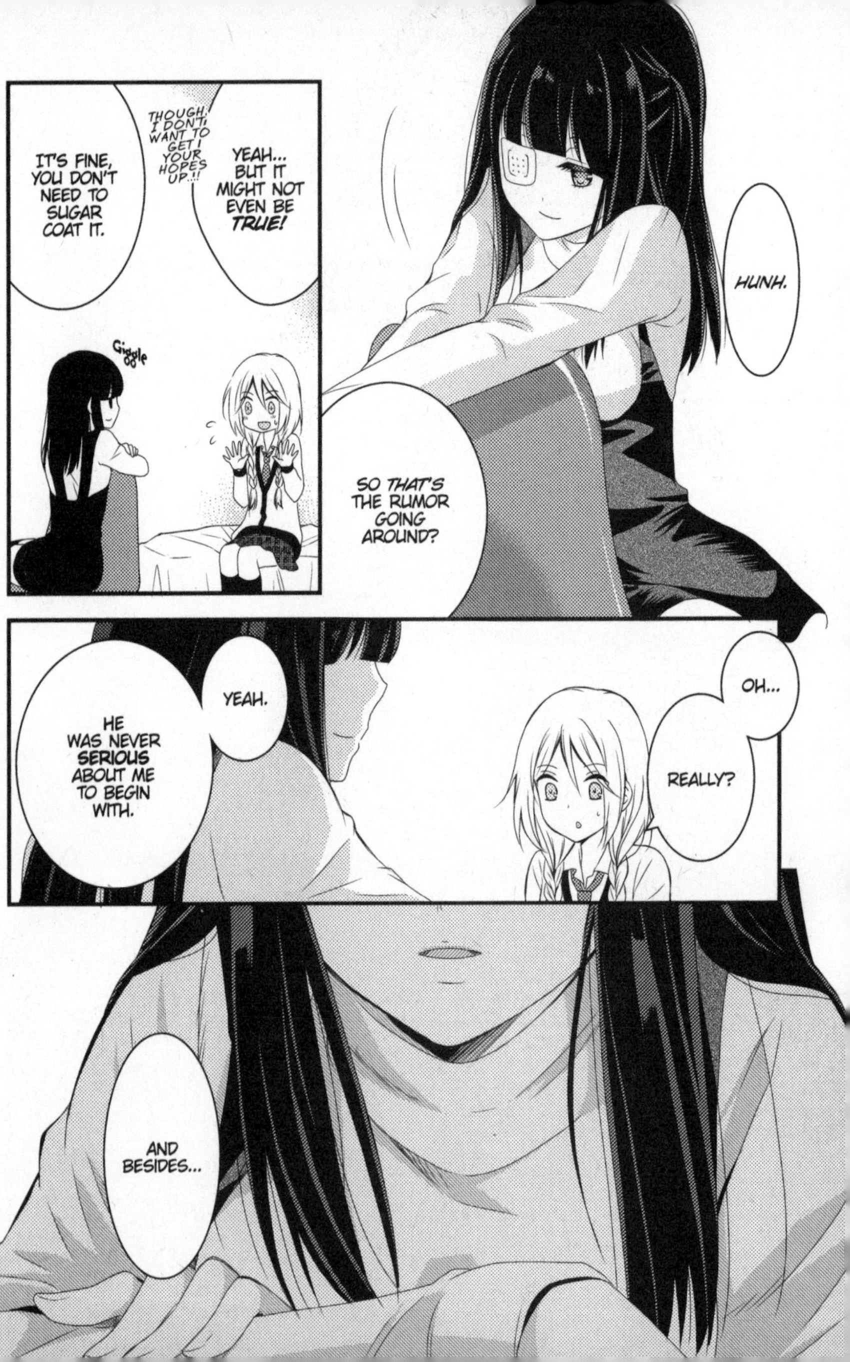
HUNH.
SO THAT'S THE RUMOR GOING AROUND?
YEAH... BUT IT MIGHT NOT EVEN BE TRUE!
THOUGH, I DON'T WANT TO GET YOUR HOPES UP..!!
IT'S FINE, YOU DON'T NEED TO SUGAR COAT IT.
Giggle
OH...
REALLY?
YEAH.
HE WAS NEVER SERIOUS ABOUT ME TO BEGIN WITH.
AND BESIDES...

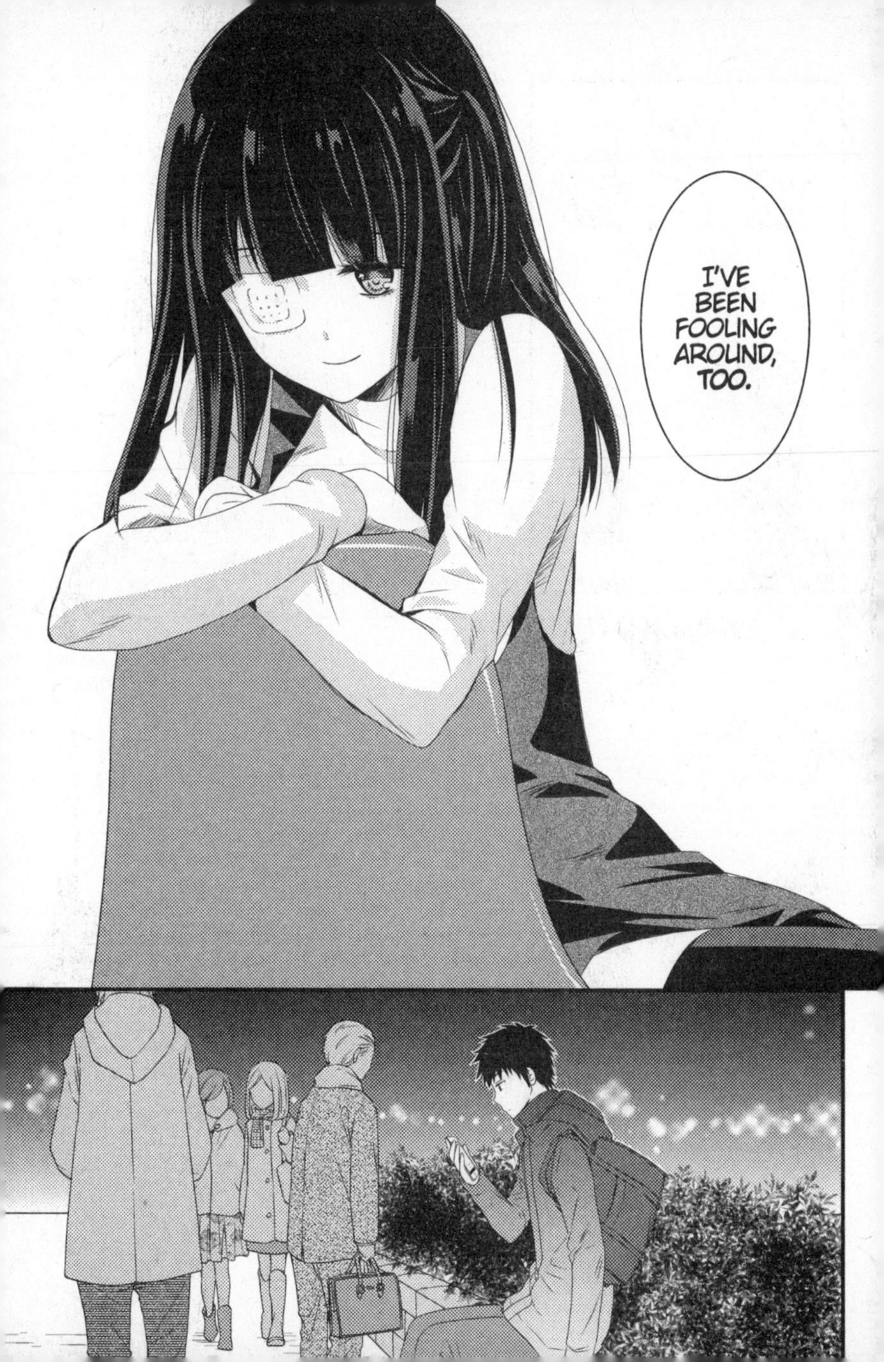
I'VE BEEN FOOLING AROUND, TOO.

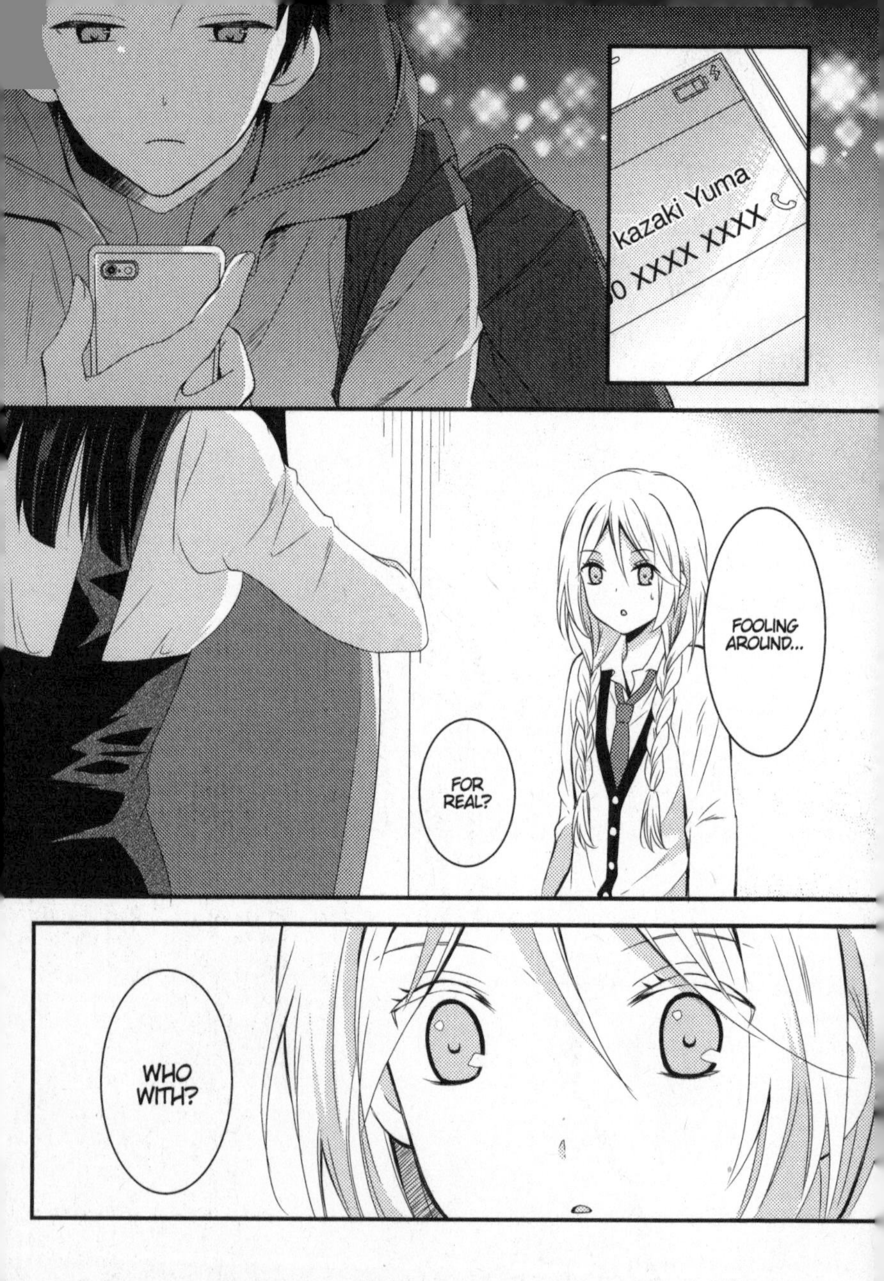
kazaki Yuma
0 XXXX XXXX
FOOLING AROUND...
FOR REAL?
WHO WITH?

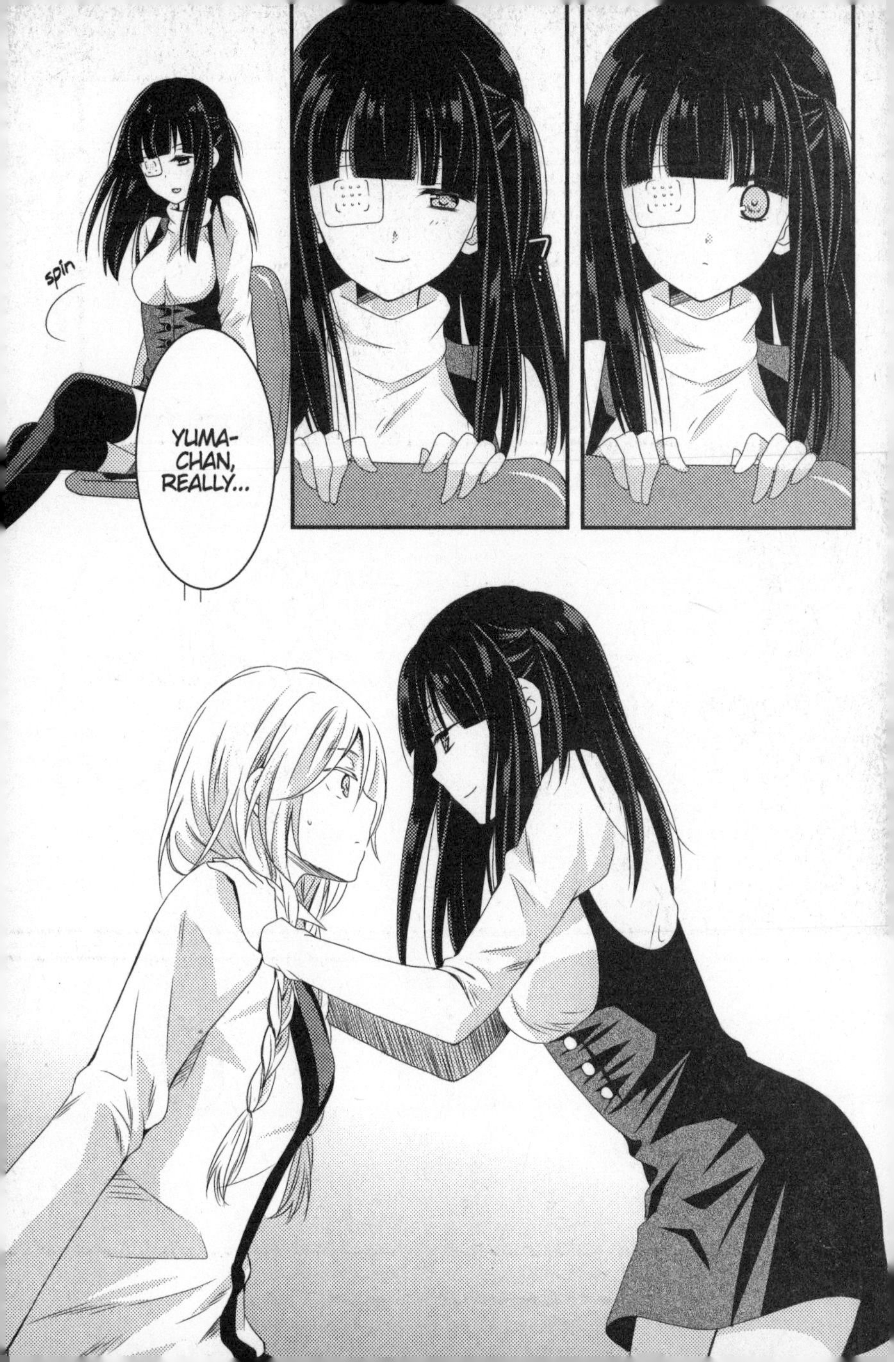
spin
YUMA-CHAN, REALLY...

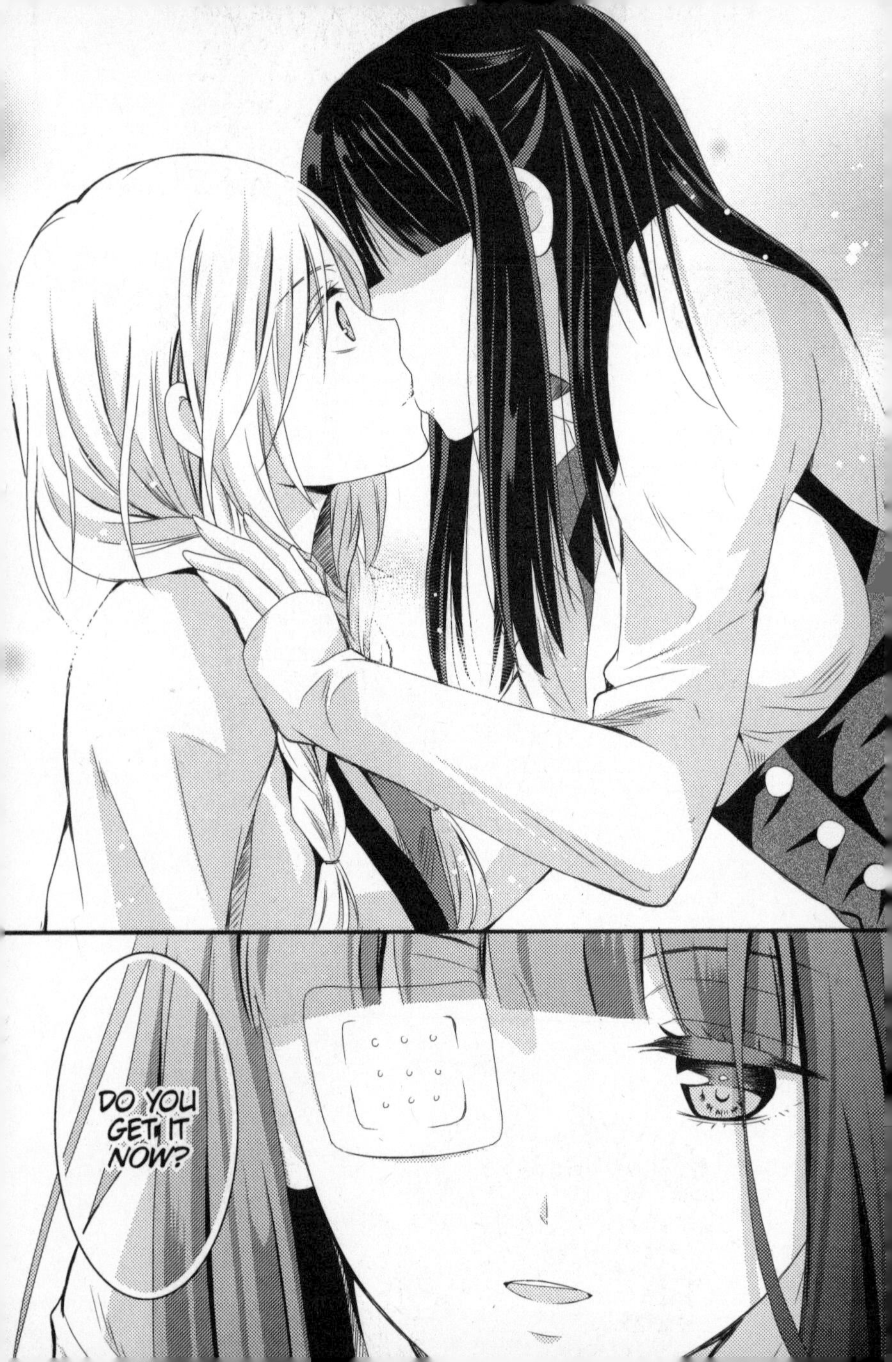
DO YOU GET IT NOW?

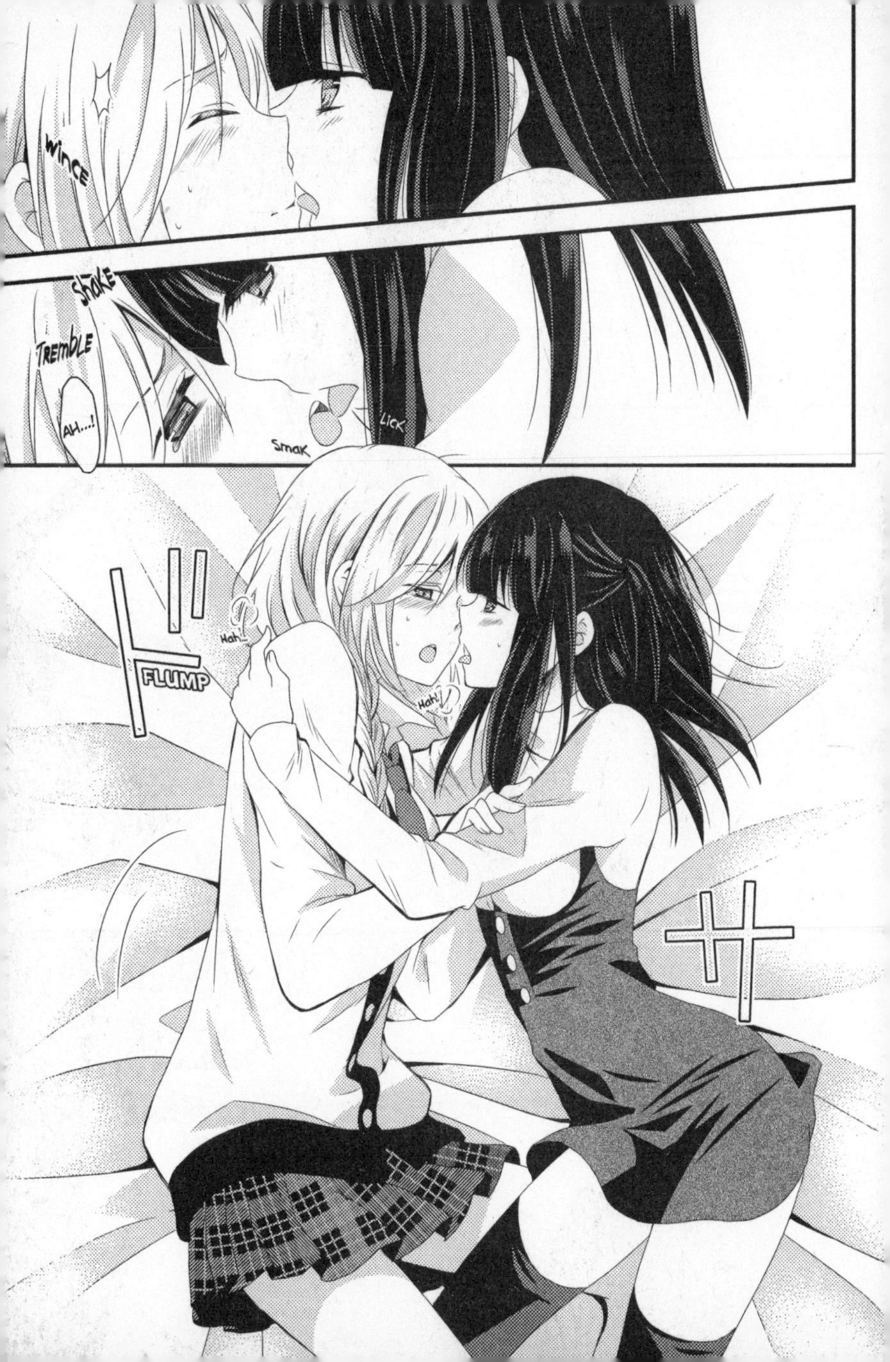
wince
Lick
Shake
Tremble
Smak
Ah...!
サ
ドサ
FLUMP
Hah...
Hah!

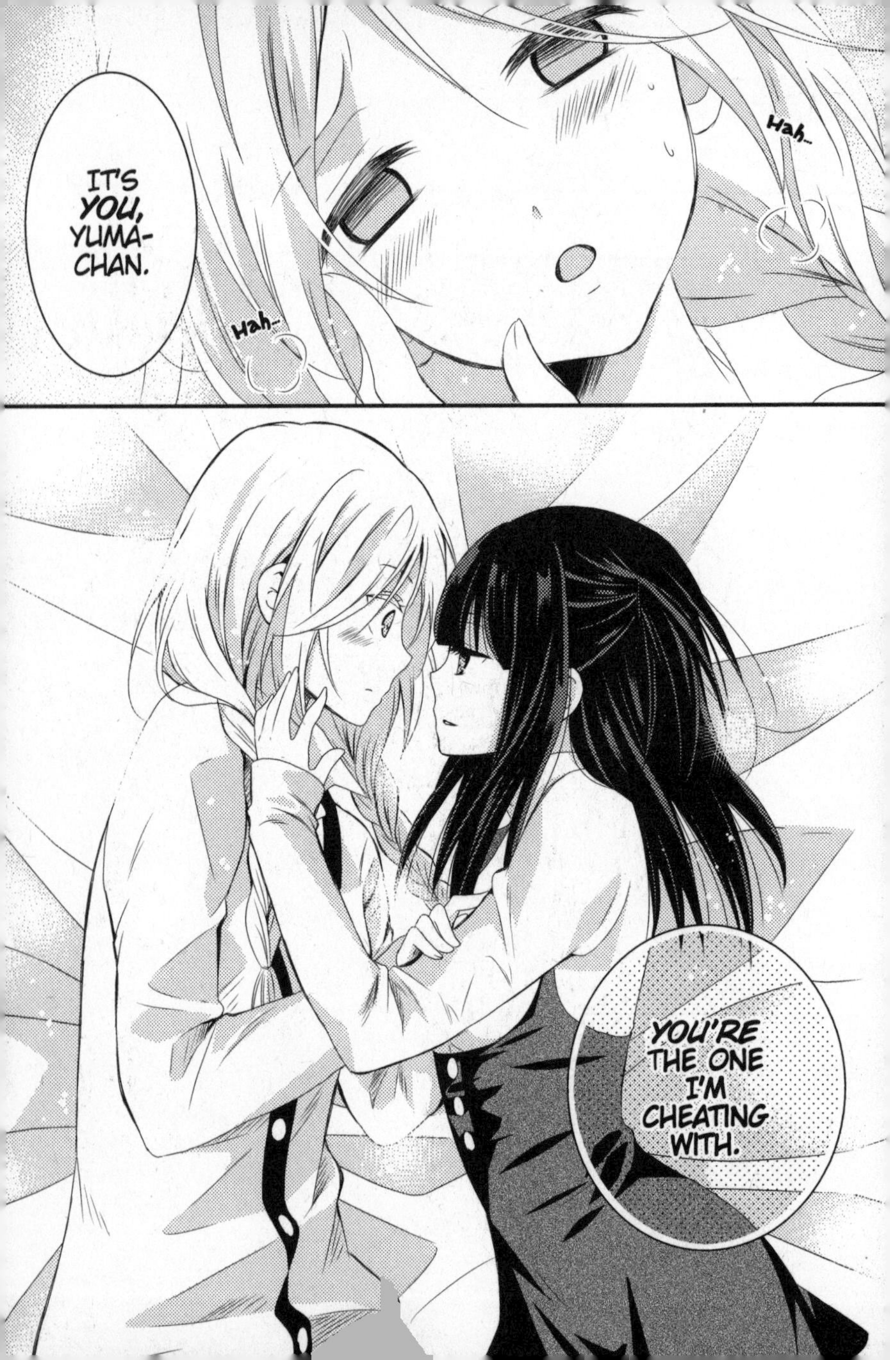
Hah...
IT'S YOU, YUMA-CHAN.
Hah...
YOU'RE THE ONE I'M CHEATING WITH.

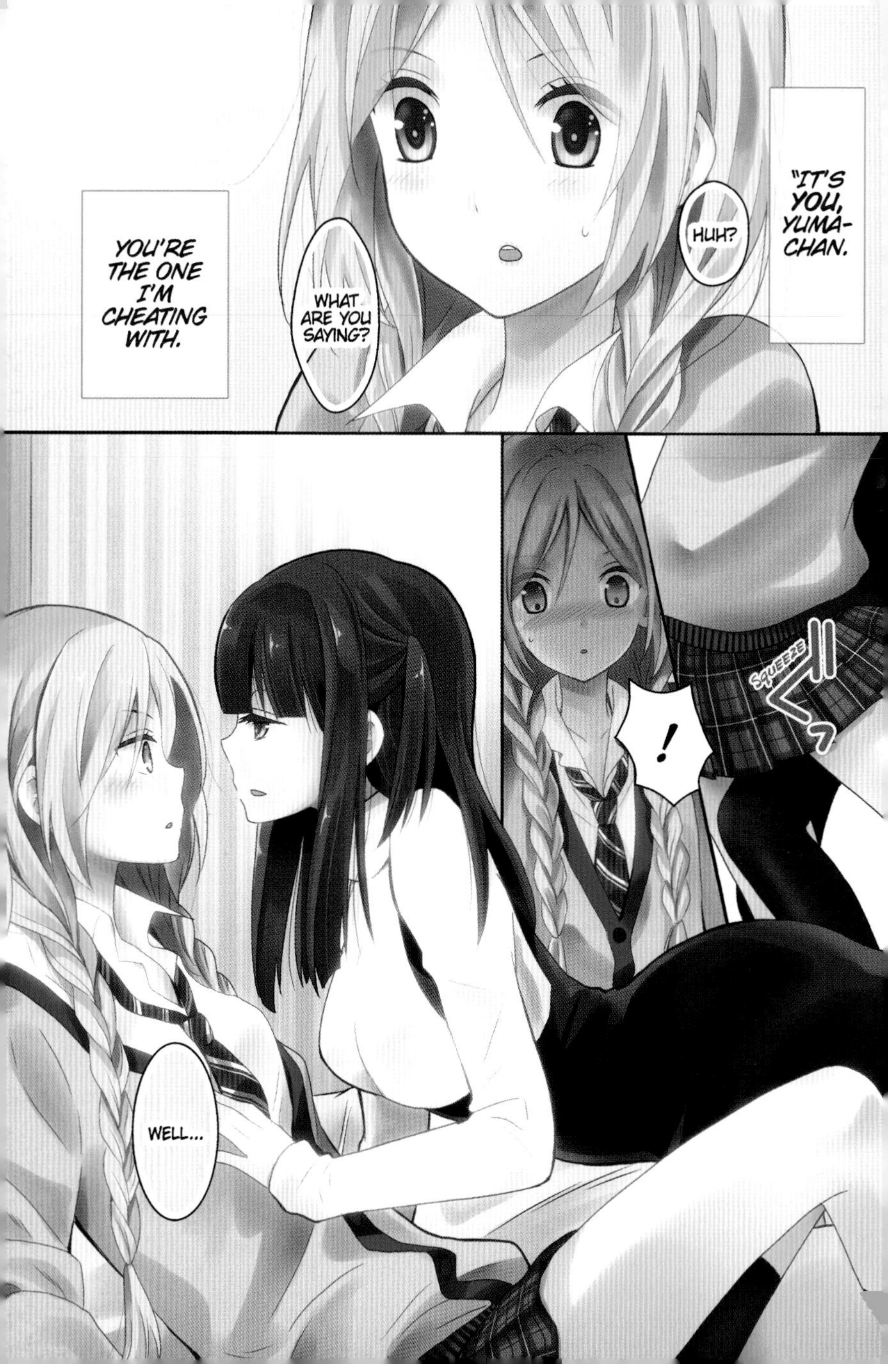
"IT'S YOU, YUMA-CHAN.
HUH?
WHAT ARE YOU SAYING?
YOU'RE THE ONE I'M CHEATING WITH.
SQUEEZE
!
WELL...

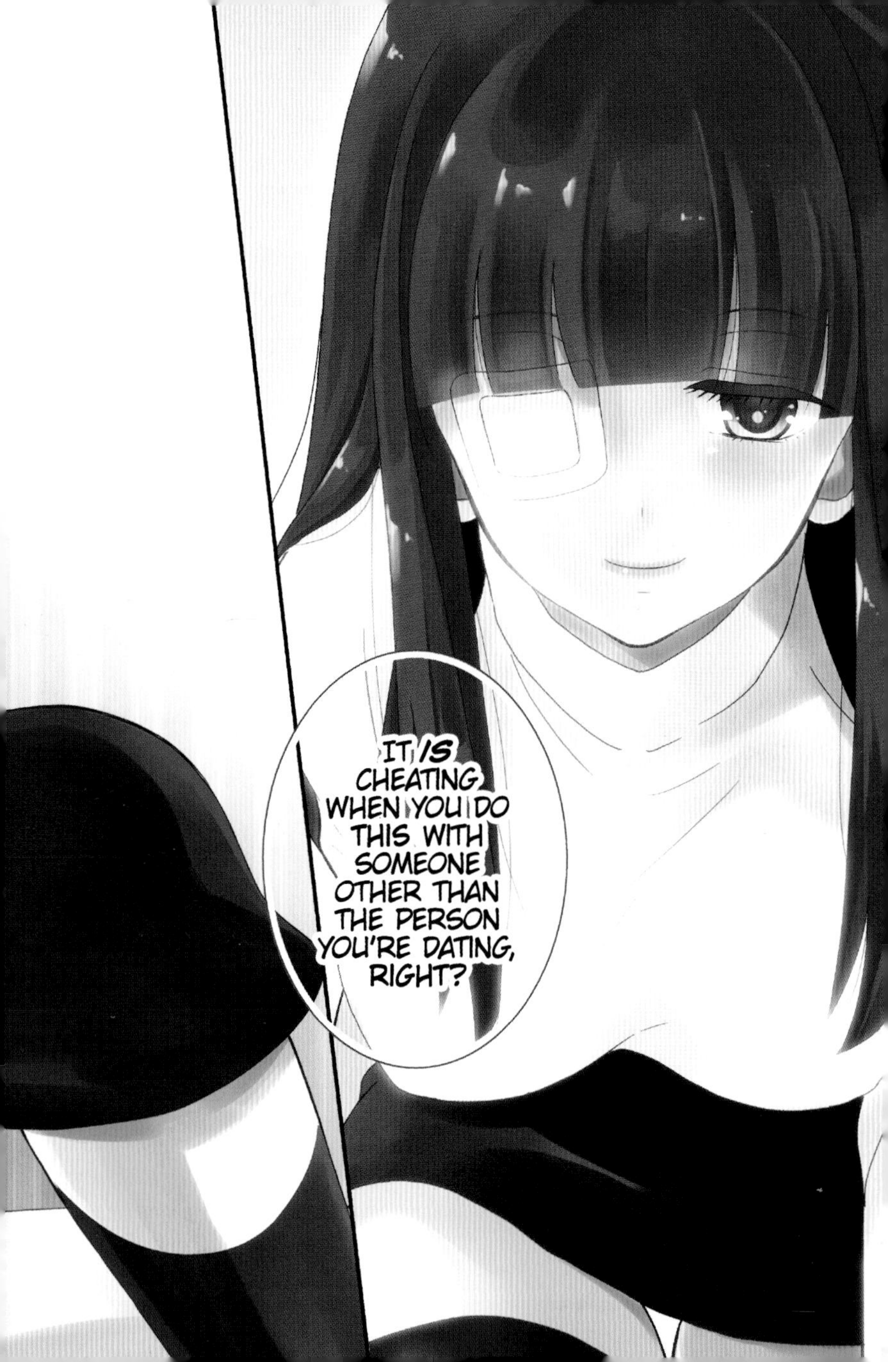
IT *IS* CHEATING WHEN YOU DO THIS WITH SOMEONE OTHER THAN THE PERSON YOU'RE DATING, RIGHT?

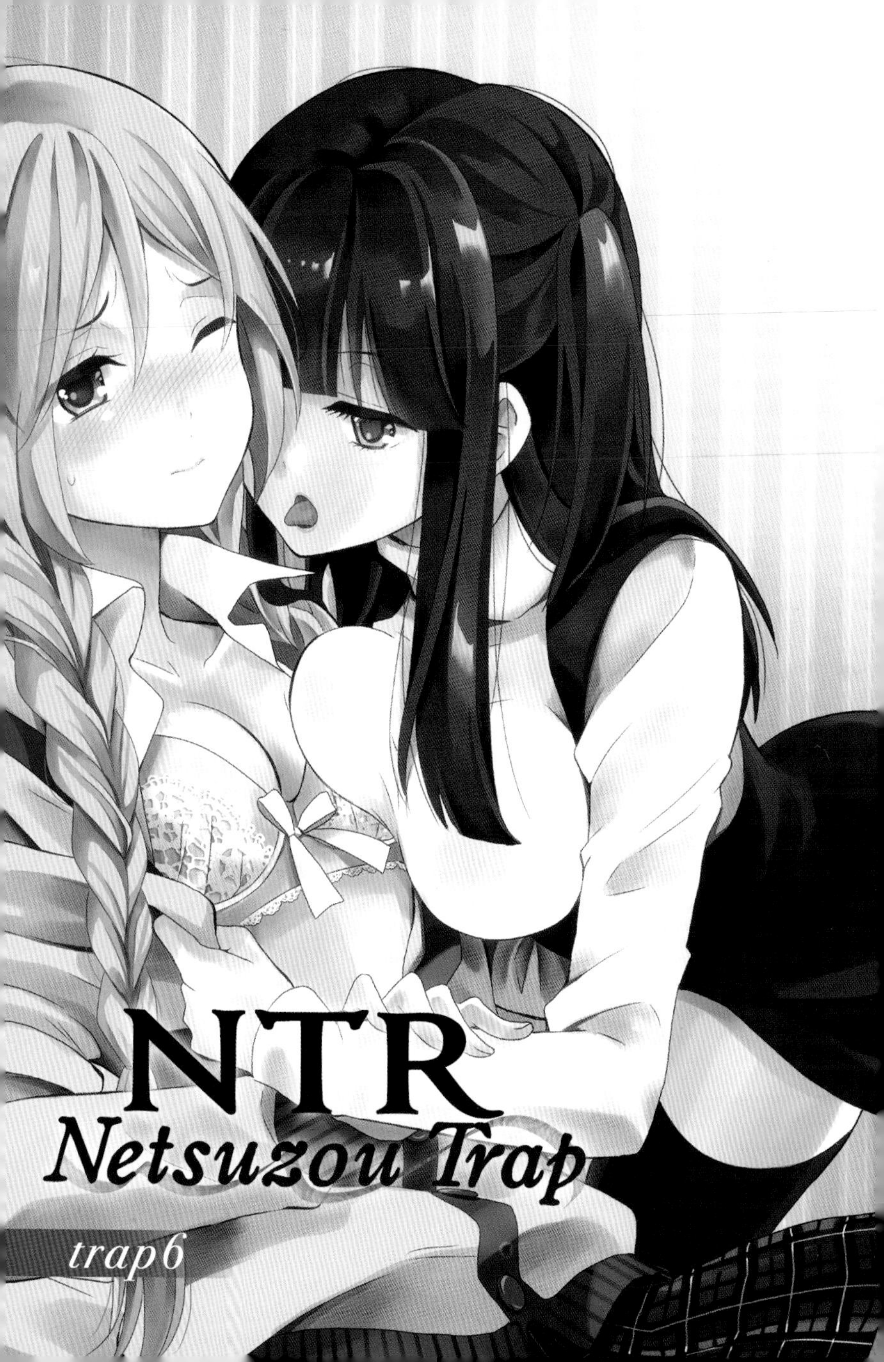
NTR
Netsuzou Trap
trap6

NTR
Netsuzou Trap

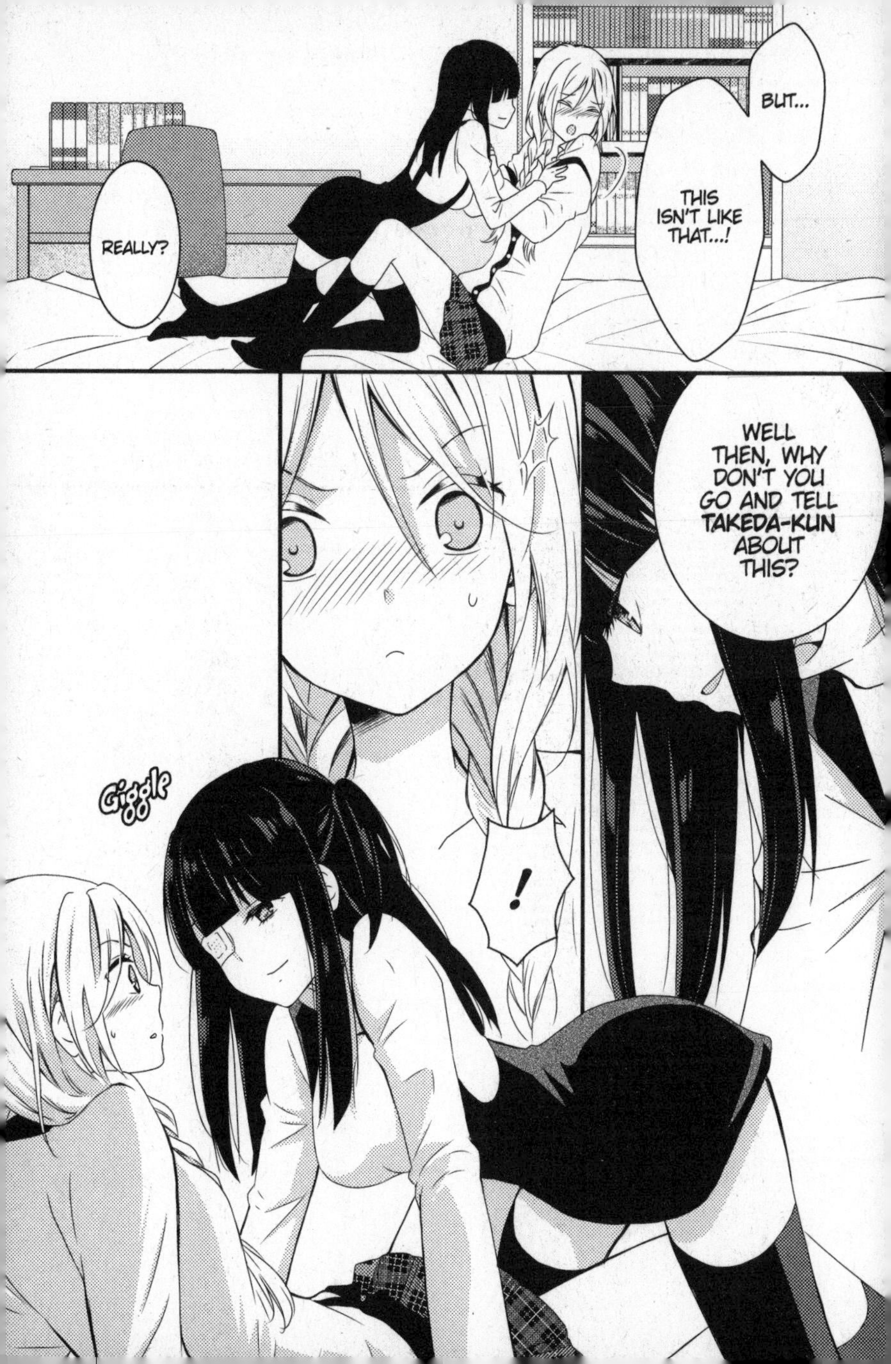
BUT...
THIS ISN'T LIKE THAT...!
REALLY?
WELL THEN, WHY DON'T YOU GO AND TELL TAKEDA-KUN ABOUT THIS?
!
Giggle

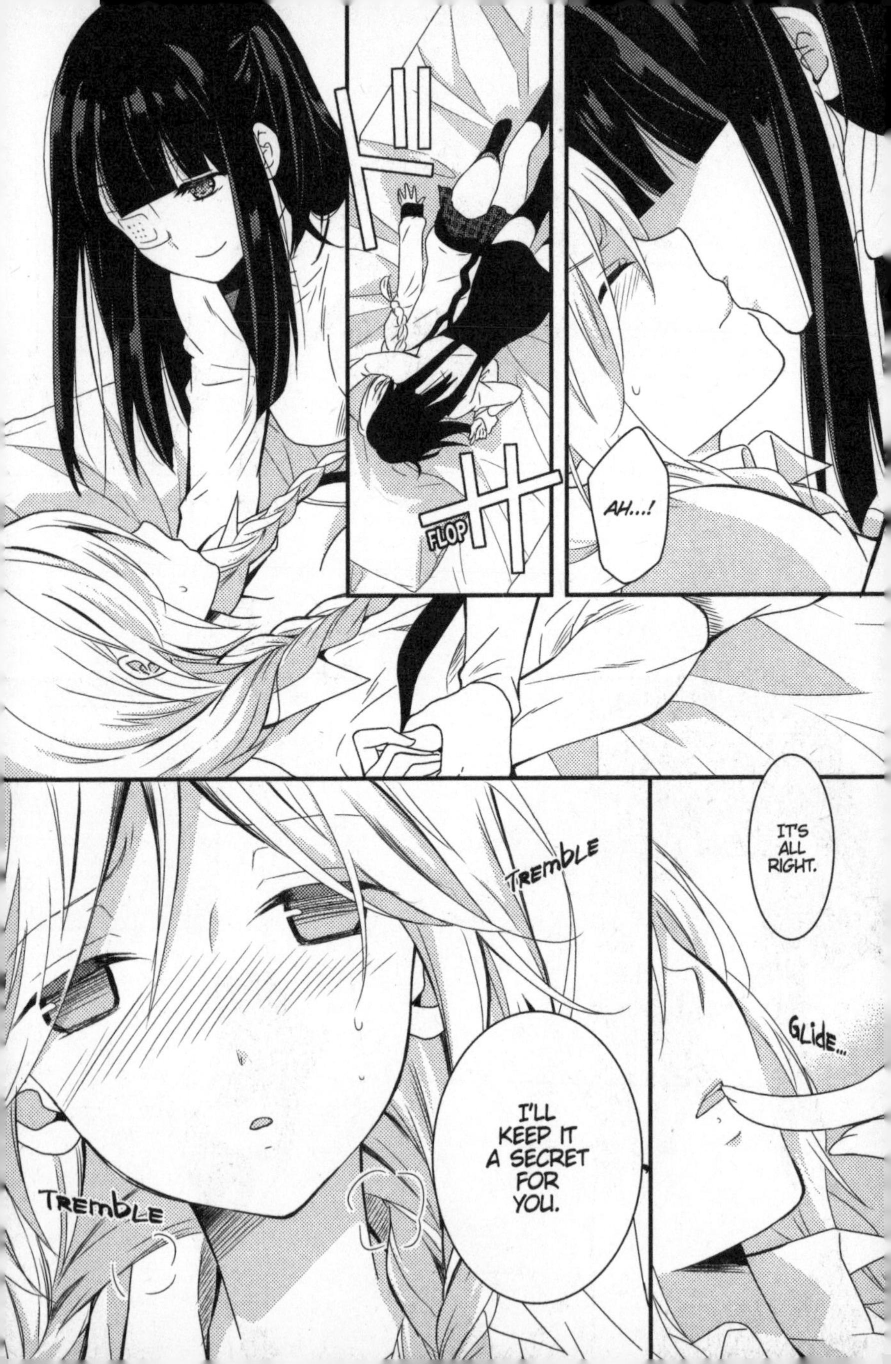
AH...!
FLOP
IT'S ALL RIGHT.
GLIDE...
TREMBLE
I'LL KEEP IT A SECRET FOR YOU.
TREMBLE

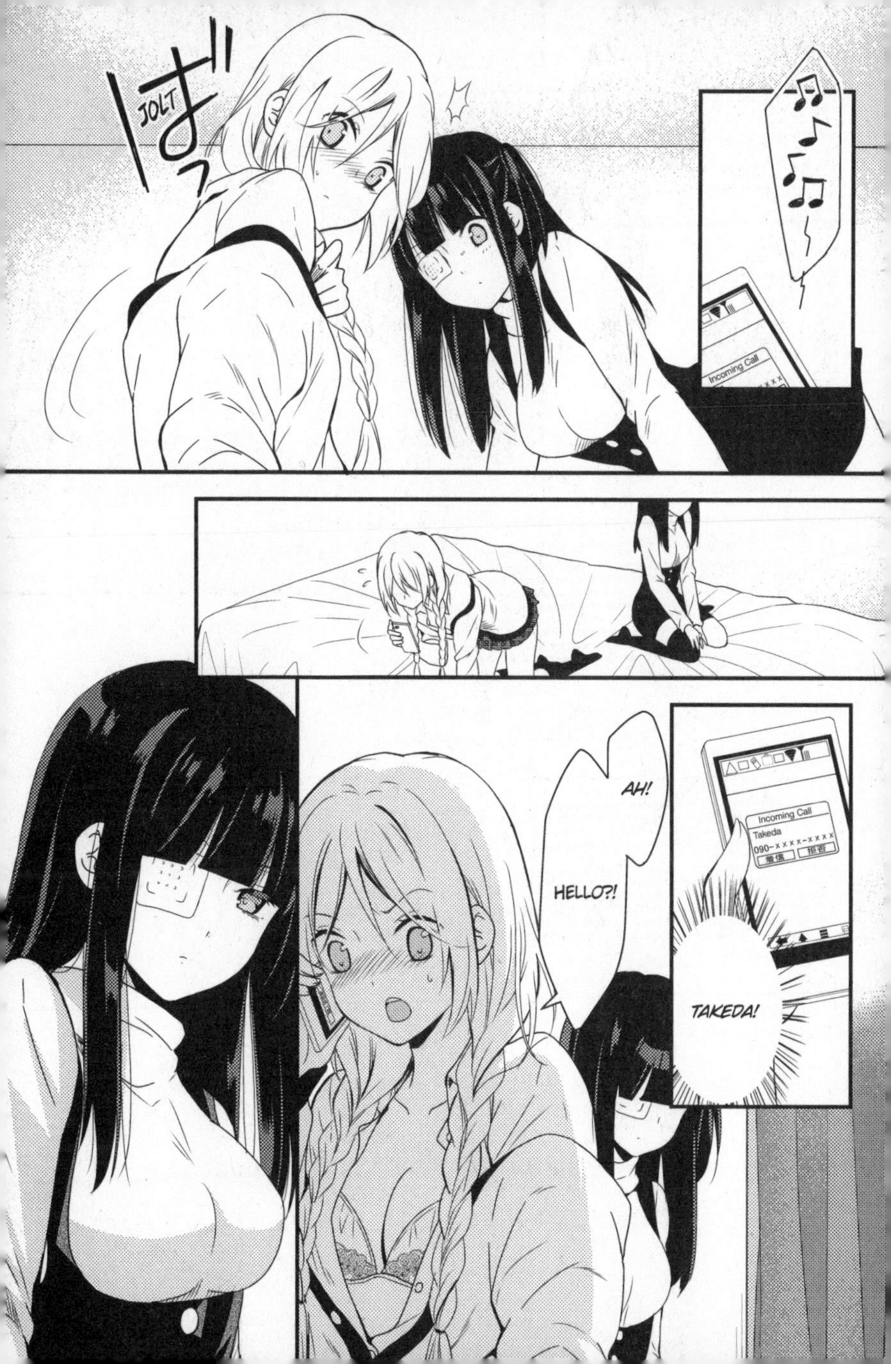
Incoming Call
JOLT
Incoming Call
Takeda
090-xxxx-xxxx
TAKEDA!
AH!
HELLO?!

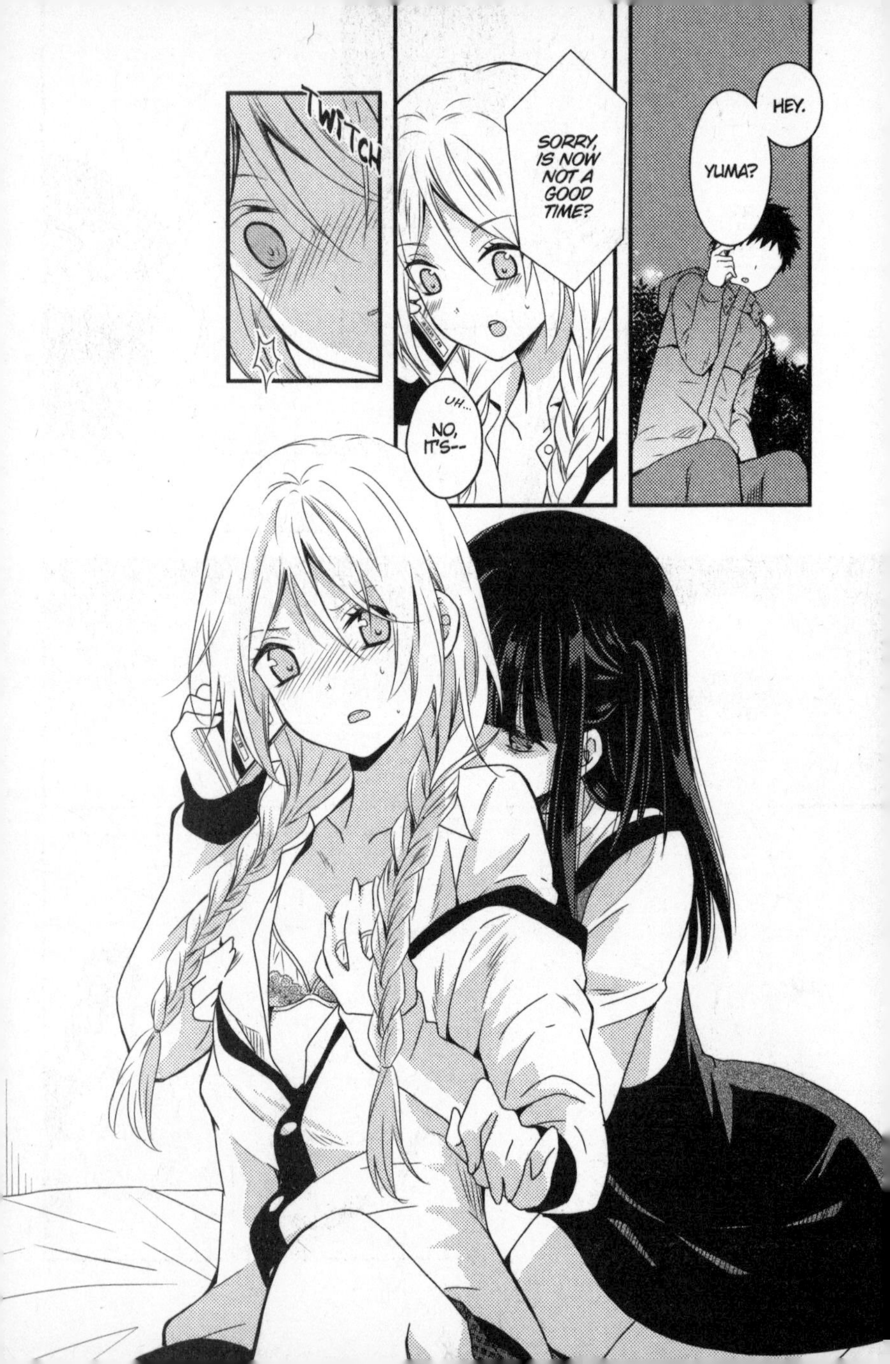
HEY.
YUMA?
SORRY, IS NOW NOT A GOOD TIME?
UH... NO, IT'S--
TWITCH

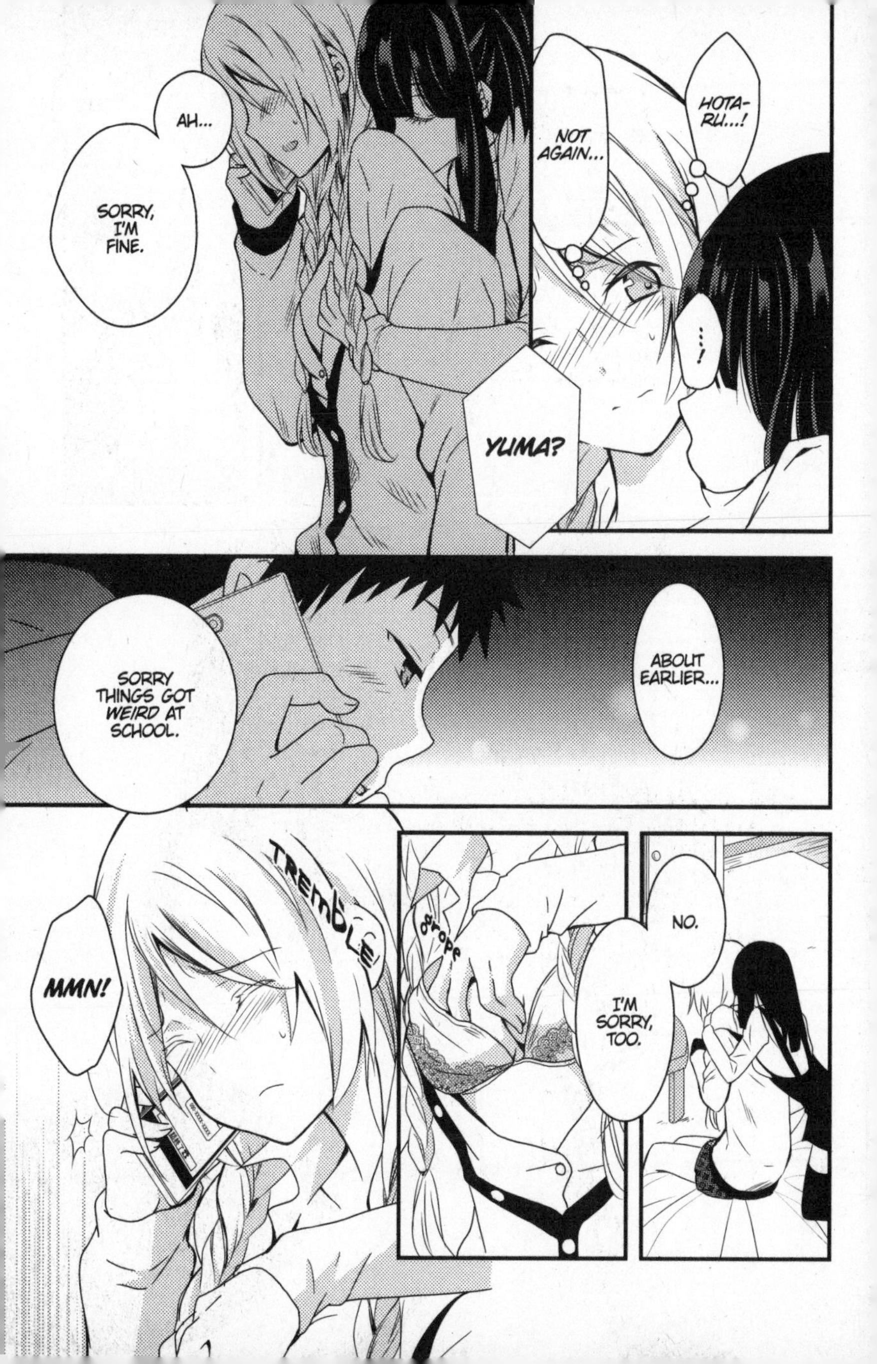
HOTA-RU...!
NOT AGAIN...
...!
YUMA?
AH...
SORRY, I'M FINE.
ABOUT EARLIER...
SORRY THINGS GOT WEIRD AT SCHOOL.
NO.
I'M SORRY, TOO.
grope
TREMBLE
MMN!

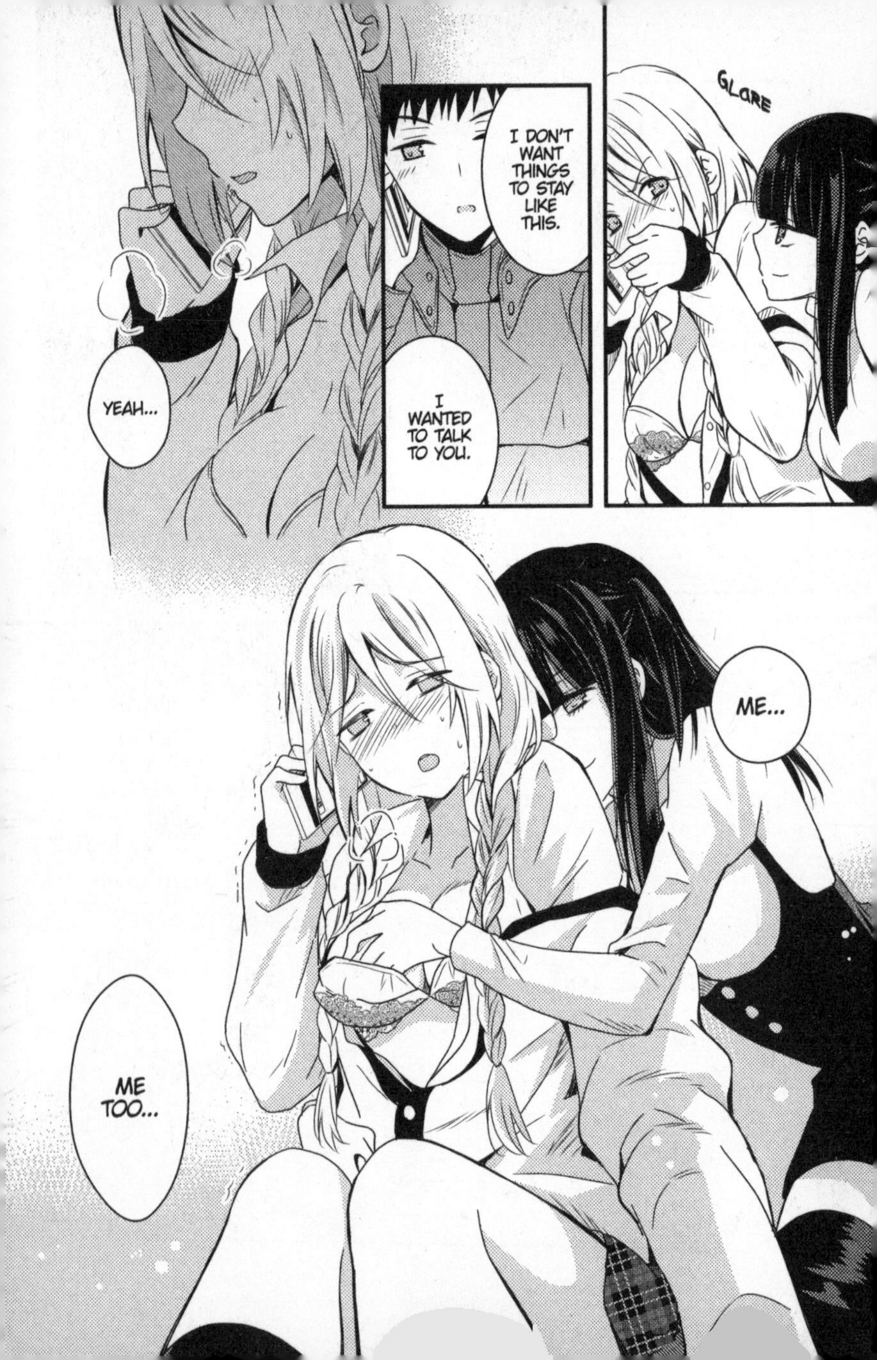
GLARE
I DON'T WANT THINGS TO STAY LIKE THIS.
I WANTED TO TALK TO YOU.
YEAH...
ME...
ME TOO...

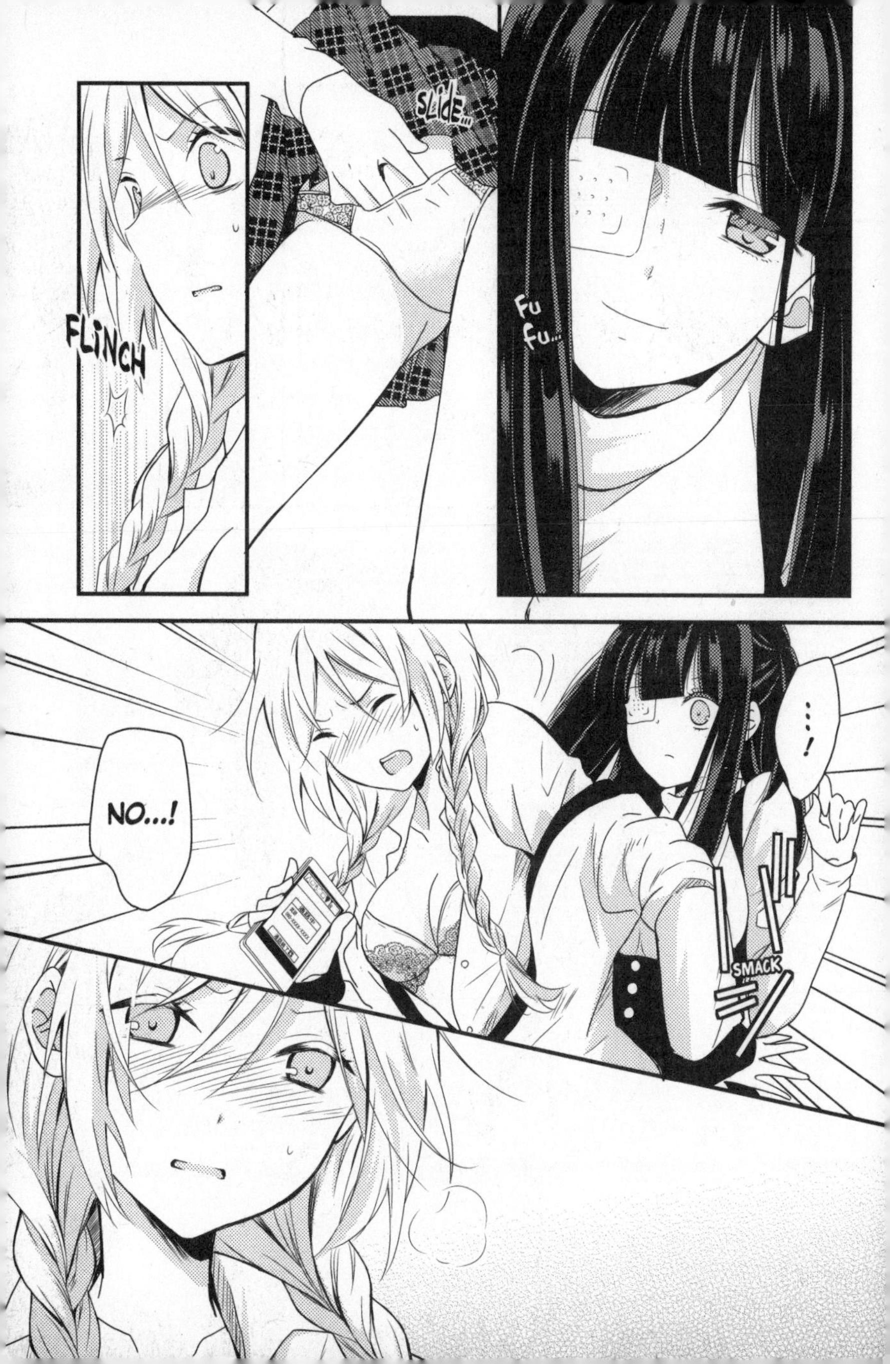
SLIDE...
Fu fu...
FLINCH
...!
SMACK
NO...!

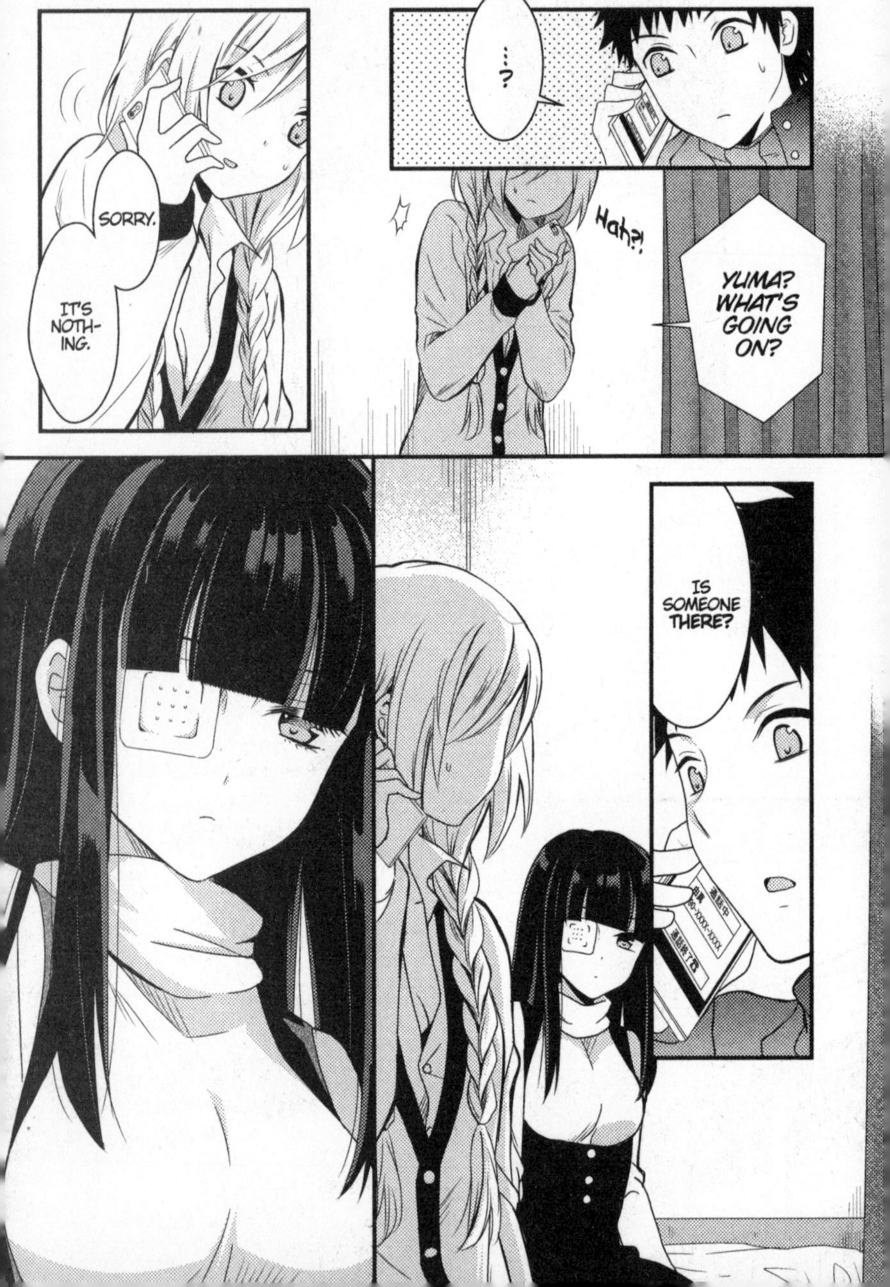
...?
YUMA? WHAT'S GOING ON?
Hah?!
SORRY.
IT'S NOTHING.
IS SOMEONE THERE?

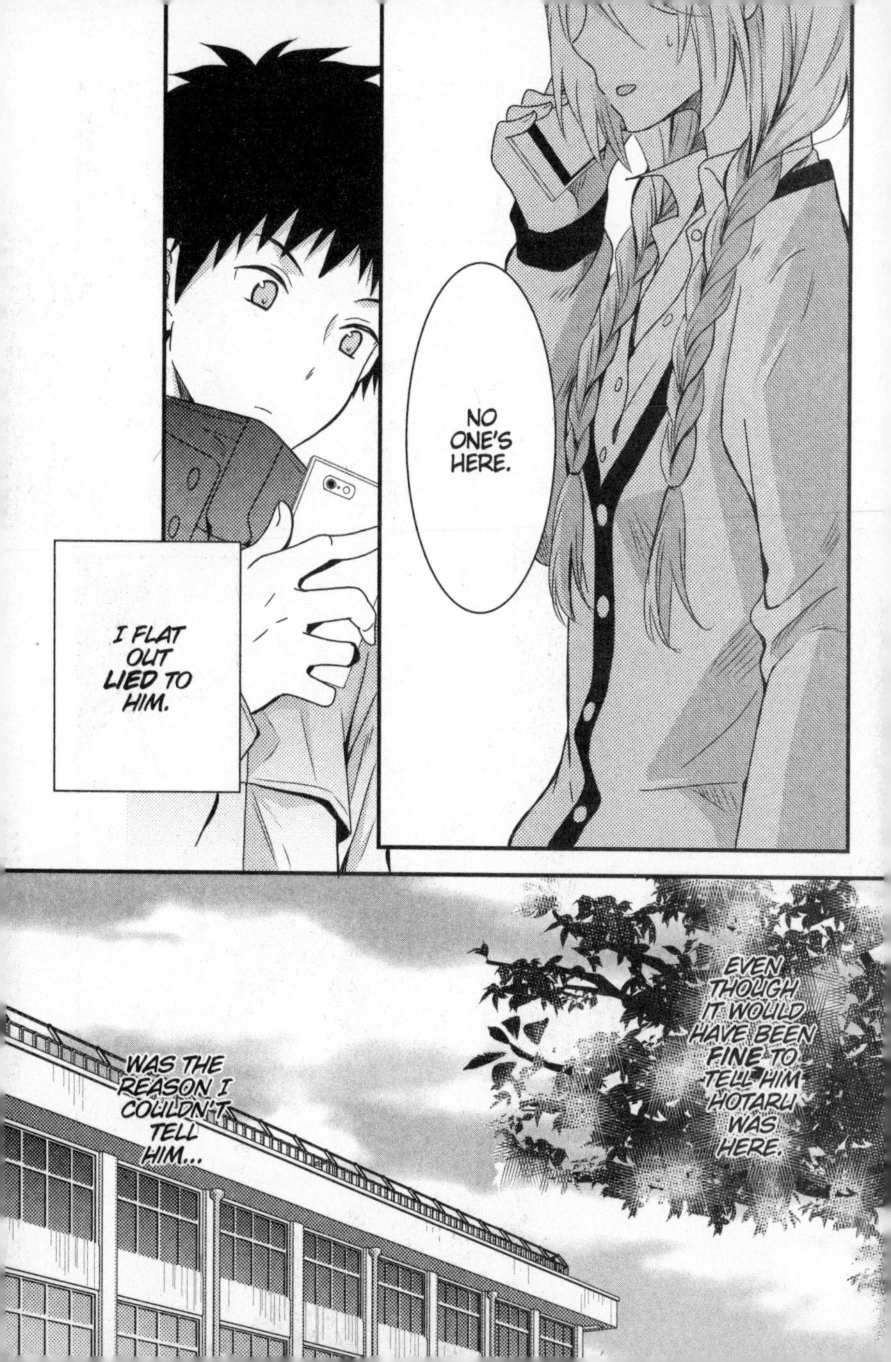
NO ONE'S HERE.
I FLAT OUT LIED TO HIM.
EVEN THOUGH IT WOULD HAVE BEEN FINE TO TELL HIM HOTARU WAS HERE.
WAS THE REASON I COULDN'T TELL HIM...

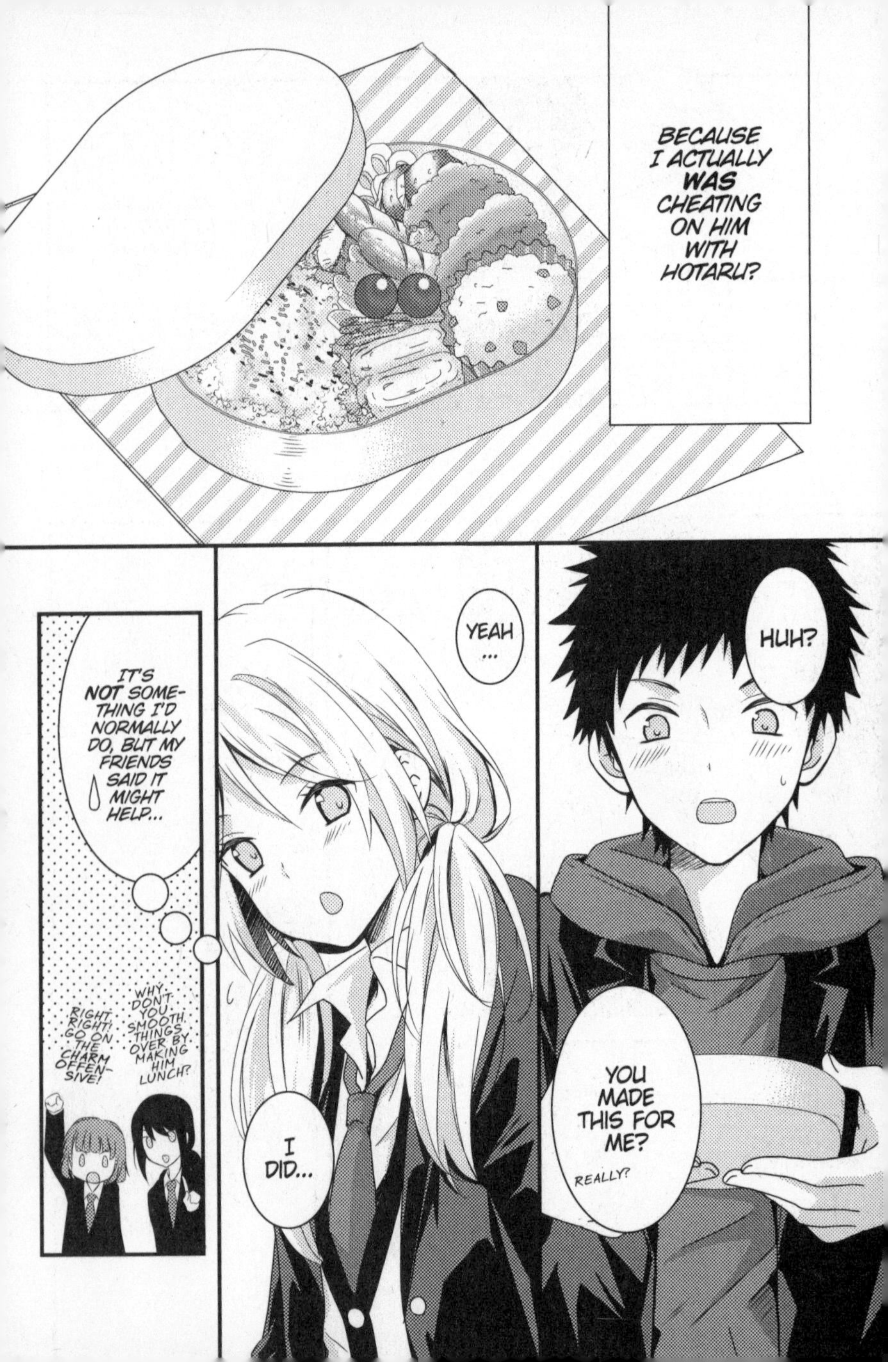
BECAUSE I ACTUALLY WAS CHEATING ON HIM WITH HOTARU?
HUH?
YOU MADE THIS FOR ME?
REALLY?
YEAH ...
I DID...
IT'S NOT SOME-THING I'D NORMALLY DO, BUT MY FRIENDS SAID IT MIGHT HELP...
WHY DON'T YOU SMOOTH THINGS OVER BY MAKING HIM LUNCH?
RIGHT RIGHT! GO ON THE CHARM OFFEN-SIVE!

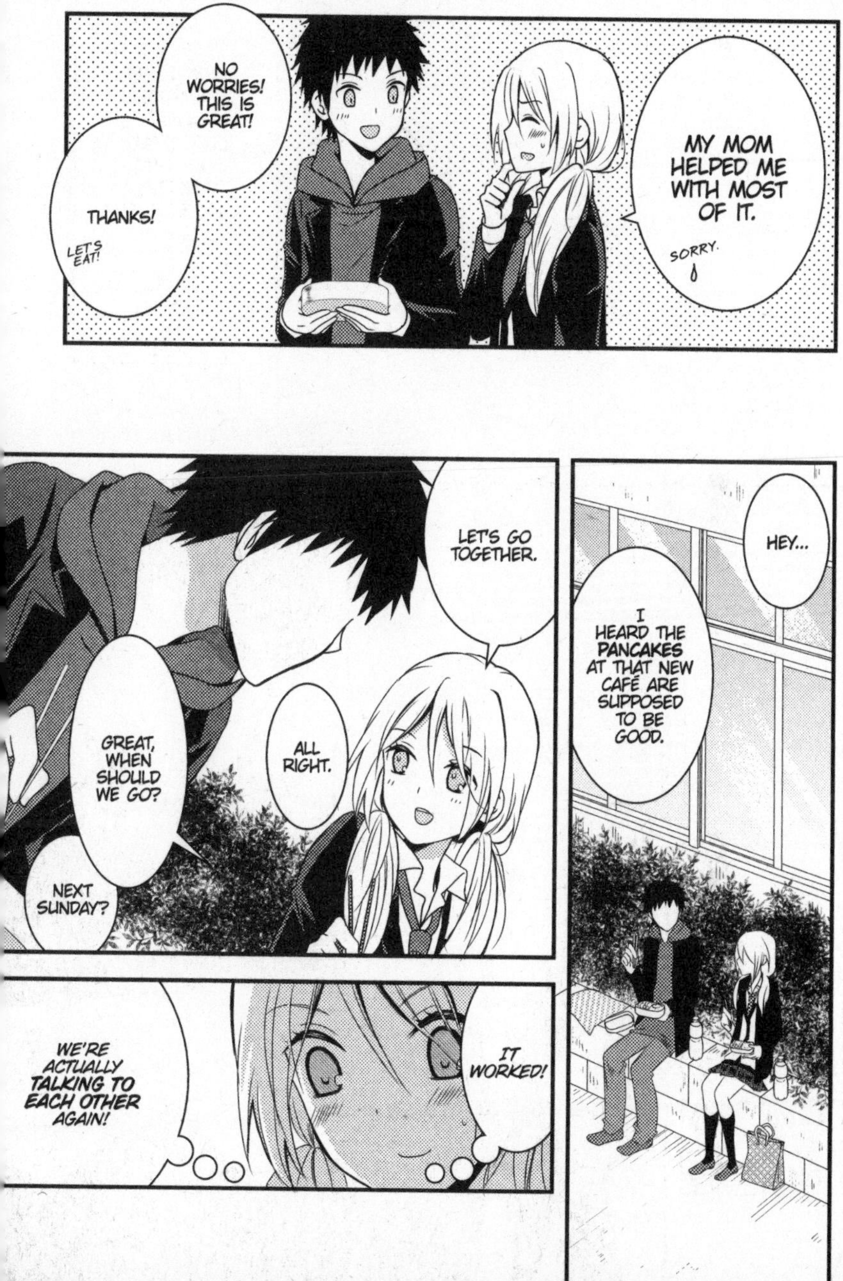

MY MOM HELPED ME WITH MOST OF IT.
SORRY.
NO WORRIES! THIS IS GREAT!
THANKS!
LET'S EAT!
HEY...
I HEARD THE **PANCAKES** AT THAT NEW CAFÉ ARE SUPPOSED TO BE GOOD.
LET'S GO TOGETHER.
ALL RIGHT.
GREAT, WHEN SHOULD WE GO?
NEXT SUNDAY?
IT WORKED!
*WE'RE ACTUALLY **TALKING** TO EACH OTHER AGAIN!*

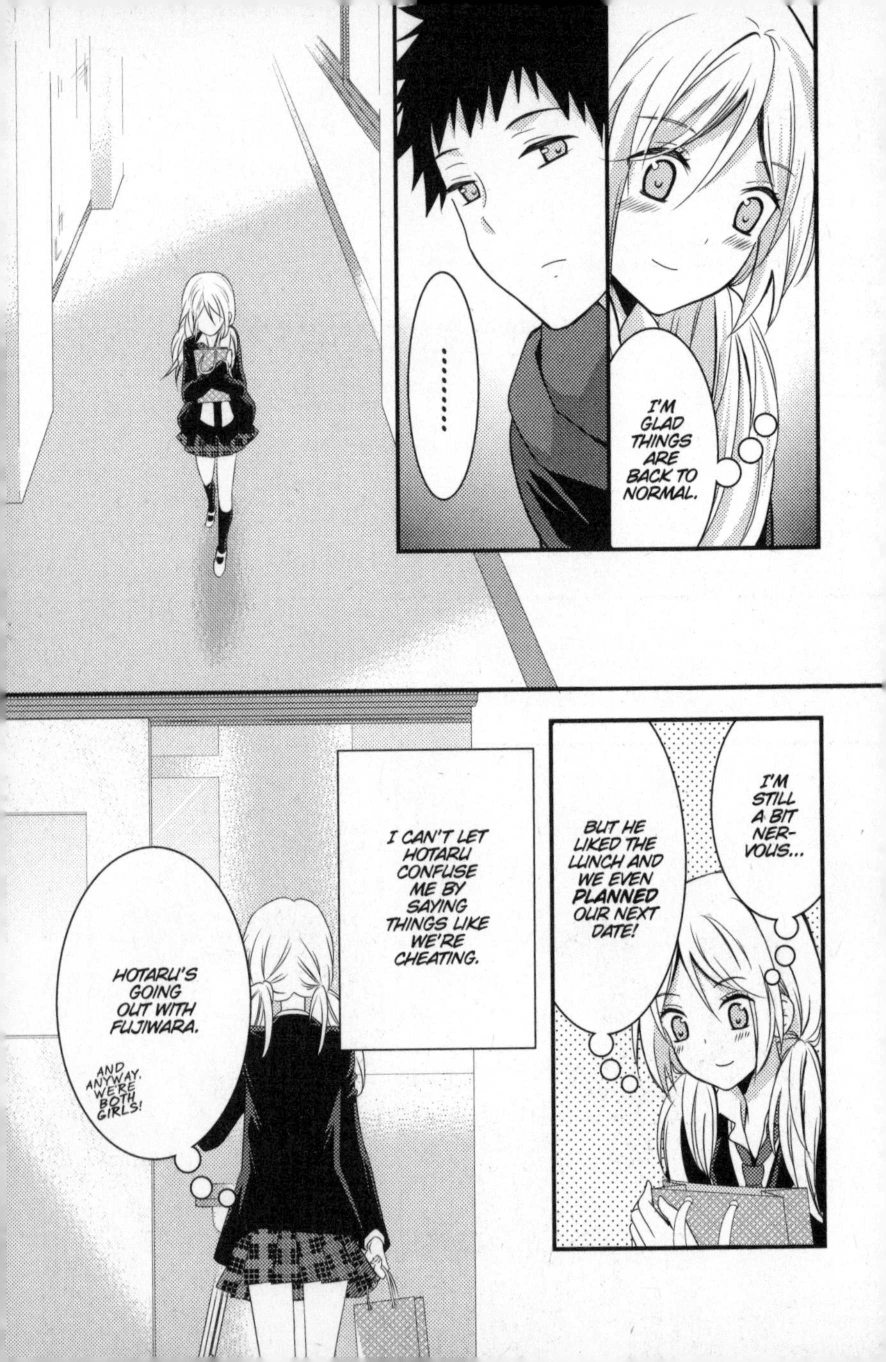
I'M GLAD THINGS ARE BACK TO NORMAL.
......
I'M STILL A BIT NERVOUS...
BUT HE LIKED THE LUNCH AND WE EVEN PLANNED OUR NEXT DATE!
I CAN'T LET HOTARU CONFUSE ME BY SAYING THINGS LIKE WE'RE CHEATING.
HOTARU'S GOING OUT WITH FUJIWARA.
AND ANYWAY, WE'RE BOTH GIRLS!

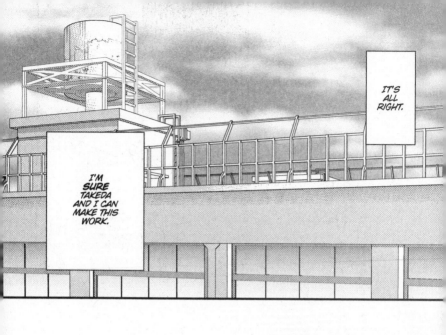

IT'S ALL RIGHT.

I'M SURE TAKEDA AND I CAN MAKE THIS WORK.

I CAN'T ACT LIKE NOTHING'S CHANGED.

AH, MAN!

IT'S NO USE!

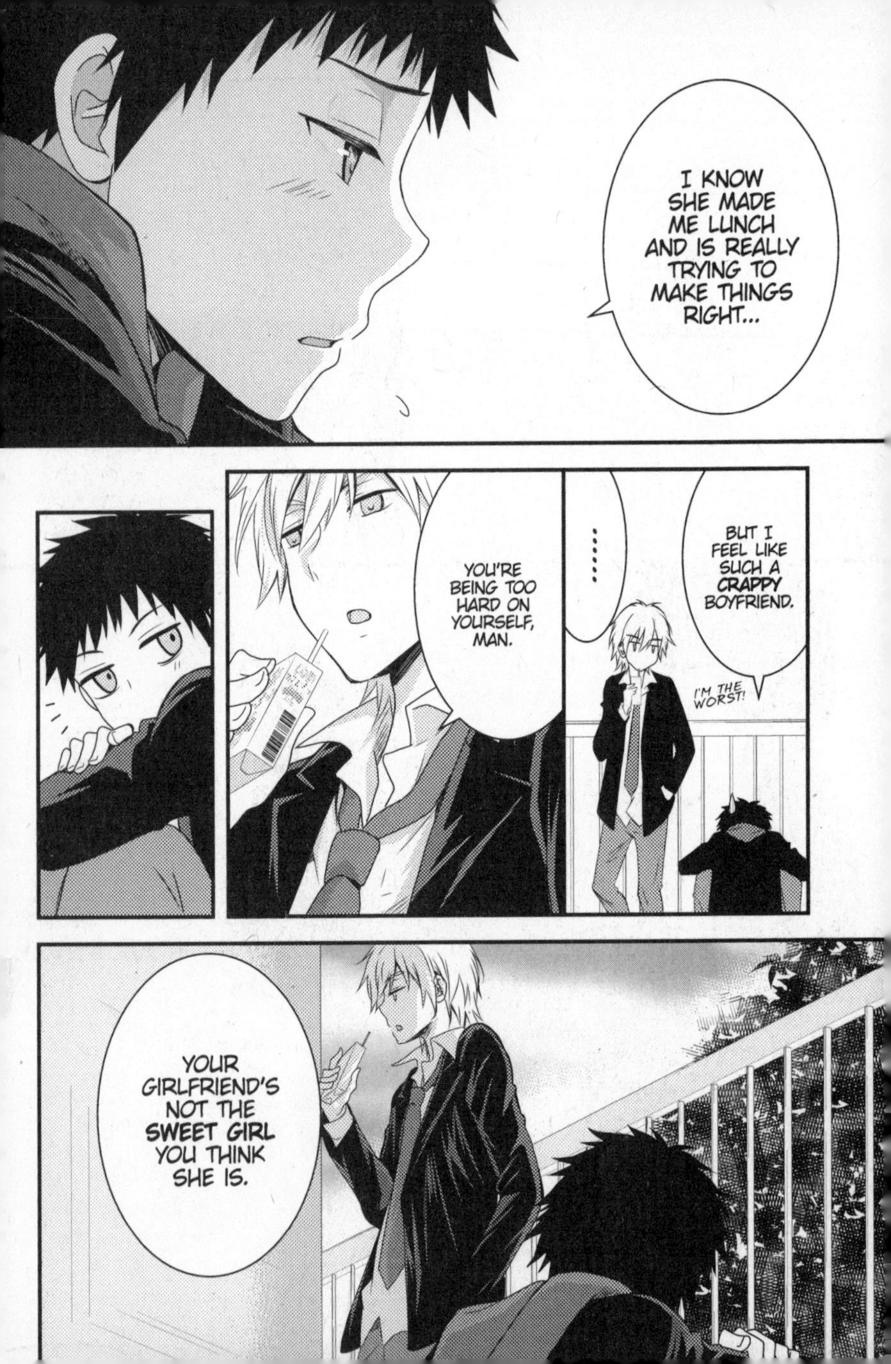
I KNOW SHE MADE ME LUNCH AND IS REALLY TRYING TO MAKE THINGS RIGHT...
BUT I FEEL LIKE SUCH A **CRAPPY** BOYFRIEND.
I'M THE WORST!
......
YOU'RE BEING TOO HARD ON YOURSELF, MAN.
YOUR GIRLFRIEND'S NOT THE **SWEET GIRL** YOU THINK SHE IS.

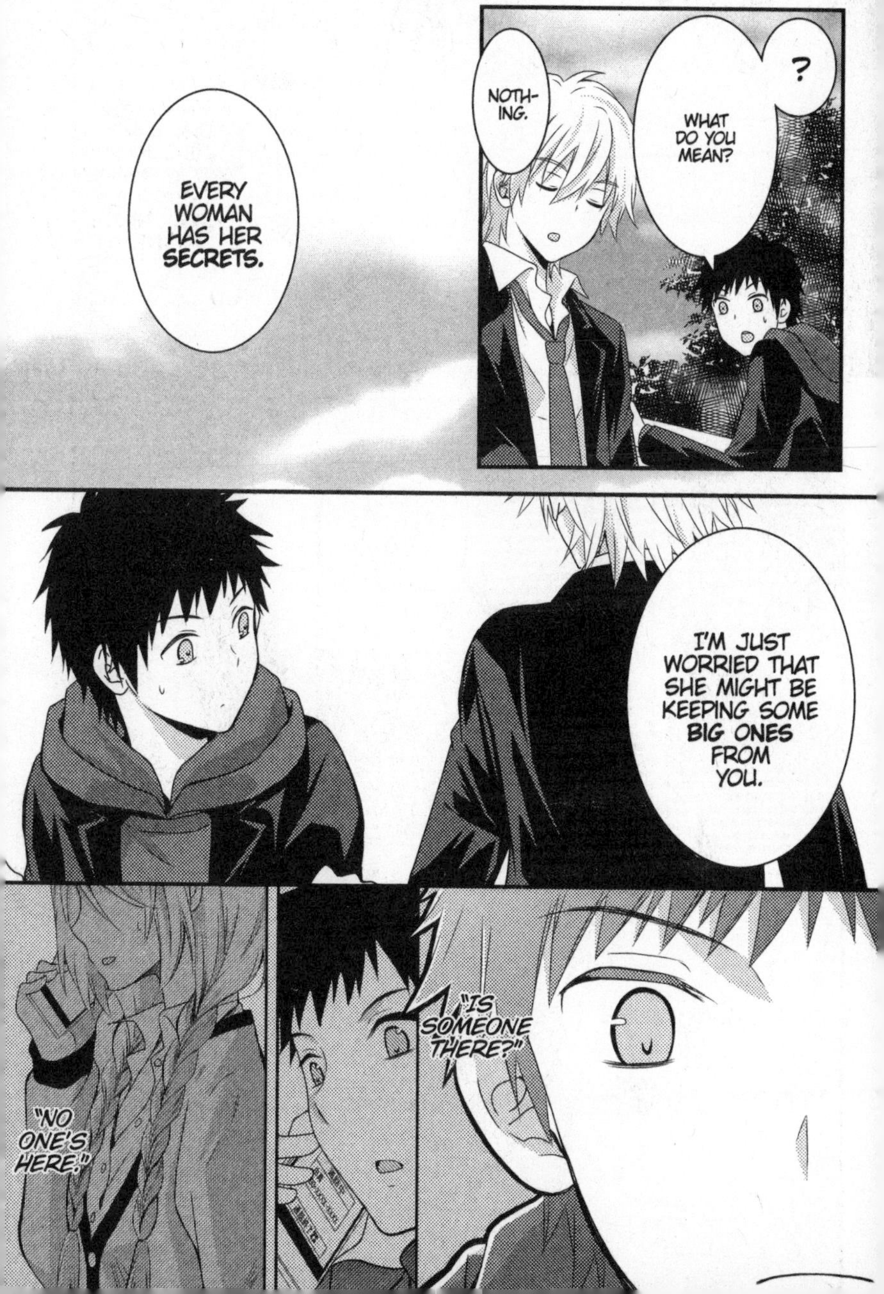
?
WHAT DO YOU MEAN?
NOTH-ING.
EVERY WOMAN HAS HER SECRETS.
I'M JUST WORRIED THAT SHE MIGHT BE KEEPING SOME BIG ONES FROM YOU.
"IS SOMEONE THERE?"
"NO ONE'S HERE."

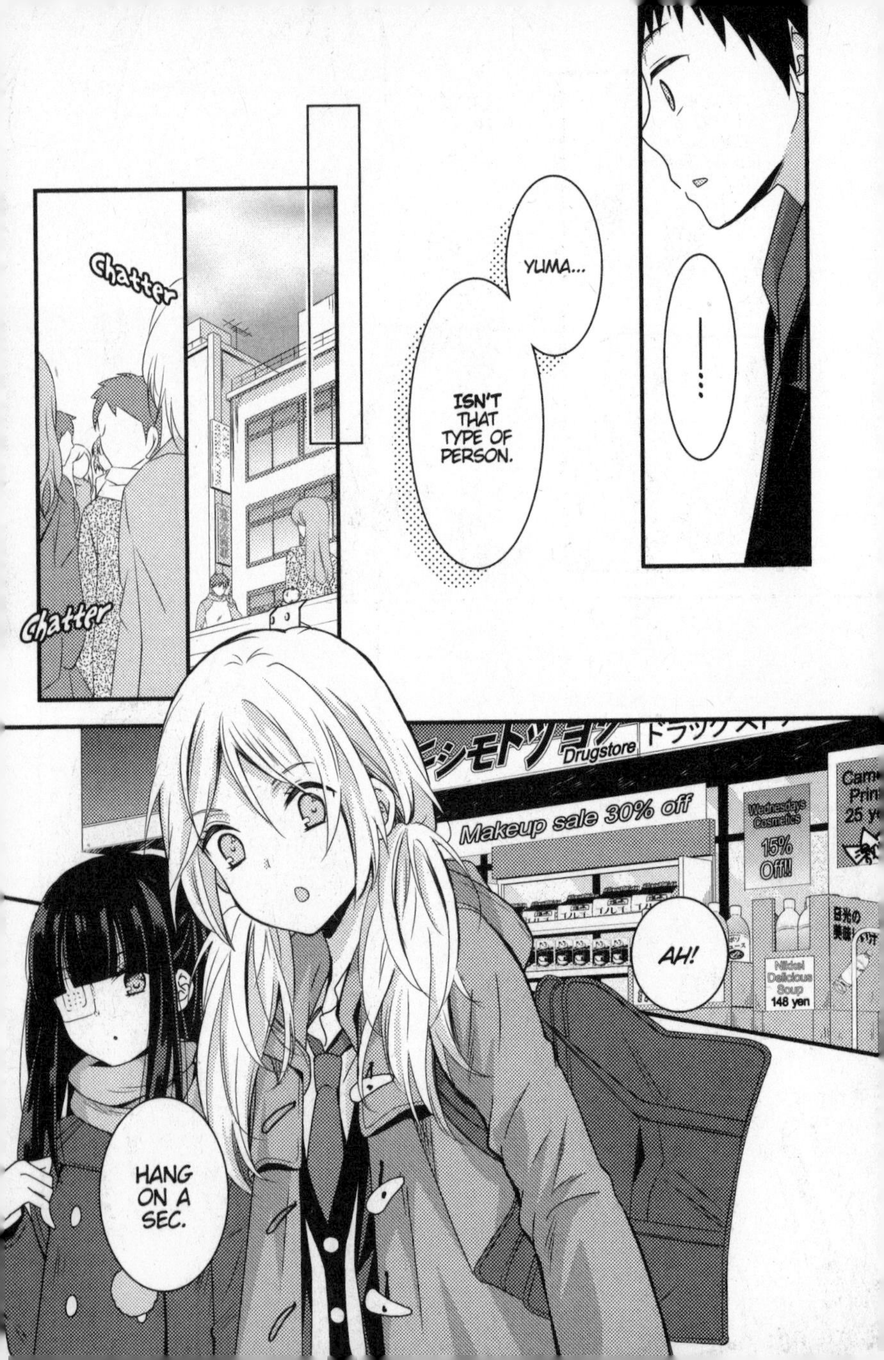
......
YUMA...
ISN'T THAT TYPE OF PERSON.
Chatter
Chatter
Drugstore
Makeup sale 30% off
Wednesdays Cosmetics 15% Off!!
Nikkei Delicious Soup 148 yen
AH!
HANG ON A SEC.

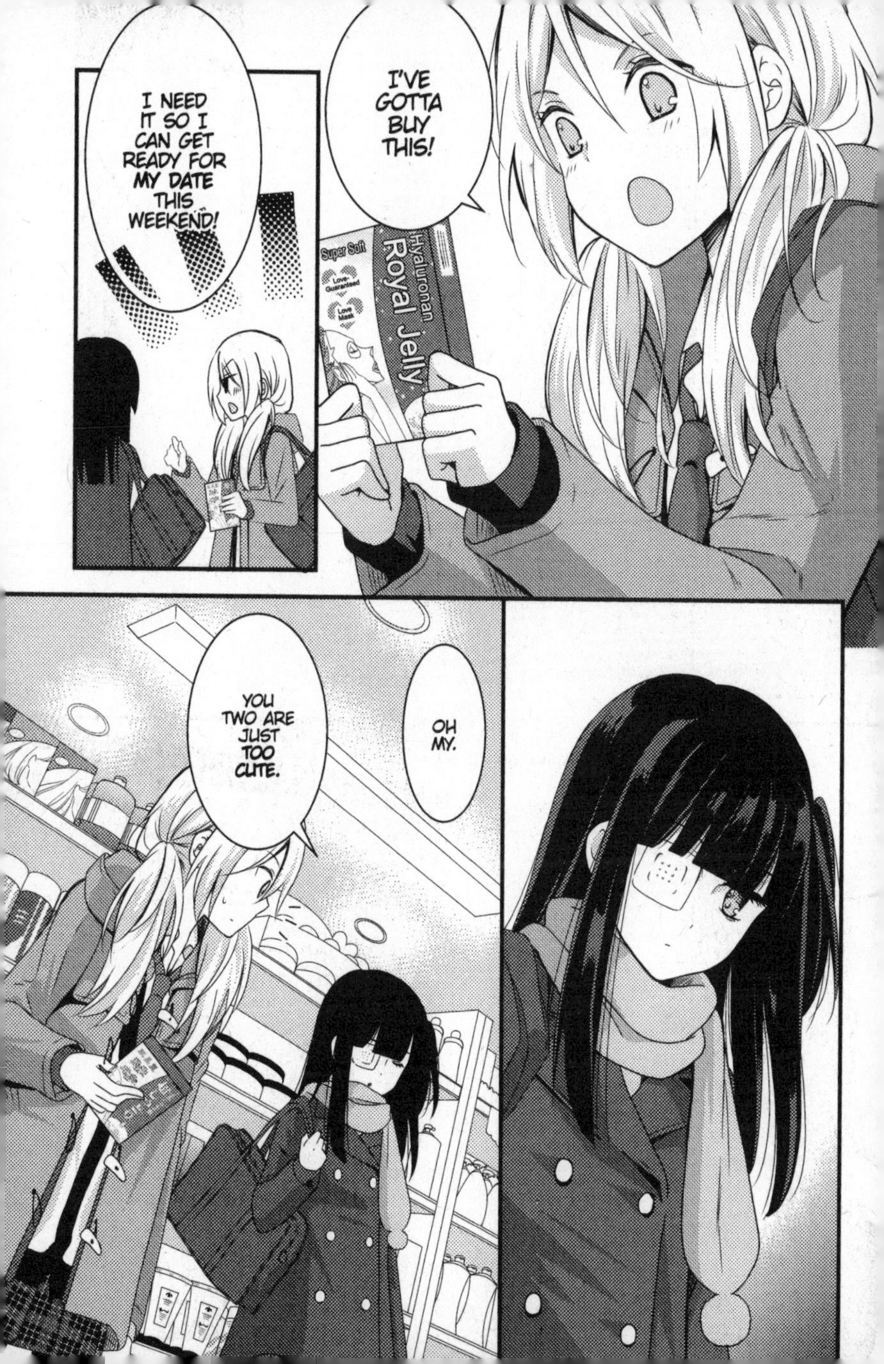
I'VE GOTTA BUY THIS!
Hyaluronan Royal Jelly
Super Soft
Love-Guaranteed
Love Mask
I NEED IT SO I CAN GET READY FOR MY DATE THIS WEEKEND!
OH MY.
YOU TWO ARE JUST TOO CUTE.

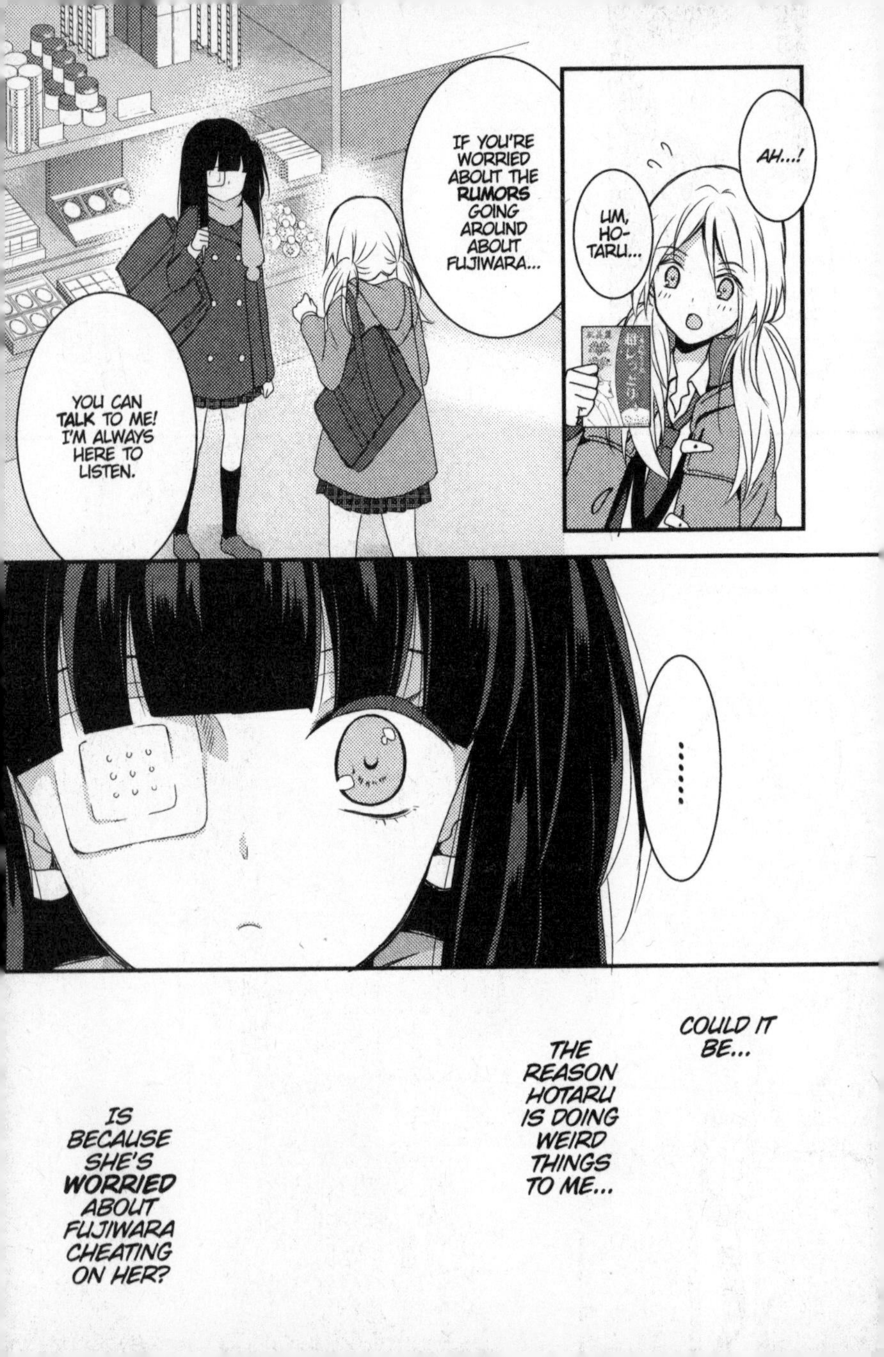
AH...!
UM, HO-TARU...
IF YOU'RE WORRIED ABOUT THE **RUMORS** GOING AROUND ABOUT FUJIWARA...
YOU CAN **TALK** TO ME! I'M ALWAYS HERE TO LISTEN.
......
COULD IT BE...
THE REASON HOTARU IS DOING WEIRD THINGS TO ME...
IS BECAUSE SHE'S **WORRIED** ABOUT FUJIWARA CHEATING ON HER?

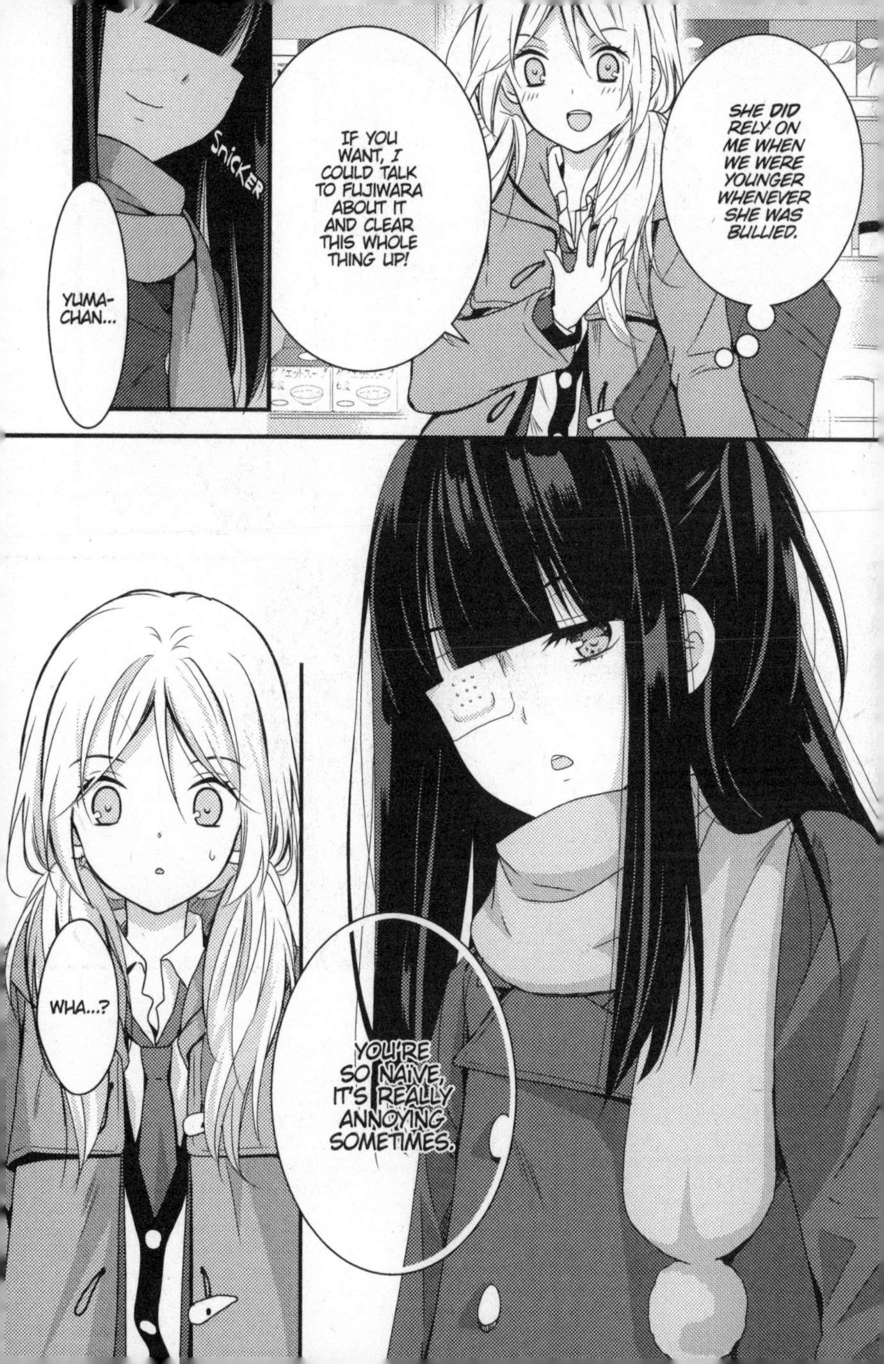
SHE DID RELY ON ME WHEN WE WERE YOUNGER WHENEVER SHE WAS BULLIED.
IF YOU WANT, I COULD TALK TO FUJIWARA ABOUT IT AND CLEAR THIS WHOLE THING UP!
SNICKER
YUMA-CHAN...
YOU'RE SO NAIVE, IT'S REALLY ANNOYING SOMETIMES.
WHA...?

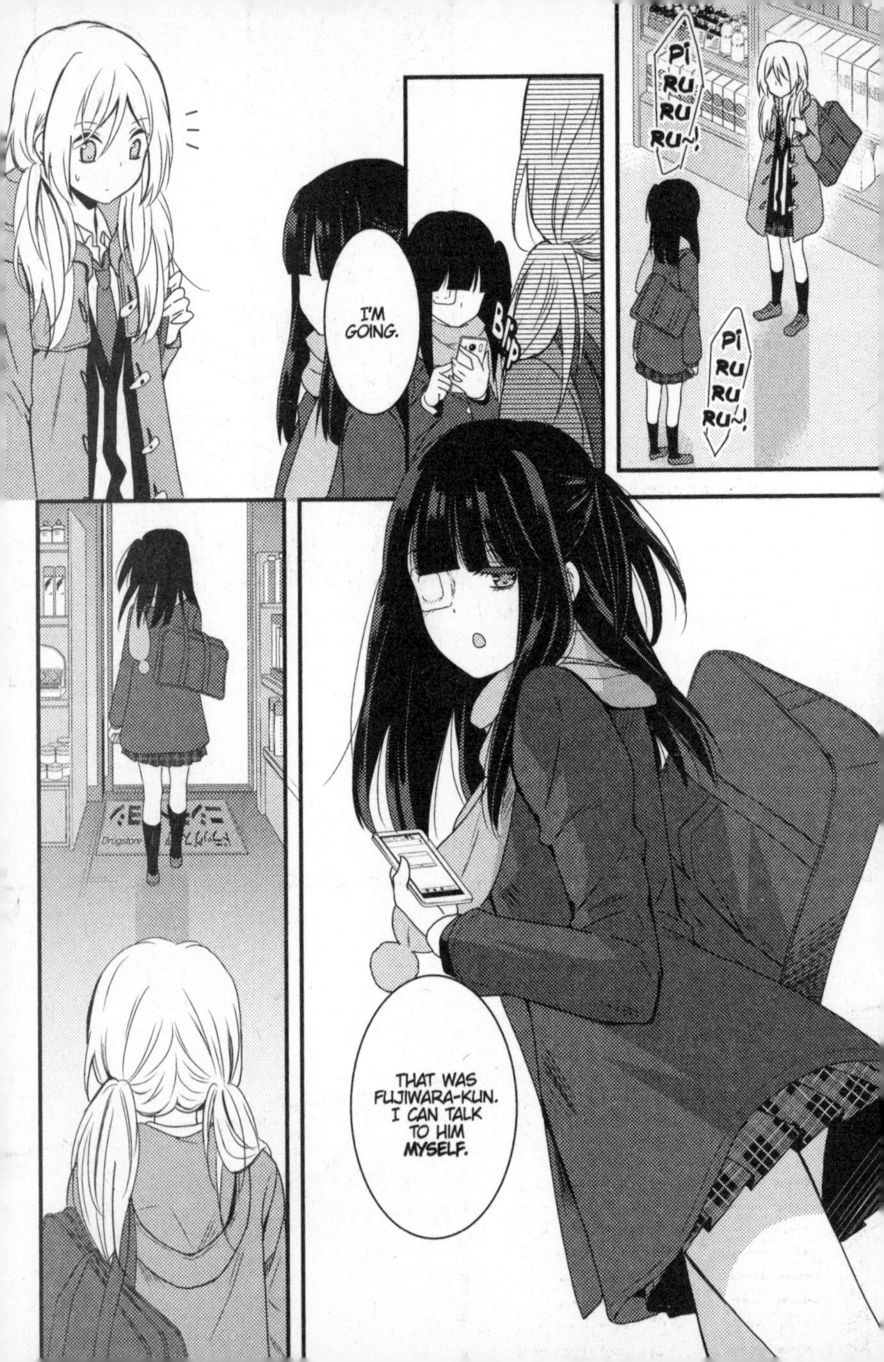
PI RU RU RU~!
PI RU RU RU~!
BIIP
I'M GOING.
THAT WAS FUJIWARA-KUN. I CAN TALK TO HIM MYSELF.
Drugstore

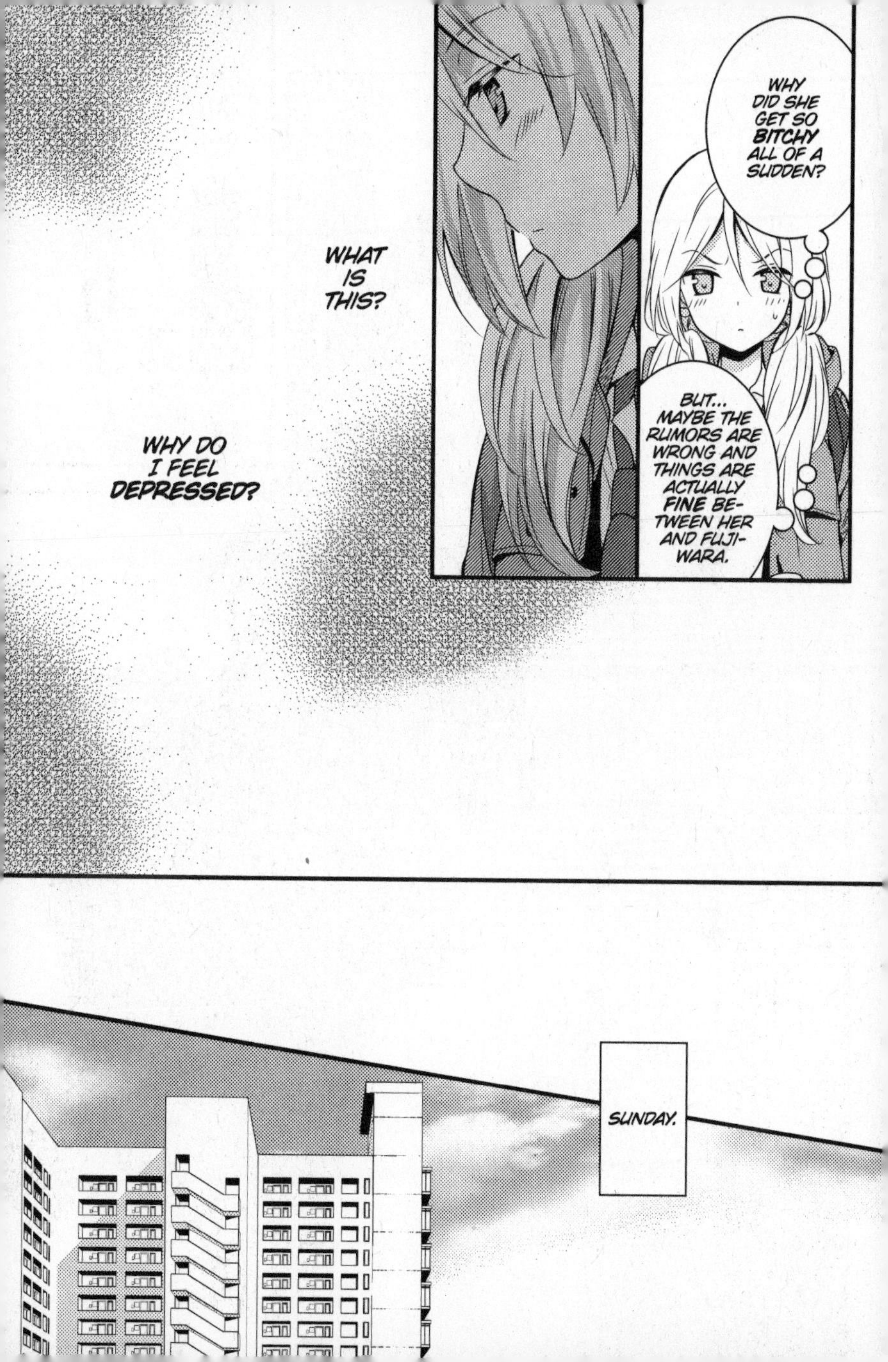
WHY DID SHE GET SO BITCHY ALL OF A SUDDEN?
BUT... MAYBE THE RUMORS ARE WRONG AND THINGS ARE ACTUALLY FINE BE-TWEEN HER AND FUJI-WARA.
WHAT IS THIS?
WHY DO I FEEL DEPRESSED?
SUNDAY.

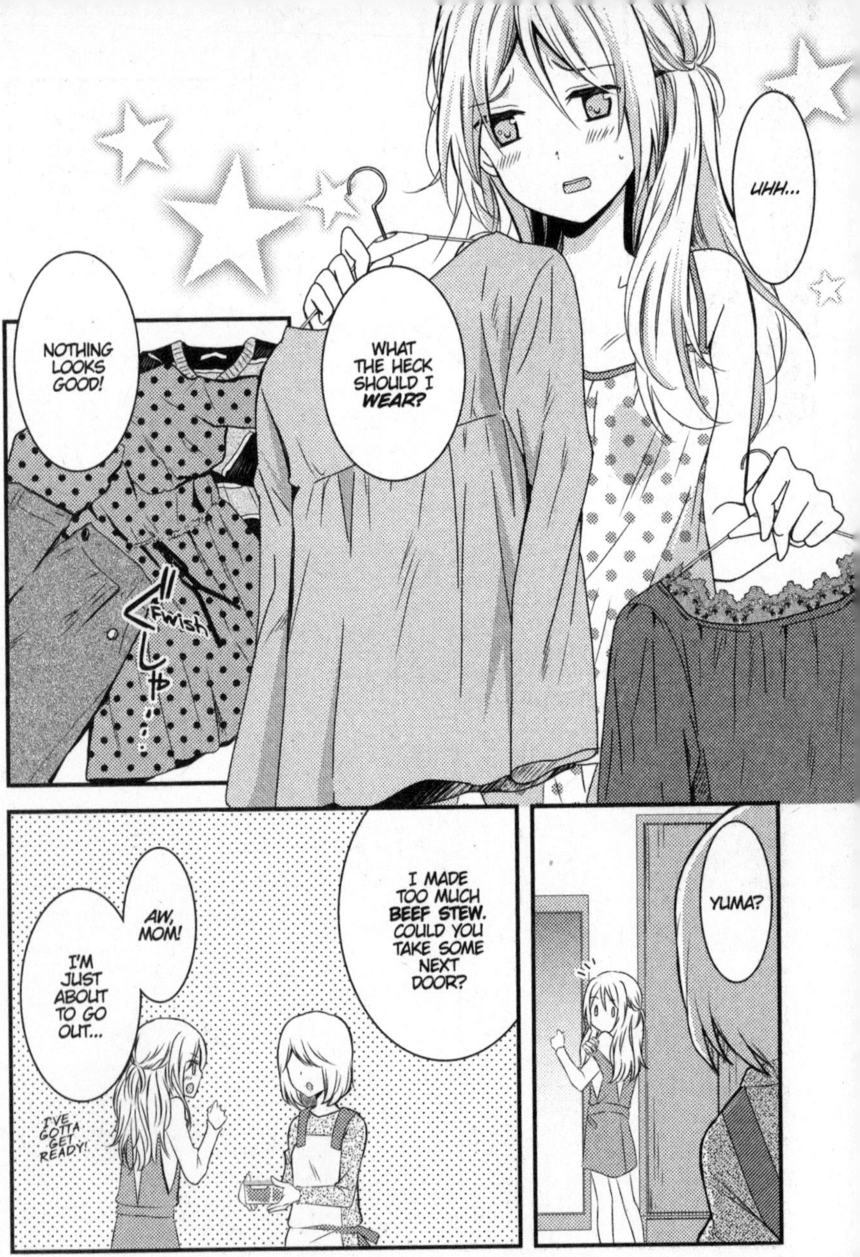
UHH...
WHAT THE HECK SHOULD I WEAR?
NOTHING LOOKS GOOD!
FWISH
YUMA?
I MADE TOO MUCH BEEF STEW. COULD YOU TAKE SOME NEXT DOOR?
AW, MOM!
I'M JUST ABOUT TO GO OUT...
I'VE GOTTA GET READY!

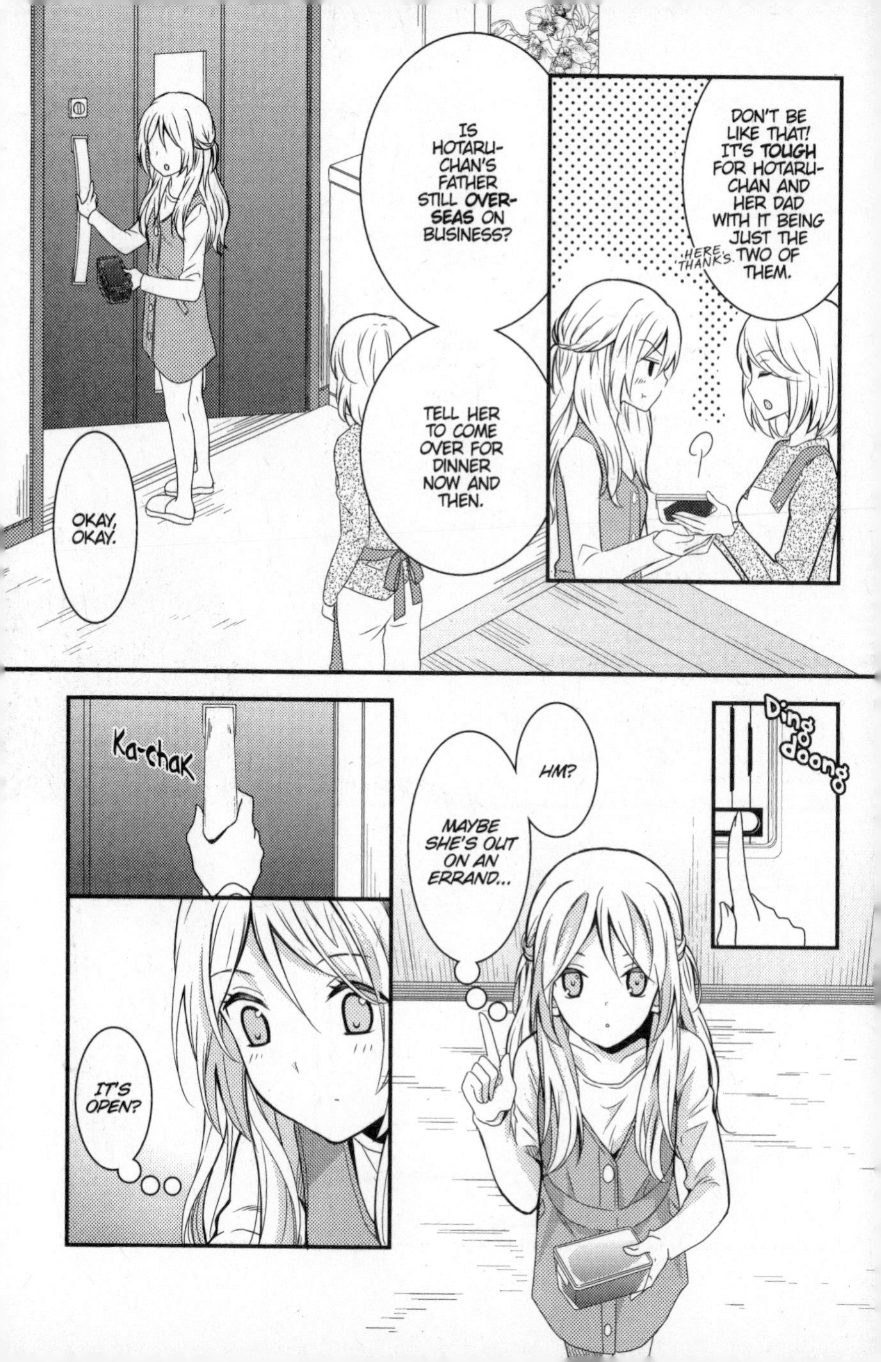
DON'T BE LIKE THAT! IT'S TOUGH FOR HOTARU-CHAN AND HER DAD WITH IT BEING JUST THE TWO OF THEM.
HERE. THANKS.
IS HOTARU-CHAN'S FATHER STILL OVER-SEAS ON BUSINESS?
TELL HER TO COME OVER FOR DINNER NOW AND THEN.
OKAY, OKAY.
Ding dong
HM?
MAYBE SHE'S OUT ON AN ERRAND...
Ka-chak
IT'S OPEN?

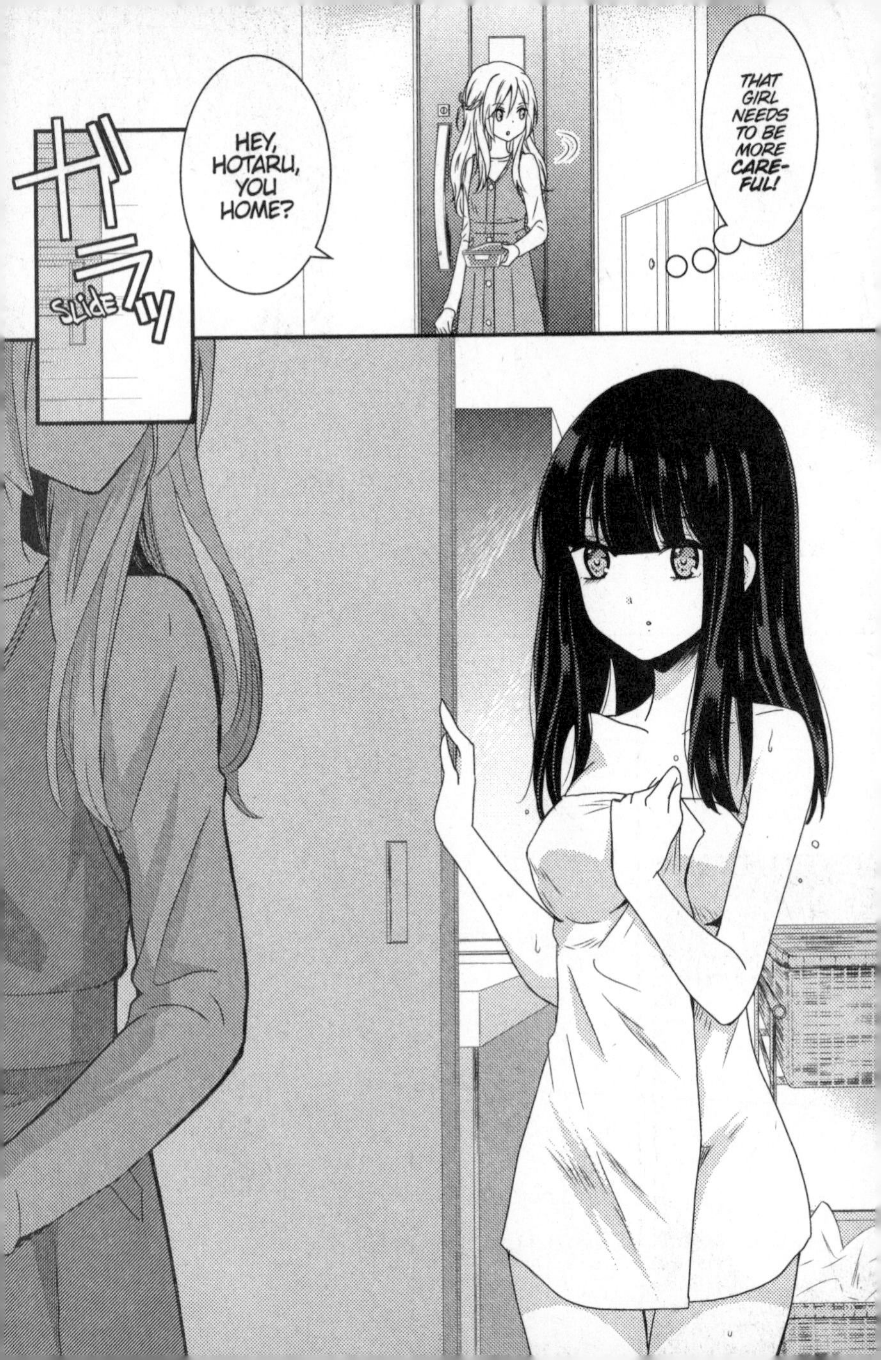
THAT GIRL NEEDS TO BE MORE CARE-FUL!
HEY, HOTARU, YOU HOME?
ガラッ
SLIDE

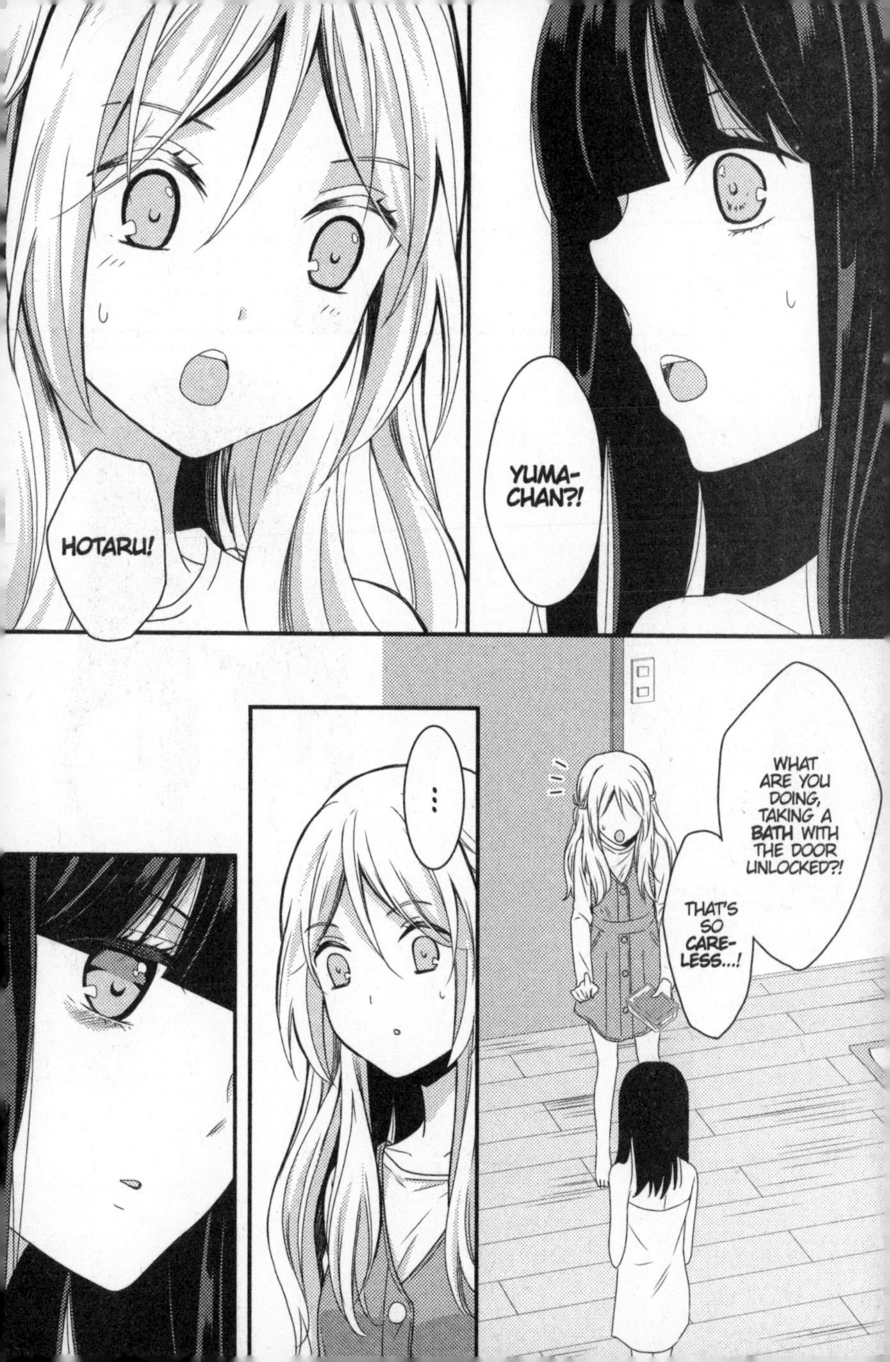
YUMA-CHAN?!
HOTARU!
WHAT ARE YOU DOING, TAKING A BATH WITH THE DOOR UNLOCKED?!
THAT'S SO CARE-LESS...!
...

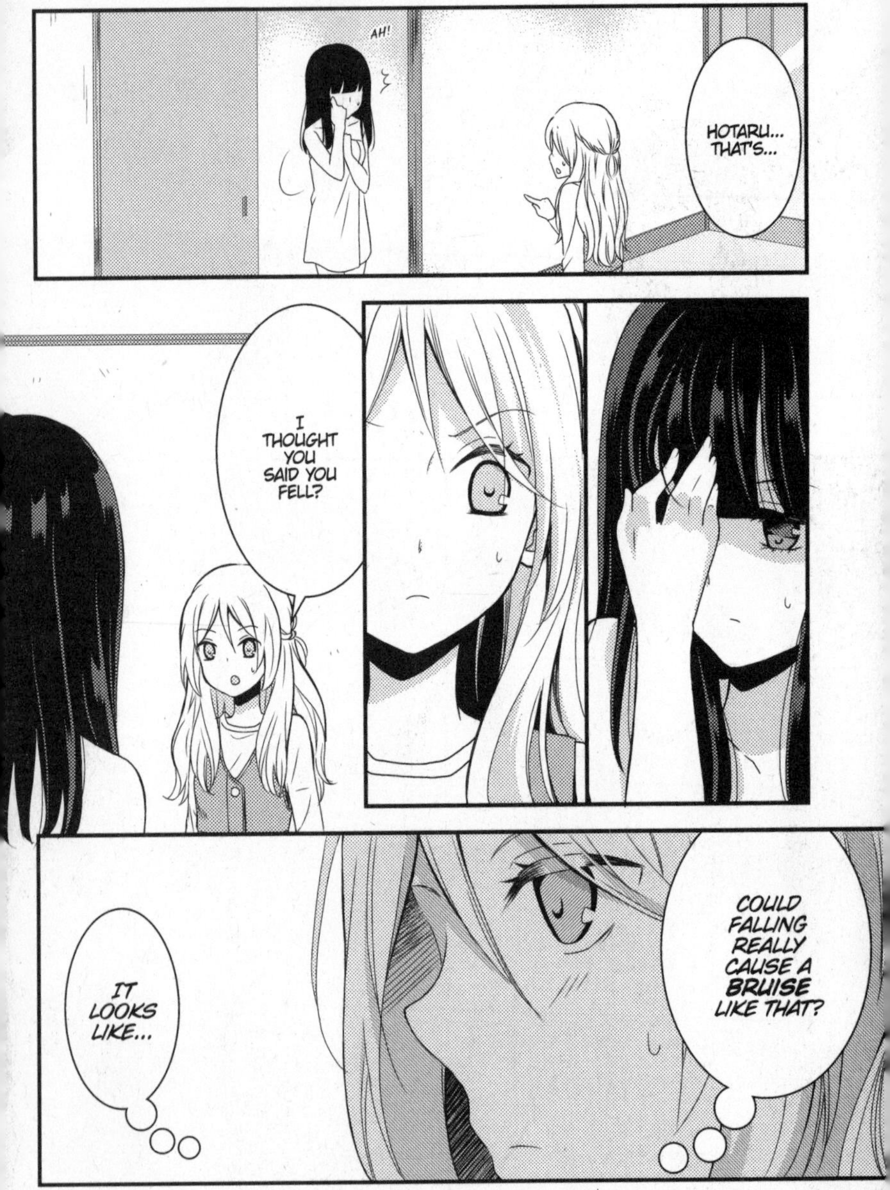
HOTARU... THAT'S...
AH!
I THOUGHT YOU SAID YOU FELL?
COULD FALLING REALLY CAUSE A BRUISE LIKE THAT?
IT LOOKS LIKE...

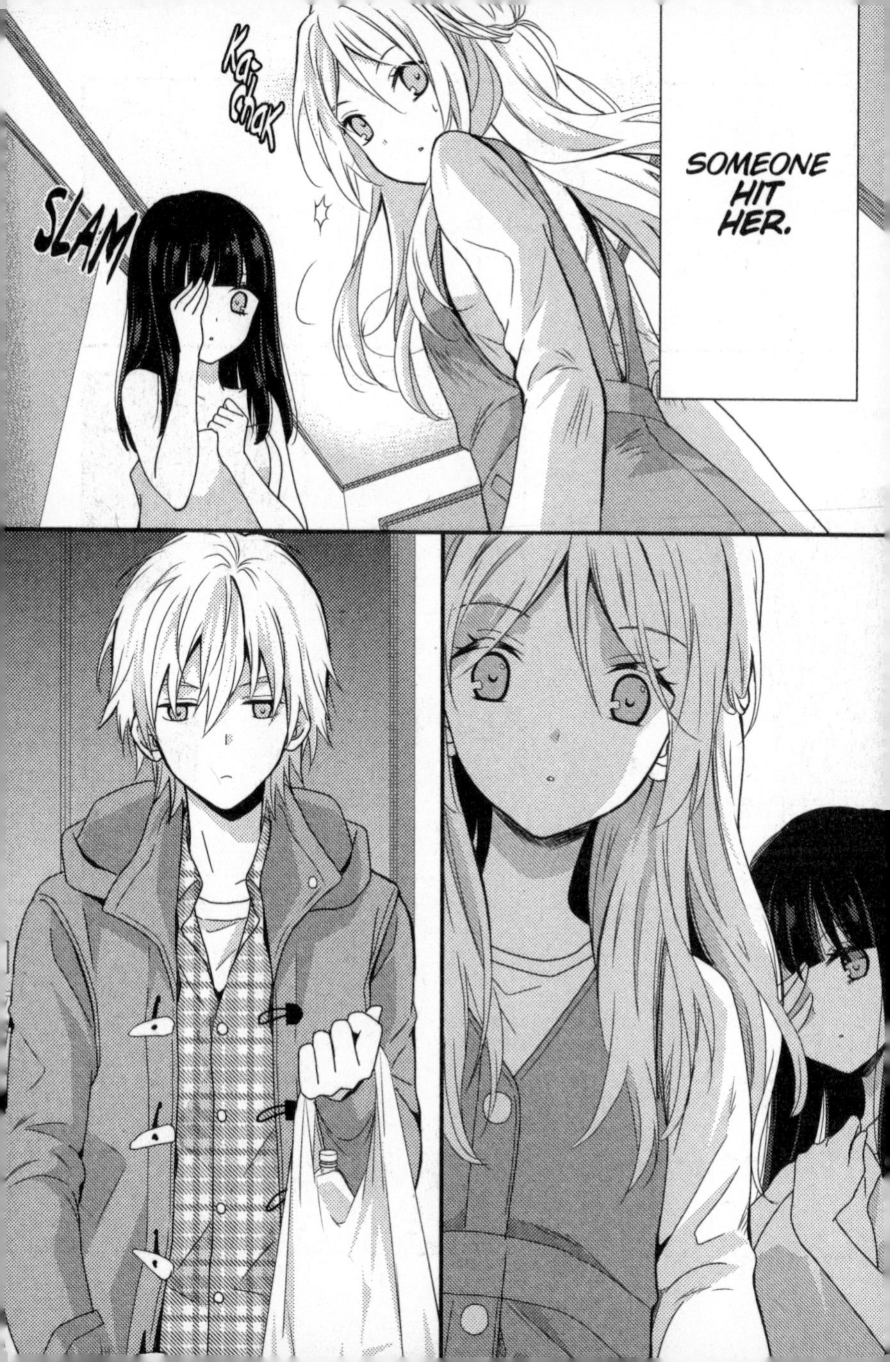
SOMEONE HIT HER.
Ka-chak
SLAM

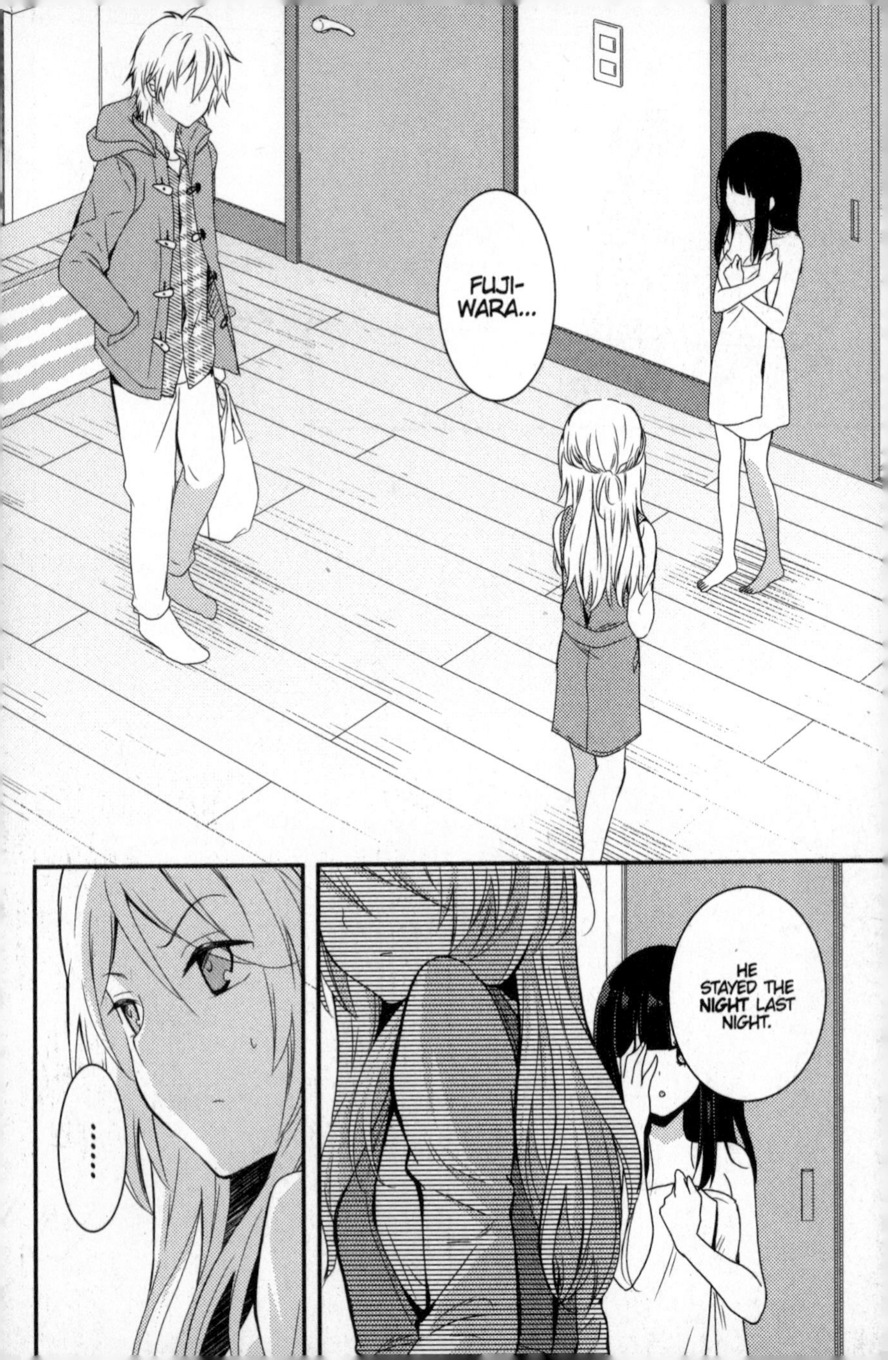
FUJI-WARA...
HE STAYED THE NIGHT LAST NIGHT.
......

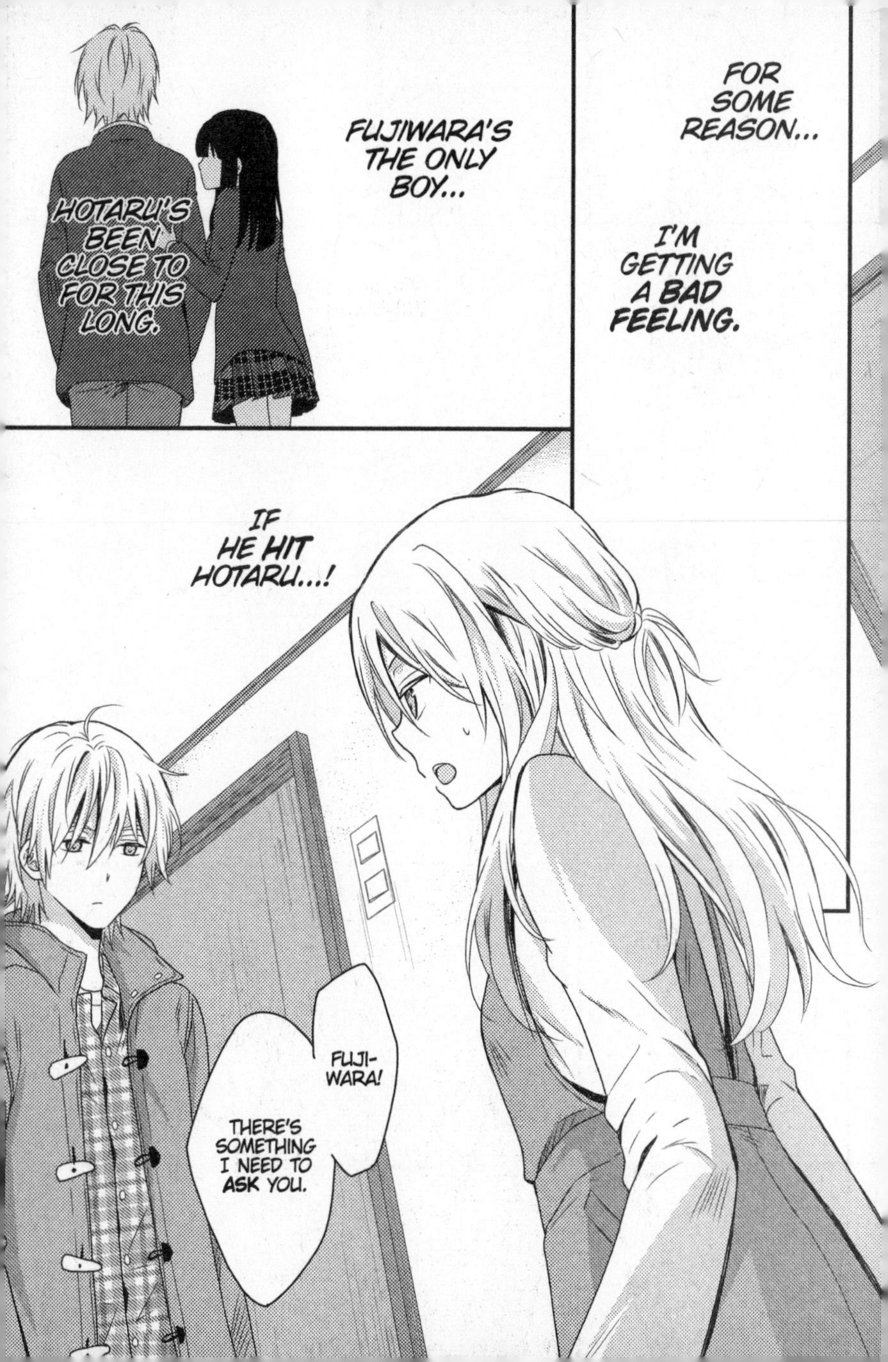

FOR SOME REASON...
I'M GETTING A BAD FEELING.
FUJIWARA'S THE ONLY BOY...
HOTARU'S BEEN CLOSE TO FOR THIS LONG.
IF HE HIT HOTARU...!
FUJI-WARA!
THERE'S SOMETHING I NEED TO ASK YOU.

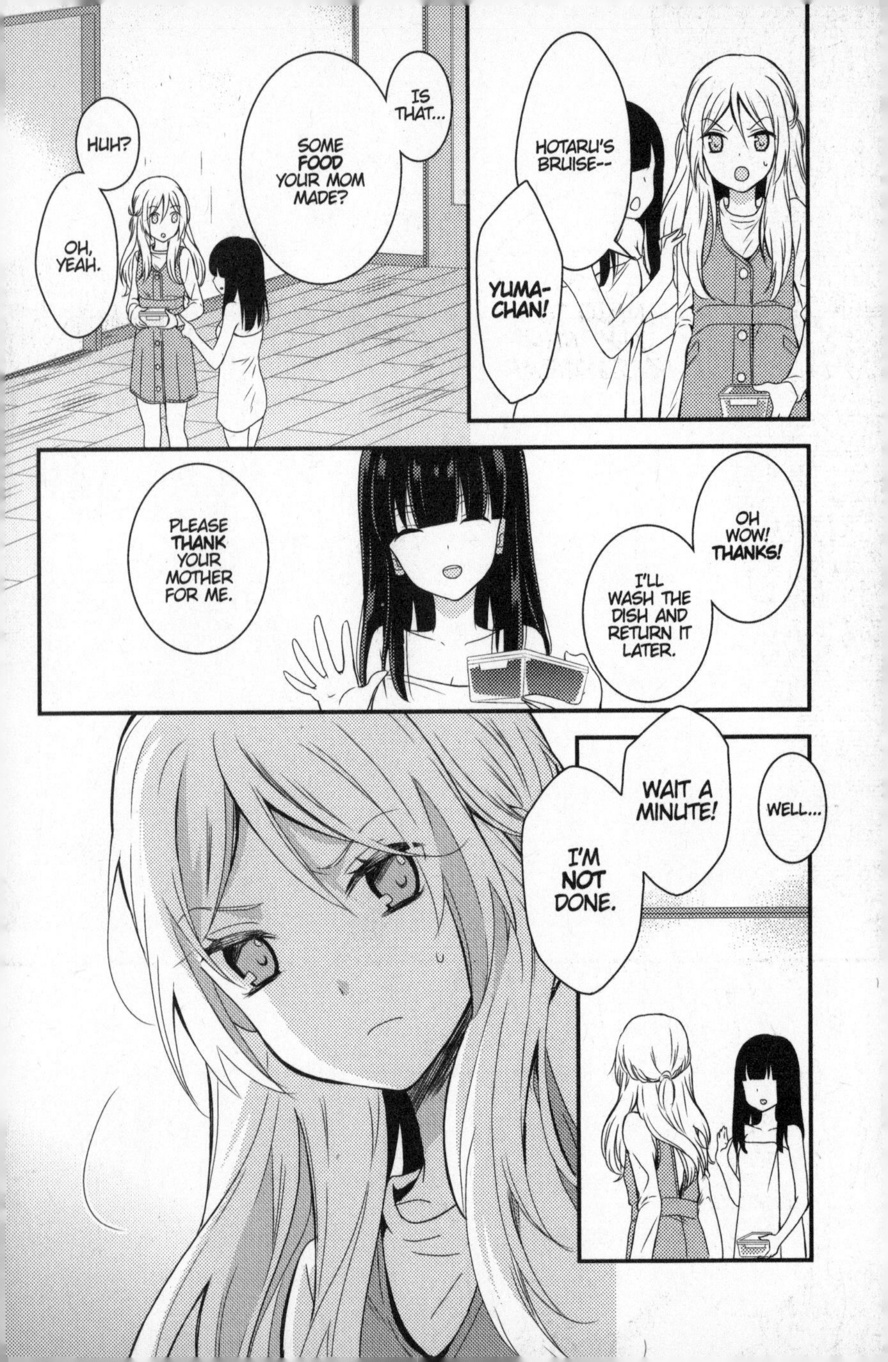
HOTARU'S BRUISE--
YUMA-CHAN!
IS THAT...
SOME FOOD YOUR MOM MADE?
HUH?
OH, YEAH.
OH WOW! THANKS!
I'LL WASH THE DISH AND RETURN IT LATER.
PLEASE THANK YOUR MOTHER FOR ME.
WELL...
WAIT A MINUTE!
I'M NOT DONE.

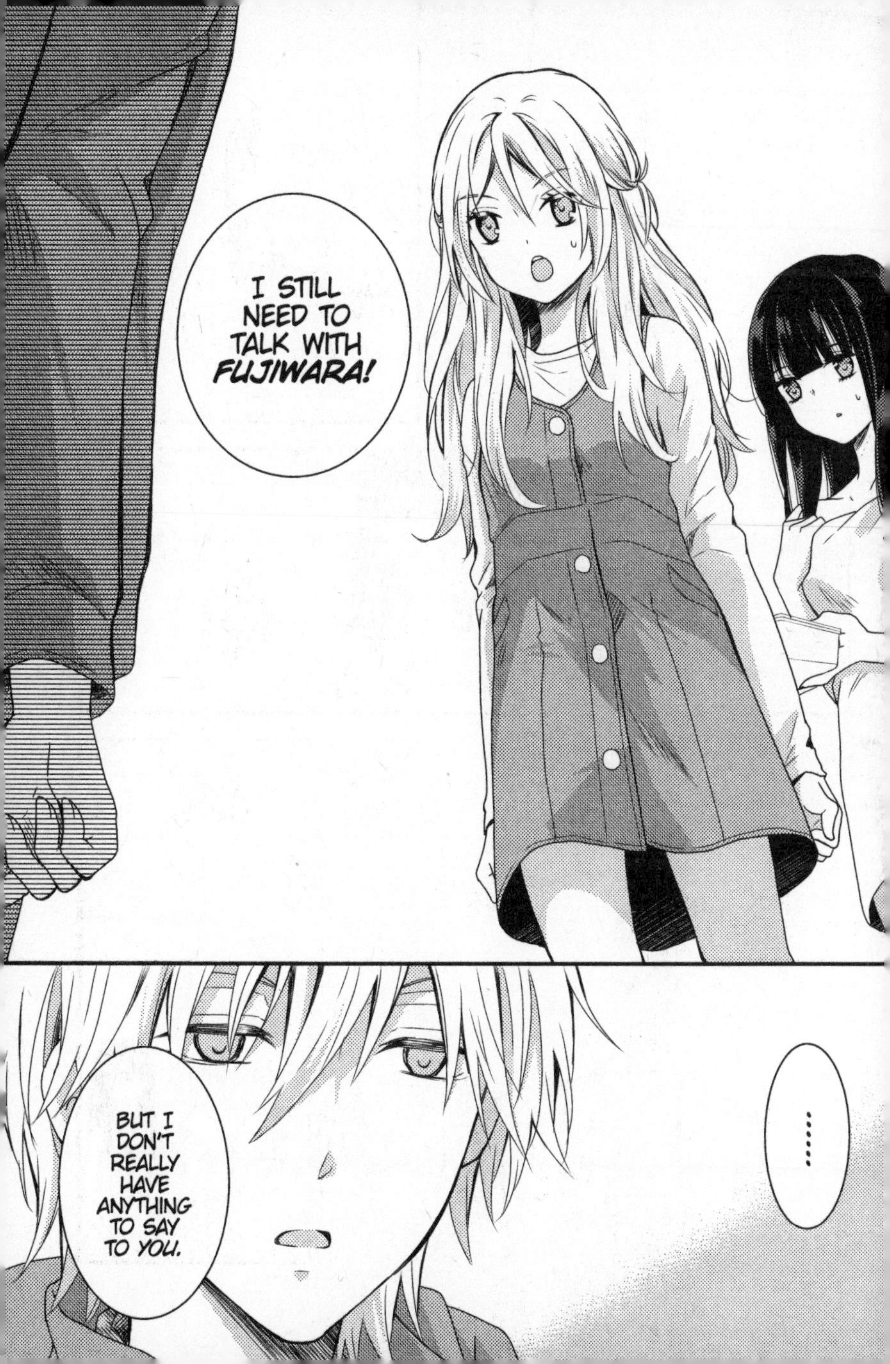
I STILL NEED TO TALK WITH *FUJIWARA!*
……
BUT I DON'T REALLY HAVE ANYTHING TO SAY TO *YOU.*

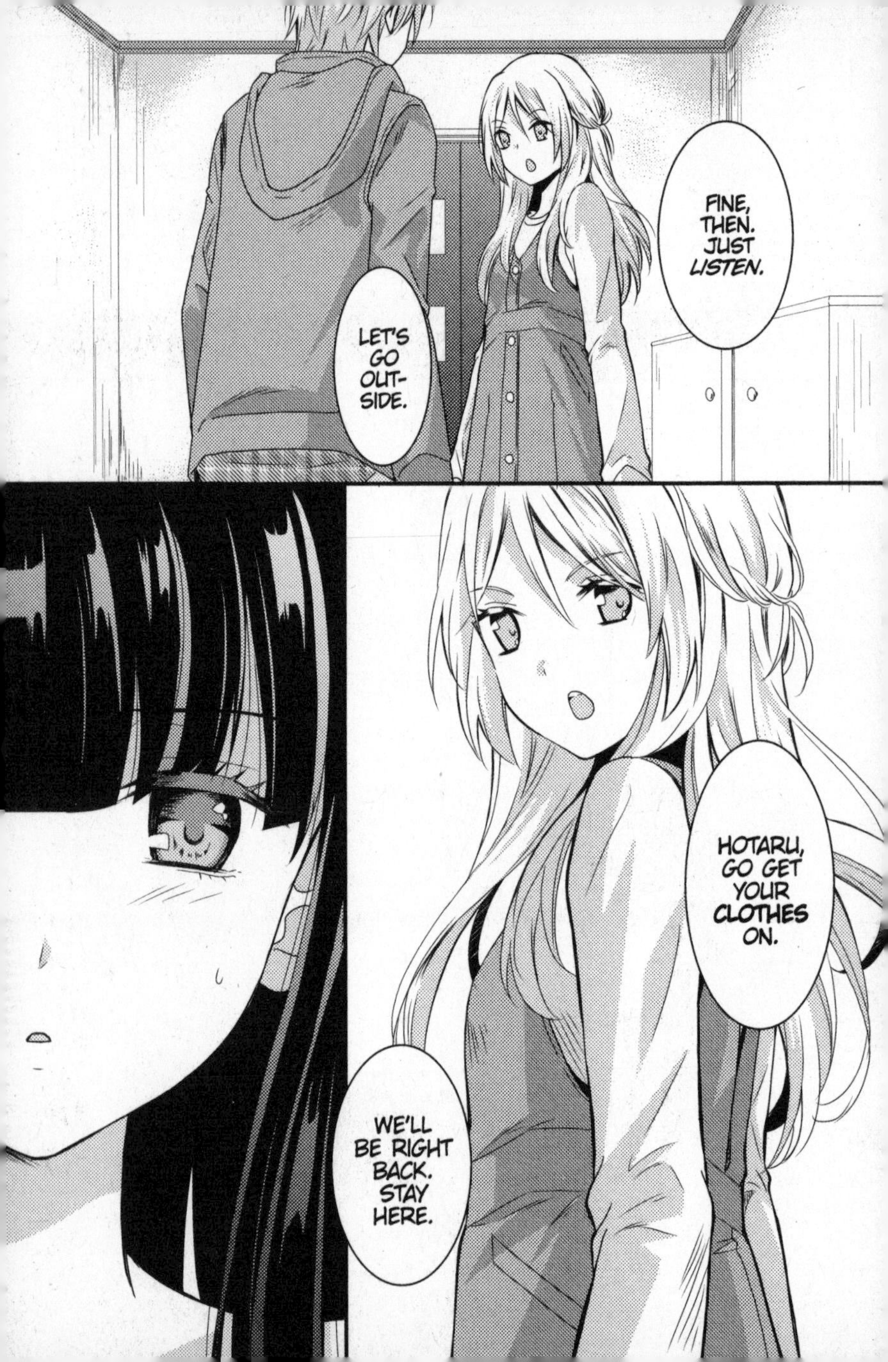
FINE, THEN. JUST LISTEN.
LET'S GO OUT-SIDE.
HOTARU, GO GET YOUR CLOTHES ON.
WE'LL BE RIGHT BACK. STAY HERE.

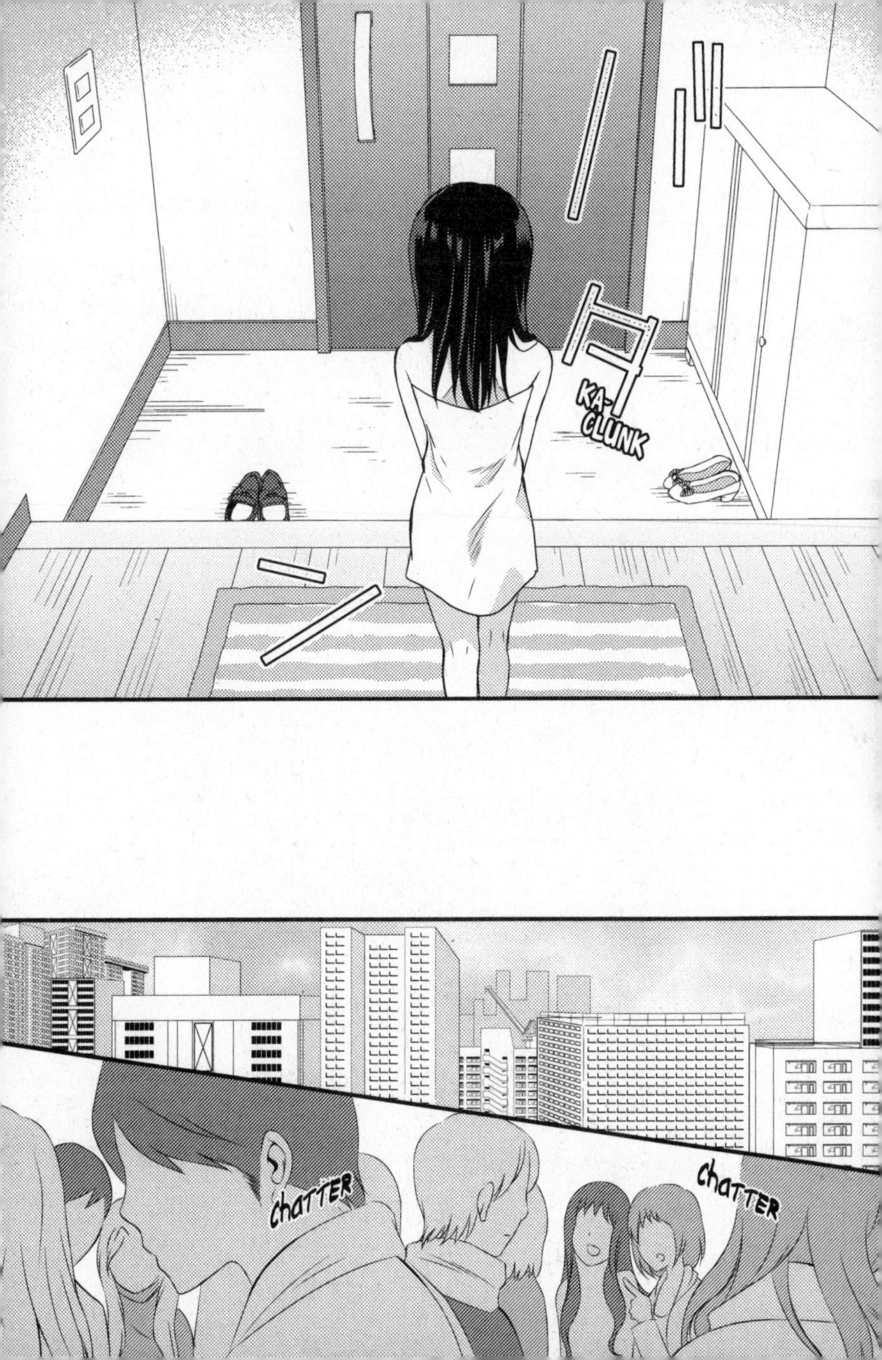
KA-CLUNK
CHATTER
CHATTER

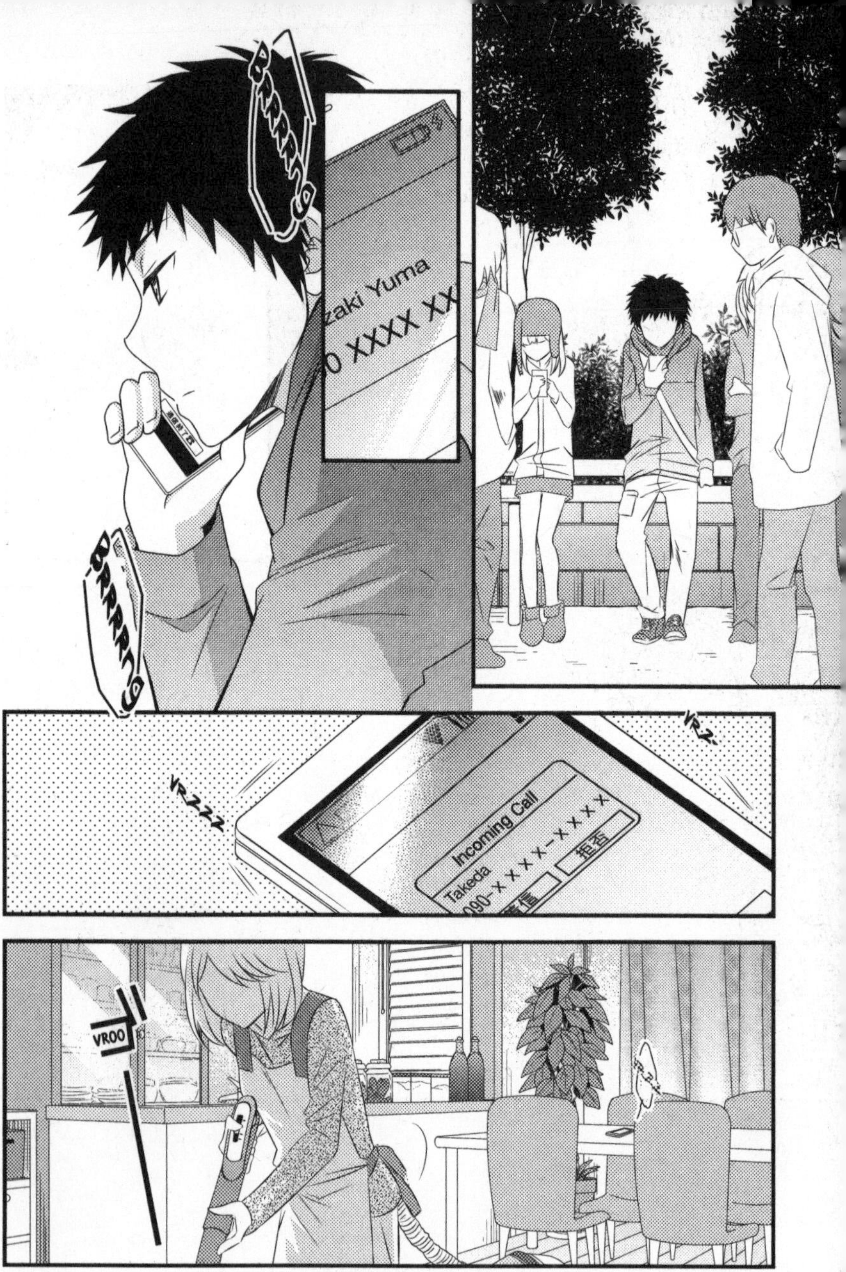
zaki Yuma
0 XXXX XX
BRRRRRO
BRRRRRO
VR-Z-
VR-Z-Z-Z
Incoming Call
Takeda
090-XXXX-XXXX
拒否
VROO

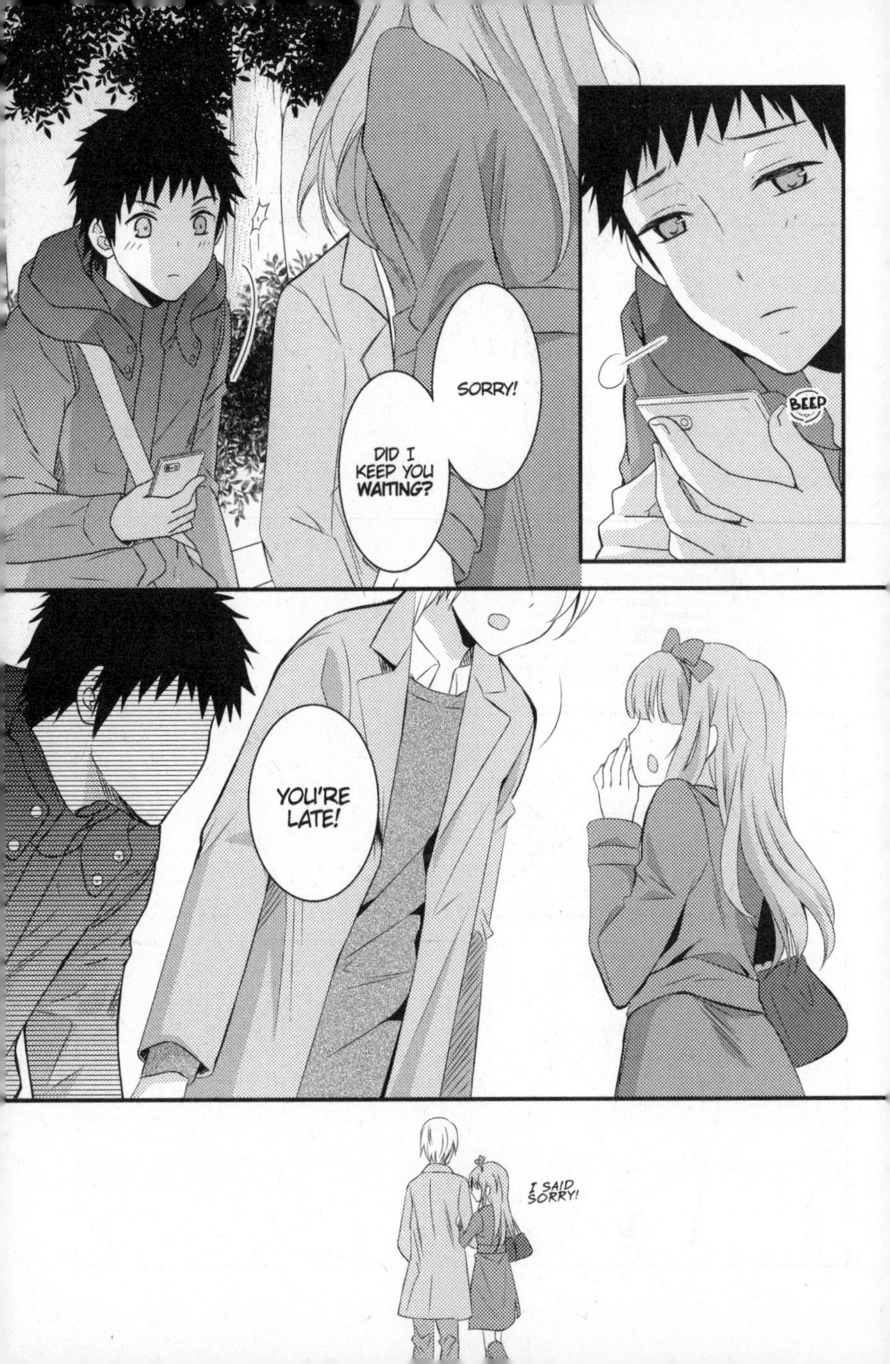
BEEP
SORRY!
DID I KEEP YOU WAITING?
YOU'RE LATE!
I SAID SORRY!

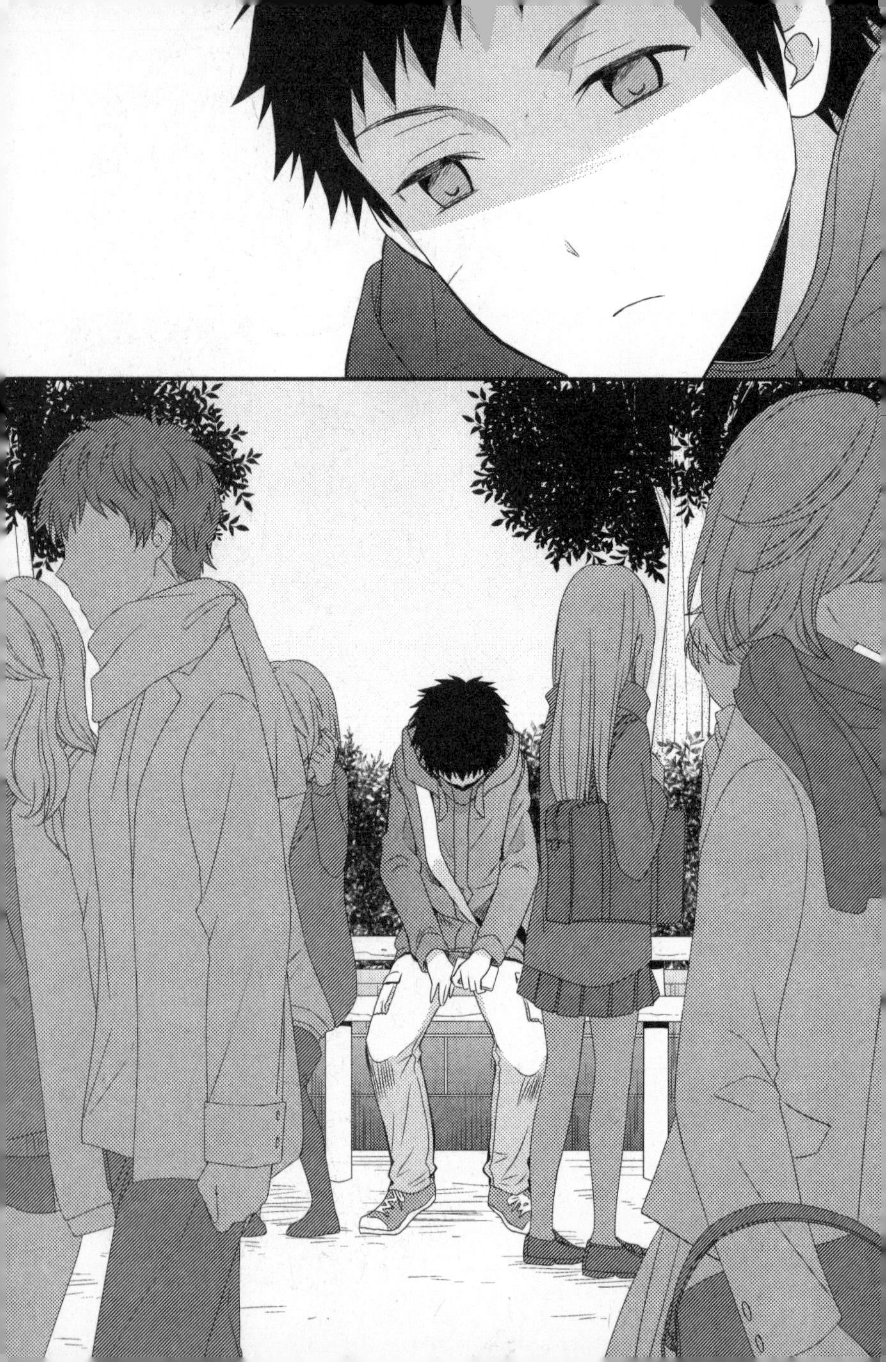

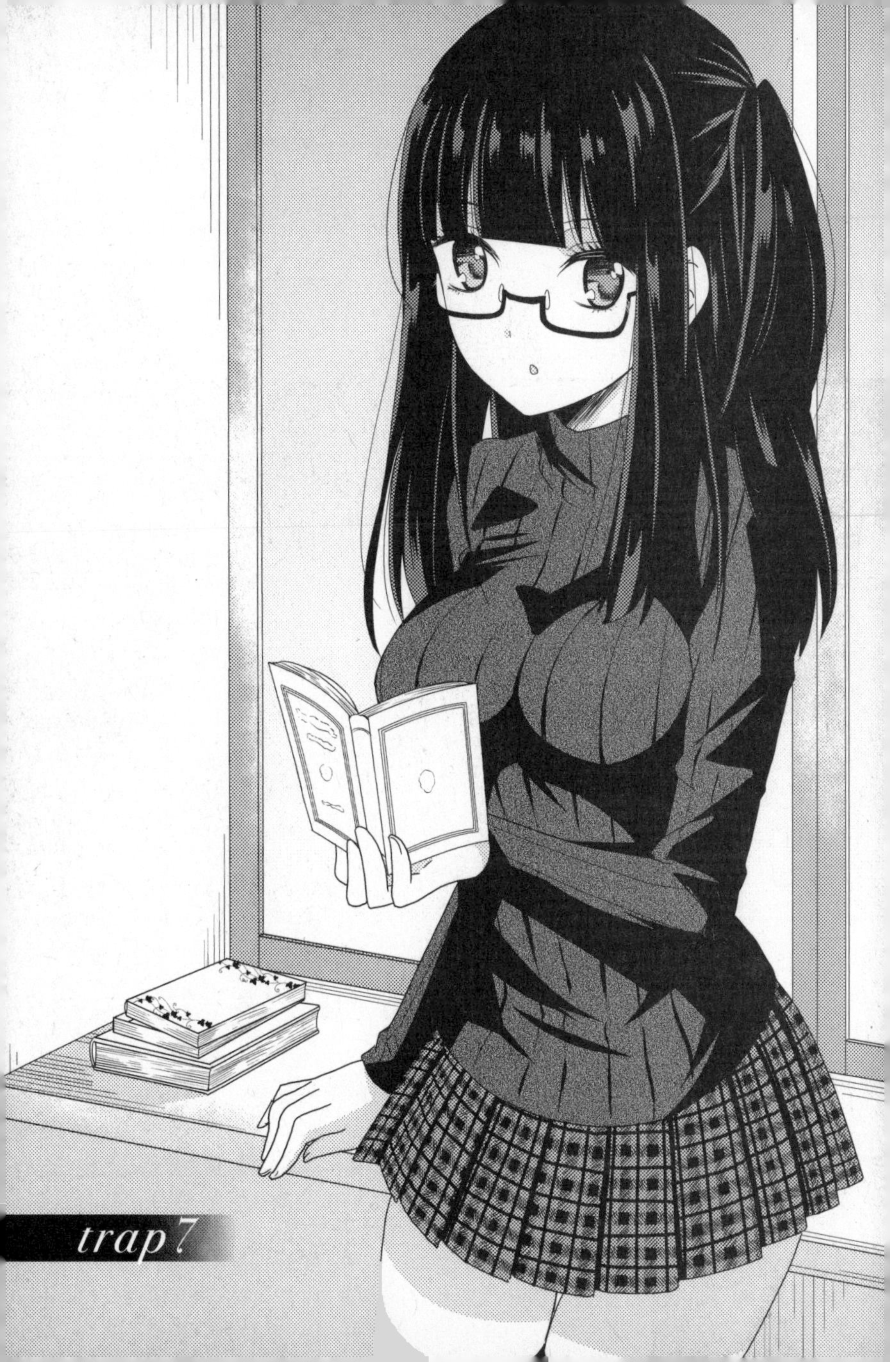
trap 7

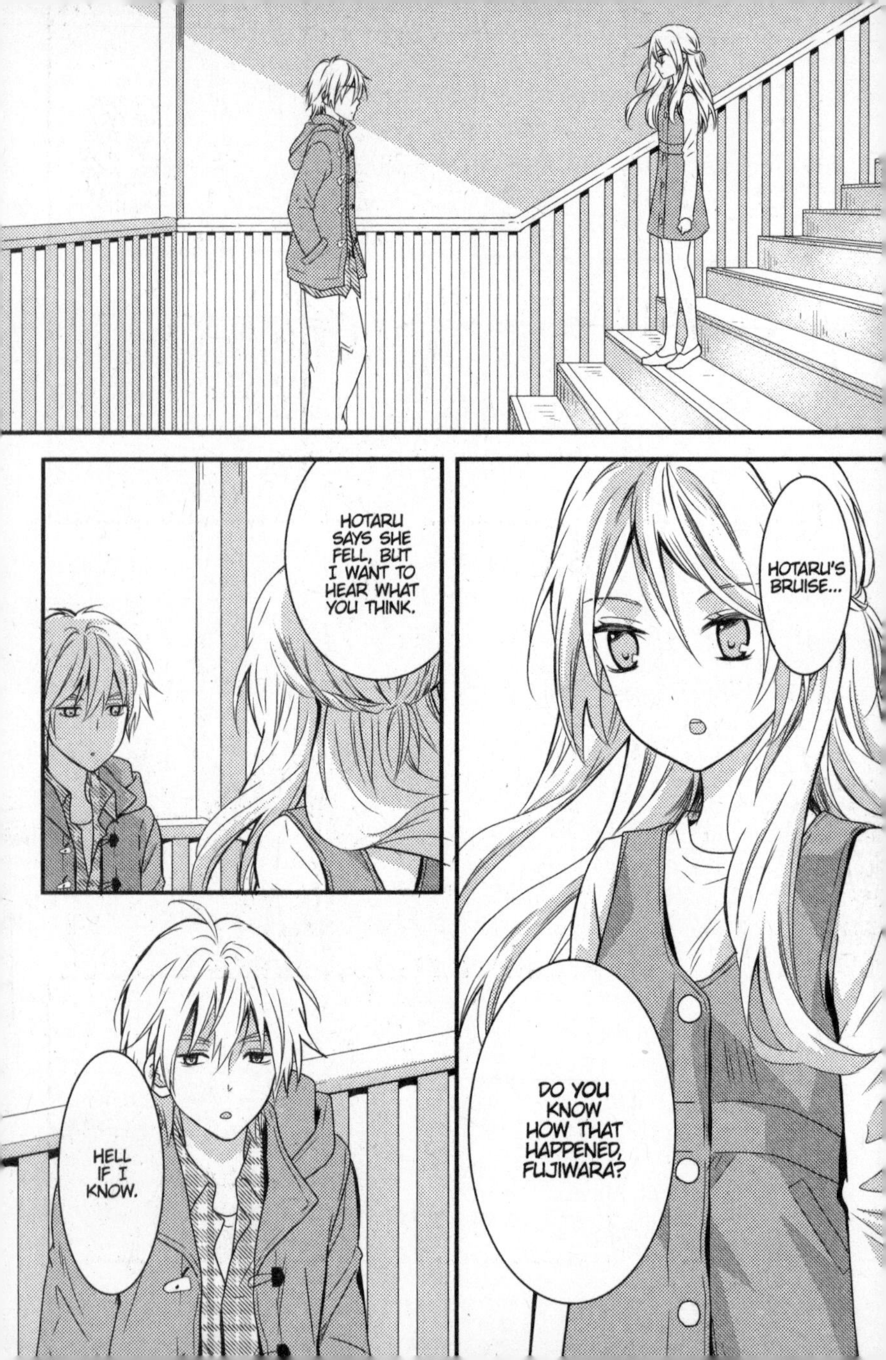
HOTARU'S BRUISE...
DO YOU KNOW HOW THAT HAPPENED, FUJIWARA?
HOTARU SAYS SHE FELL, BUT I WANT TO HEAR WHAT YOU THINK.
HELL IF I KNOW.

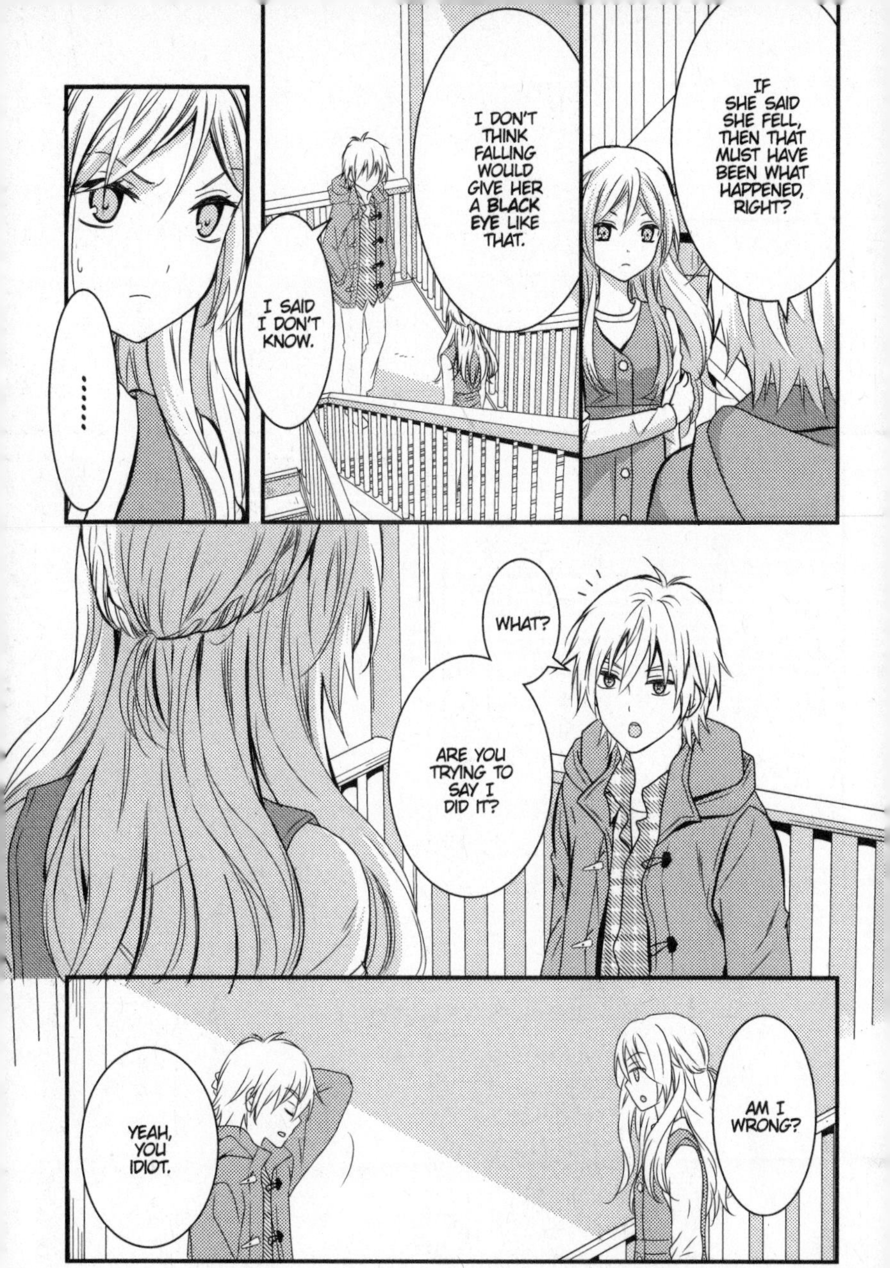
IF SHE SAID SHE FELL, THEN THAT MUST HAVE BEEN WHAT HAPPENED, RIGHT?
I DON'T THINK FALLING WOULD GIVE HER A BLACK EYE LIKE THAT.
I SAID I DON'T KNOW.
......
WHAT?
ARE YOU TRYING TO SAY I DID IT?
AM I WRONG?
YEAH, YOU IDIOT.

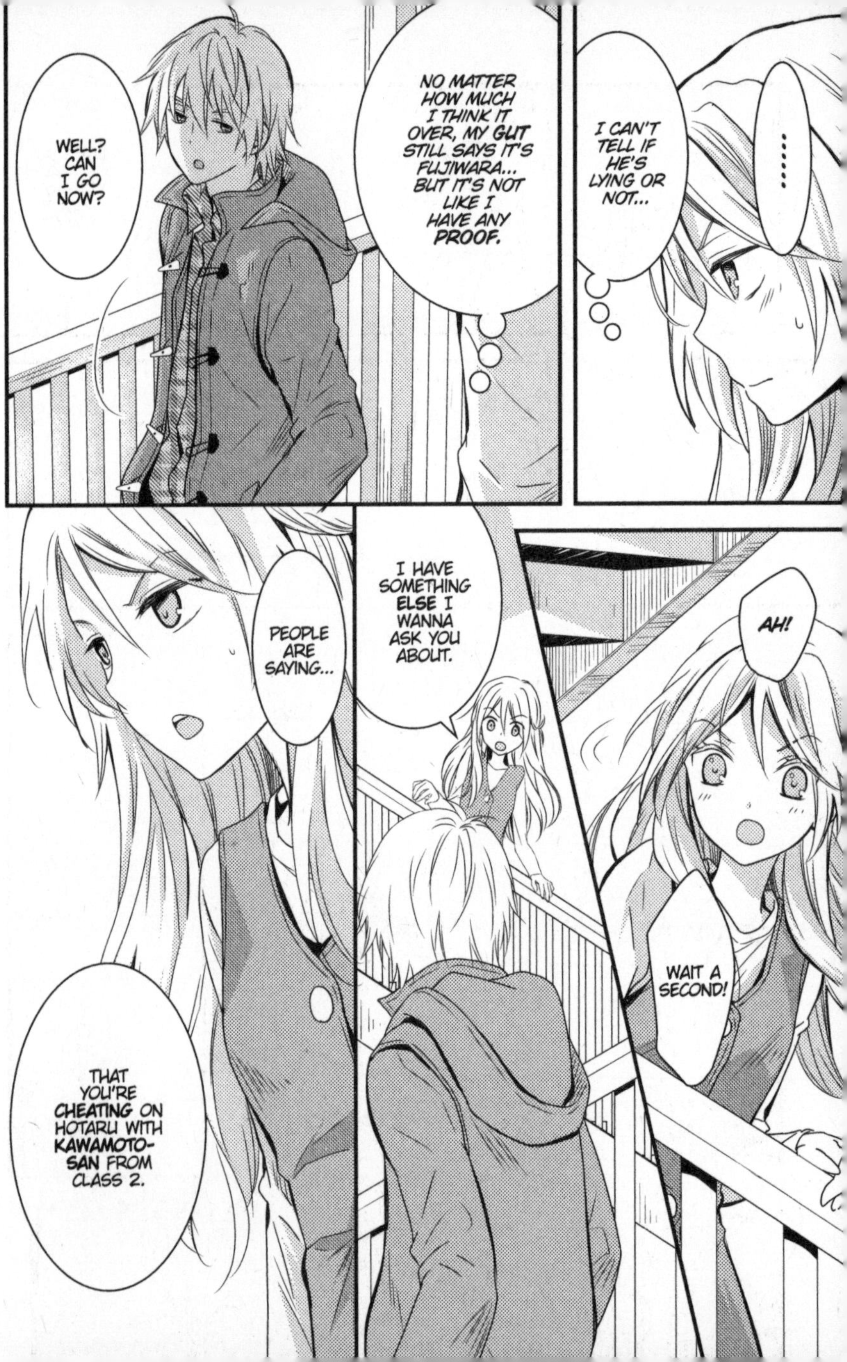
......
I CAN'T TELL IF HE'S LYING OR NOT...
NO MATTER HOW MUCH I THINK IT OVER, MY GUT STILL SAYS IT'S FUJIWARA... BUT IT'S NOT LIKE I HAVE ANY PROOF.
WELL? CAN I GO NOW?
AH!
WAIT A SECOND!
I HAVE SOMETHING ELSE I WANNA ASK YOU ABOUT.
PEOPLE ARE SAYING...
THAT YOU'RE CHEATING ON HOTARU WITH KAWAMOTO-SAN FROM CLASS 2.

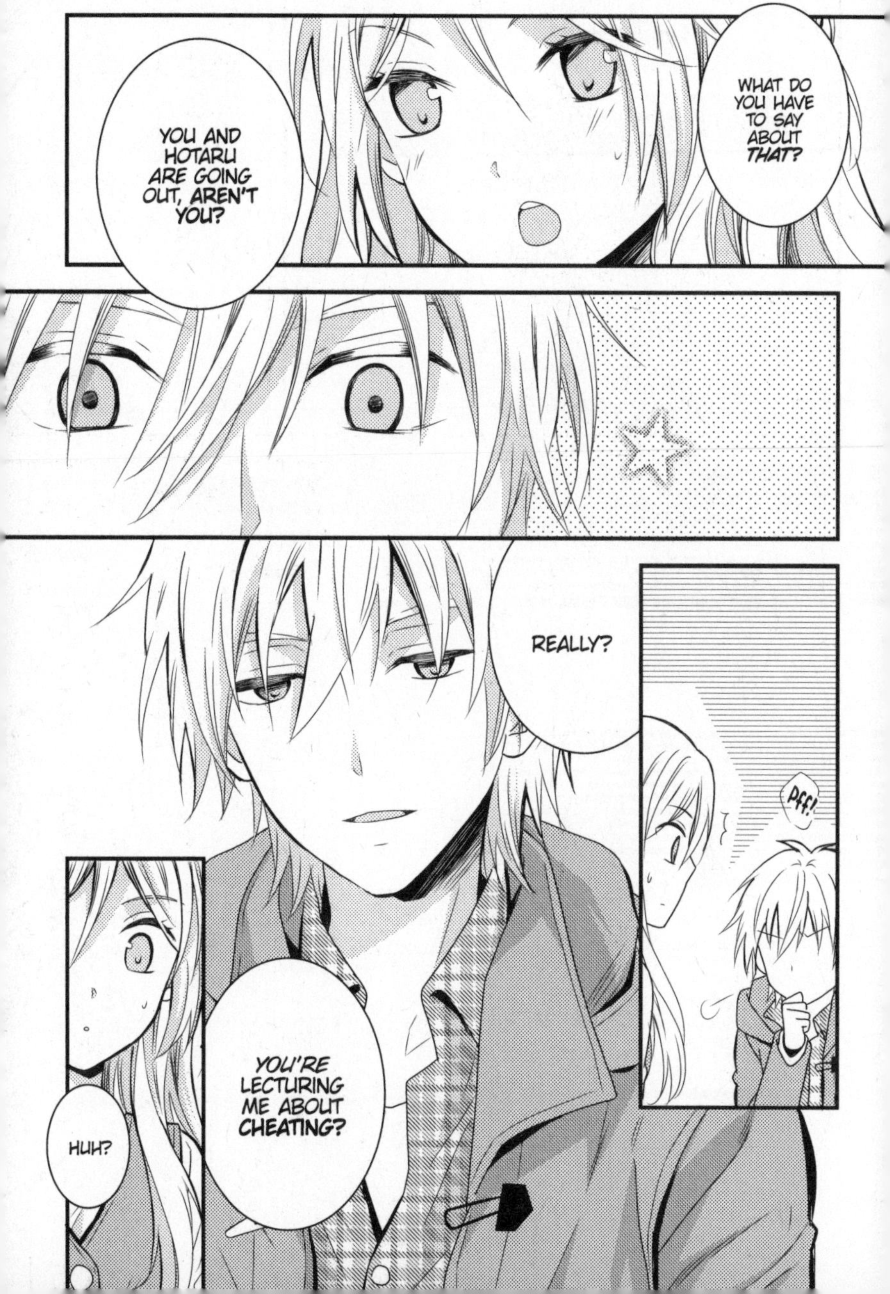
WHAT DO YOU HAVE TO SAY ABOUT *THAT?*
YOU AND HOTARU ARE GOING OUT, AREN'T YOU?
REALLY?
Pff!
YOU'RE LECTURING ME ABOUT CHEATING?
HUH?

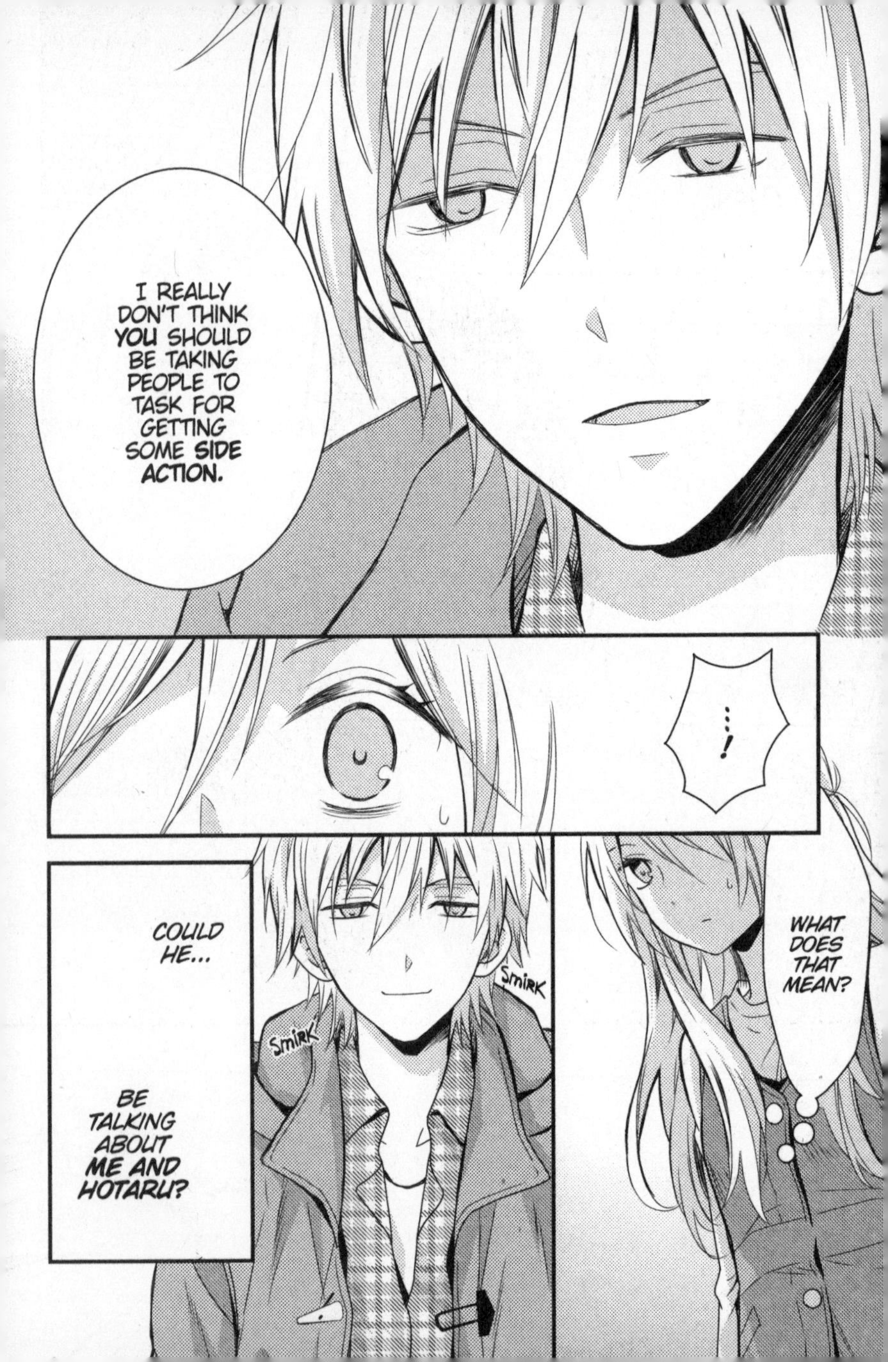
I REALLY DON'T THINK YOU SHOULD BE TAKING PEOPLE TO TASK FOR GETTING SOME SIDE ACTION.
...!
WHAT DOES THAT MEAN?
COULD HE...
Smirk
Smirk
BE TALKING ABOUT ME AND HOTARU?

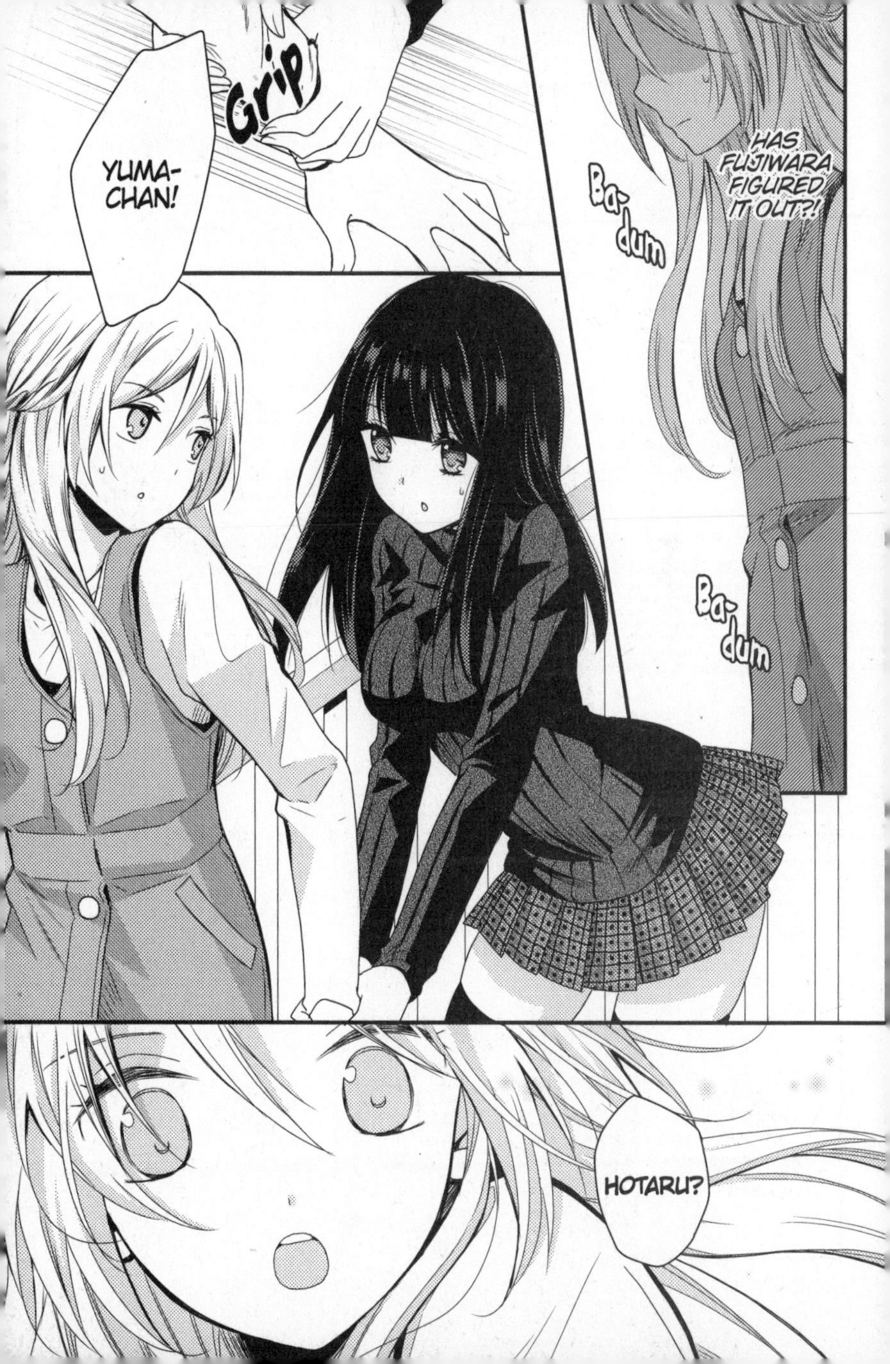
HAS FUJIWARA FIGURED IT OUT?!
Ba-dum
Ba-dum
Grip
YUMA-CHAN!
HOTARU?

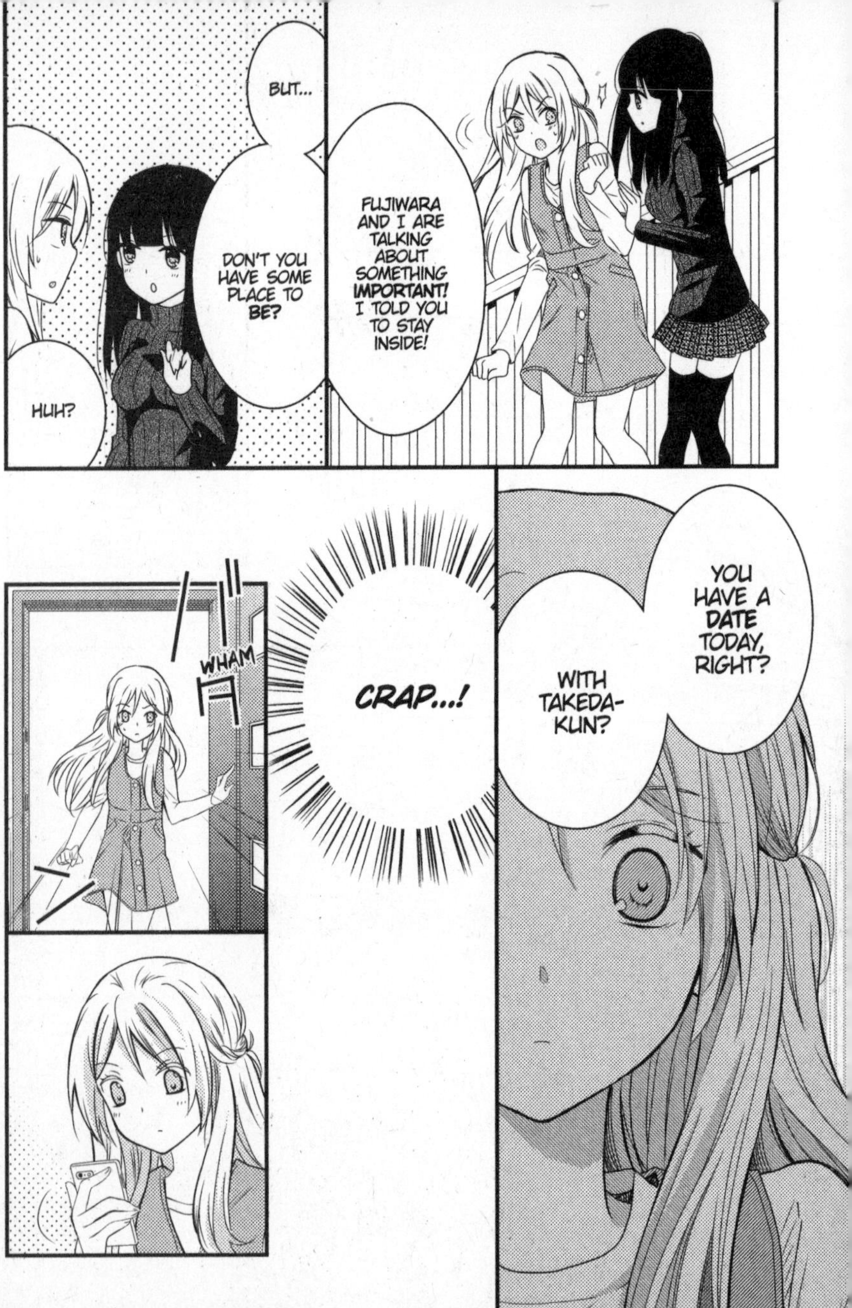
FUJIWARA AND I ARE TALKING ABOUT SOMETHING IMPORTANT! I TOLD YOU TO STAY INSIDE!
BUT...
DON'T YOU HAVE SOME PLACE TO BE?
HUH?
YOU HAVE A DATE TODAY, RIGHT?
WITH TAKEDA-KUN?
CRAP...!
WHAM

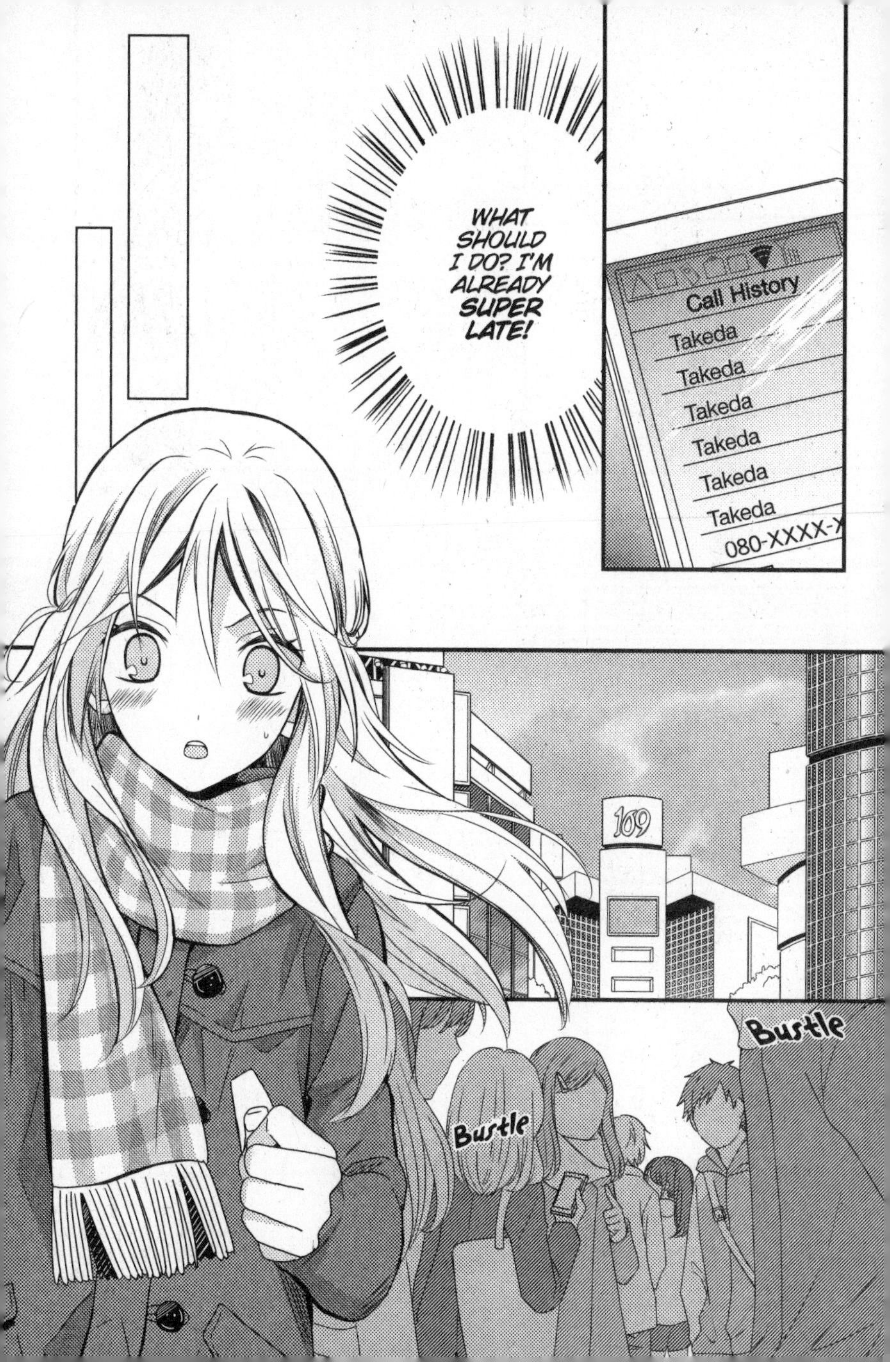
Call History
Takeda
Takeda
Takeda
Takeda
Takeda
Takeda
080-XXXX-X
WHAT SHOULD I DO? I'M ALREADY SUPER LATE!
Bustle
Bustle

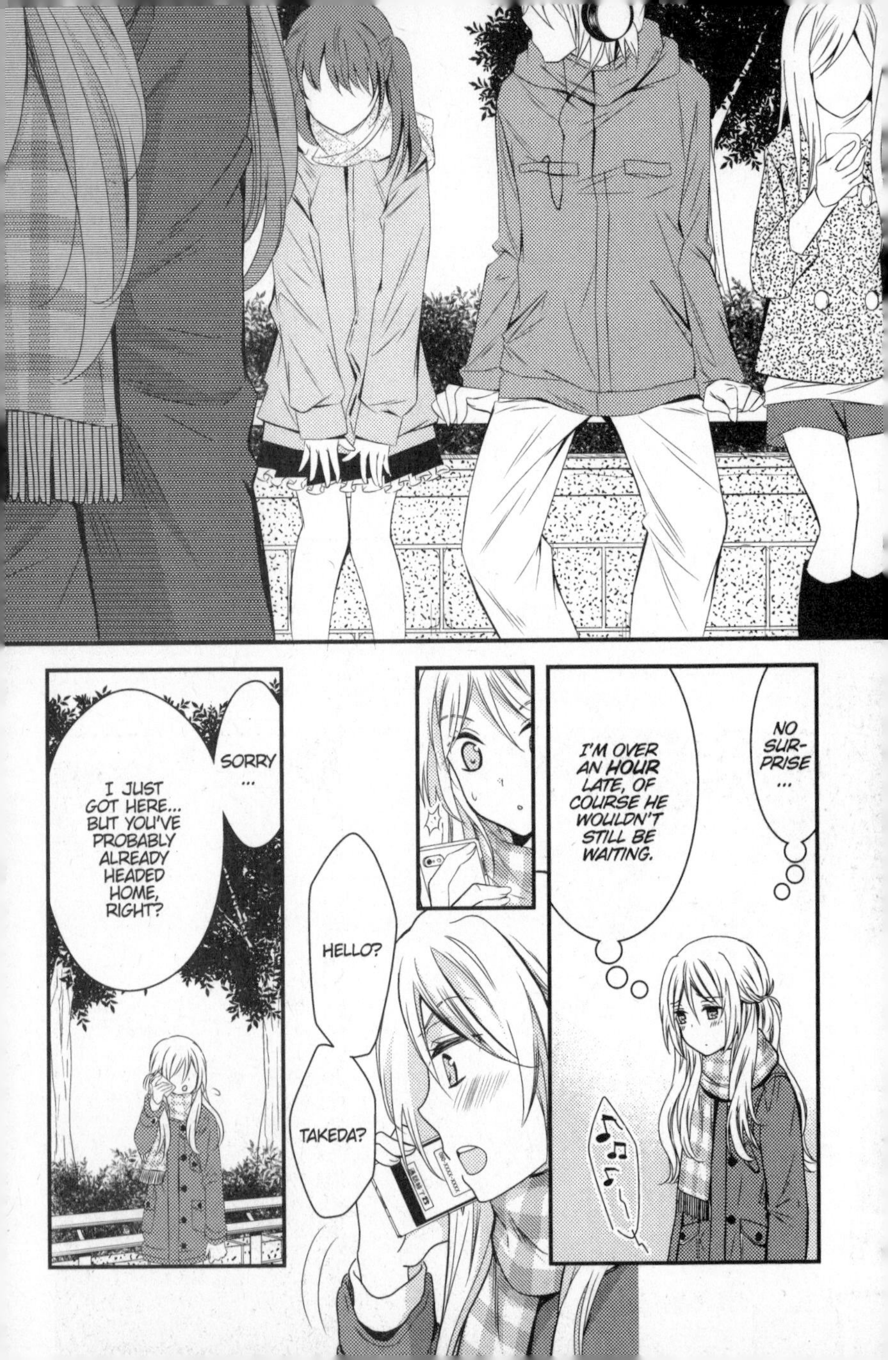
NO SURPRISE...
I'M OVER AN HOUR LATE, OF COURSE HE WOULDN'T STILL BE WAITING.
HELLO?
TAKEDA?
SORRY...
I JUST GOT HERE... BUT YOU'VE PROBABLY ALREADY HEADED HOME, RIGHT?

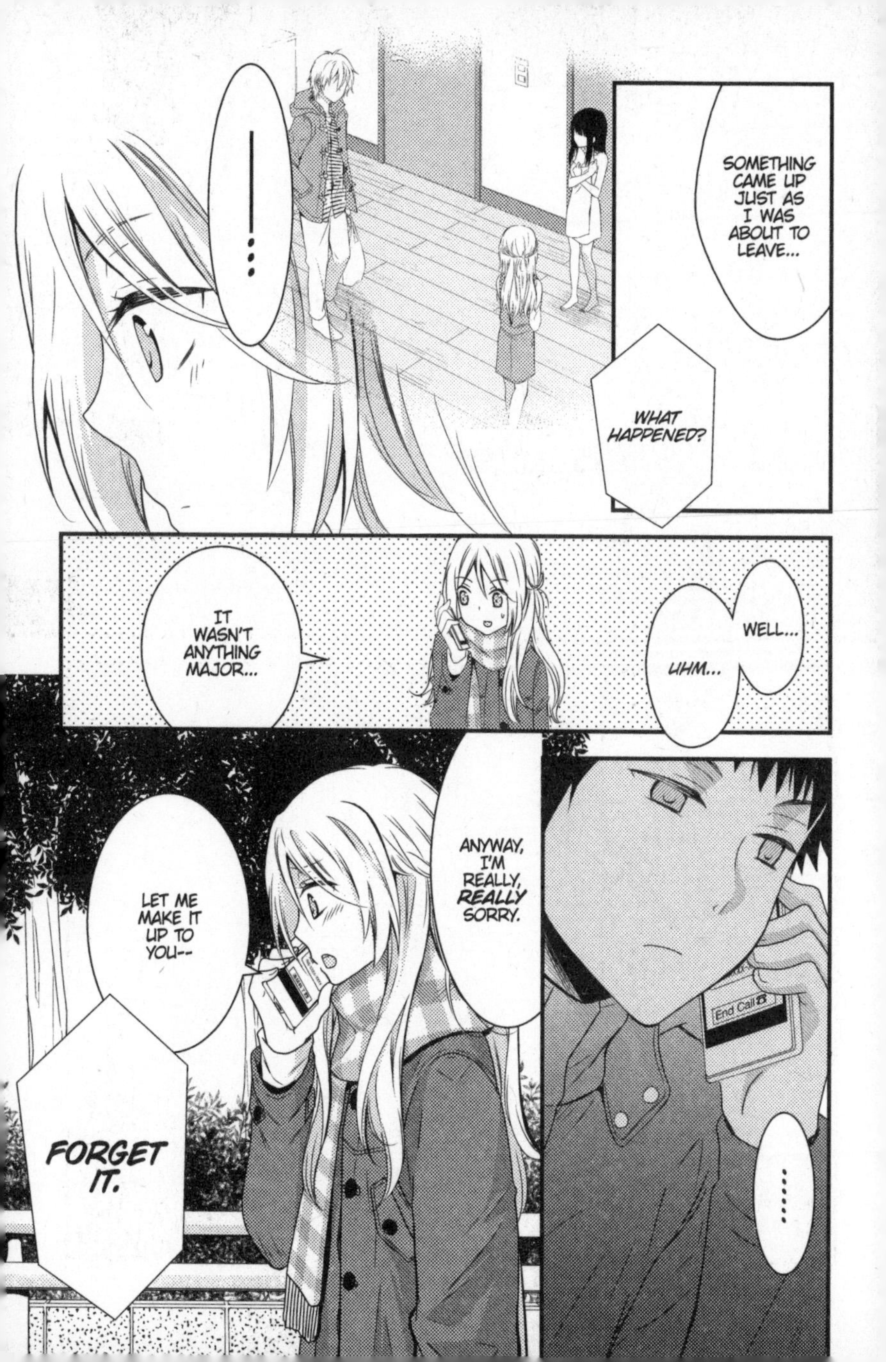
SOMETHING CAME UP JUST AS I WAS ABOUT TO LEAVE...
WHAT HAPPENED?
......
WELL...
UHM...
IT WASN'T ANYTHING MAJOR...
End Call
......
ANYWAY, I'M REALLY, REALLY SORRY.
LET ME MAKE IT UP TO YOU--
FORGET IT.

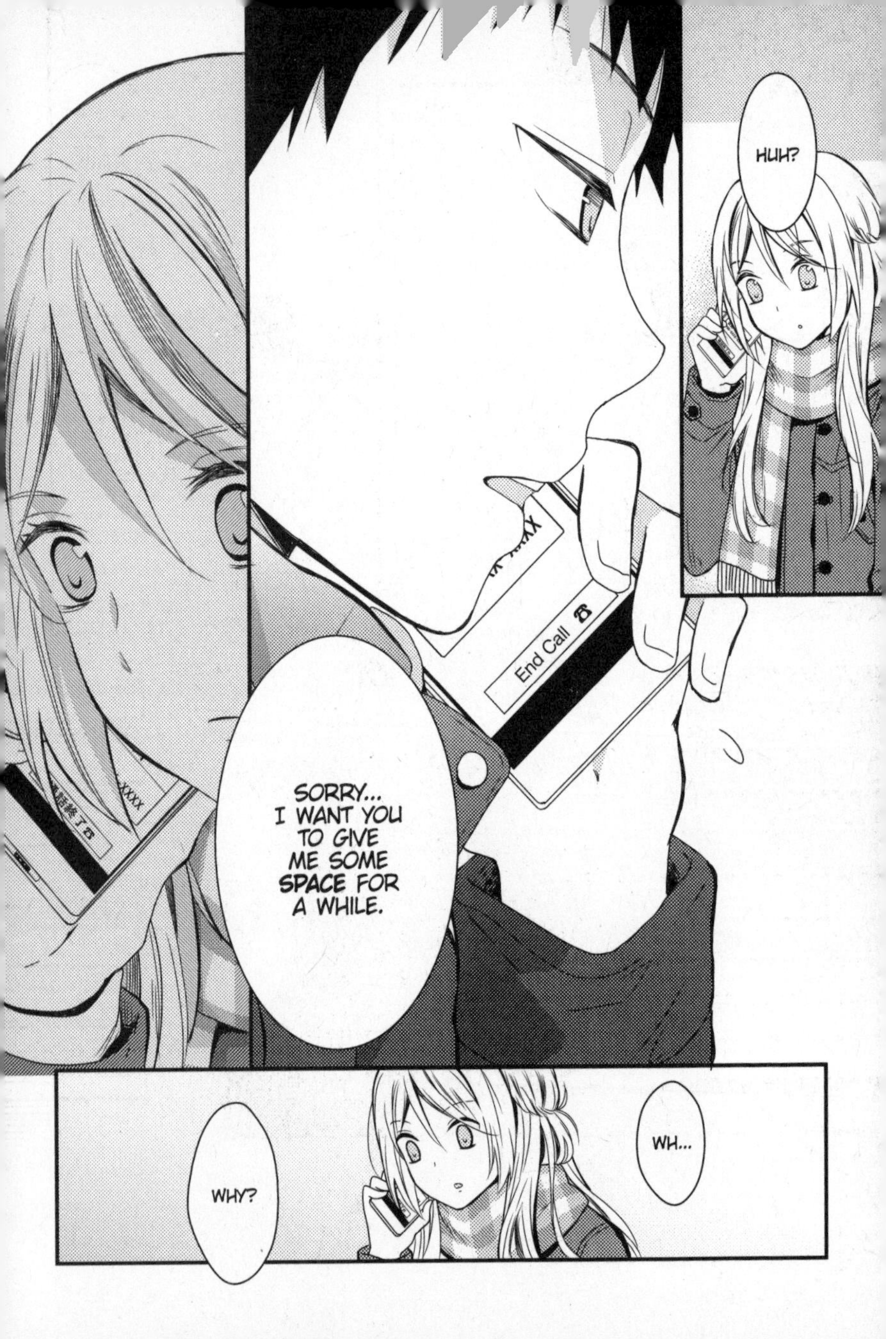
HUH?
End Call
SORRY... I WANT YOU TO GIVE ME SOME SPACE FOR A WHILE.
WH...
WHY?

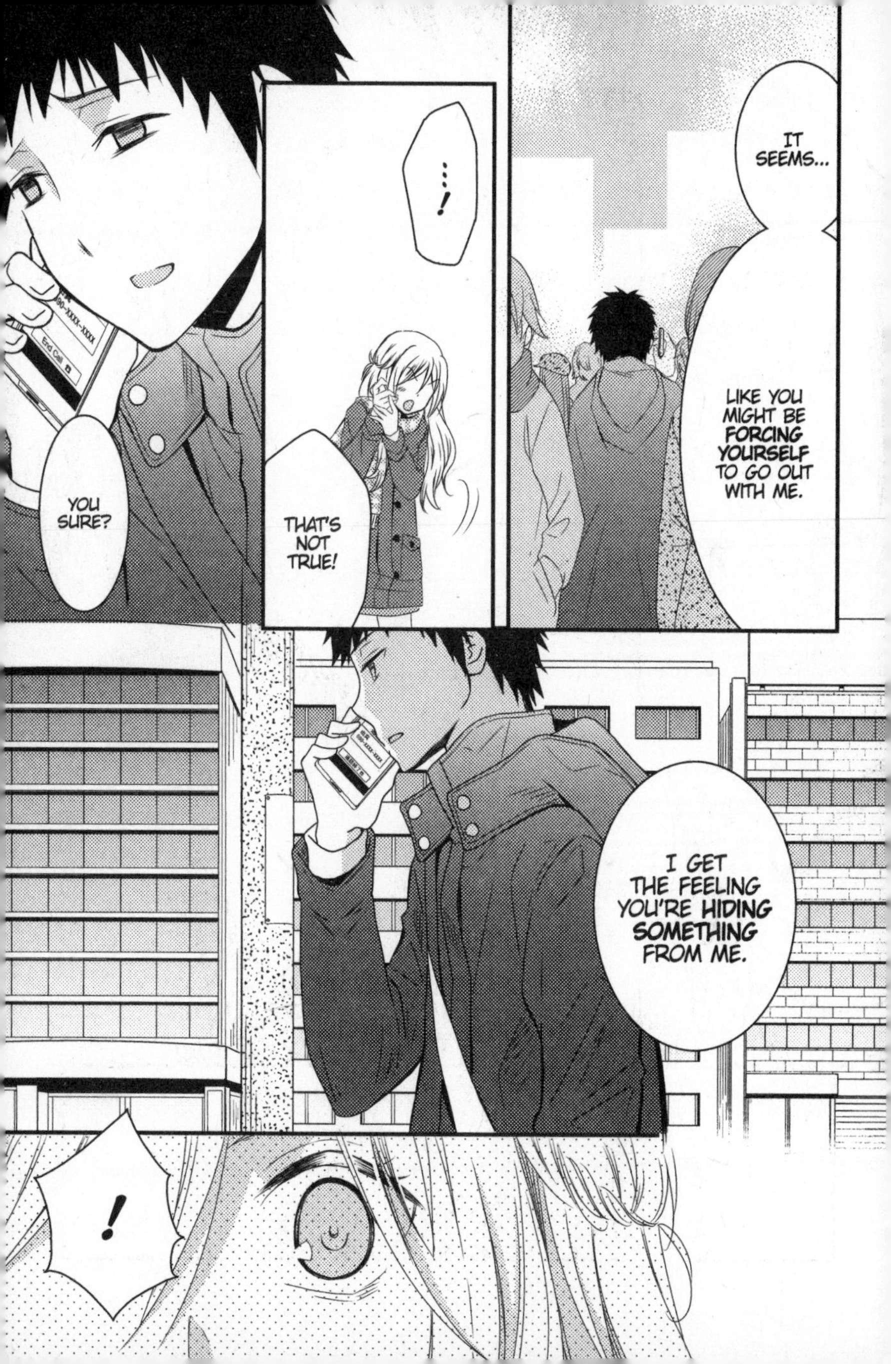
IT SEEMS...
LIKE YOU MIGHT BE FORCING YOURSELF TO GO OUT WITH ME.
...!
THAT'S NOT TRUE!
YOU SURE?
I GET THE FEELING YOU'RE HIDING SOMETHING FROM ME.
!

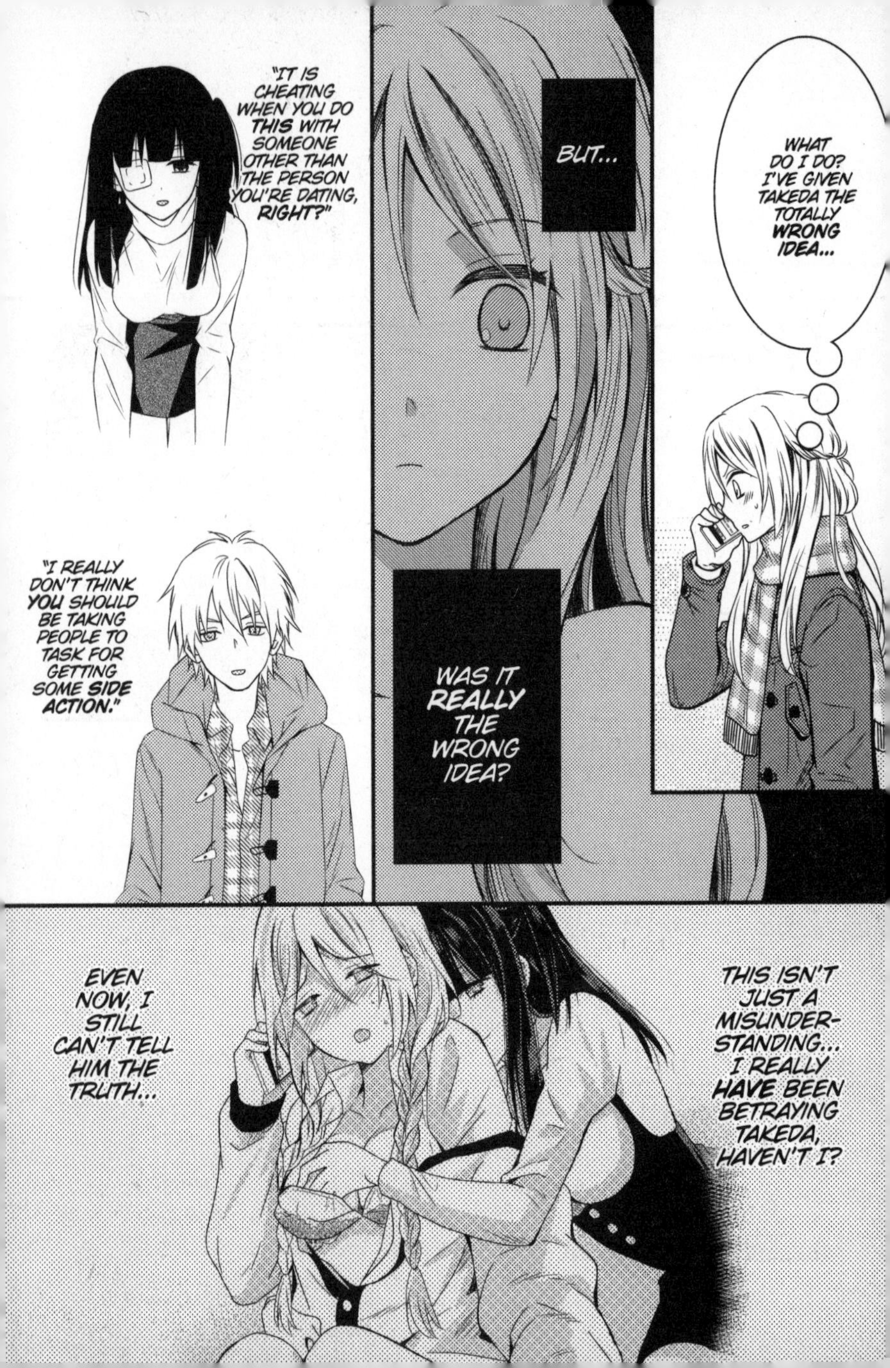
WHAT DO I DO? I'VE GIVEN TAKEDA THE TOTALLY WRONG IDEA...
BUT...
WAS IT REALLY THE WRONG IDEA?
"IT IS CHEATING WHEN YOU DO THIS WITH SOMEONE OTHER THAN THE PERSON YOU'RE DATING, RIGHT?"
"I REALLY DON'T THINK YOU SHOULD BE TAKING PEOPLE TO TASK FOR GETTING SOME SIDE ACTION."
THIS ISN'T JUST A MISUNDER-STANDING... I REALLY HAVE BEEN BETRAYING TAKEDA, HAVEN'T I?
EVEN NOW, I STILL CAN'T TELL HIM THE TRUTH...

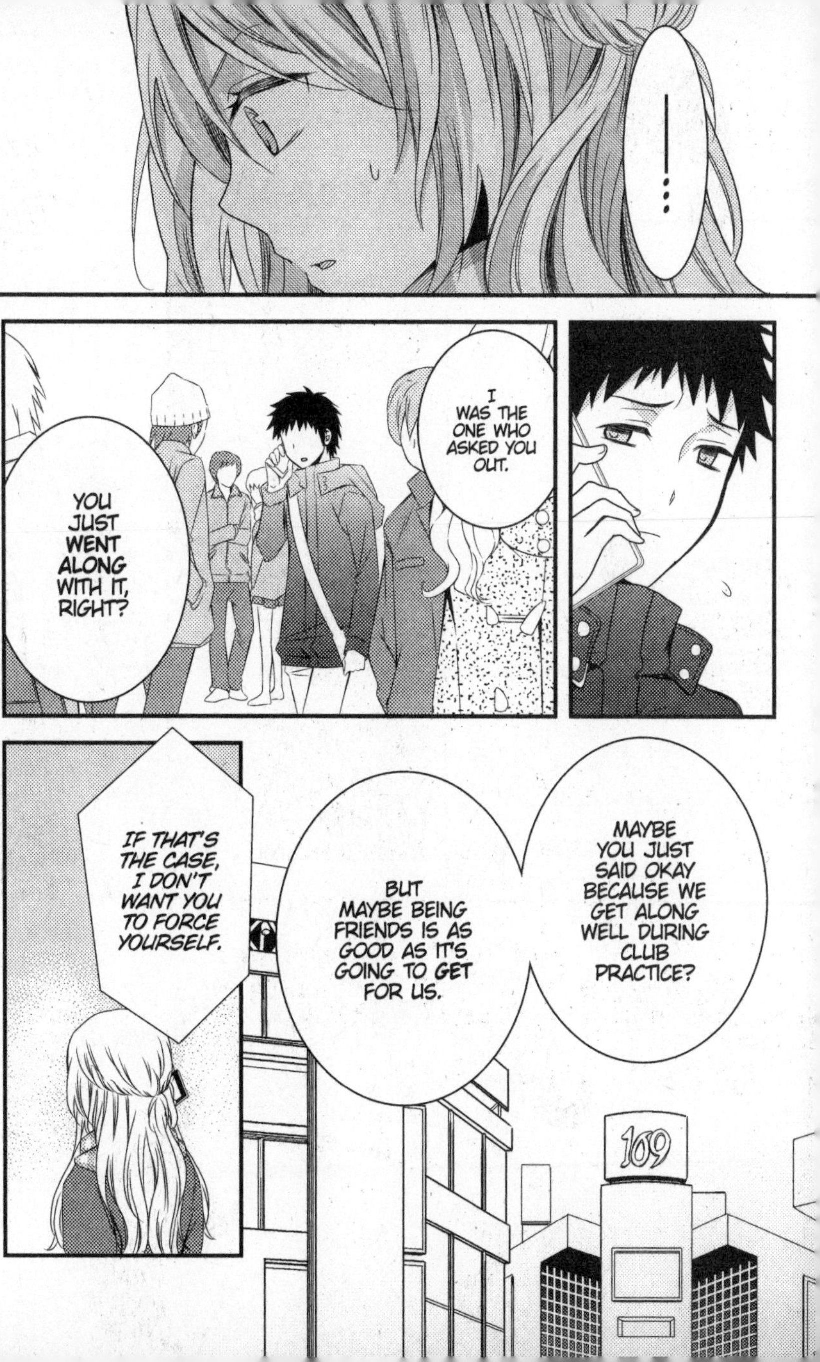
—…
I WAS THE ONE WHO ASKED YOU OUT.
YOU JUST WENT ALONG WITH IT, RIGHT?
MAYBE YOU JUST SAID OKAY BECAUSE WE GET ALONG WELL DURING CLUB PRACTICE?
BUT MAYBE BEING FRIENDS IS AS GOOD AS IT'S GOING TO GET FOR US.
IF THAT'S THE CASE, I DON'T WANT YOU TO FORCE YOURSELF.
109

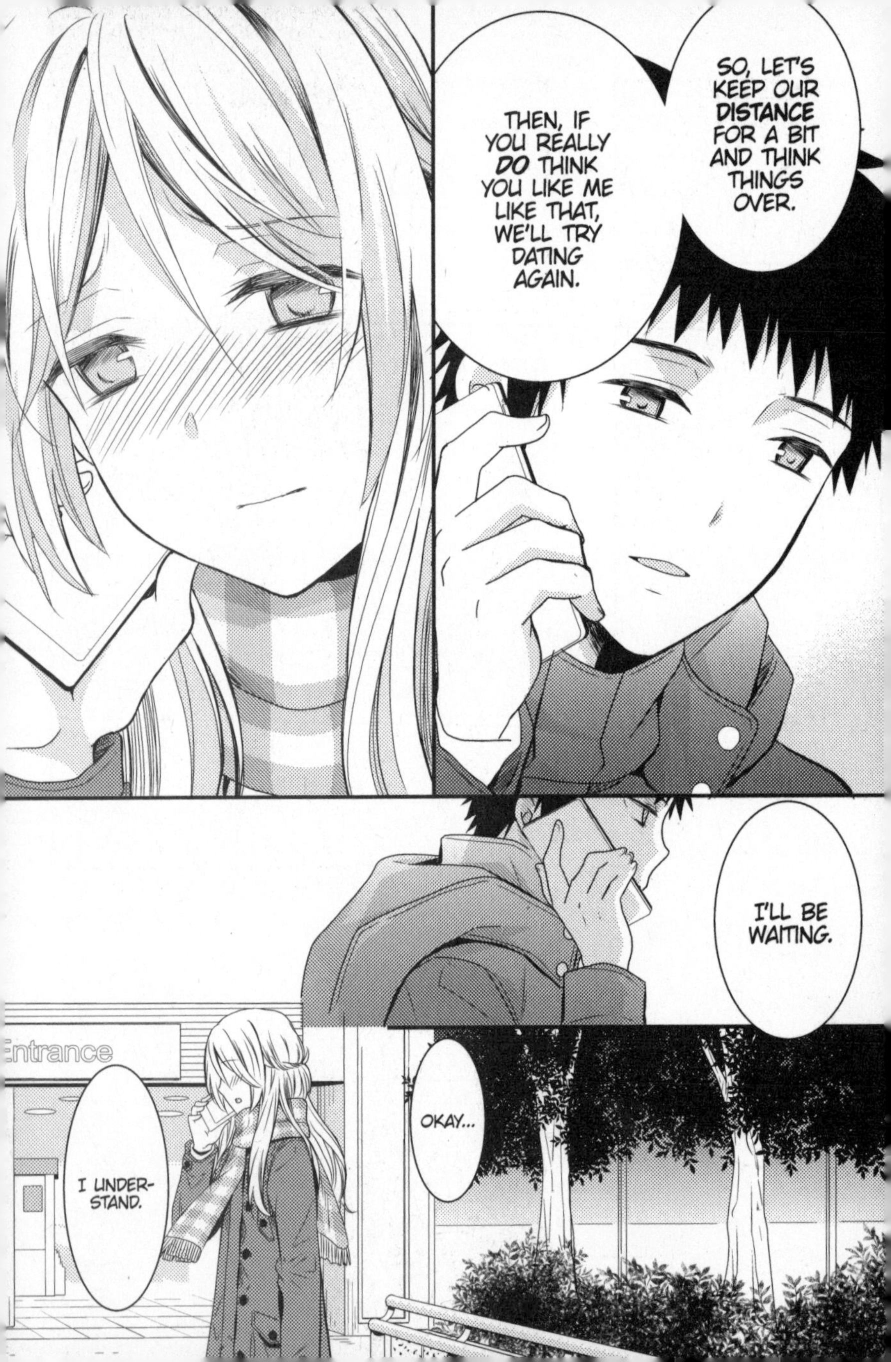
SO, LET'S KEEP OUR DISTANCE FOR A BIT AND THINK THINGS OVER.
THEN, IF YOU REALLY DO THINK YOU LIKE ME LIKE THAT, WE'LL TRY DATING AGAIN.
I'LL BE WAITING.
OKAY...
Entrance
I UNDER-STAND.

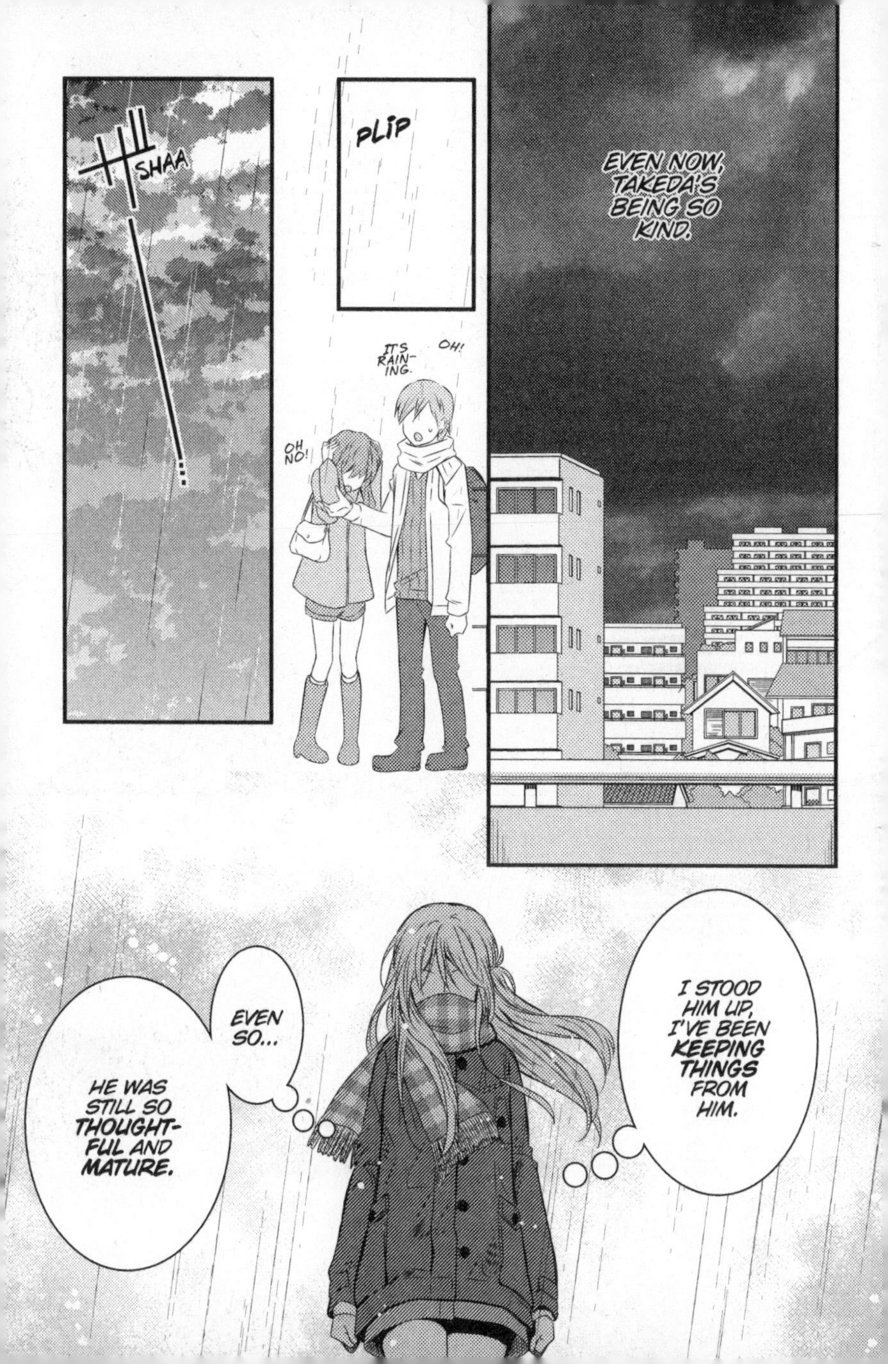
EVEN NOW, TAKEDA'S BEING SO KIND.
PLIP
OH!
IT'S RAINING.
OH NO!
SHAA
I STOOD HIM UP, I'VE BEEN KEEPING THINGS FROM HIM.
EVEN SO...
HE WAS STILL SO THOUGHTFUL AND MATURE.

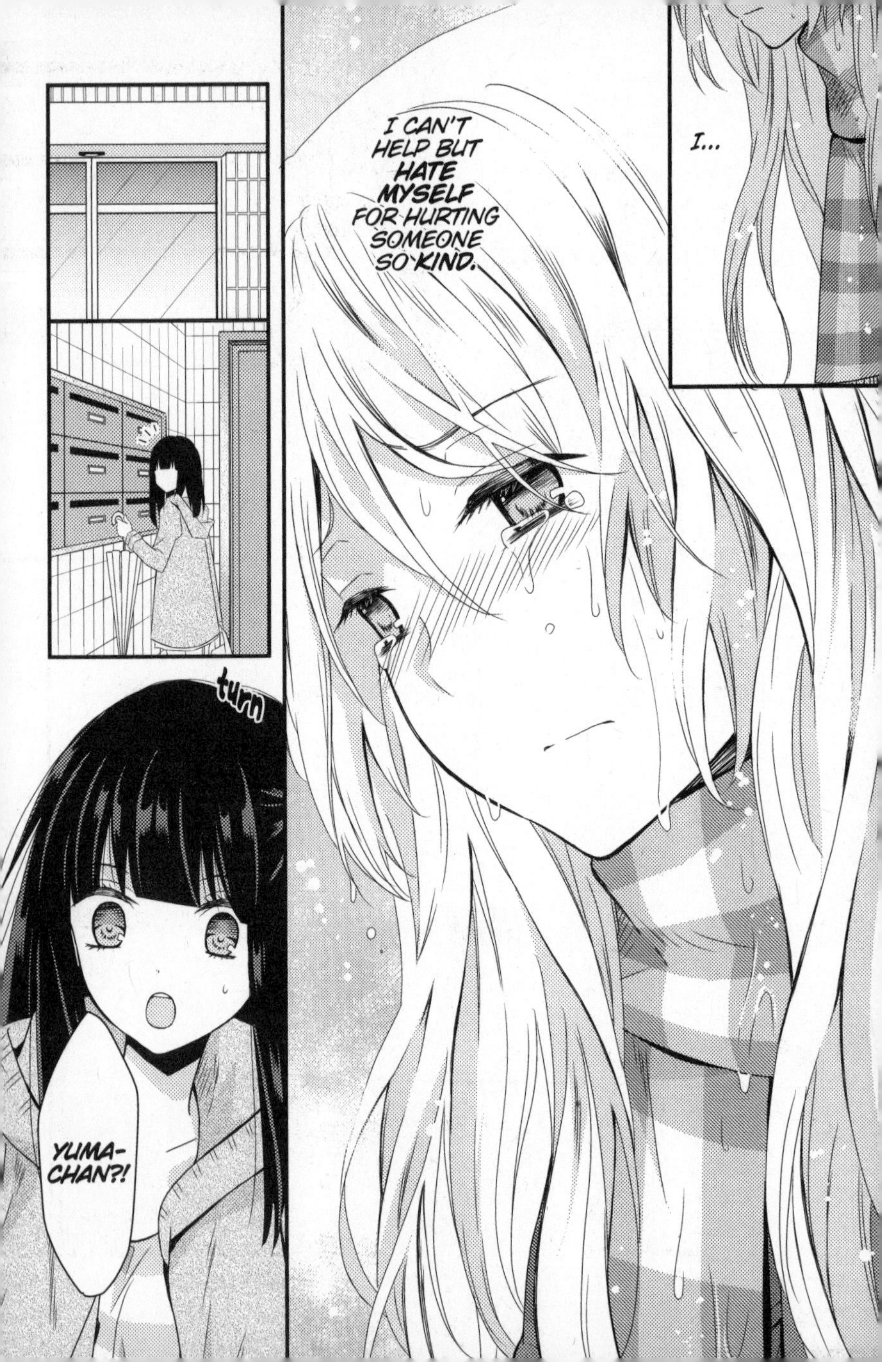
I...
I CAN'T HELP BUT HATE MYSELF FOR HURTING SOMEONE SO KIND.
turn
YUMA-CHAN?!

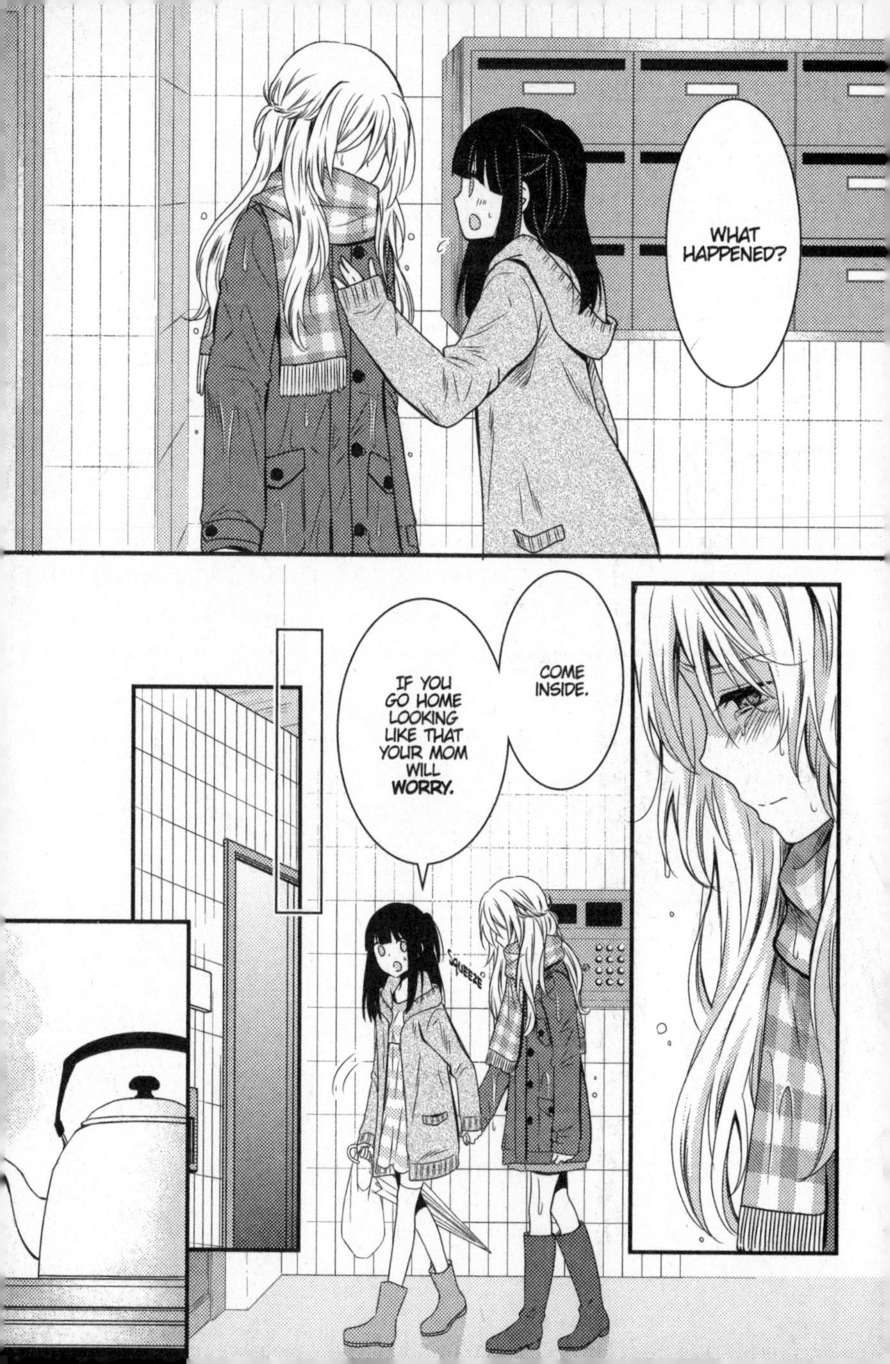
WHAT HAPPENED?
COME INSIDE.
IF YOU GO HOME LOOKING LIKE THAT YOUR MOM WILL WORRY.
SQUEEZE

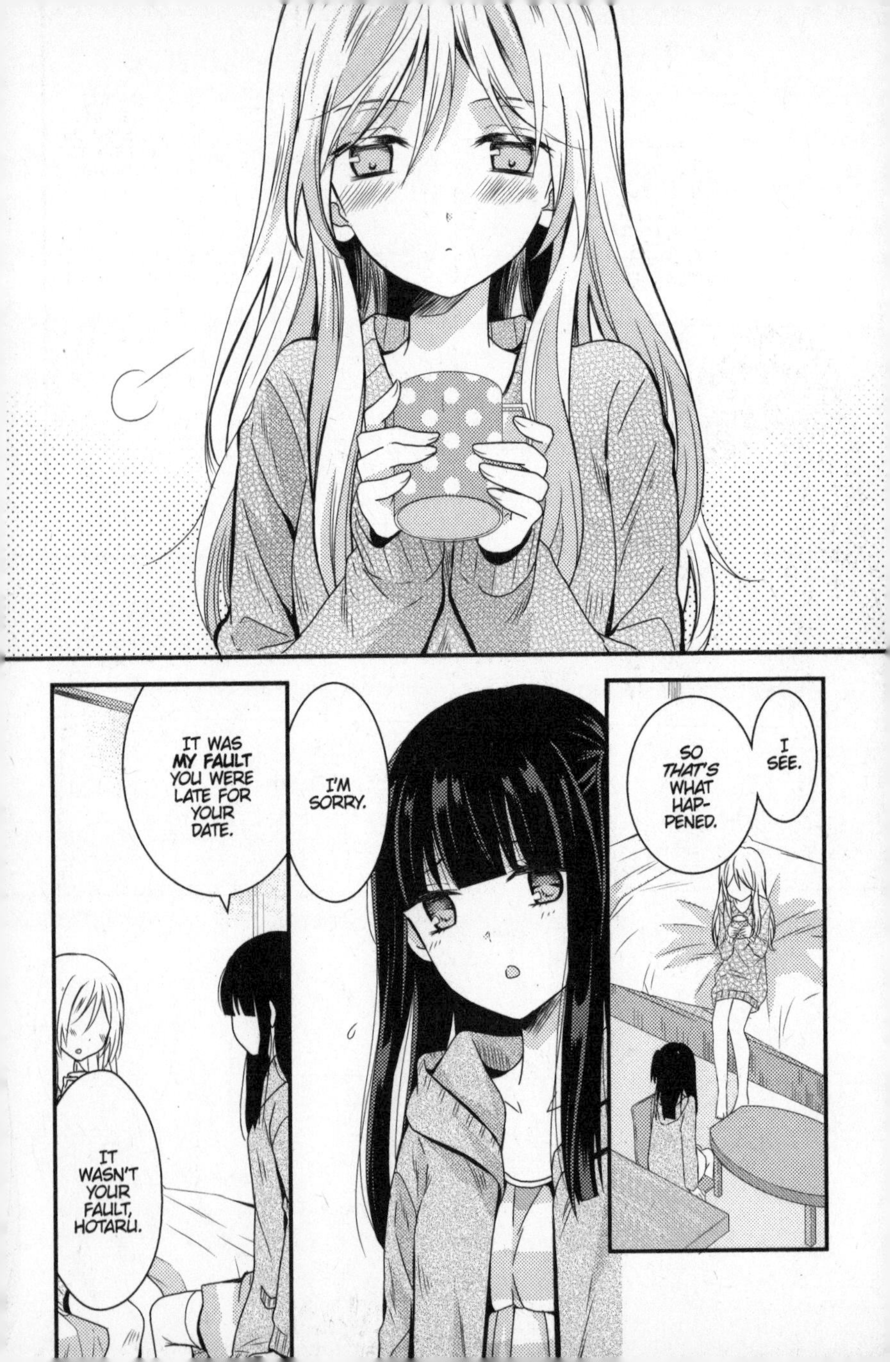
I SEE.
SO *THAT'S* WHAT HAPPENED.
I'M SORRY.
IT WAS **MY FAULT** YOU WERE LATE FOR YOUR DATE.
IT WASN'T YOUR FAULT, HOTARU.

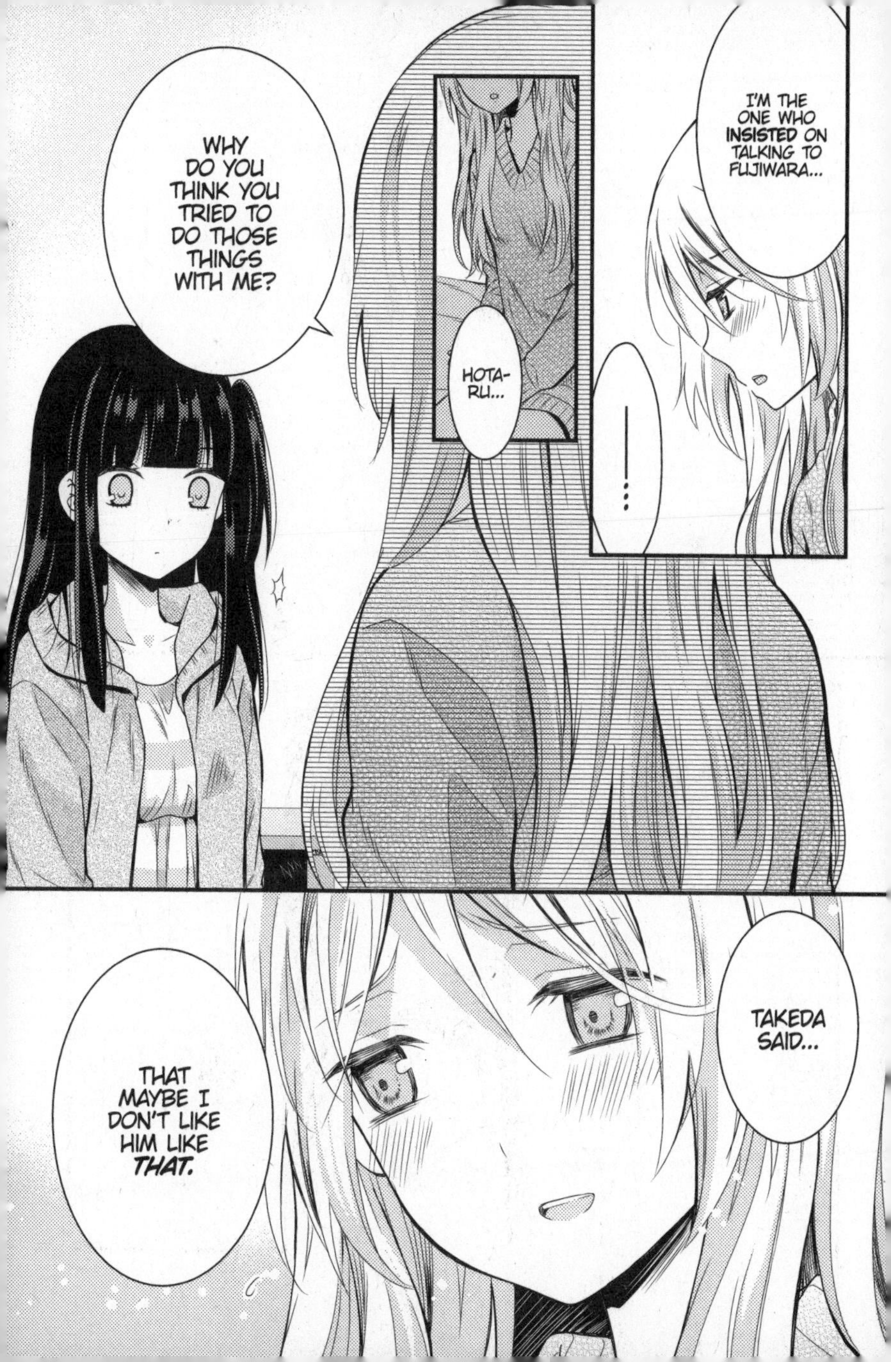
I'M THE ONE WHO INSISTED ON TALKING TO FUJIWARA...
...
HOTA-RU...
WHY DO YOU THINK YOU TRIED TO DO THOSE THINGS WITH ME?
TAKEDA SAID...
THAT MAYBE I DON'T LIKE HIM LIKE *THAT.*

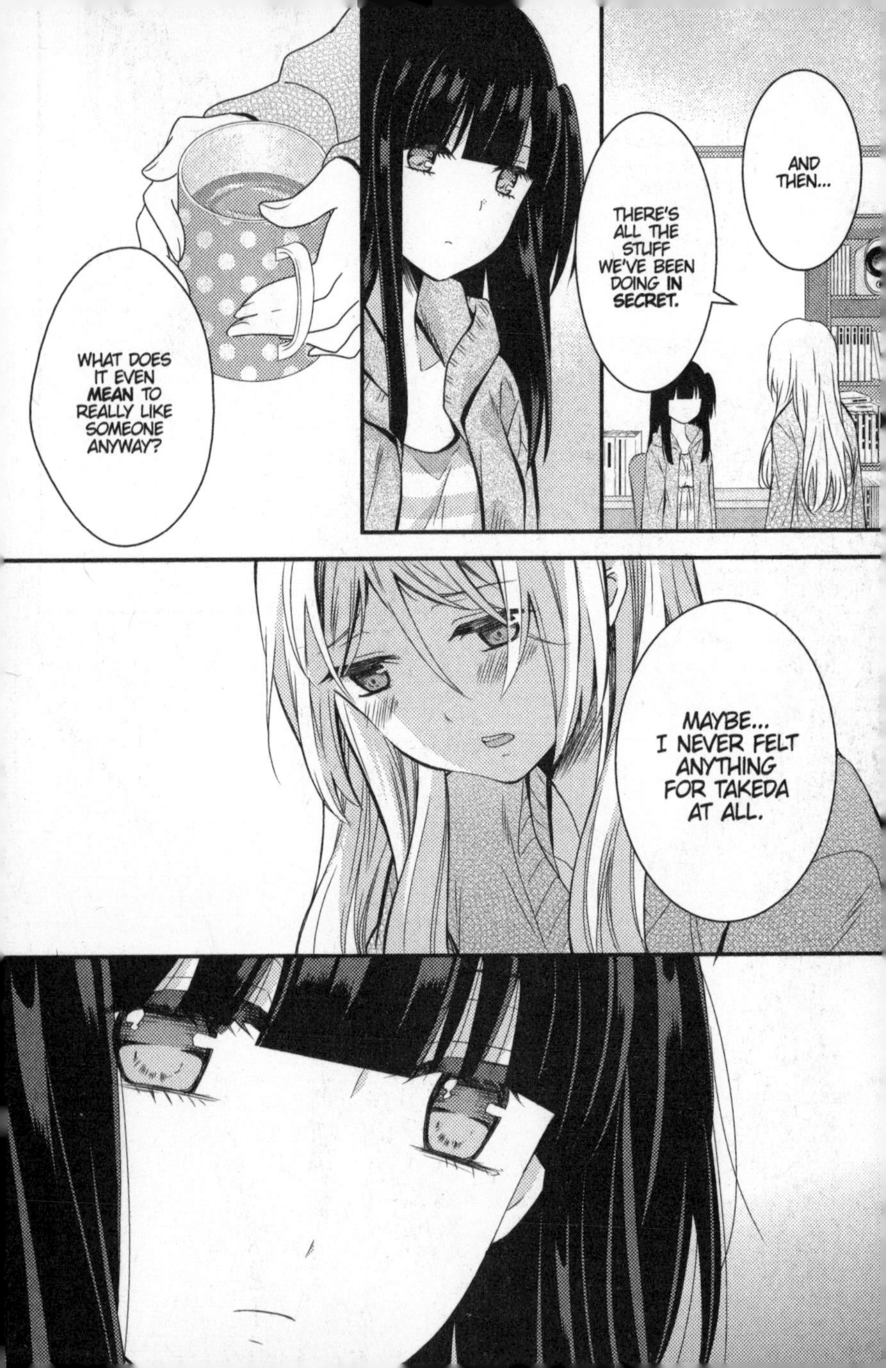
AND THEN...
THERE'S ALL THE STUFF WE'VE BEEN DOING IN SECRET.
WHAT DOES IT EVEN MEAN TO REALLY LIKE SOMEONE ANYWAY?
MAYBE... I NEVER FELT ANYTHING FOR TAKEDA AT ALL.

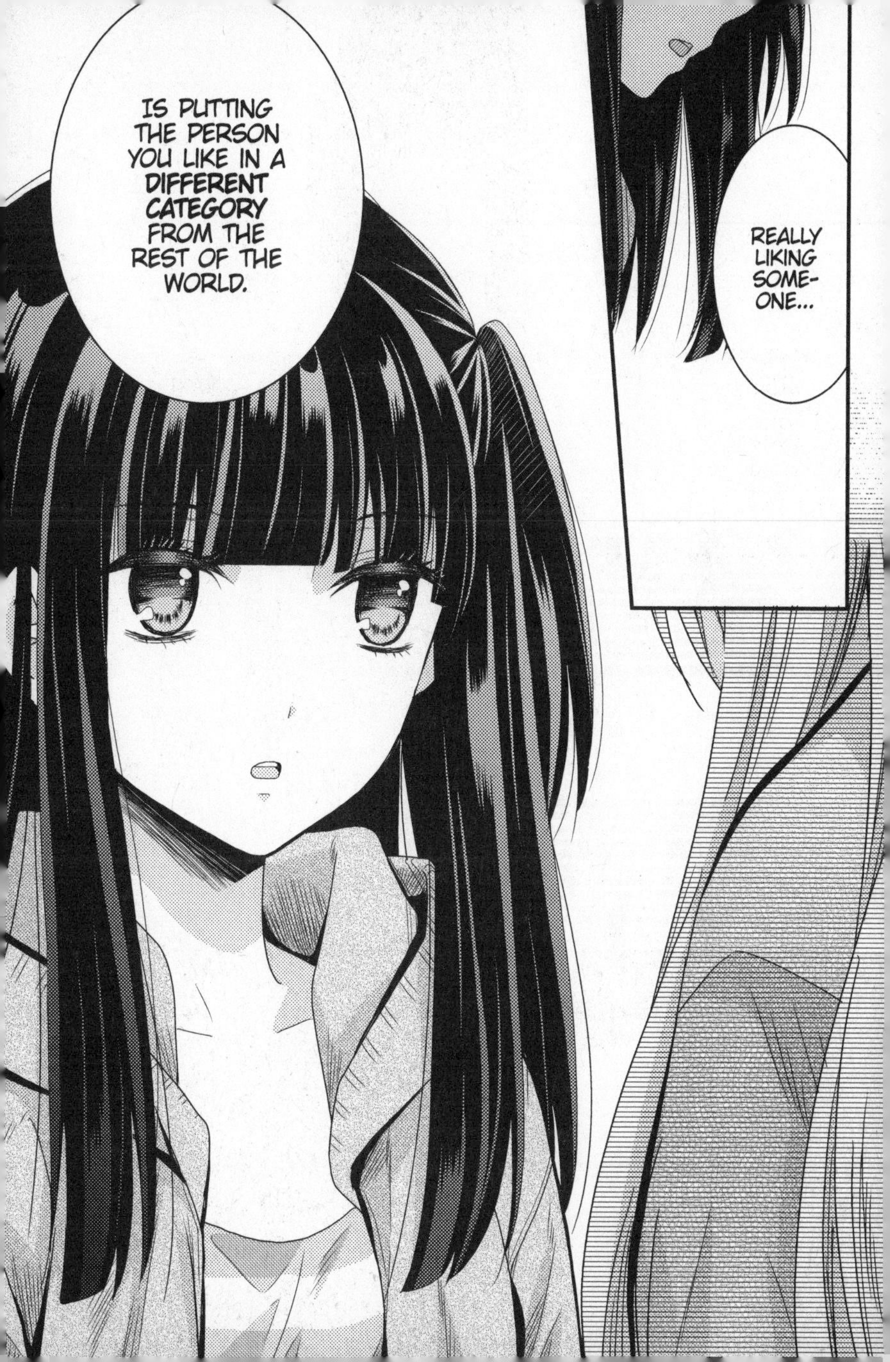
REALLY LIKING SOME-ONE...
IS PUTTING THE PERSON YOU LIKE IN A DIFFERENT CATEGORY FROM THE REST OF THE WORLD.

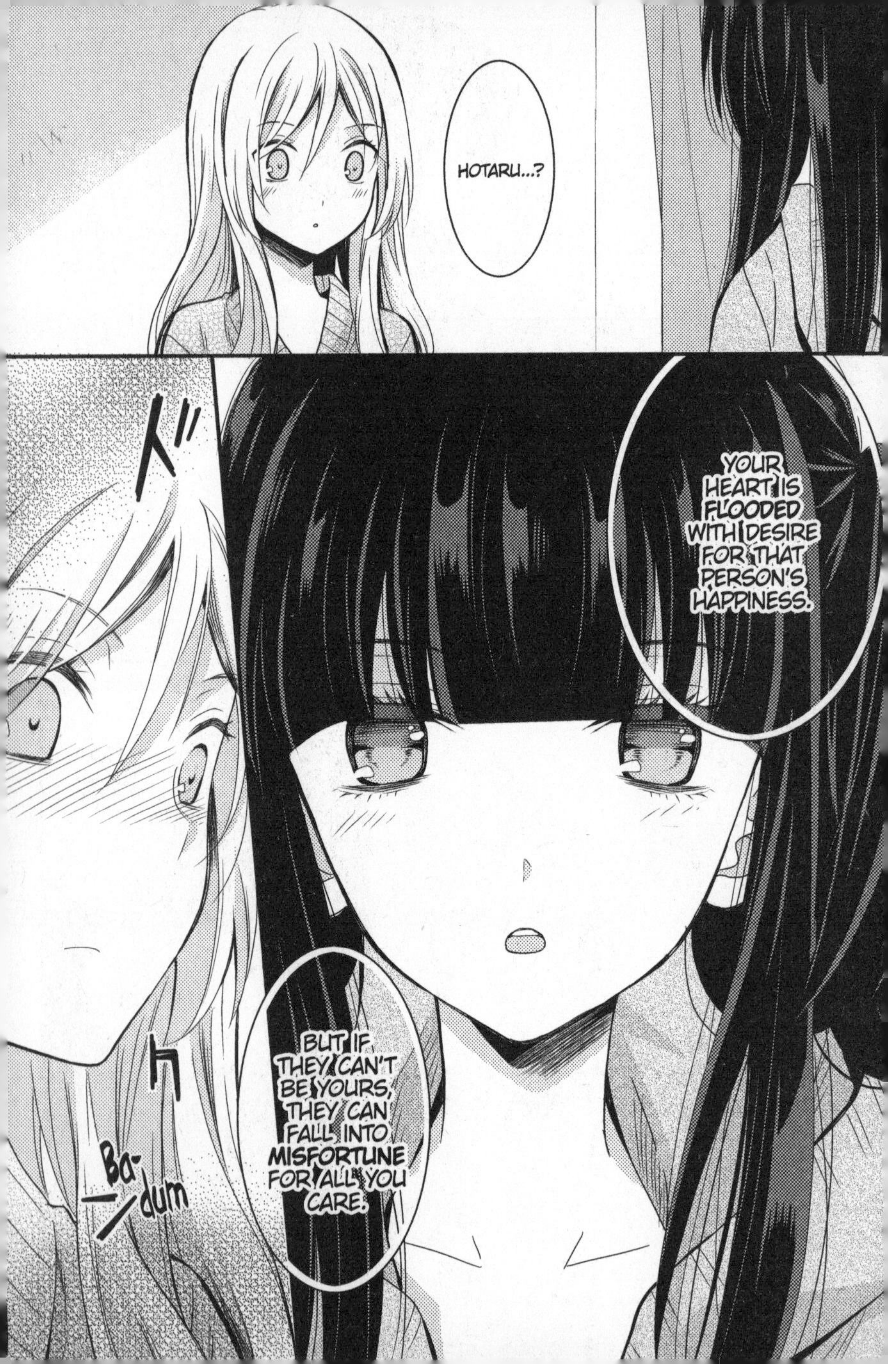
HOTARU...?
YOUR HEART IS FLOODED WITH DESIRE FOR THAT PERSON'S HAPPINESS.
ド
BUT IF THEY CAN'T BE YOURS, THEY CAN FALL INTO MISFORTUNE FOR ALL YOU CARE.
Ba-dum

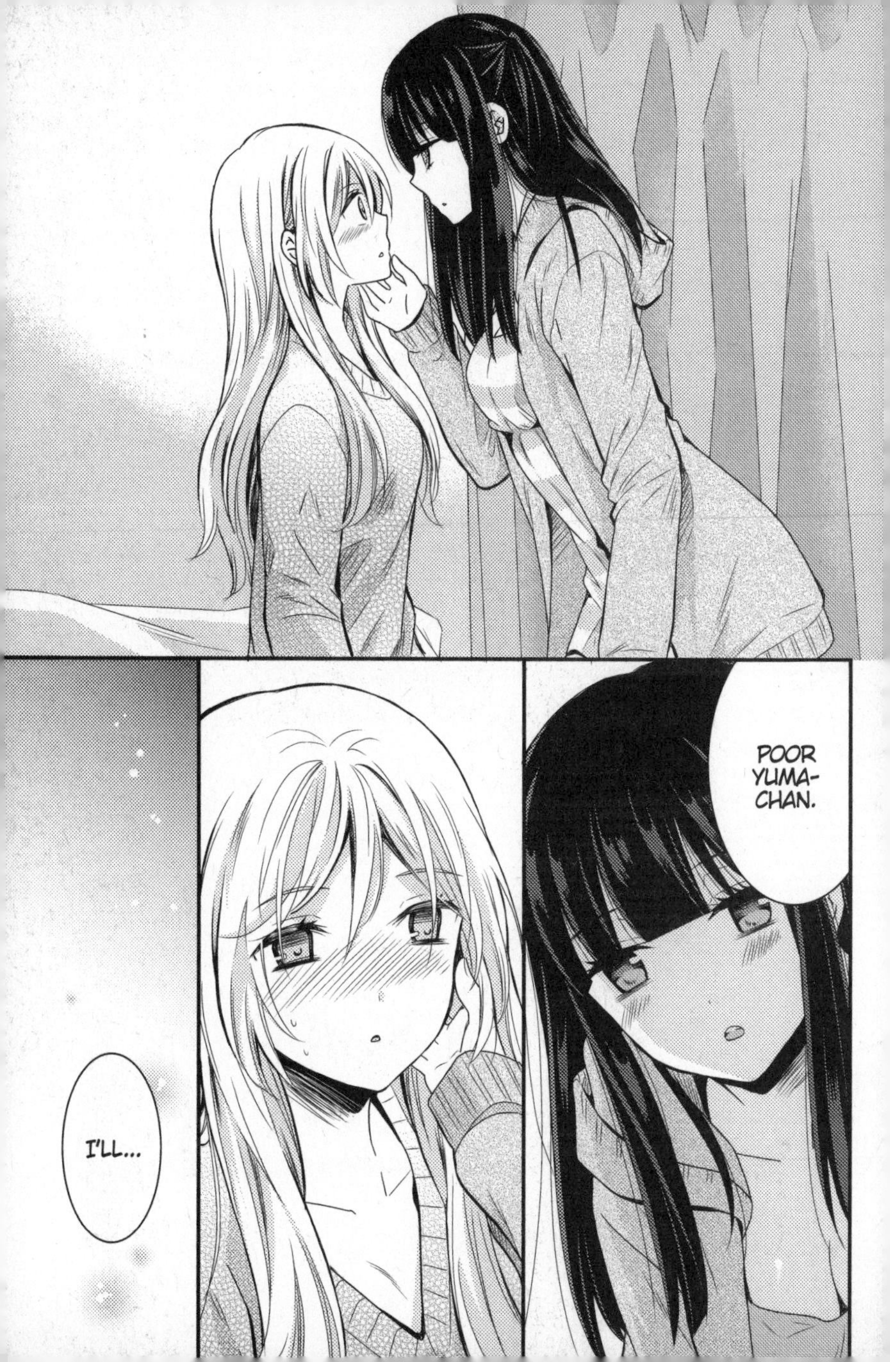
POOR YUMA-CHAN.
I'LL...

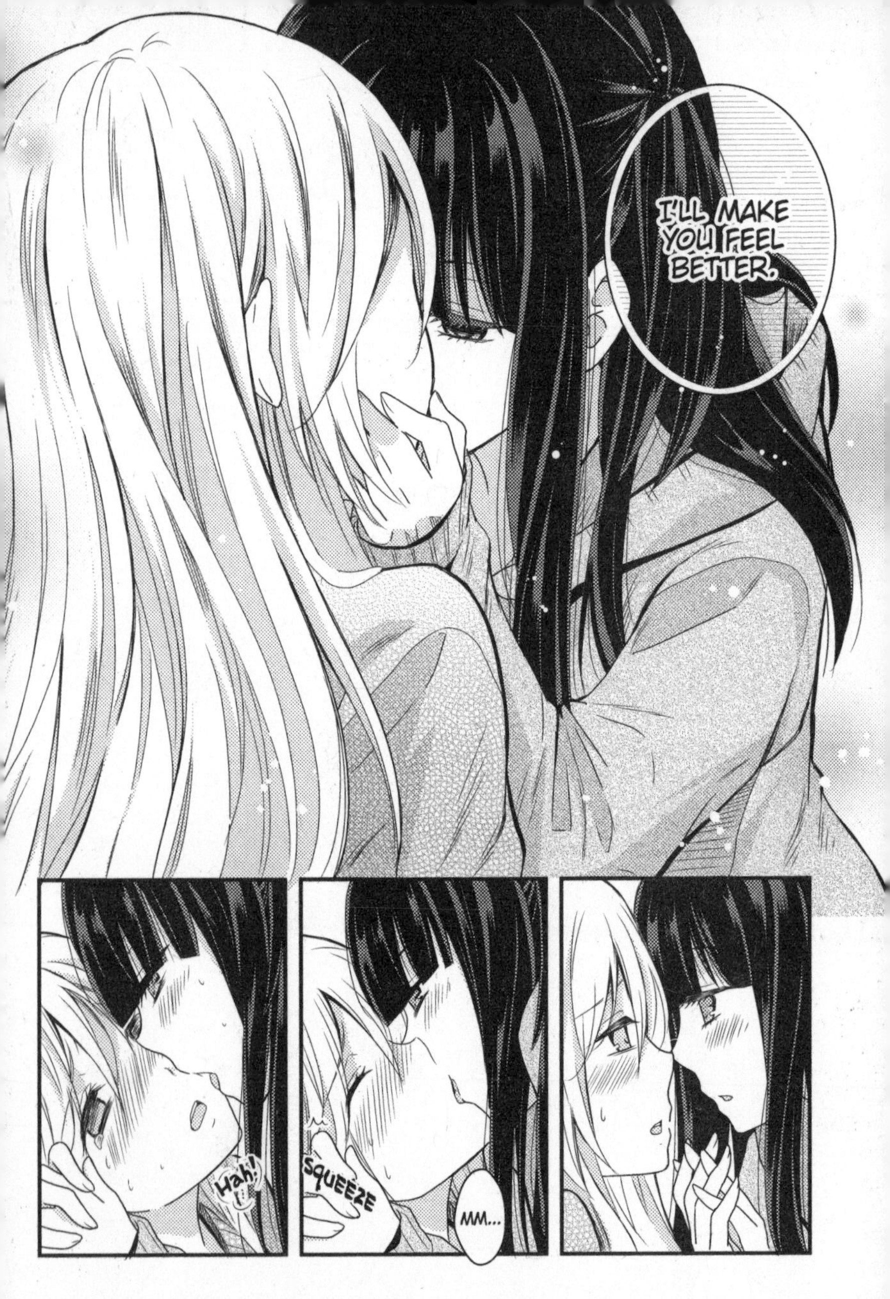
I'LL MAKE YOU FEEL BETTER.
MM...
SQUEEZE
Hah!

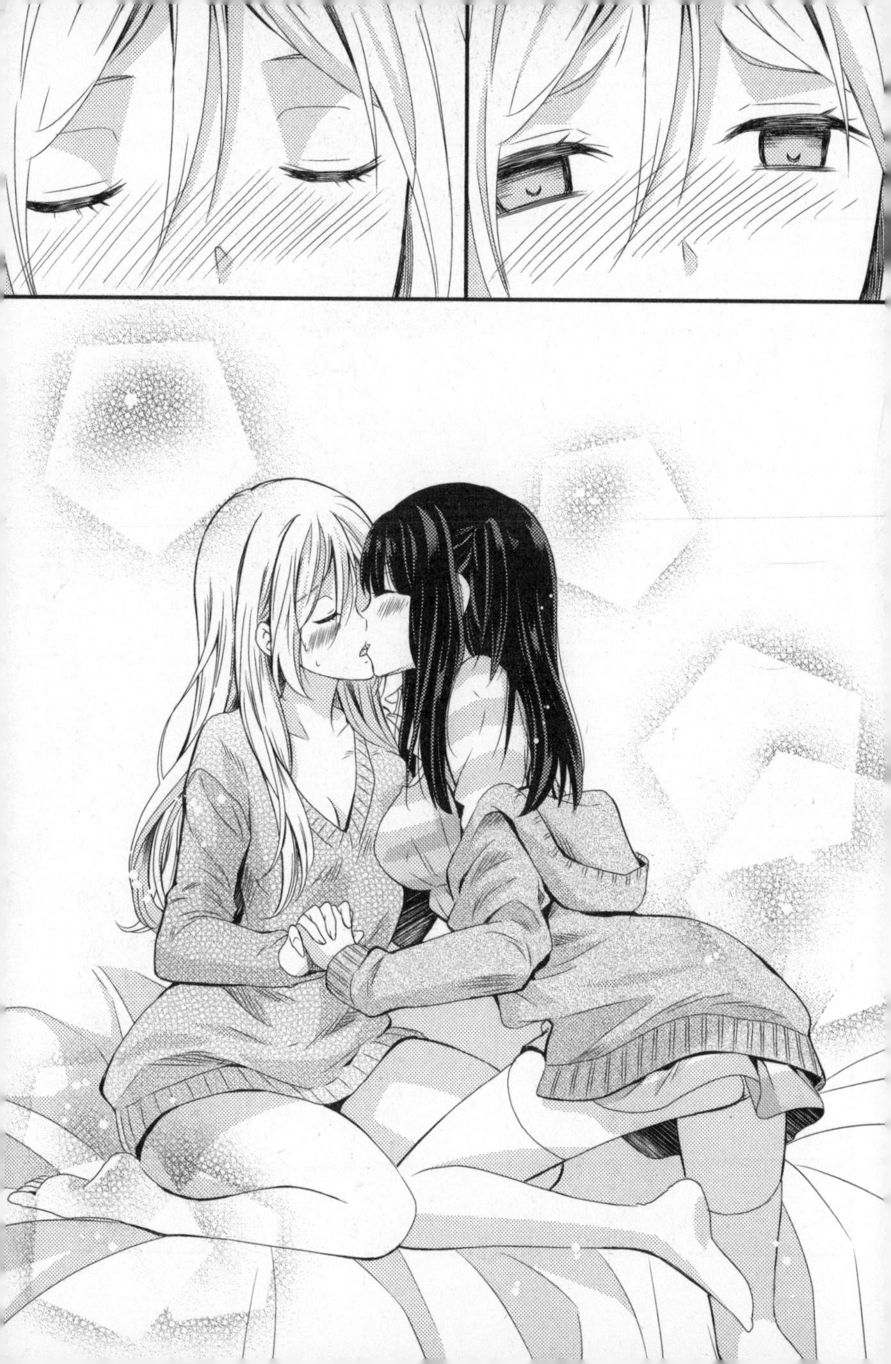

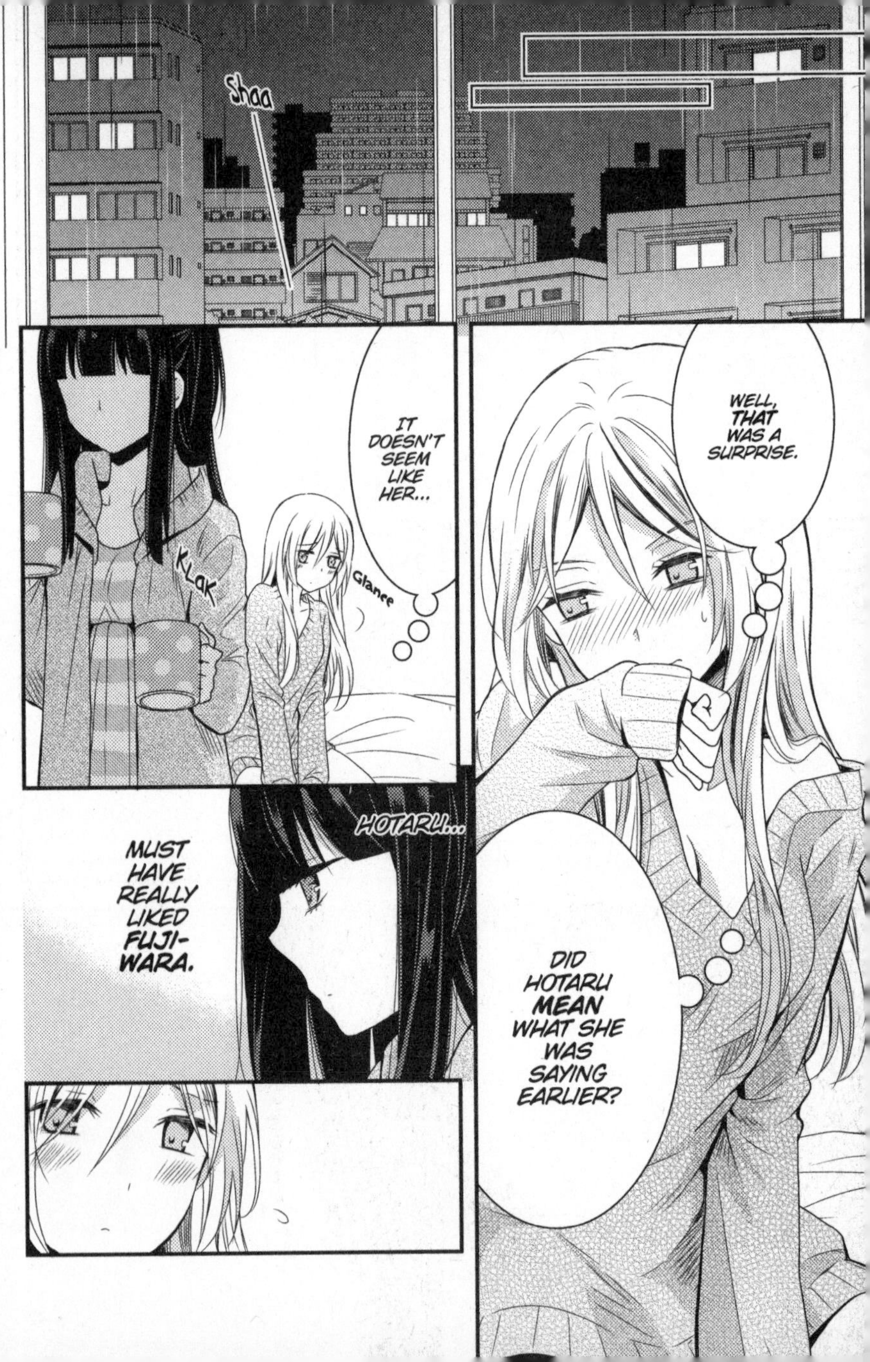
Shaa
WELL, THAT WAS A SURPRISE.
DID HOTARU MEAN WHAT SHE WAS SAYING EARLIER?
IT DOESN'T SEEM LIKE HER...
Glance
KLAK
HOTARU...
MUST HAVE REALLY LIKED FUJI-WARA.

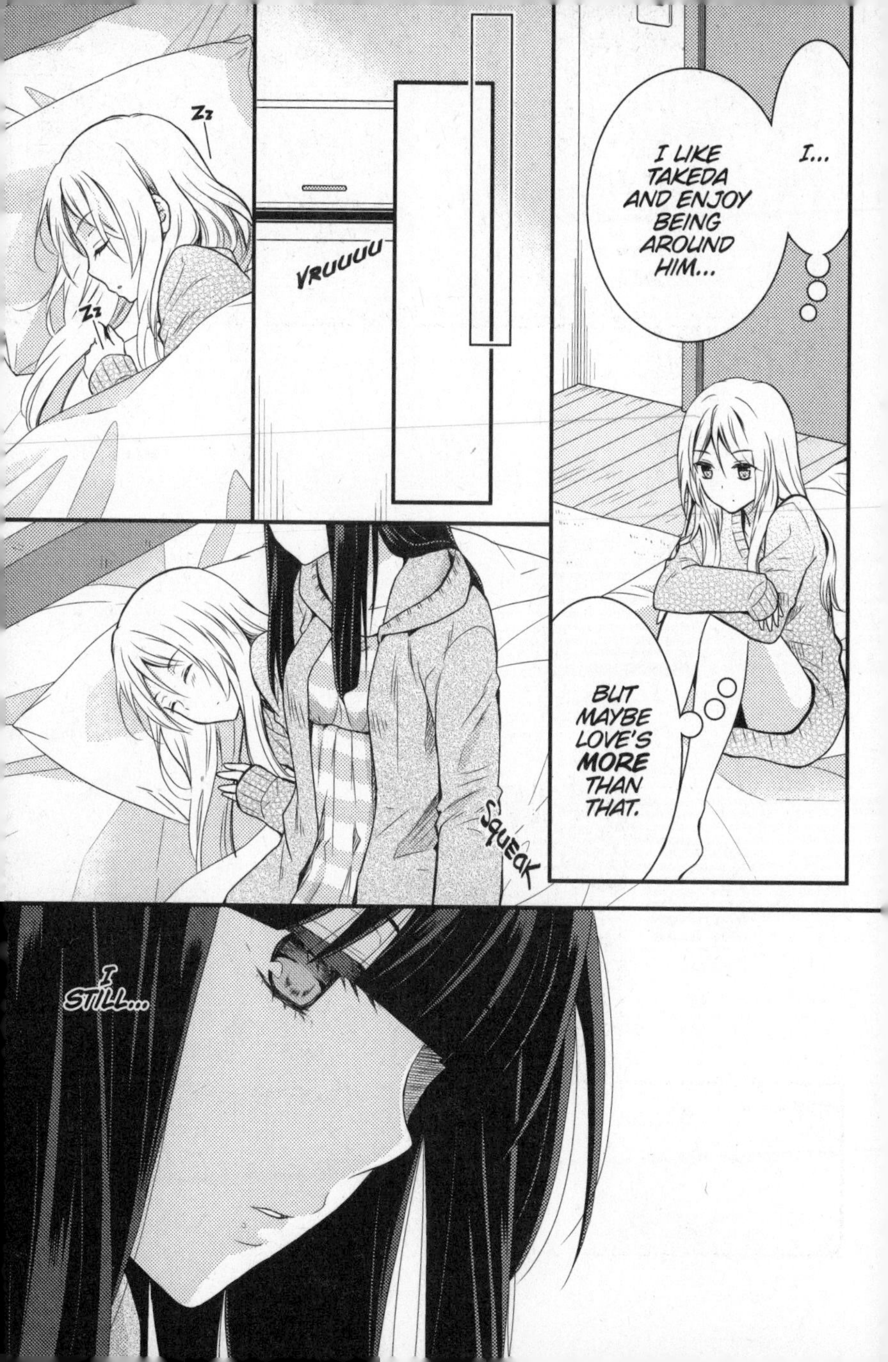
I...
I LIKE TAKEDA AND ENJOY BEING AROUND HIM...
BUT MAYBE LOVE'S MORE THAN THAT.
VRUUUU
Zz
Zz
SQUEAK
I STILL...

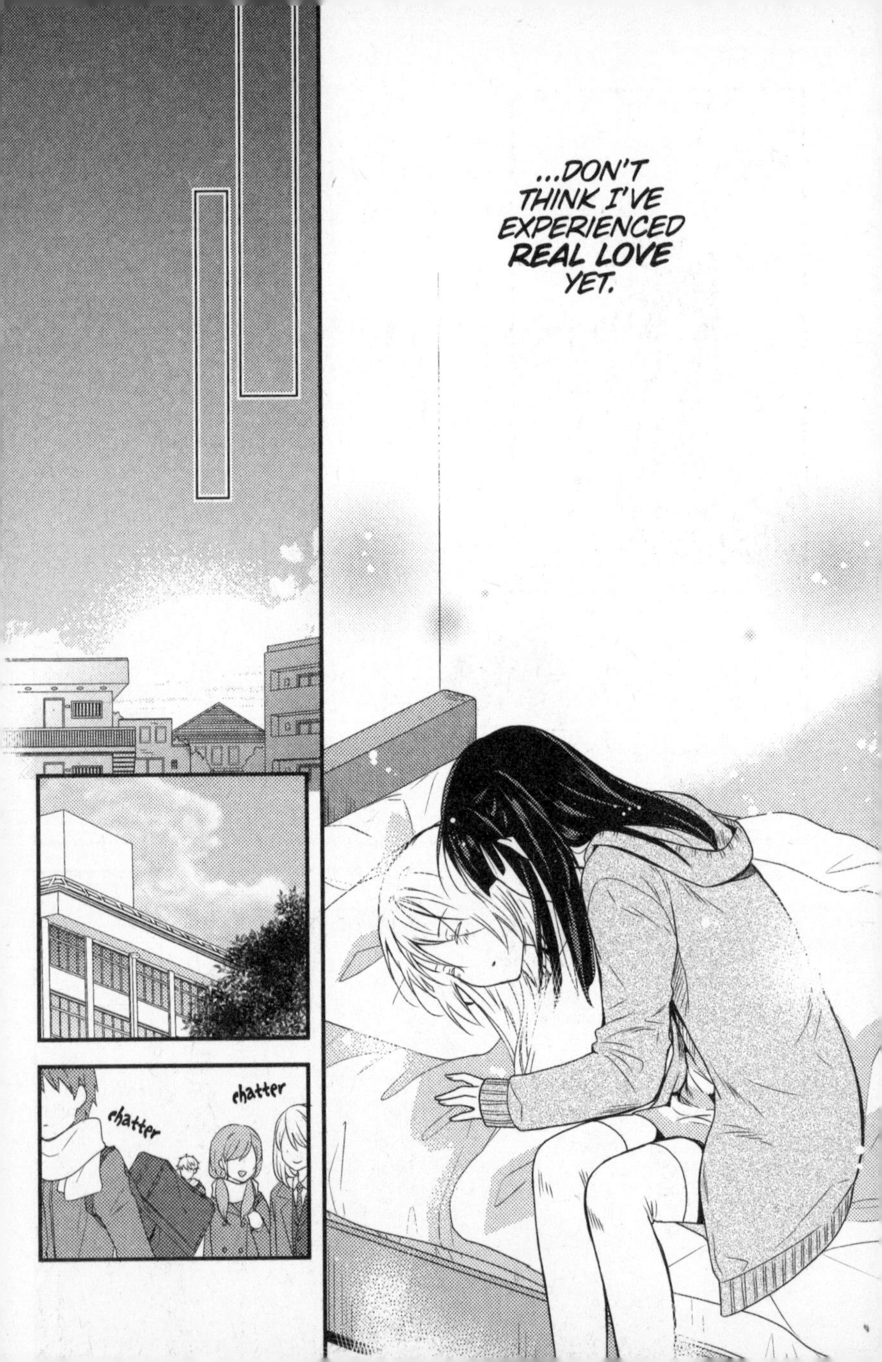
...DON'T THINK I'VE EXPERIENCED REAL LOVE YET.
chatter
chatter

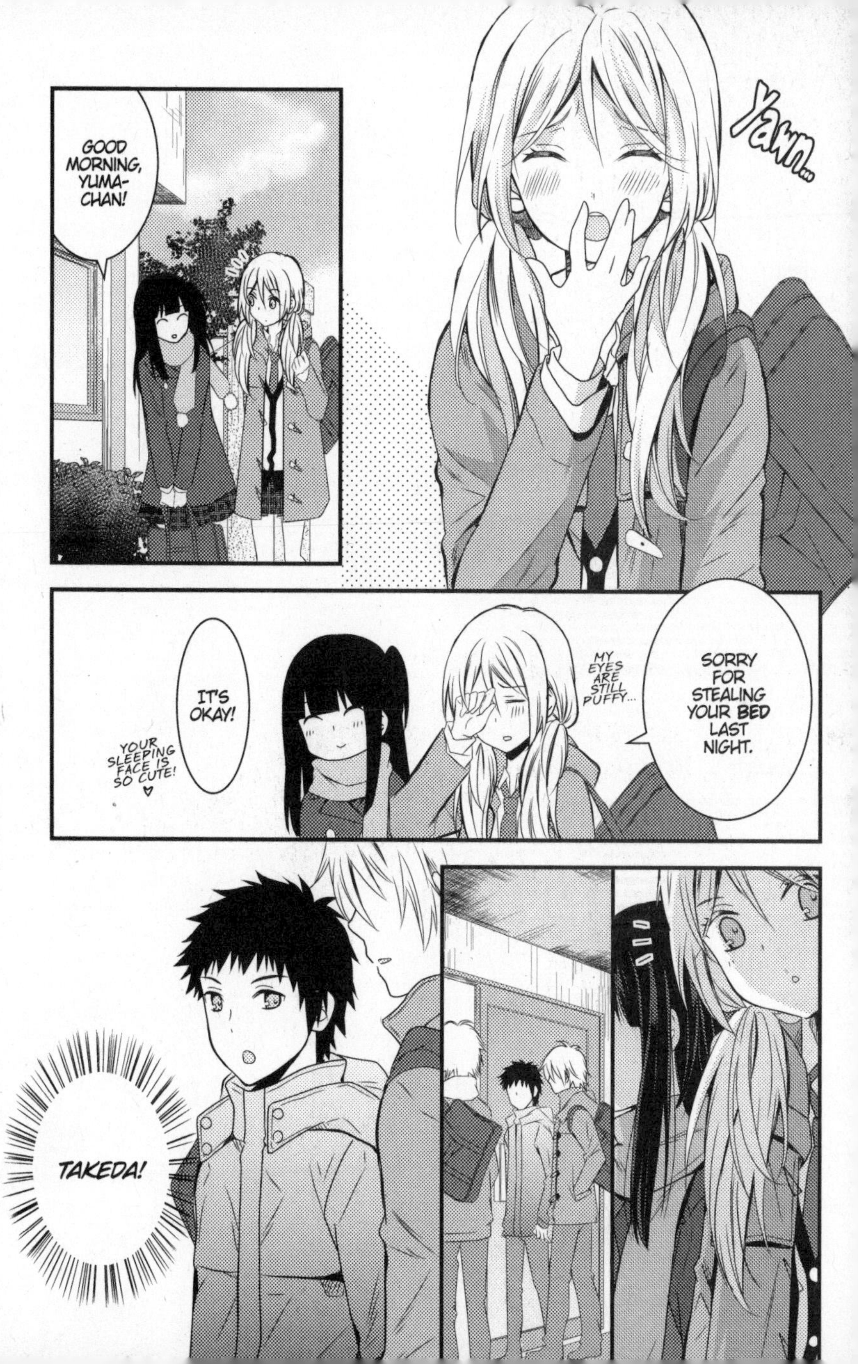
Yawn...
GOOD MORNING, YUMA-CHAN!
SORRY FOR STEALING YOUR BED LAST NIGHT.
MY EYES ARE STILL PUFFY...
IT'S OKAY!
YOUR SLEEPING FACE IS SO CUTE! ♥
TAKEDA!

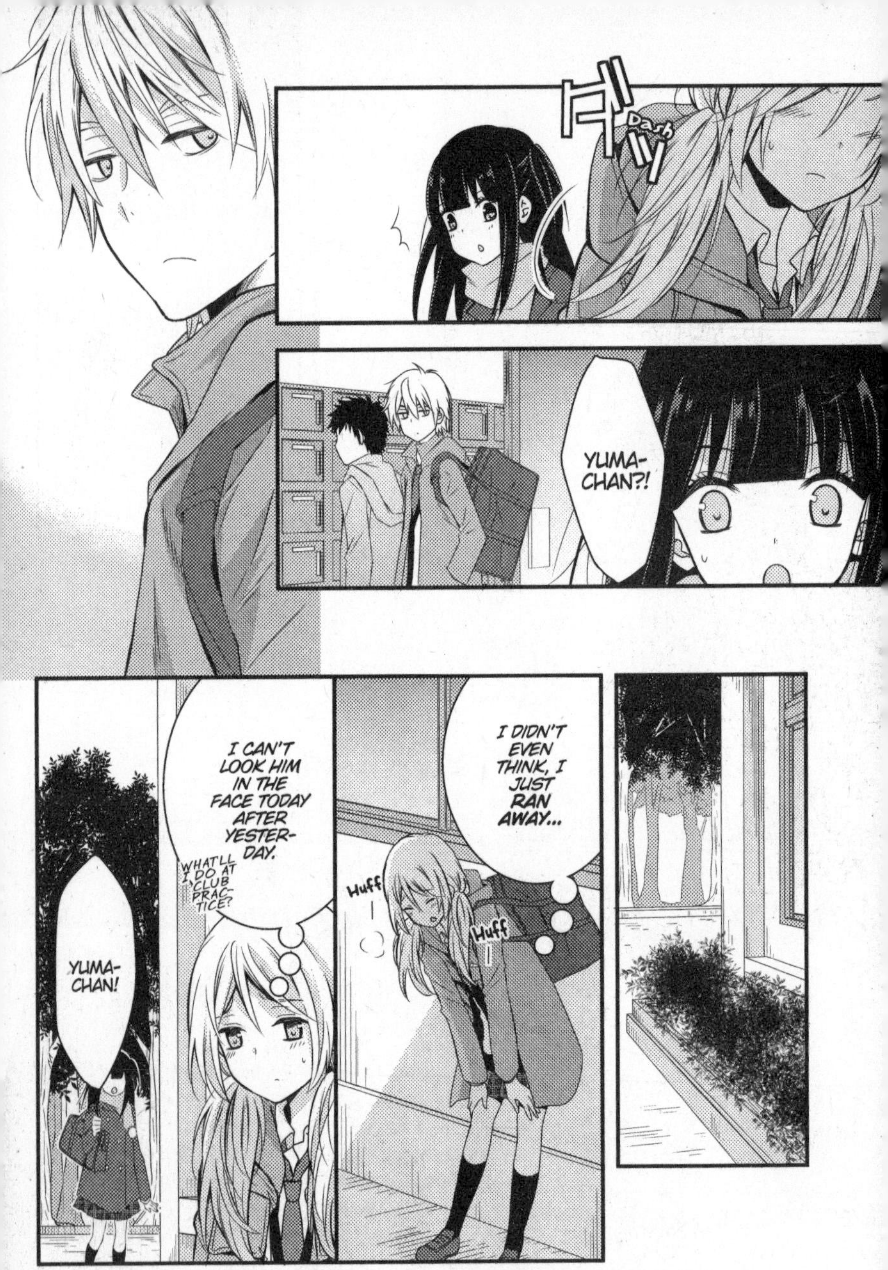
Dash
YUMA-CHAN?!
I DIDN'T EVEN THINK, I JUST RAN AWAY...
Huff
Huff
I CAN'T LOOK HIM IN THE FACE TODAY AFTER YESTER-DAY.
WHAT'LL I DO AT CLUB PRACTICE?
YUMA-CHAN!

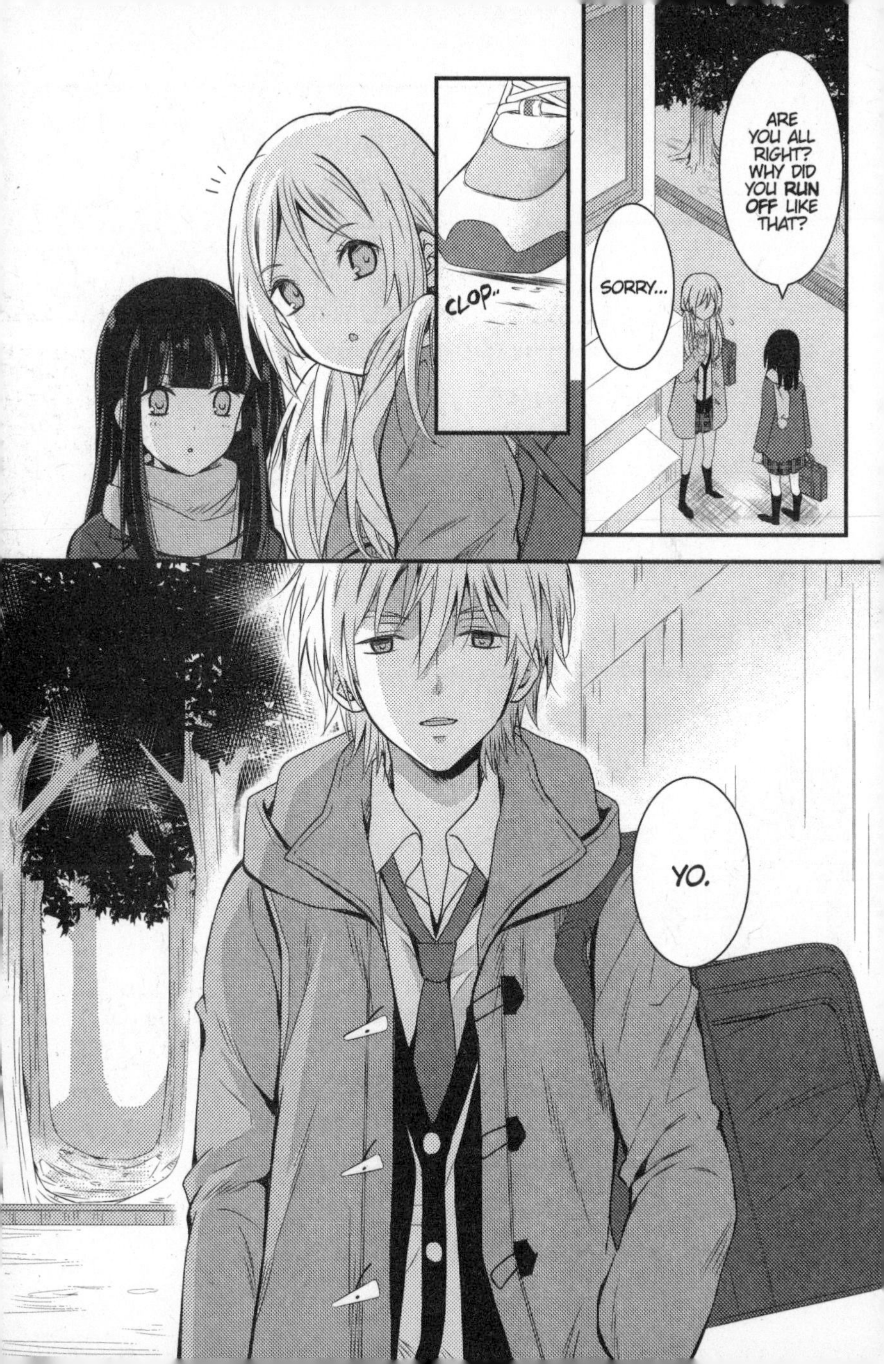
ARE YOU ALL RIGHT? WHY DID YOU RUN OFF LIKE THAT?
SORRY...
CLOP..
YO.

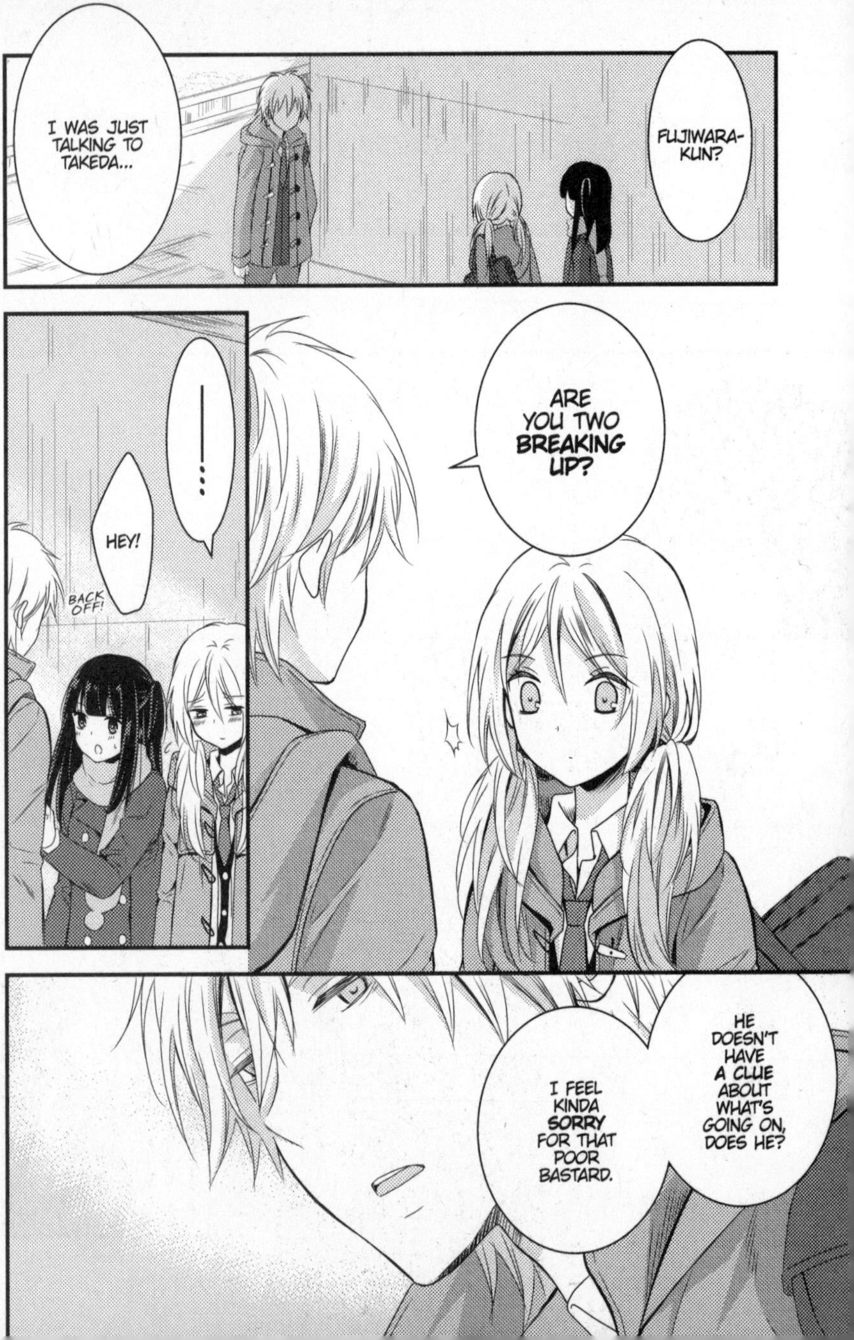
FUJIWARA-KUN?
I WAS JUST TALKING TO TAKEDA...
ARE YOU TWO BREAKING UP?
—...
HEY!
BACK OFF!
HE DOESN'T HAVE A CLUE ABOUT WHAT'S GOING ON, DOES HE?
I FEEL KINDA SORRY FOR THAT POOR BASTARD.

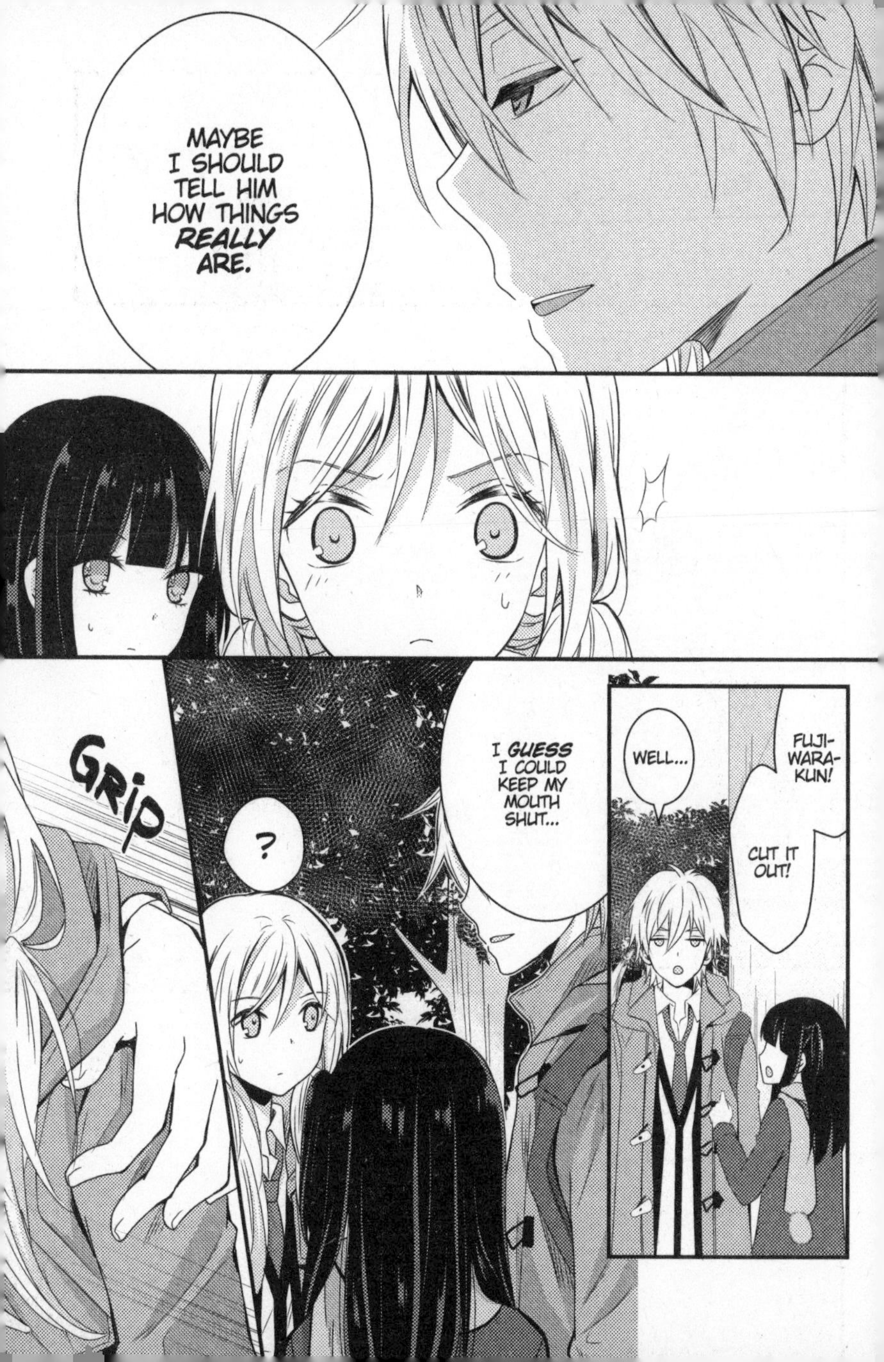
MAYBE I SHOULD TELL HIM HOW THINGS *REALLY* ARE.
FUJI-WARA-KUN!
WELL...
CUT IT OUT!
I *GUESS* I COULD KEEP MY MOUTH SHUT...
?
Grip

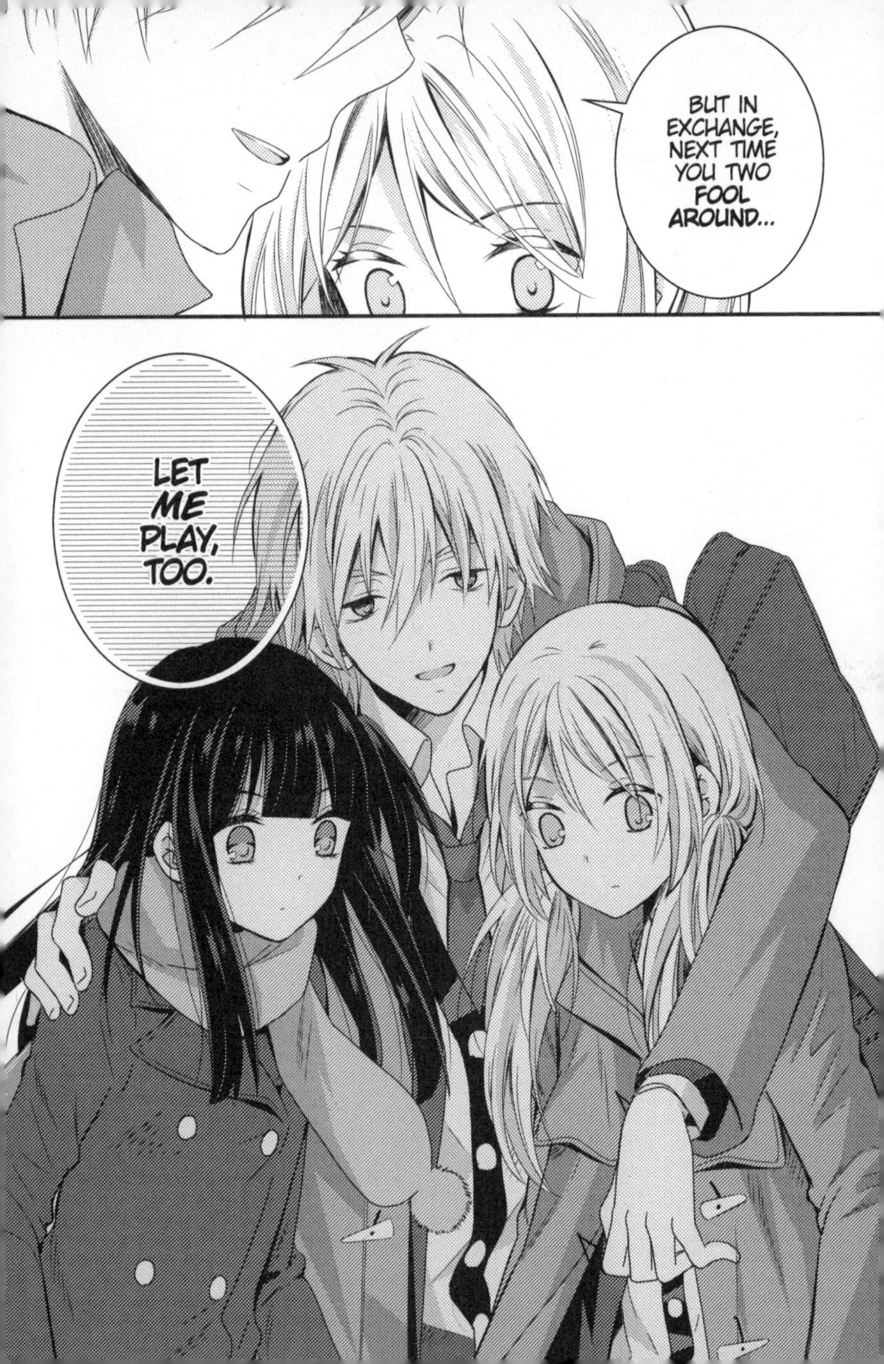
BUT IN EXCHANGE, NEXT TIME YOU TWO FOOL AROUND...
LET ME PLAY, TOO.

NTR *Netsuzou Trap*

NTR
Netsuzou Trap

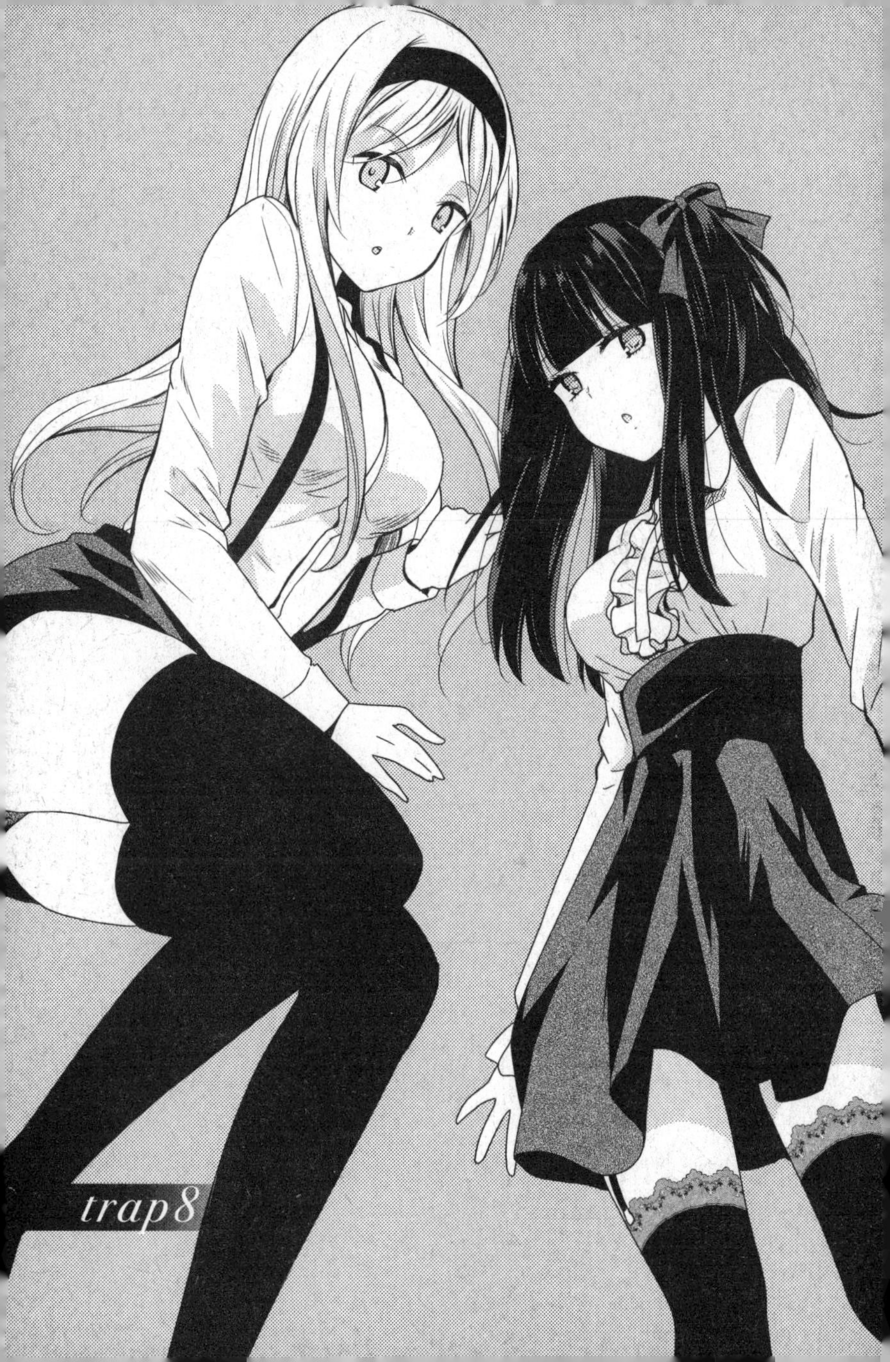
trap 8

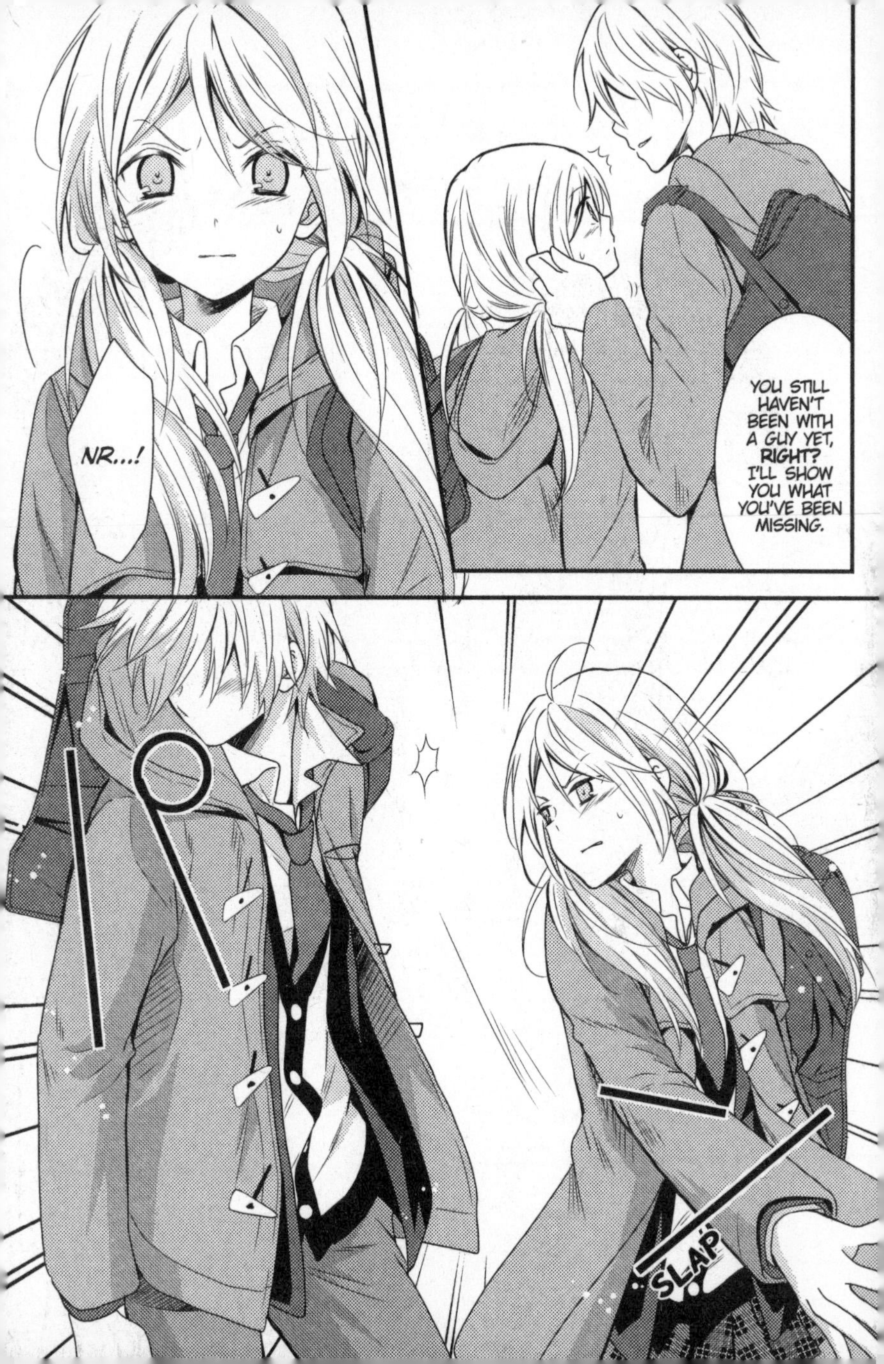
YOU STILL HAVEN'T BEEN WITH A GUY YET, RIGHT? I'LL SHOW YOU WHAT YOU'VE BEEN MISSING.
NR...!
SLAP

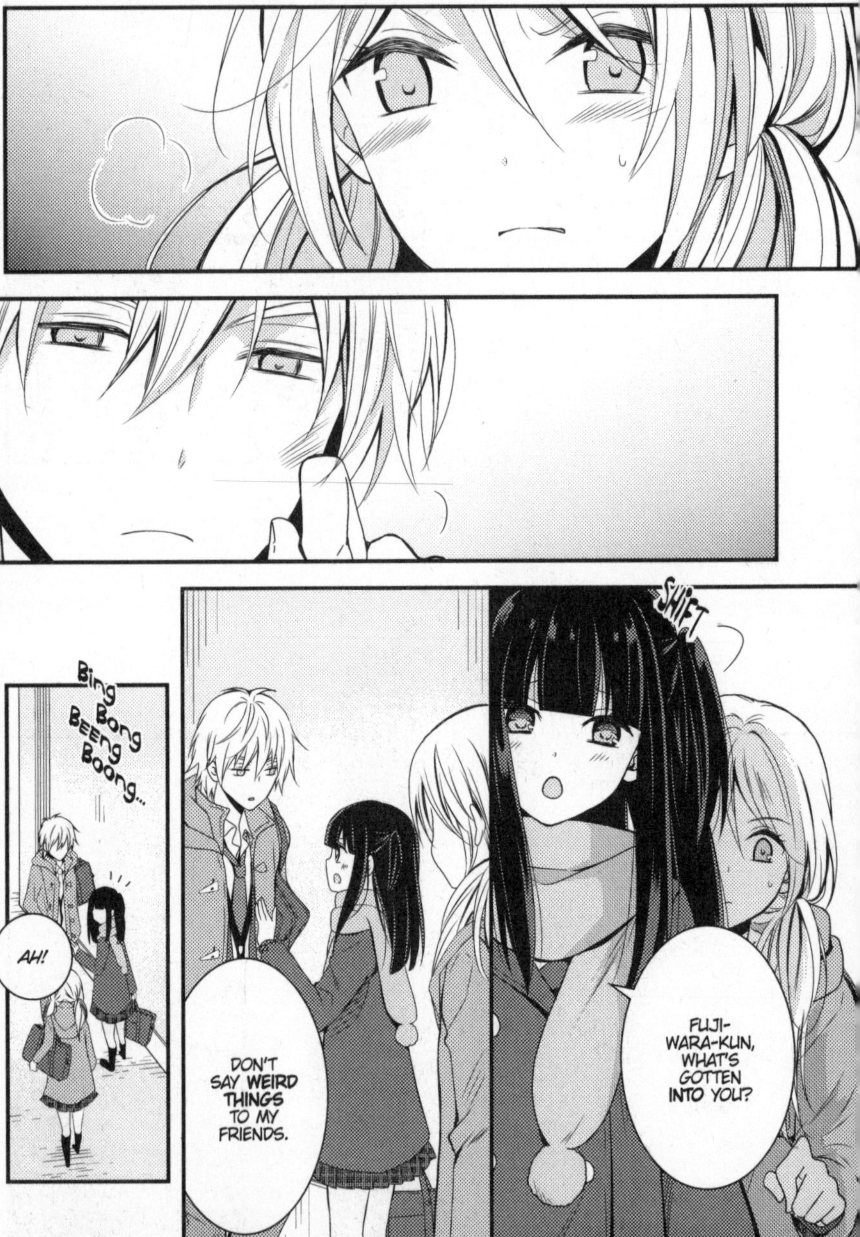
SHIFT
FUJI-WARA-KUN, WHAT'S GOTTEN INTO YOU?
DON'T SAY WEIRD THINGS TO MY FRIENDS.
Bing Bong BEEng Boong...
AH!

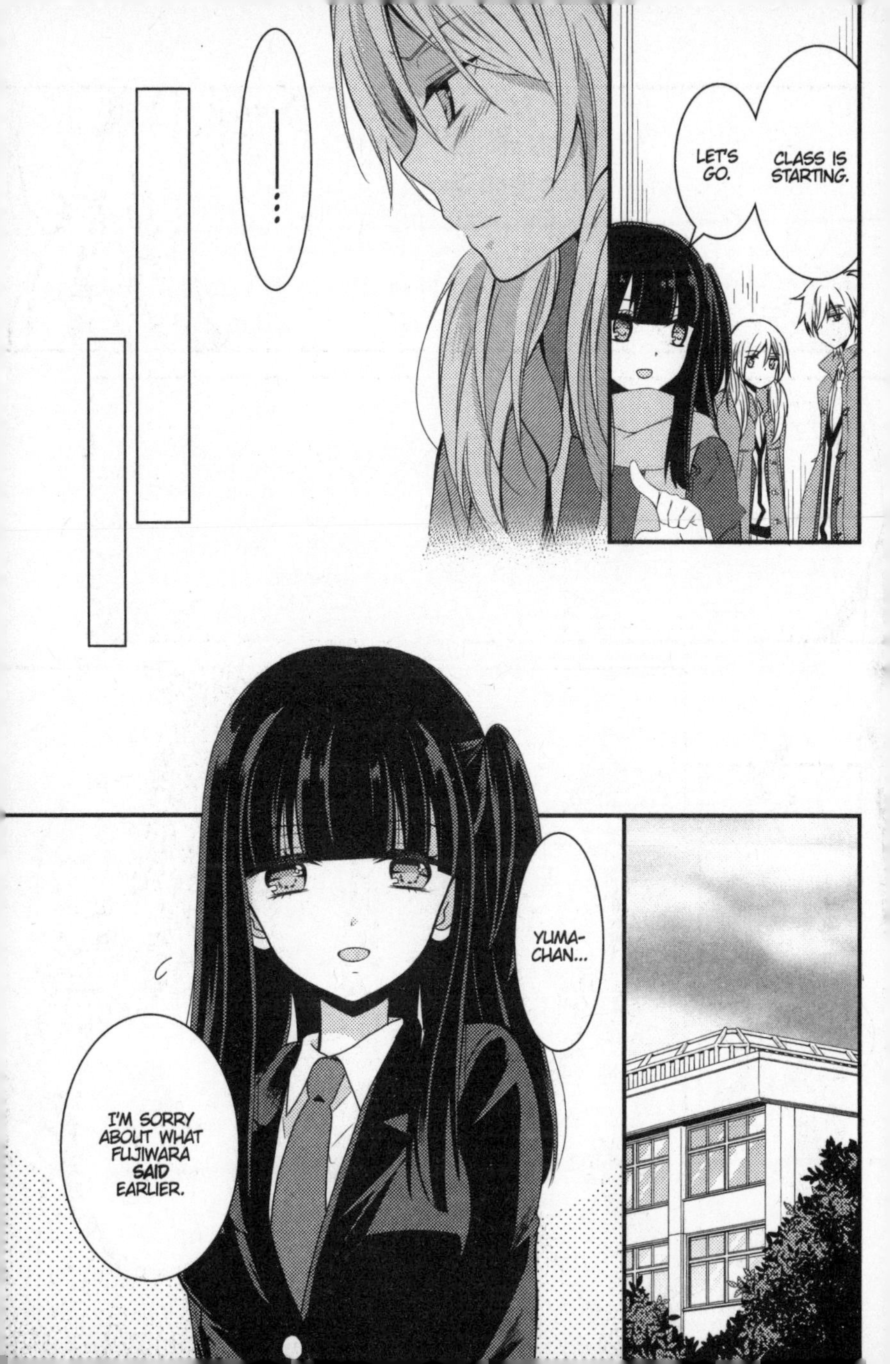
CLASS IS STARTING.
LET'S GO.
—…
YUMA-CHAN...
I'M SORRY ABOUT WHAT FUJIWARA SAID EARLIER.

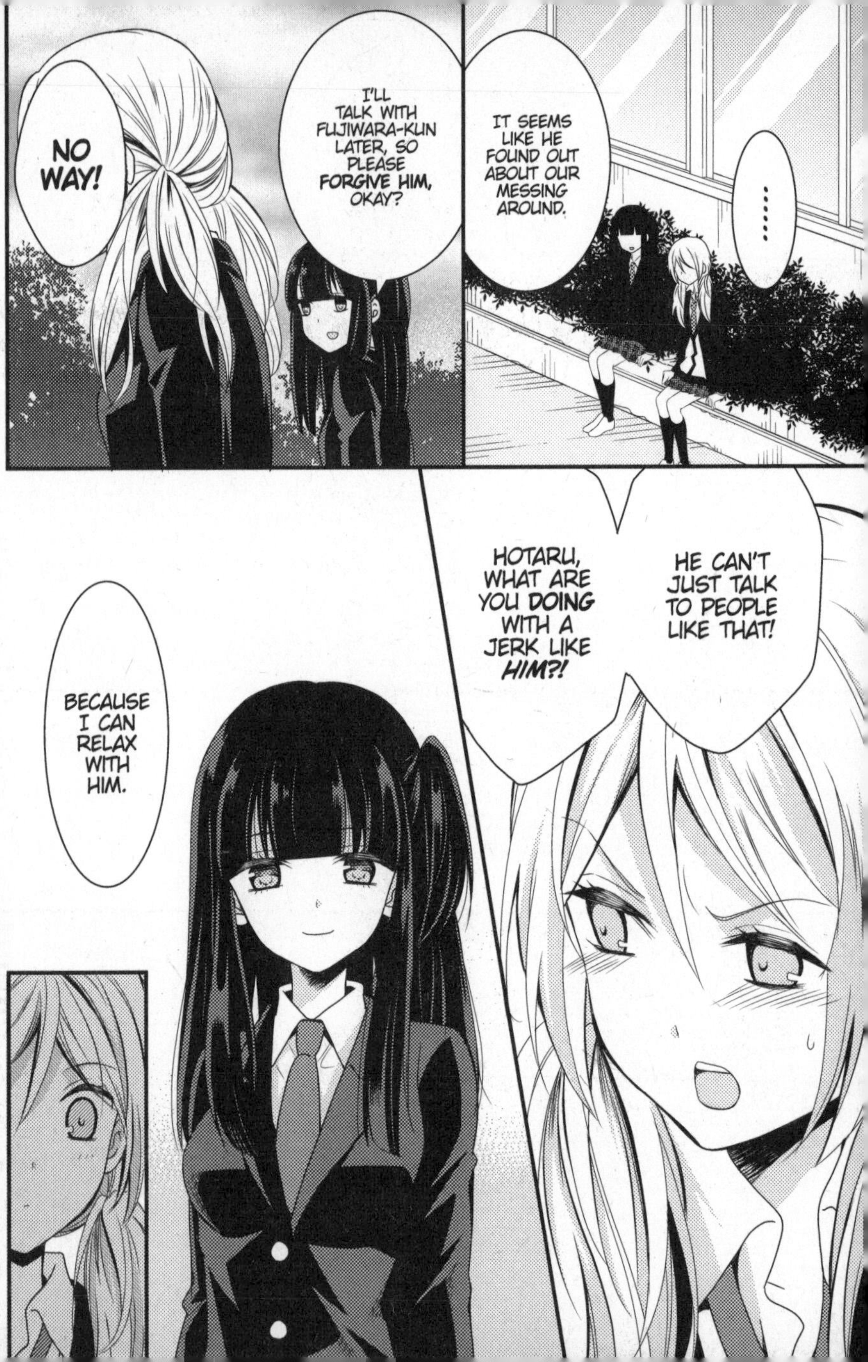
IT SEEMS LIKE HE FOUND OUT ABOUT OUR MESSING AROUND.
......
I'LL TALK WITH FUJIWARA-KUN LATER, SO PLEASE FORGIVE HIM, OKAY?
NO WAY!
HE CAN'T JUST TALK TO PEOPLE LIKE THAT!
HOTARU, WHAT ARE YOU DOING WITH A JERK LIKE HIM?!
BECAUSE I CAN RELAX WITH HIM.

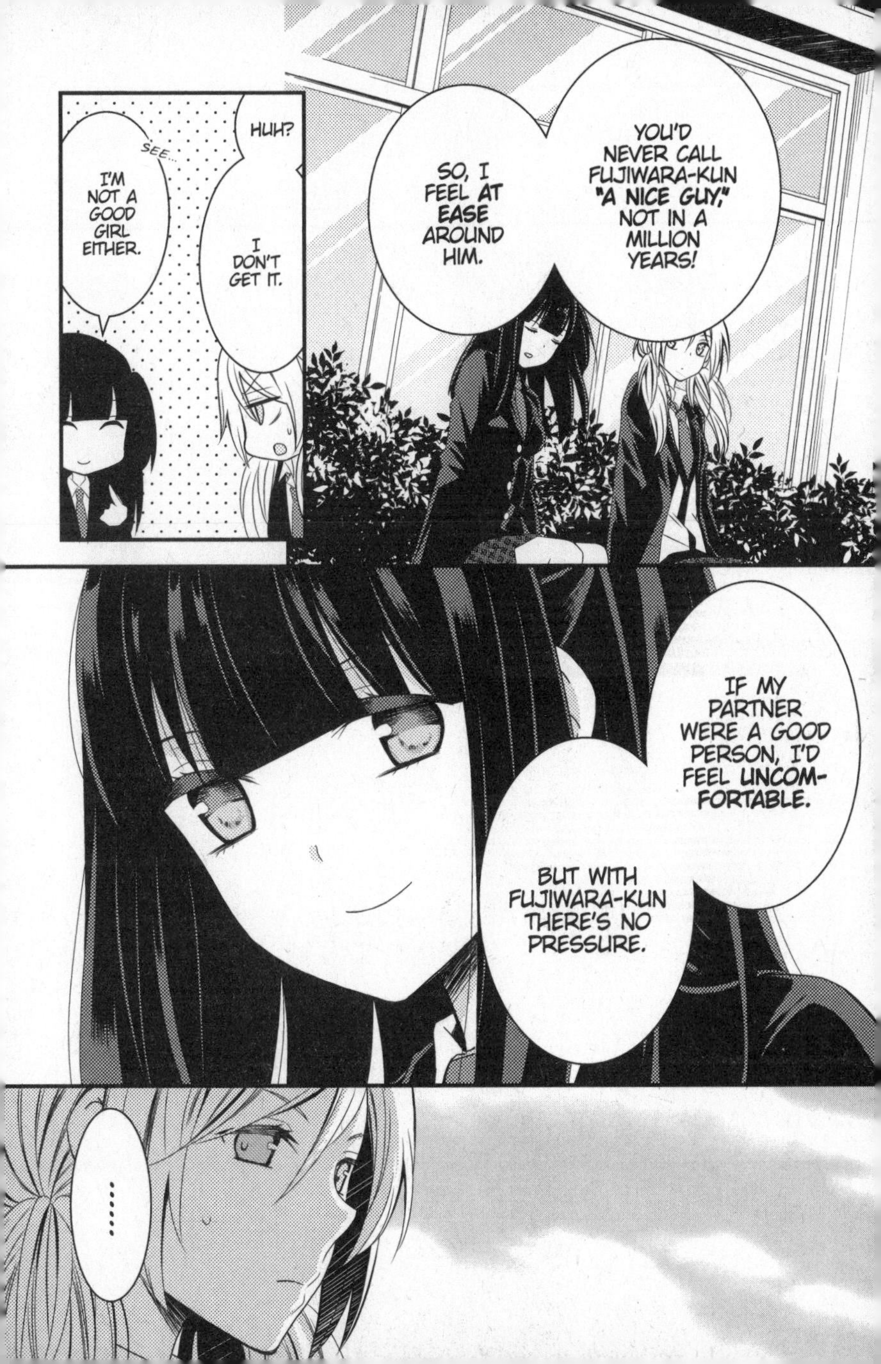
YOU'D NEVER CALL FUJIWARA-KUN "A NICE GUY," NOT IN A MILLION YEARS!
SO, I FEEL AT EASE AROUND HIM.
HUH?
I DON'T GET IT.
SEE...
I'M NOT A GOOD GIRL EITHER.
IF MY PARTNER WERE A GOOD PERSON, I'D FEEL UNCOM-FORTABLE.
BUT WITH FUJIWARA-KUN THERE'S NO PRESSURE.
......

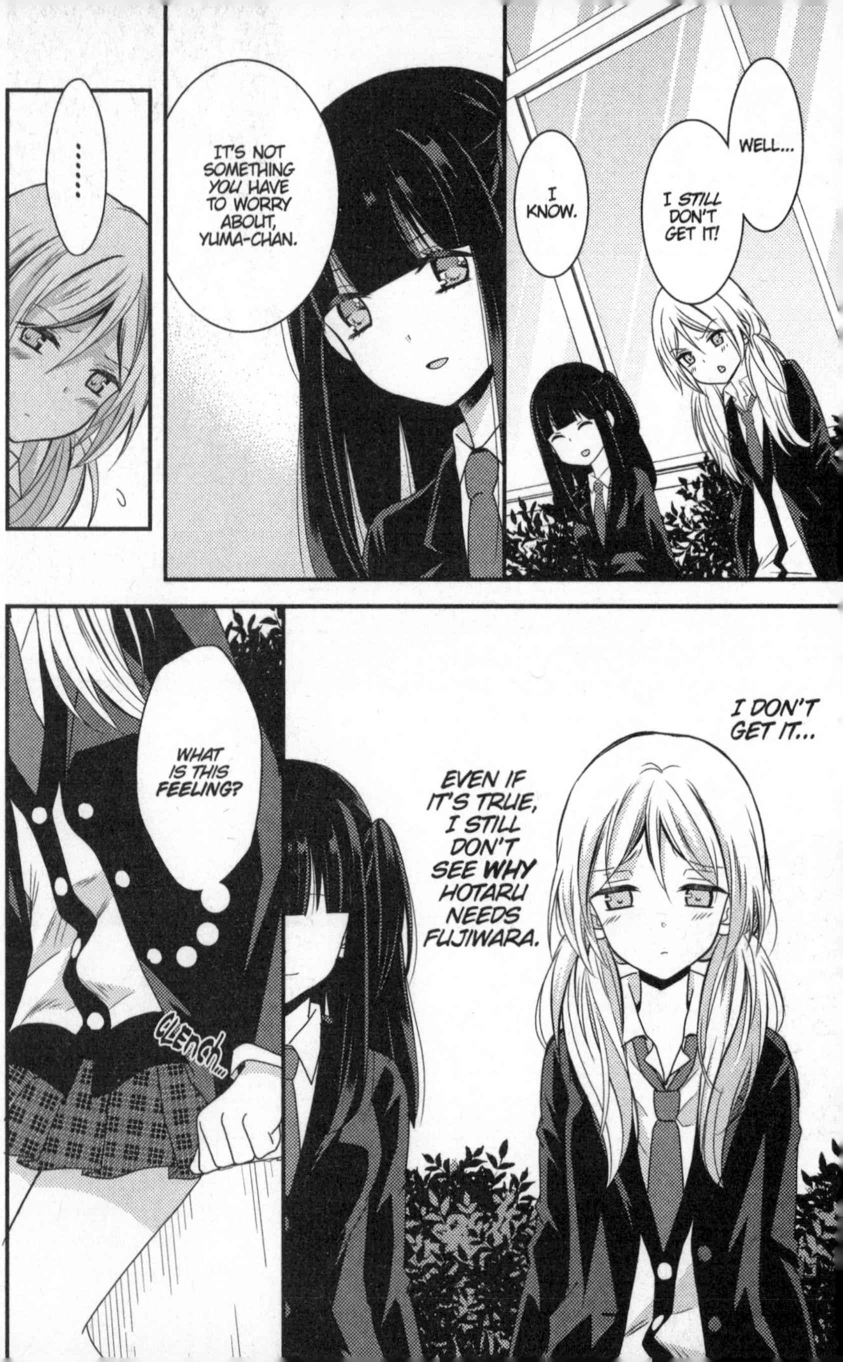
WELL...
I STILL DON'T GET IT!
I KNOW.
IT'S NOT SOMETHING YOU HAVE TO WORRY ABOUT, YUMA-CHAN.
......
I DON'T GET IT...
EVEN IF IT'S TRUE, I STILL DON'T SEE WHY HOTARU NEEDS FUJIWARA.
WHAT IS THIS FEELING?
CLENCH...

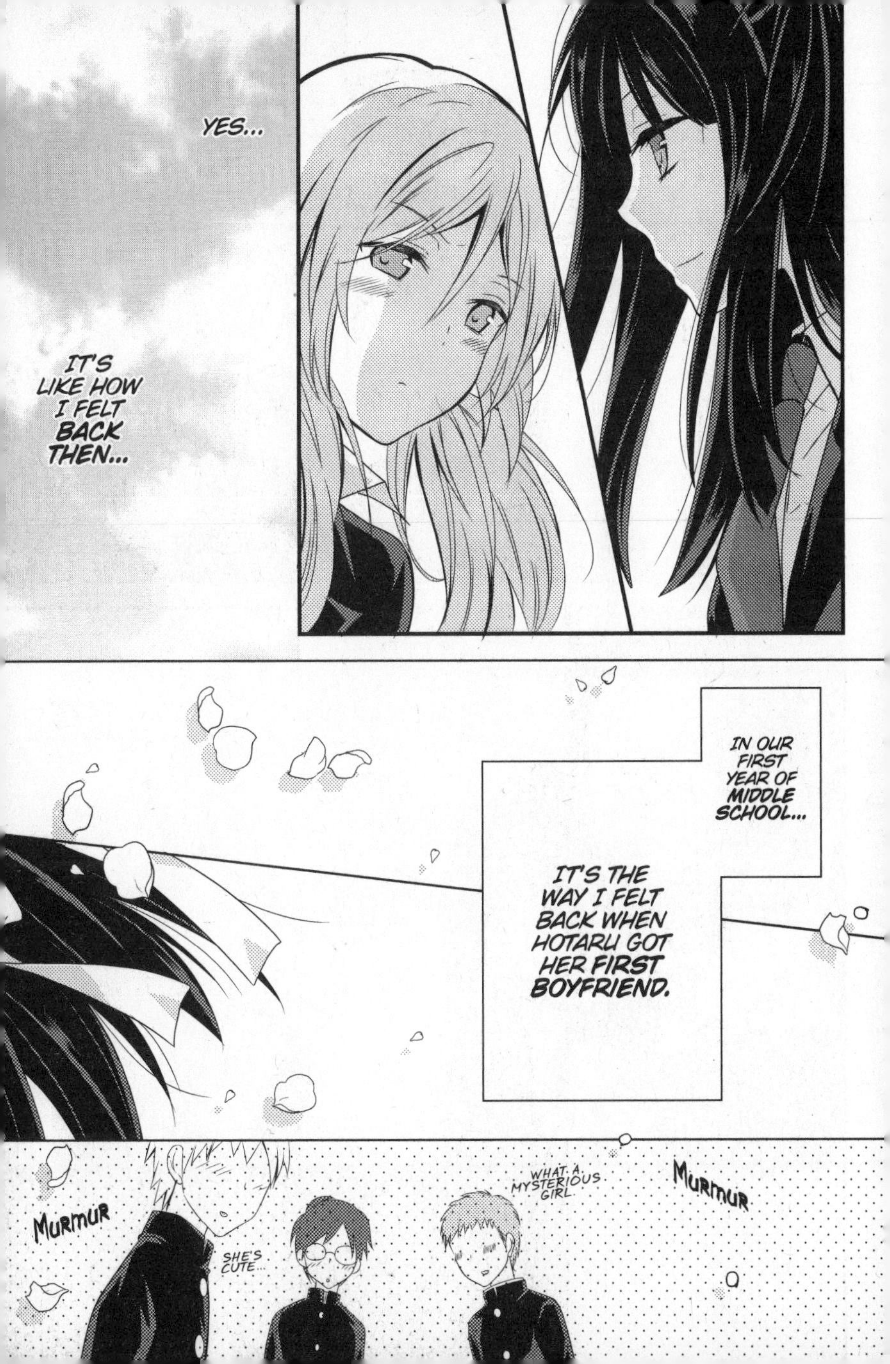
YES...
IT'S LIKE HOW I FELT BACK THEN...
IN OUR FIRST YEAR OF MIDDLE SCHOOL...
IT'S THE WAY I FELT BACK WHEN HOTARU GOT HER FIRST BOYFRIEND.
Murmur
WHAT A MYSTERIOUS GIRL.
SHE'S CUTE...
Murmur

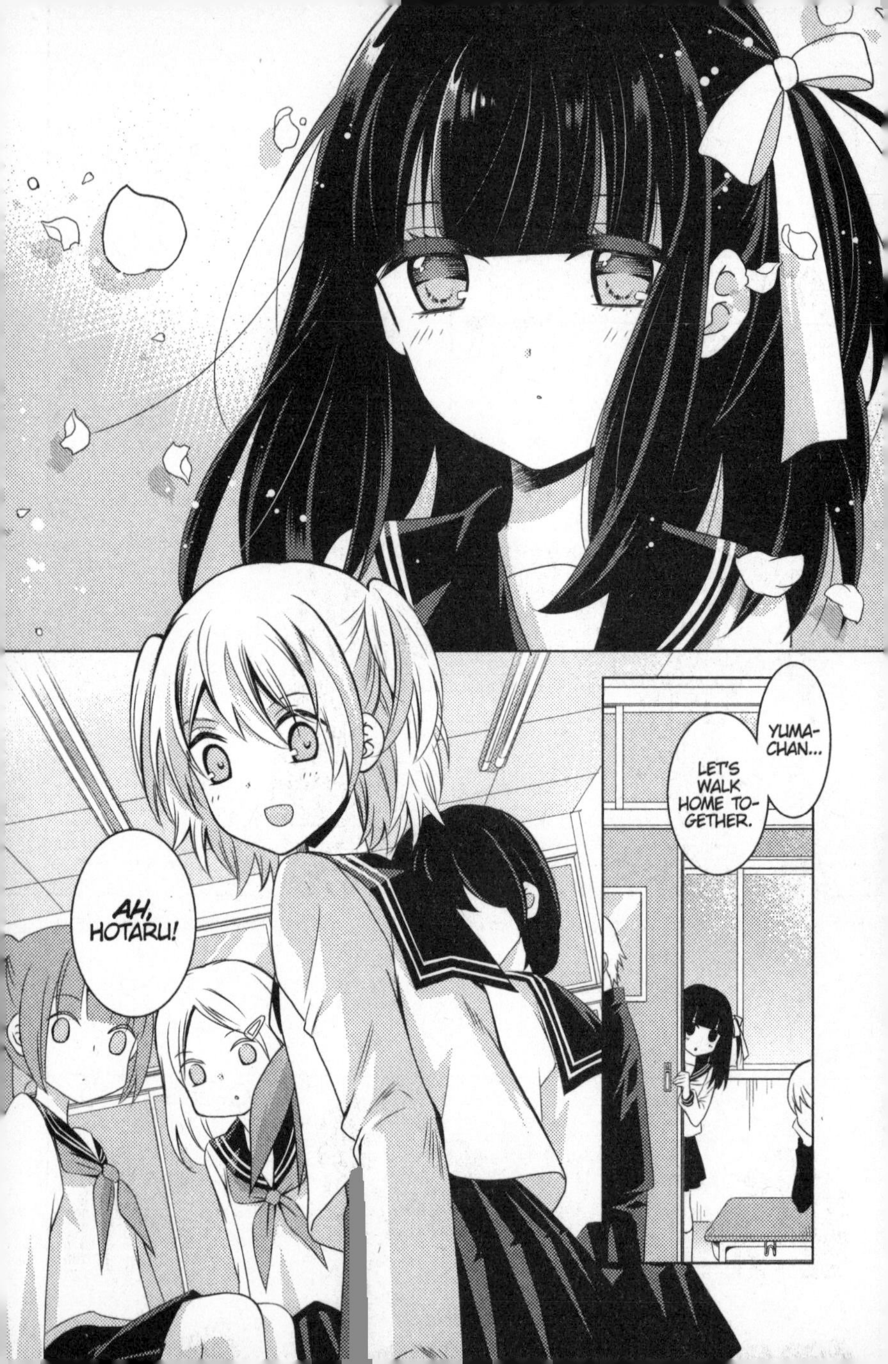
YUMA-CHAN...
LET'S WALK HOME TO-GETHER.
AH, HOTARU!

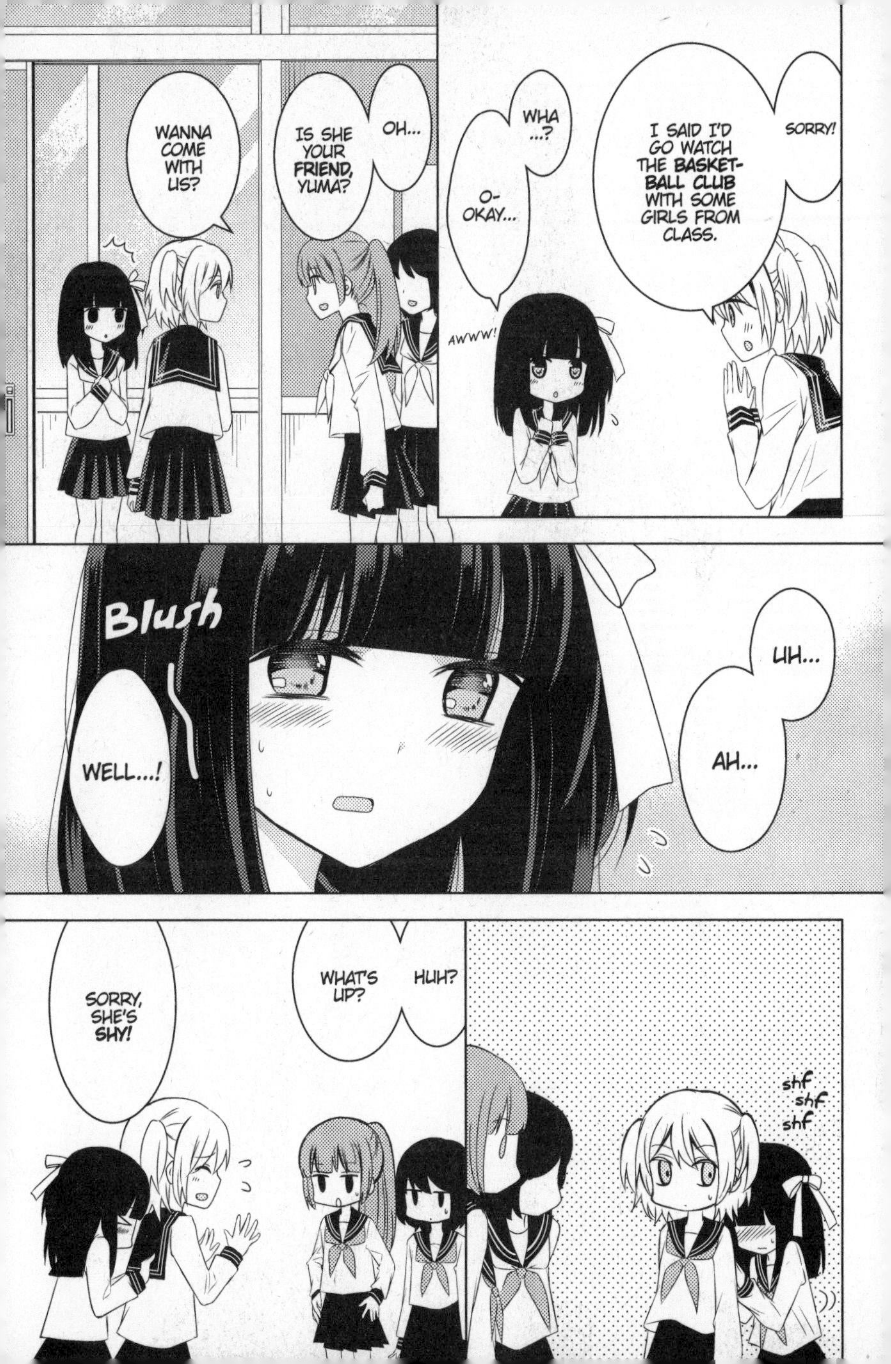
SORRY!
I SAID I'D GO WATCH THE BASKETBALL CLUB WITH SOME GIRLS FROM CLASS.
WHA ...?
O-OKAY...
AWWW!
OH...
IS SHE YOUR FRIEND, YUMA?
WANNA COME WITH US?
UH...
AH...
Blush
WELL...!
shf shf shf
HUH?
WHAT'S UP?
SORRY, SHE'S SHY!

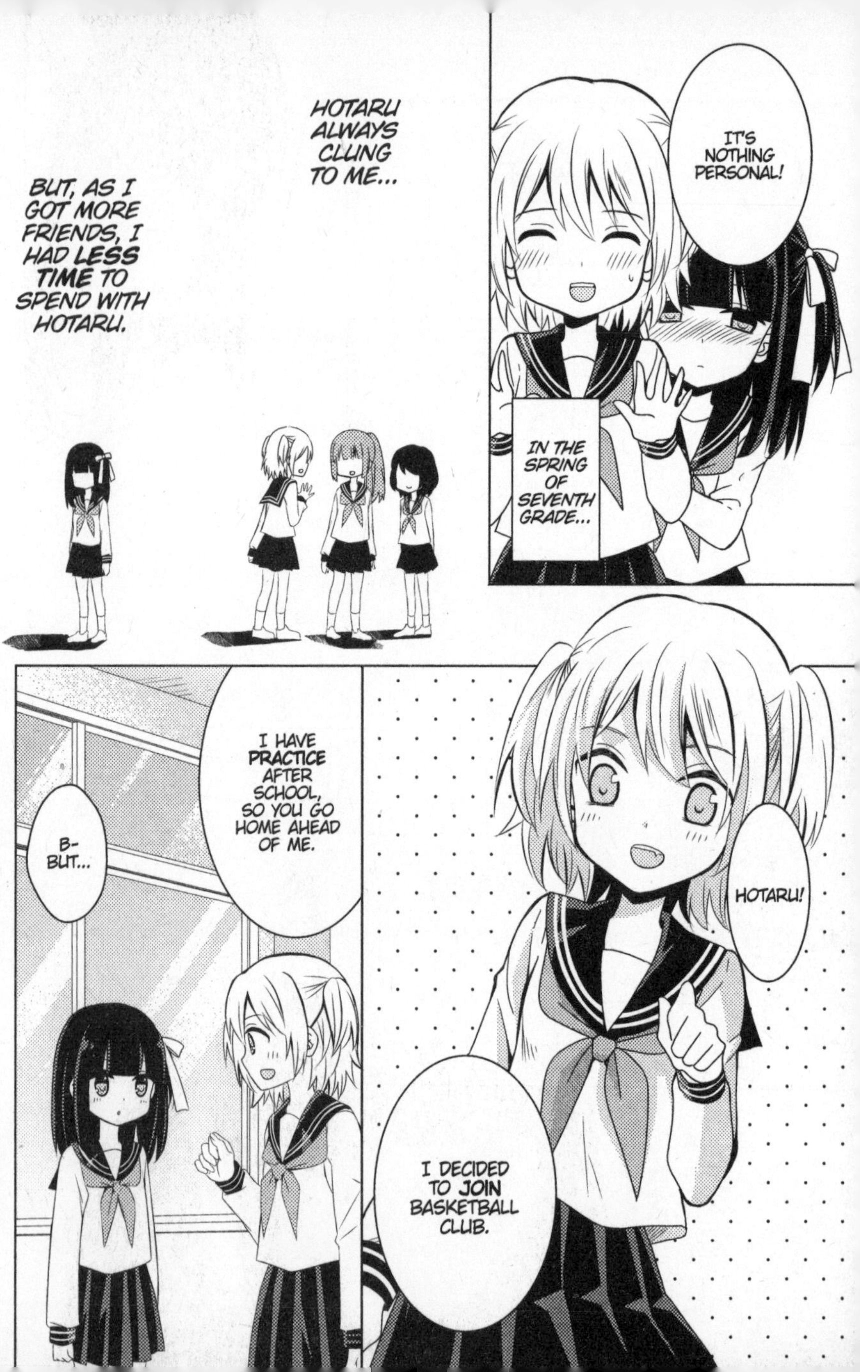

IT'S NOTHING PERSONAL!
IN THE SPRING OF SEVENTH GRADE...
HOTARU ALWAYS CLUNG TO ME...
BUT, AS I GOT MORE FRIENDS, I HAD LESS TIME TO SPEND WITH HOTARU.
HOTARU!
I DECIDED TO JOIN BASKETBALL CLUB.
I HAVE PRACTICE AFTER SCHOOL, SO YOU GO HOME AHEAD OF ME.
B-BUT...

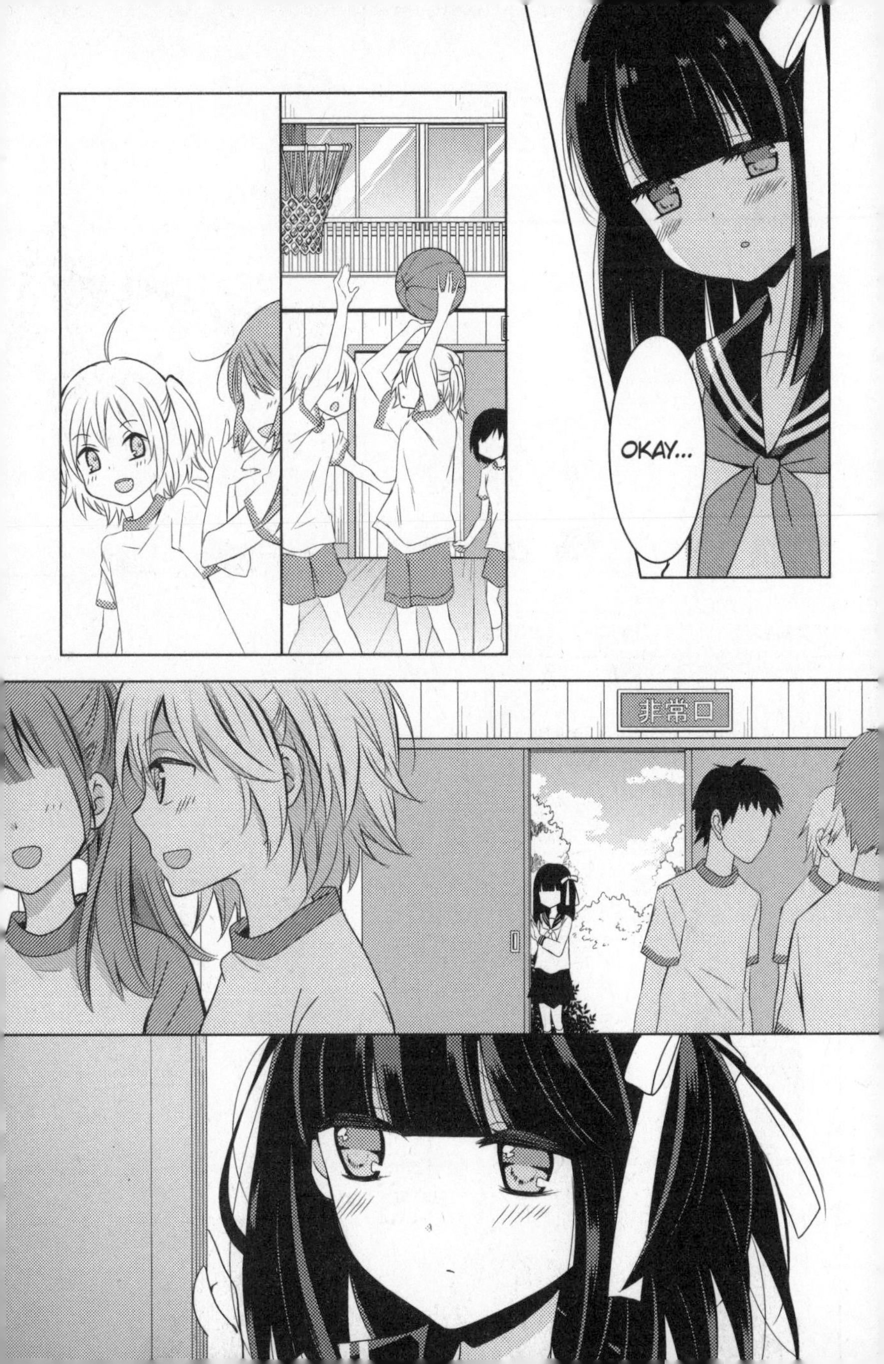
OKAY...
非常口

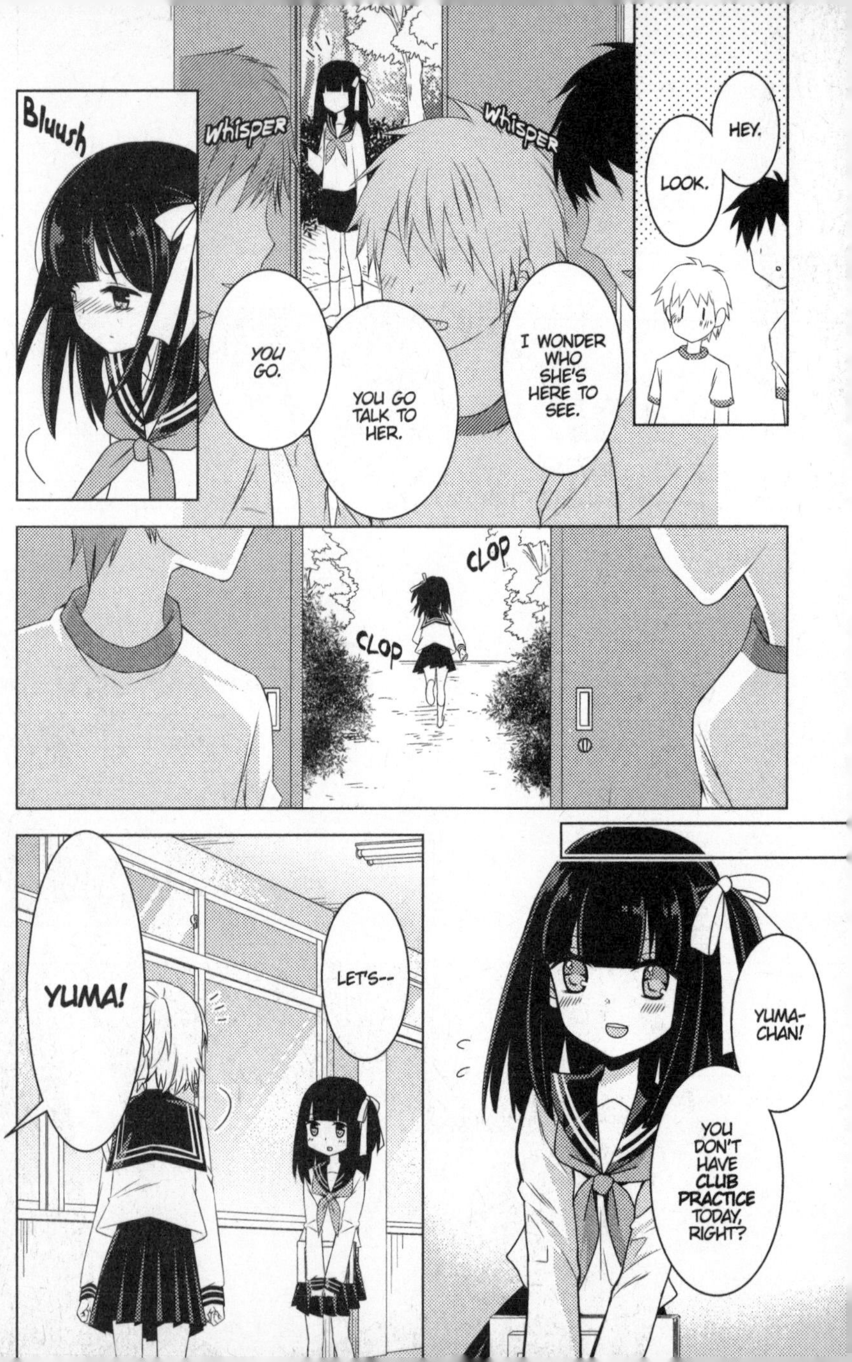
HEY.
LOOK.
Whisper
Whisper
I WONDER WHO SHE'S HERE TO SEE.
YOU GO TALK TO HER.
YOU GO.
Bluush
CLOP
CLOP
YUMA-CHAN!
YOU DON'T HAVE CLUB PRACTICE TODAY, RIGHT?
LET'S--
YUMA!

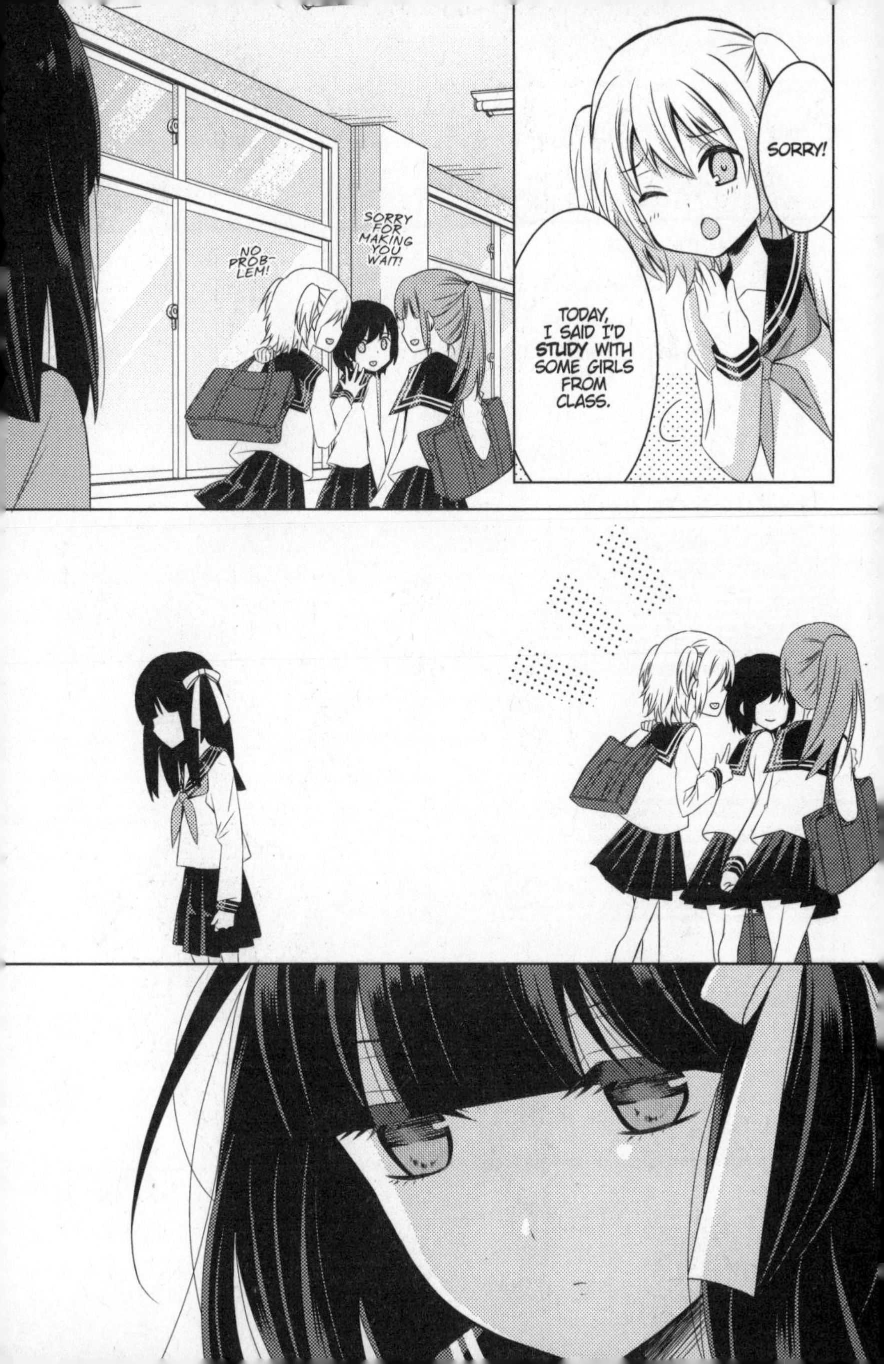
SORRY!
TODAY, I SAID I'D STUDY WITH SOME GIRLS FROM CLASS.
SORRY FOR MAKING YOU WAIT!
NO PROB-LEM!

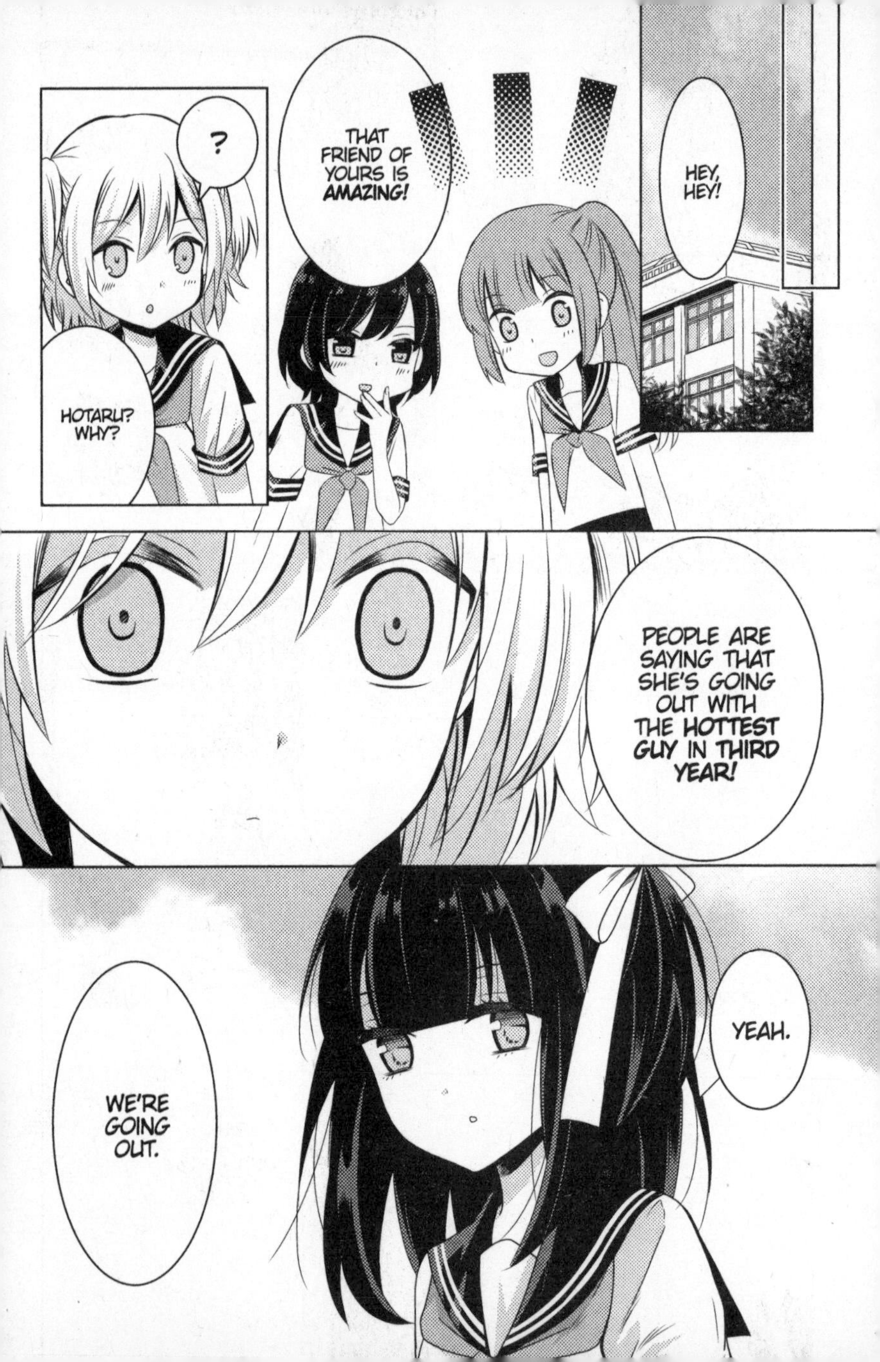
HEY, HEY!
THAT FRIEND OF YOURS IS AMAZING!
?
HOTARU? WHY?
PEOPLE ARE SAYING THAT SHE'S GOING OUT WITH THE HOTTEST GUY IN THIRD YEAR!
YEAH.
WE'RE GOING OUT.

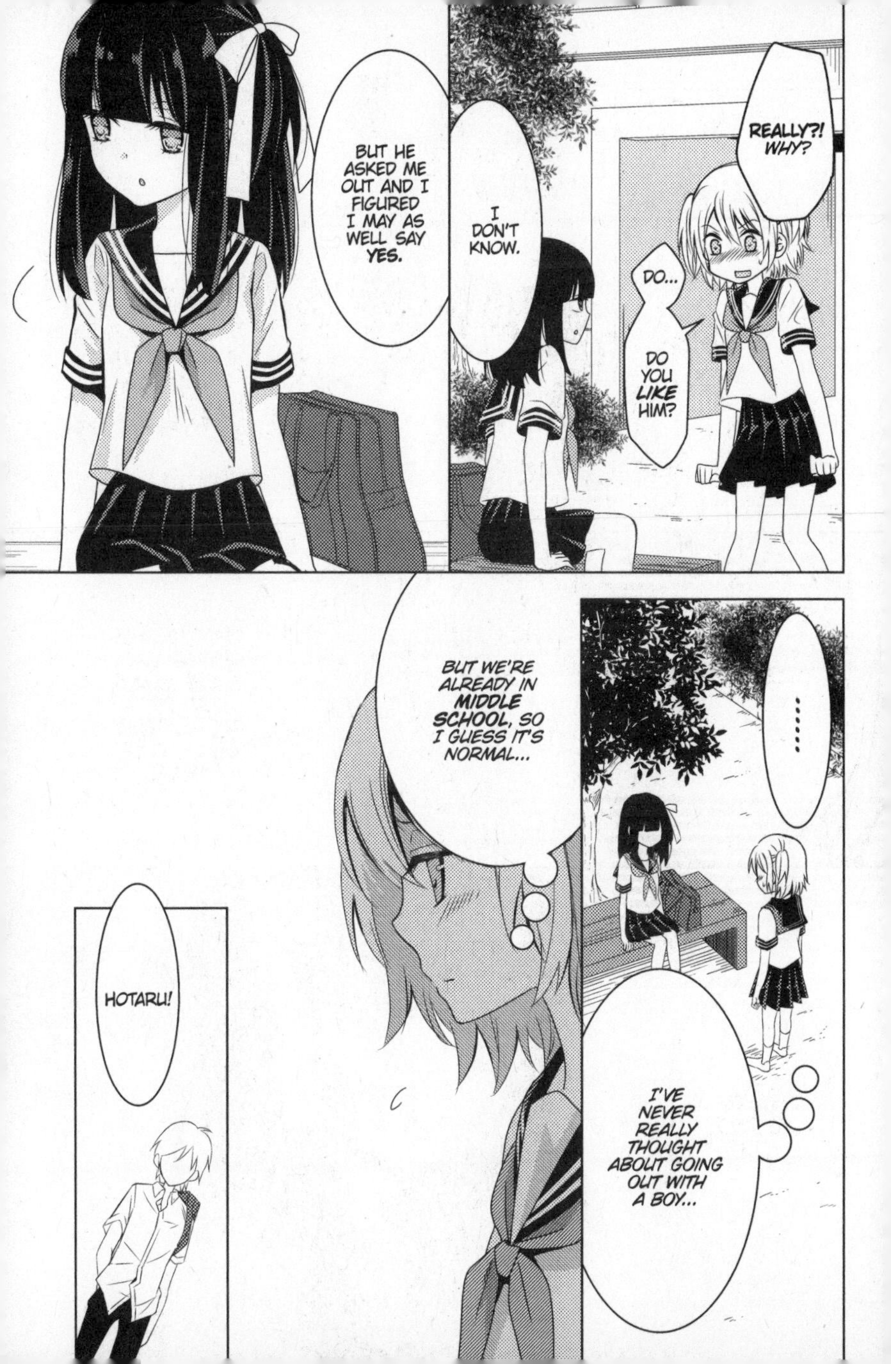
REALLY?! WHY?
DO...
DO YOU LIKE HIM?
I DON'T KNOW.
BUT HE ASKED ME OUT AND I FIGURED I MAY AS WELL SAY YES.
......
I'VE NEVER REALLY THOUGHT ABOUT GOING OUT WITH A BOY...
BUT WE'RE ALREADY IN MIDDLE SCHOOL, SO I GUESS IT'S NORMAL...
HOTARU!

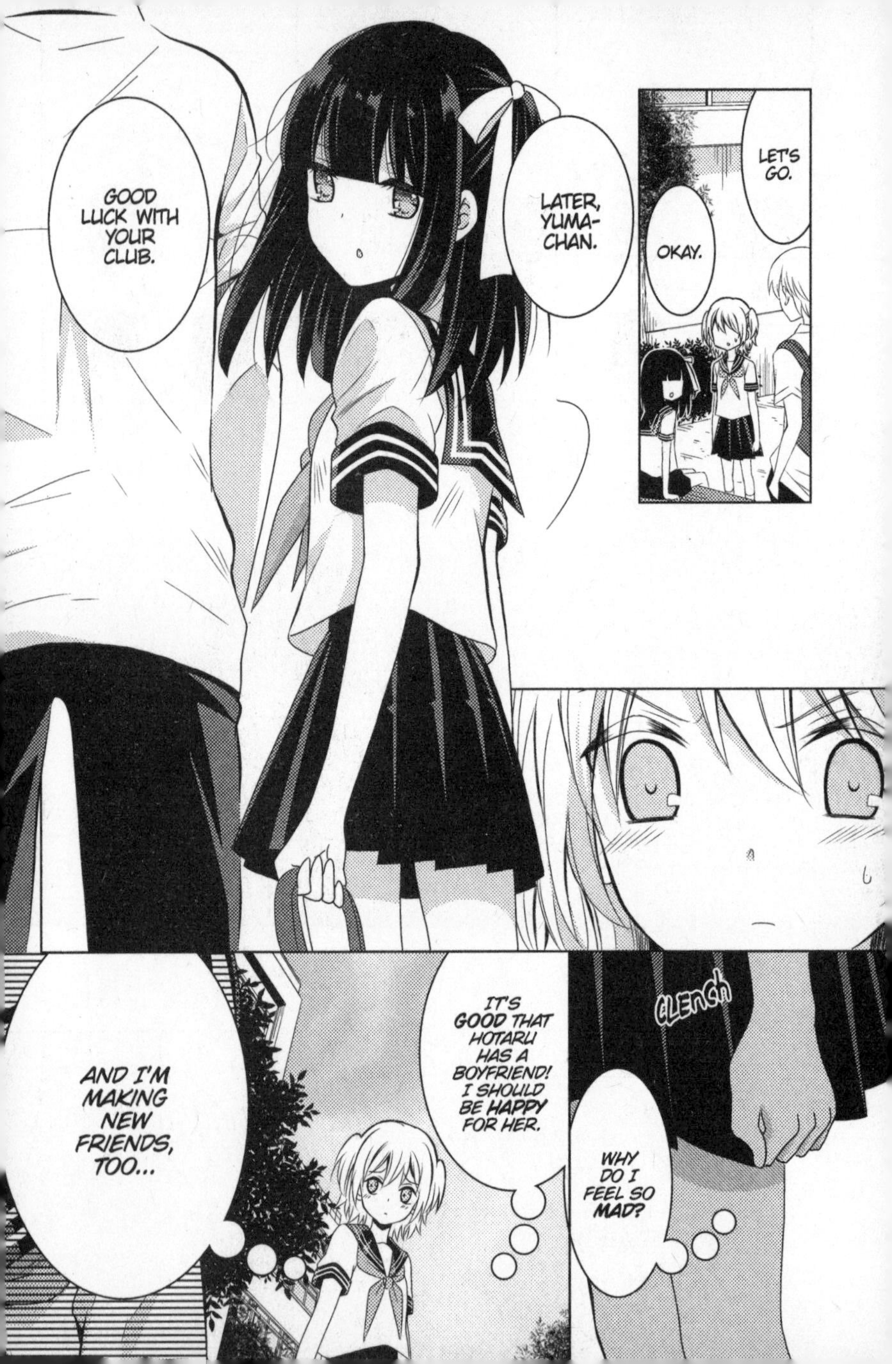
LET'S GO.
OKAY.
LATER, YUMA-CHAN.
GOOD LUCK WITH YOUR CLUB.
CLENCH
WHY DO I FEEL SO MAD?
IT'S GOOD THAT HOTARU HAS A BOYFRIEND! I SHOULD BE HAPPY FOR HER.
AND I'M MAKING NEW FRIENDS, TOO...

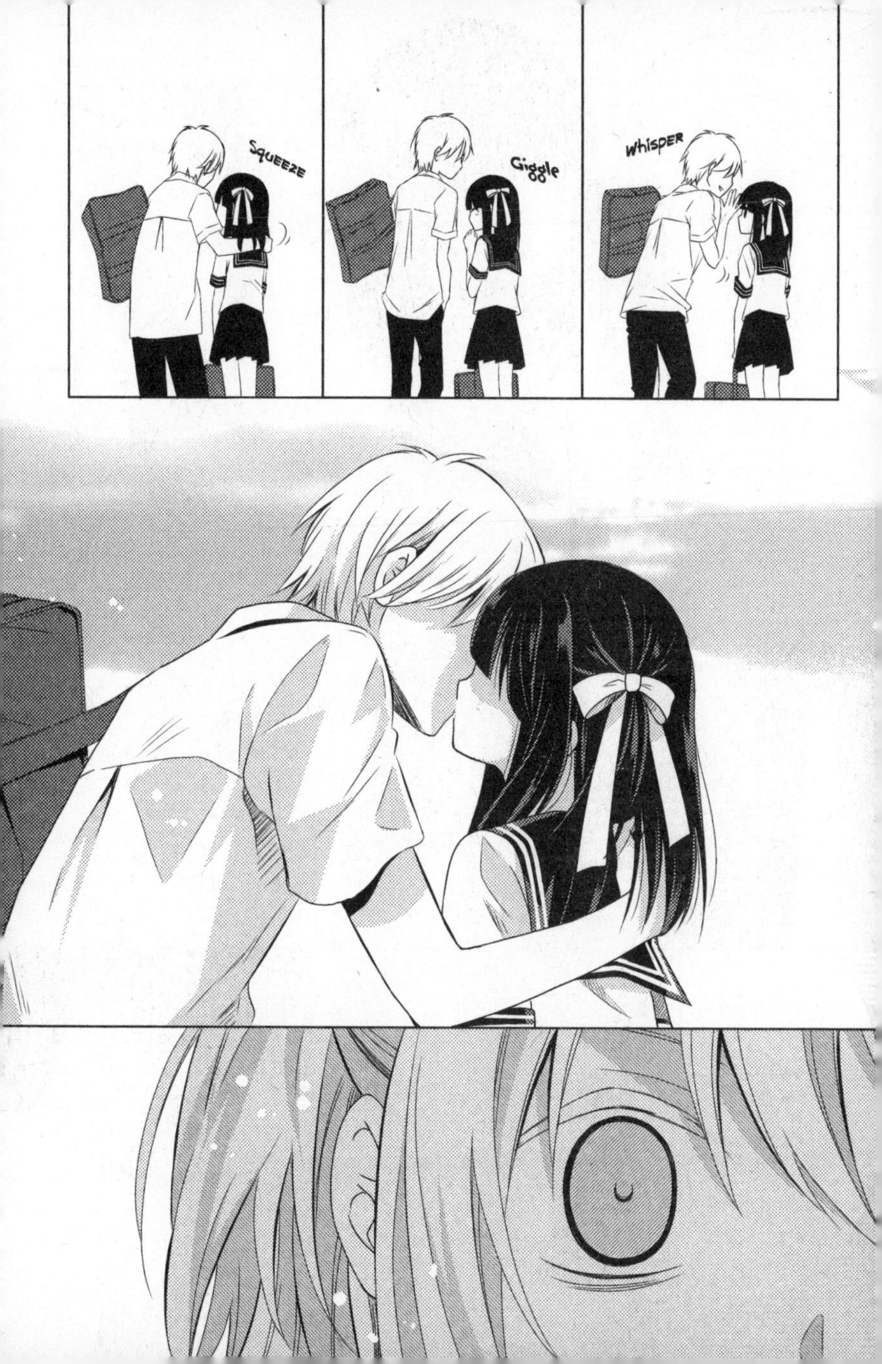
Whisper
Giggle
Squeeze

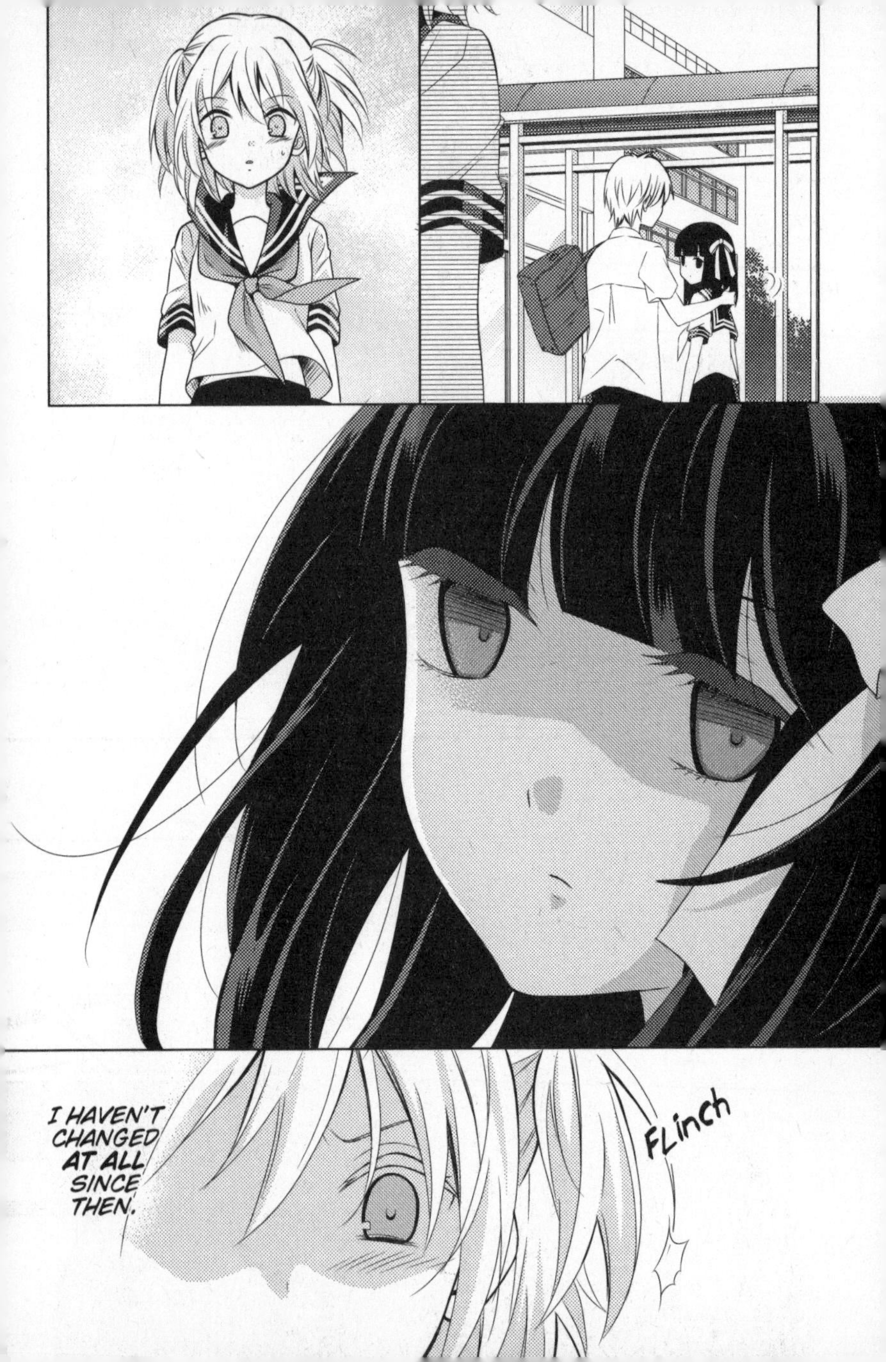
FLinch
I HAVEN'T CHANGED AT ALL SINCE THEN.

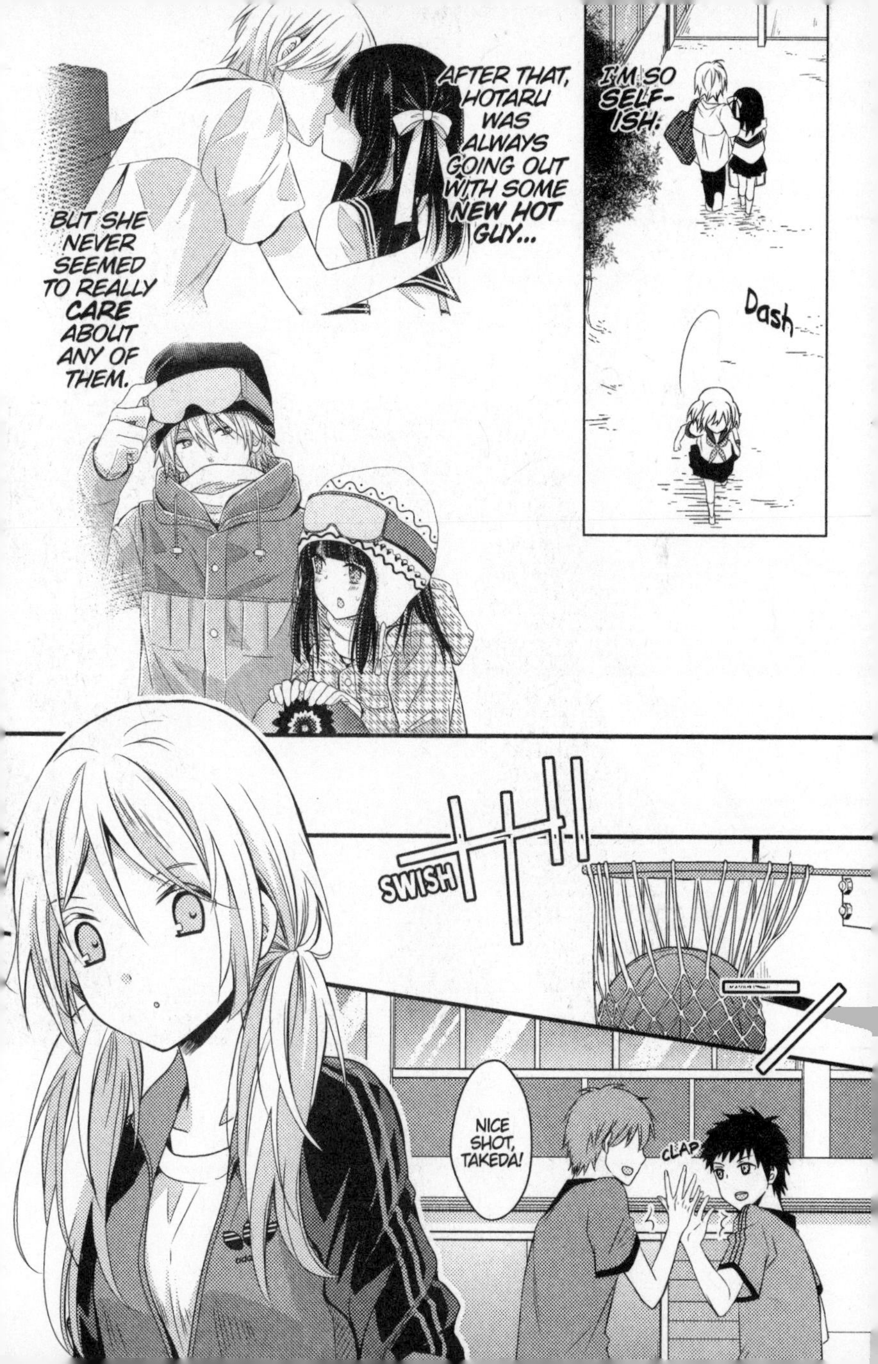
I'M SO SELFISH.
Dash
AFTER THAT, HOTARU WAS ALWAYS GOING OUT WITH SOME NEW HOT GUY...
BUT SHE NEVER SEEMED TO REALLY CARE ABOUT ANY OF THEM.
SWISH
NICE SHOT, TAKEDA!
CLAP

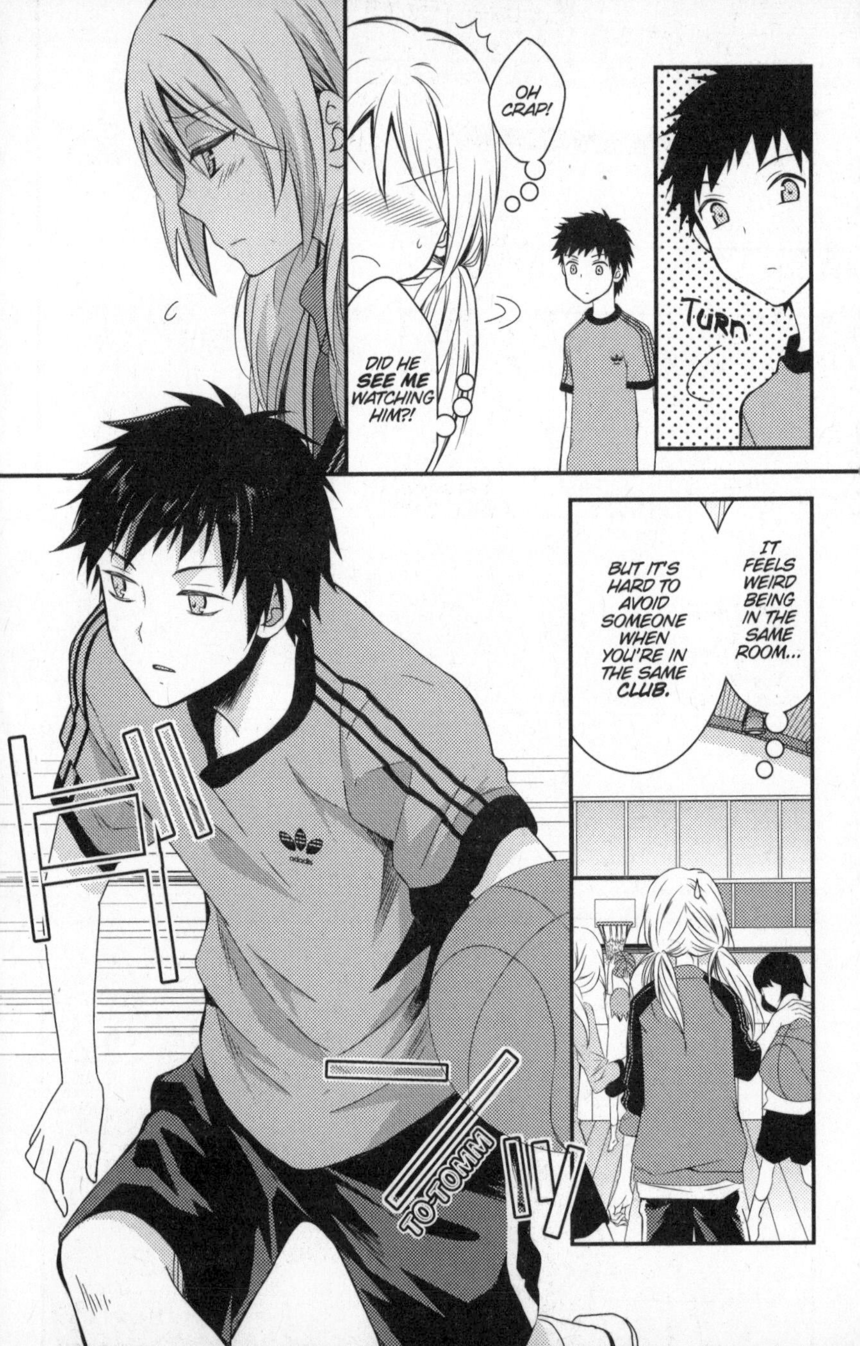
Turn
OH CRAP!
DID HE SEE ME WATCHING HIM?!
IT FEELS WEIRD BEING IN THE SAME ROOM...
BUT IT'S HARD TO AVOID SOMEONE WHEN YOU'RE IN THE SAME CLUB.
TO-TOMM

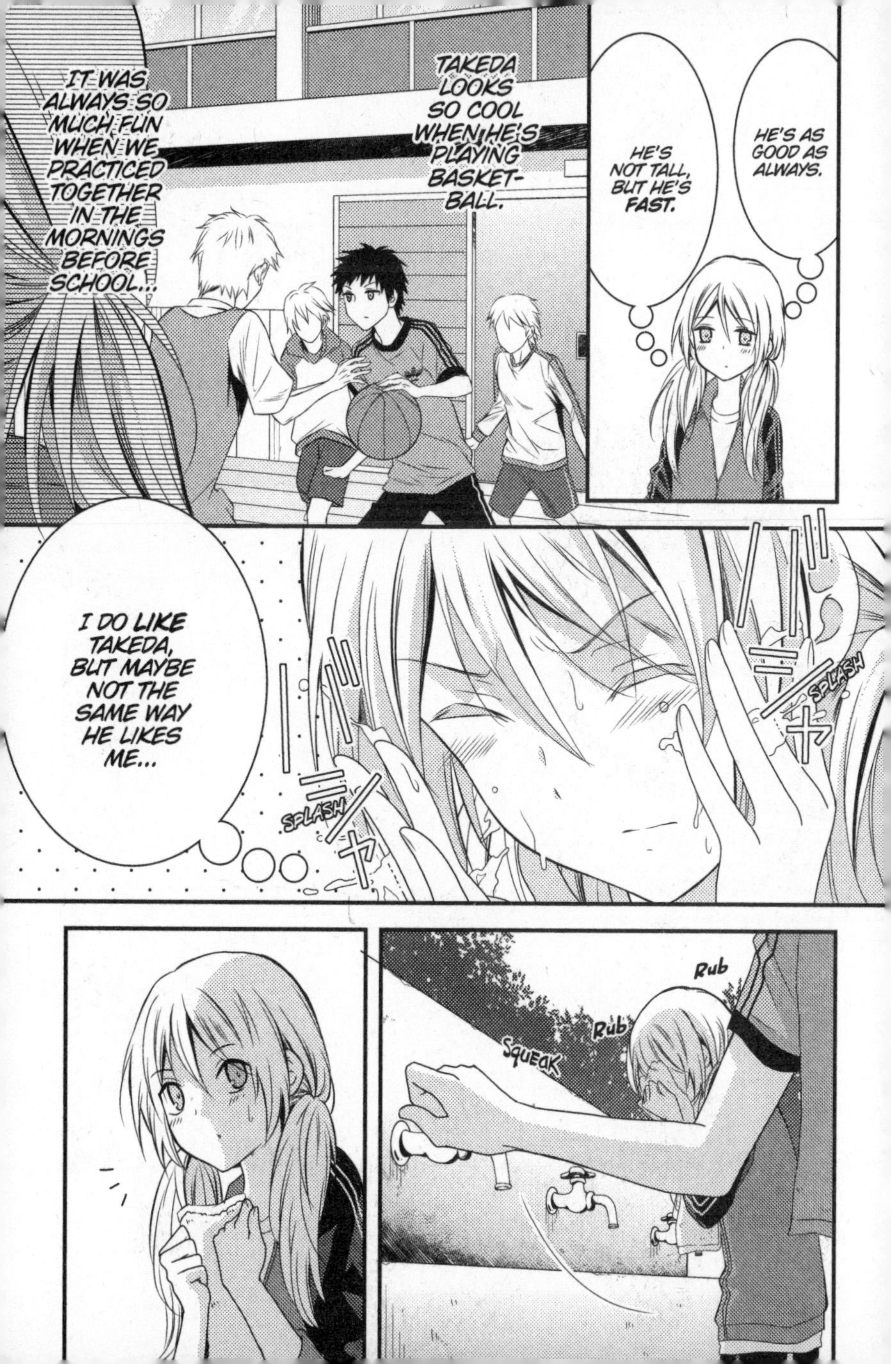
HE'S AS GOOD AS ALWAYS.
HE'S NOT TALL, BUT HE'S FAST.
TAKEDA LOOKS SO COOL WHEN HE'S PLAYING BASKET-BALL.
IT WAS ALWAYS SO MUCH FUN WHEN WE PRACTICED TOGETHER IN THE MORNINGS BEFORE SCHOOL...
SPLASH
SPLASH
I DO LIKE TAKEDA, BUT MAYBE NOT THE SAME WAY HE LIKES ME...
Rub
Rub
Squeak

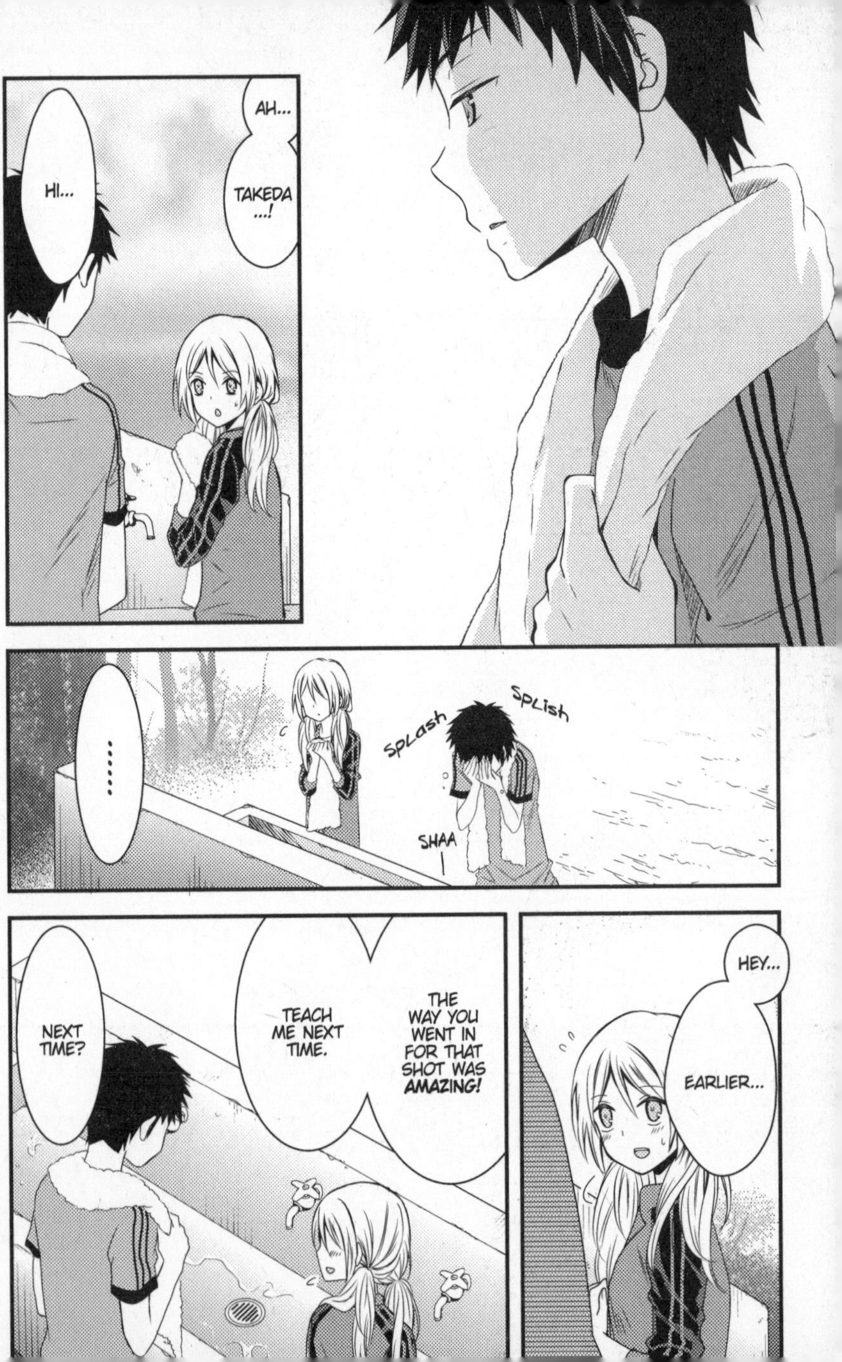
AH...
TAKEDA ...!
HI...
Splish
Splash
SHAA
......
HEY...
EARLIER...
THE WAY YOU WENT IN FOR THAT SHOT WAS AMAZING!
TEACH ME NEXT TIME.
NEXT TIME?

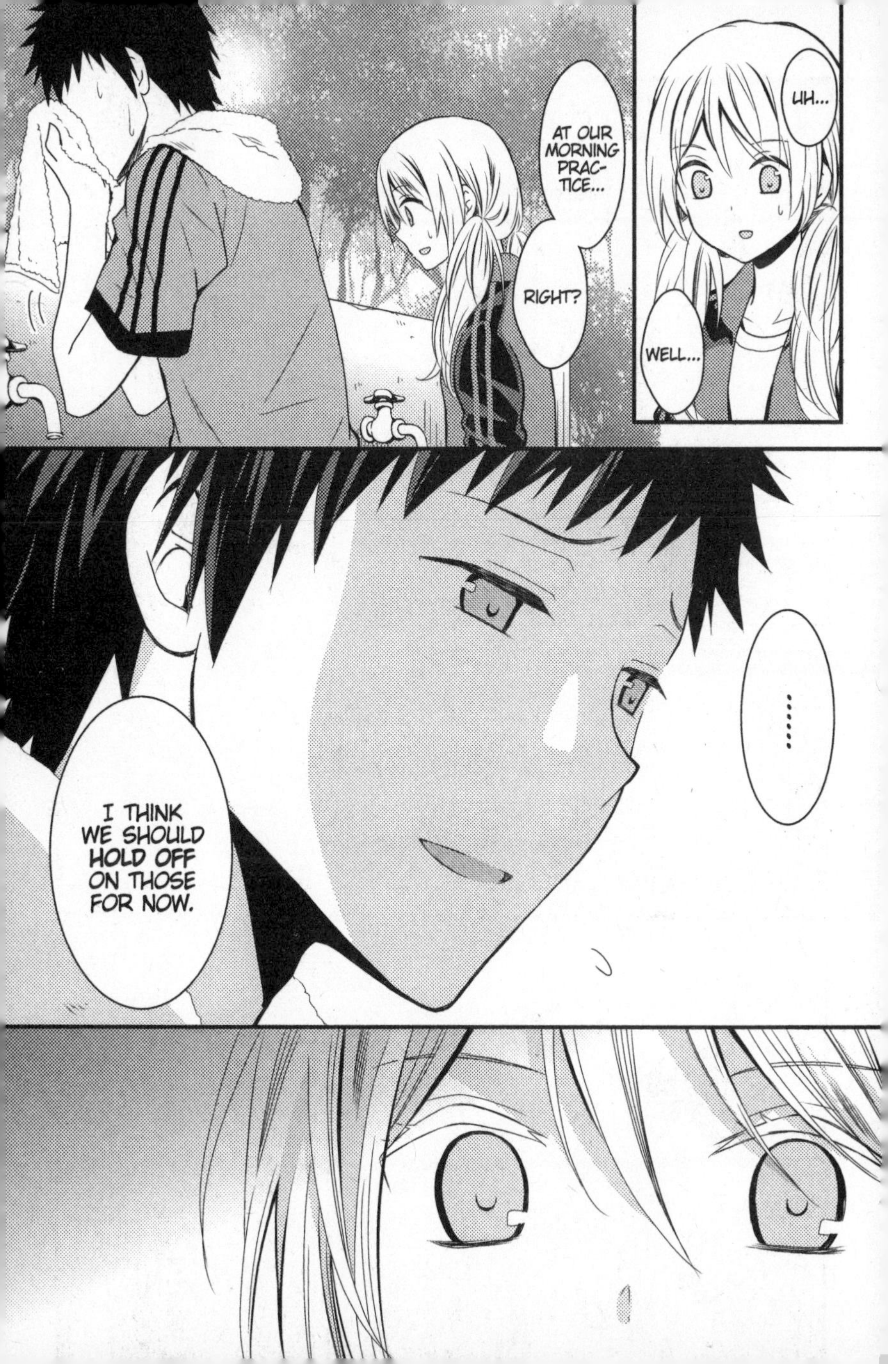
UH...
WELL...
AT OUR MORNING PRAC-TICE...
RIGHT?
......
I THINK WE SHOULD HOLD OFF ON THOSE FOR NOW.

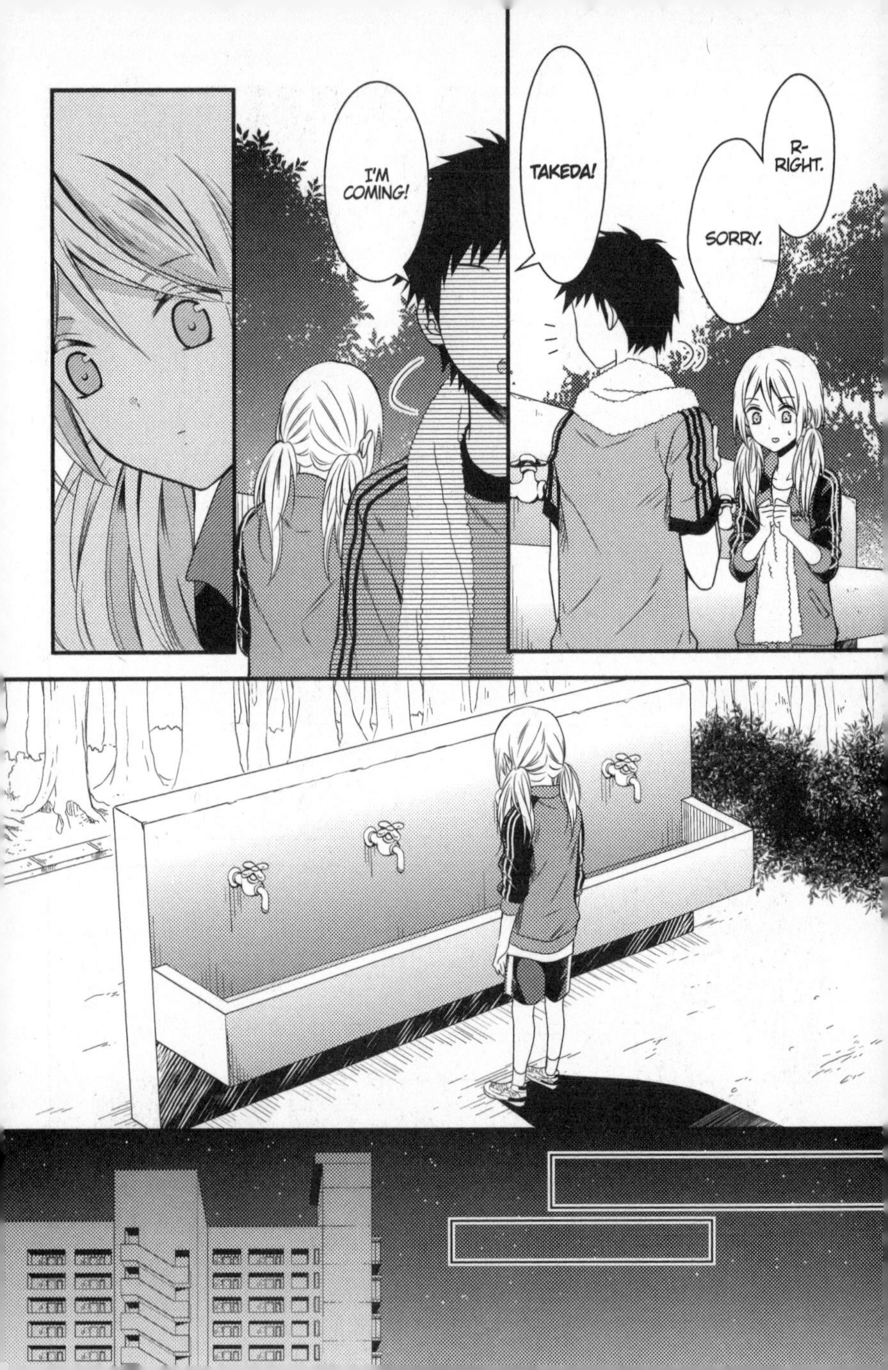
TAKEDA!
R-RIGHT.
SORRY.
I'M COMING!

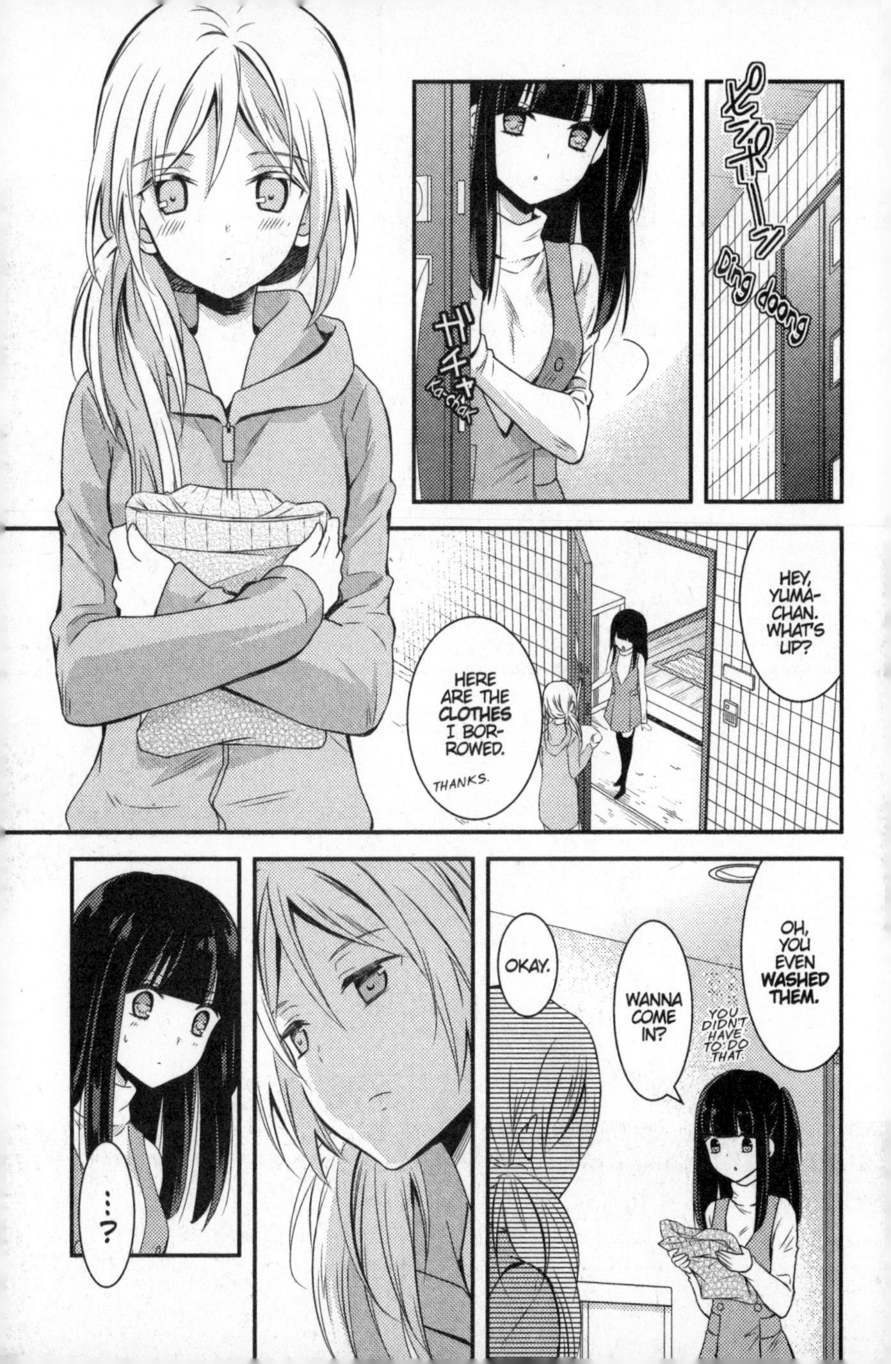
ピンポーン
Ding doong
ガチャ
Ka-chak
HEY, YUMA-CHAN. WHAT'S UP?
HERE ARE THE CLOTHES I BOR-ROWED.
THANKS.
OH, YOU EVEN WASHED THEM.
YOU DIDN'T HAVE TO DO THAT.
WANNA COME IN?
OKAY.
…?

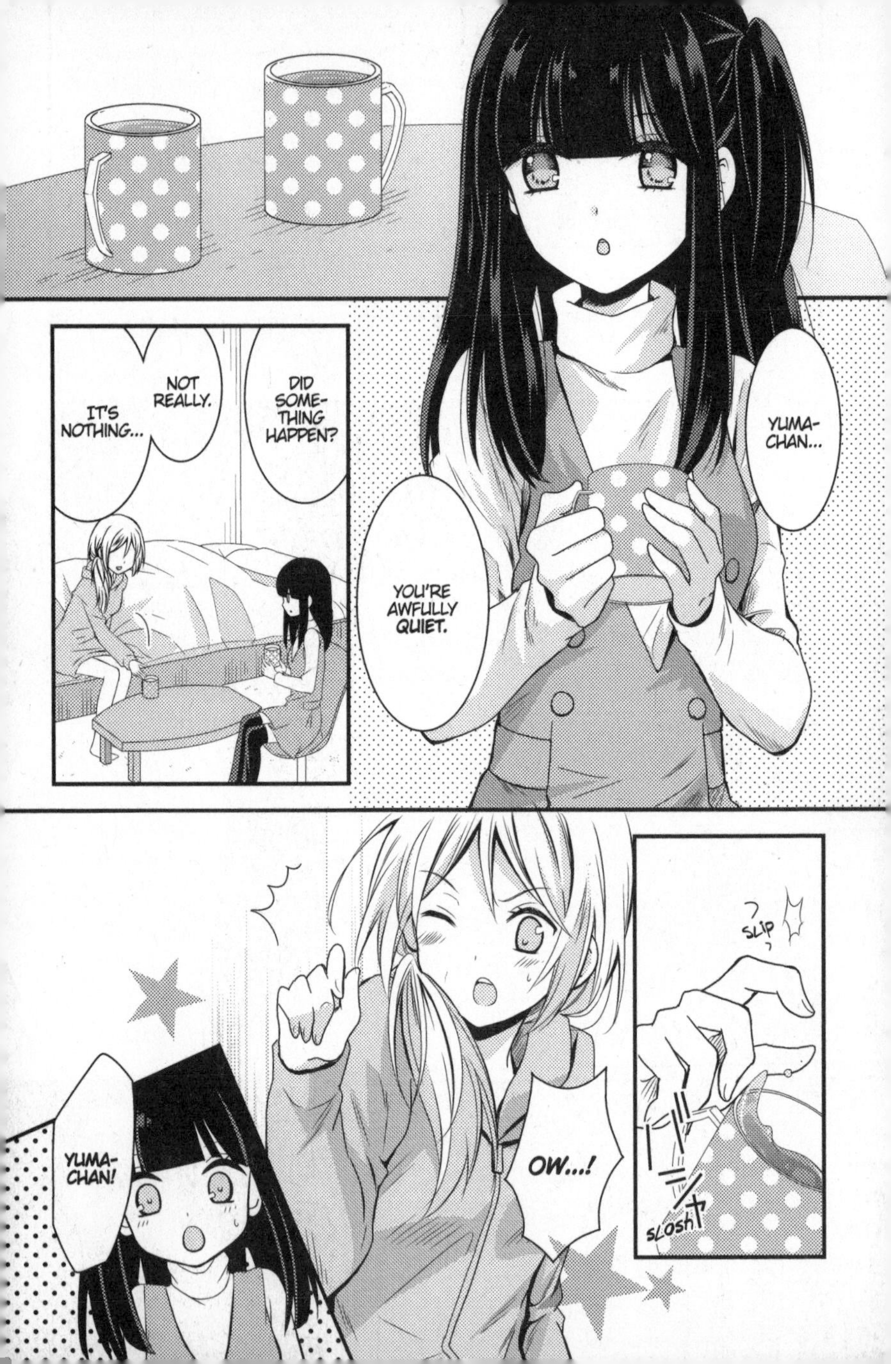
YUMA-CHAN...
YOU'RE AWFULLY QUIET.
DID SOME-THING HAPPEN?
NOT REALLY.
IT'S NOTHING...
SLIP
SLOSH
OW...!
YUMA-CHAN!

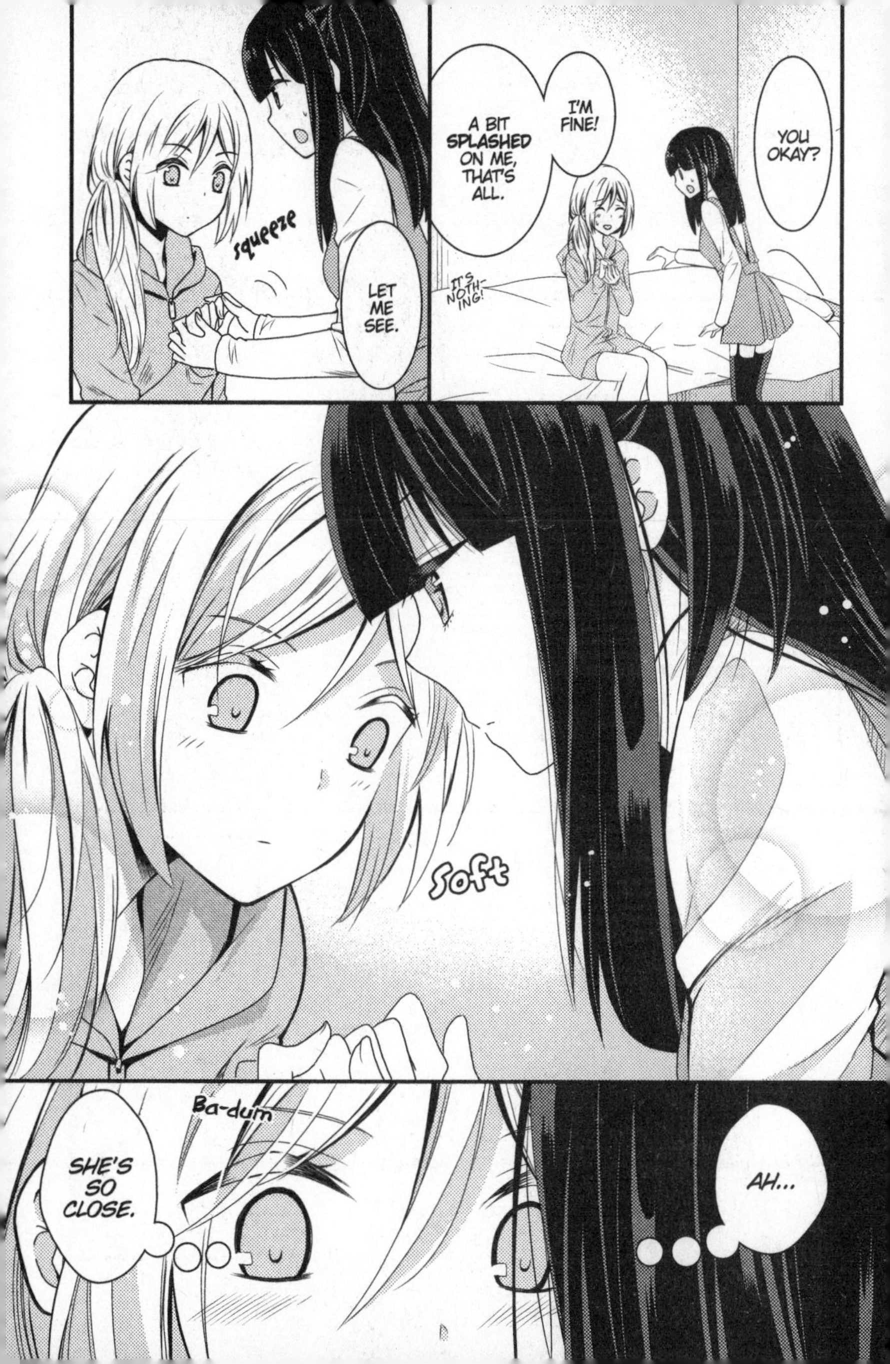
YOU OKAY?
I'M FINE!
A BIT SPLASHED ON ME, THAT'S ALL.
IT'S NOTHING!
squeeze
LET ME SEE.
Soft
AH...
Ba-dum
SHE'S SO CLOSE.

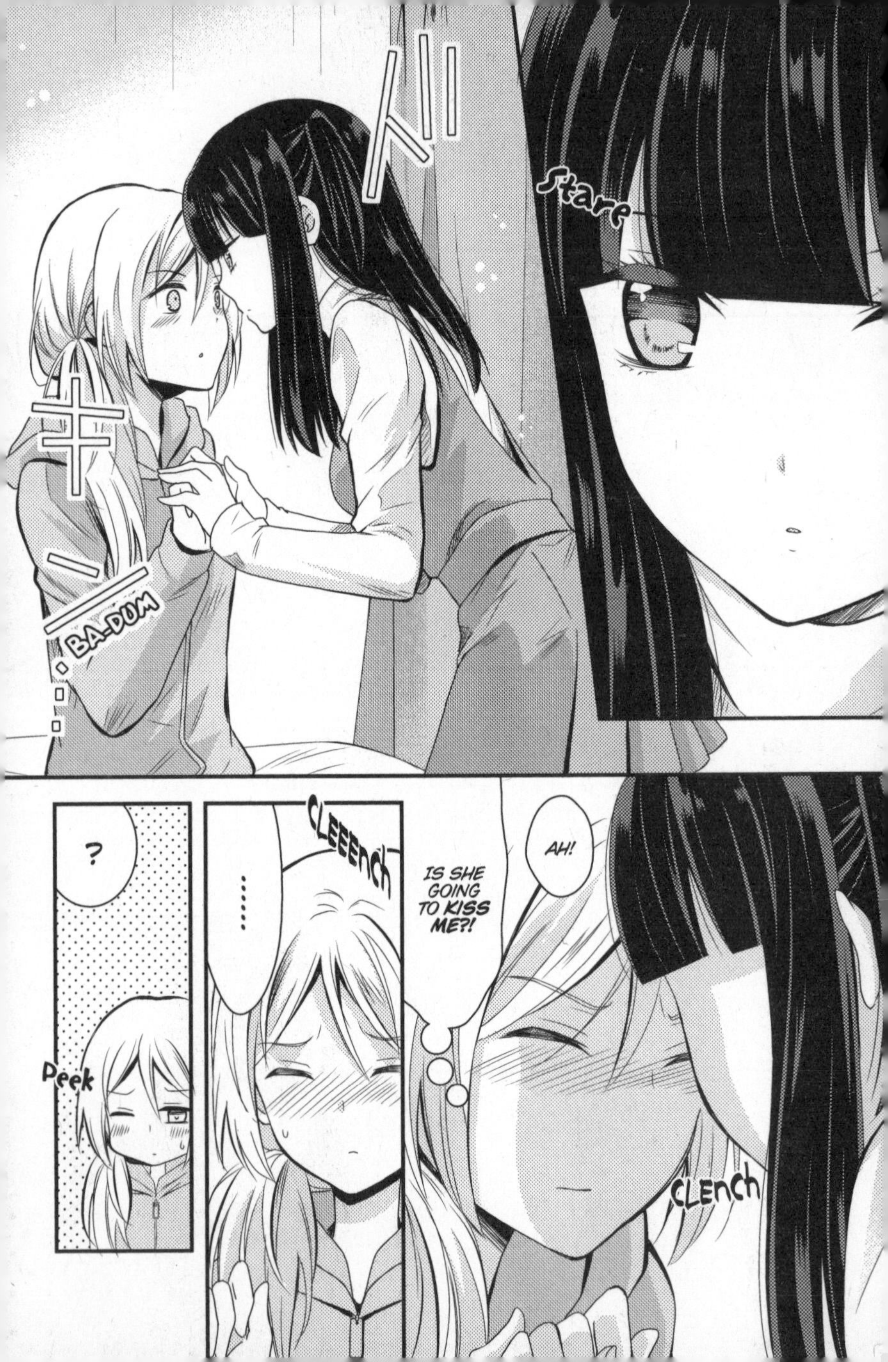
Stare
BA-DUM
...
AH!
IS SHE GOING TO KISS ME?!
CLENCH
CLEEEnch
......
?
Peek

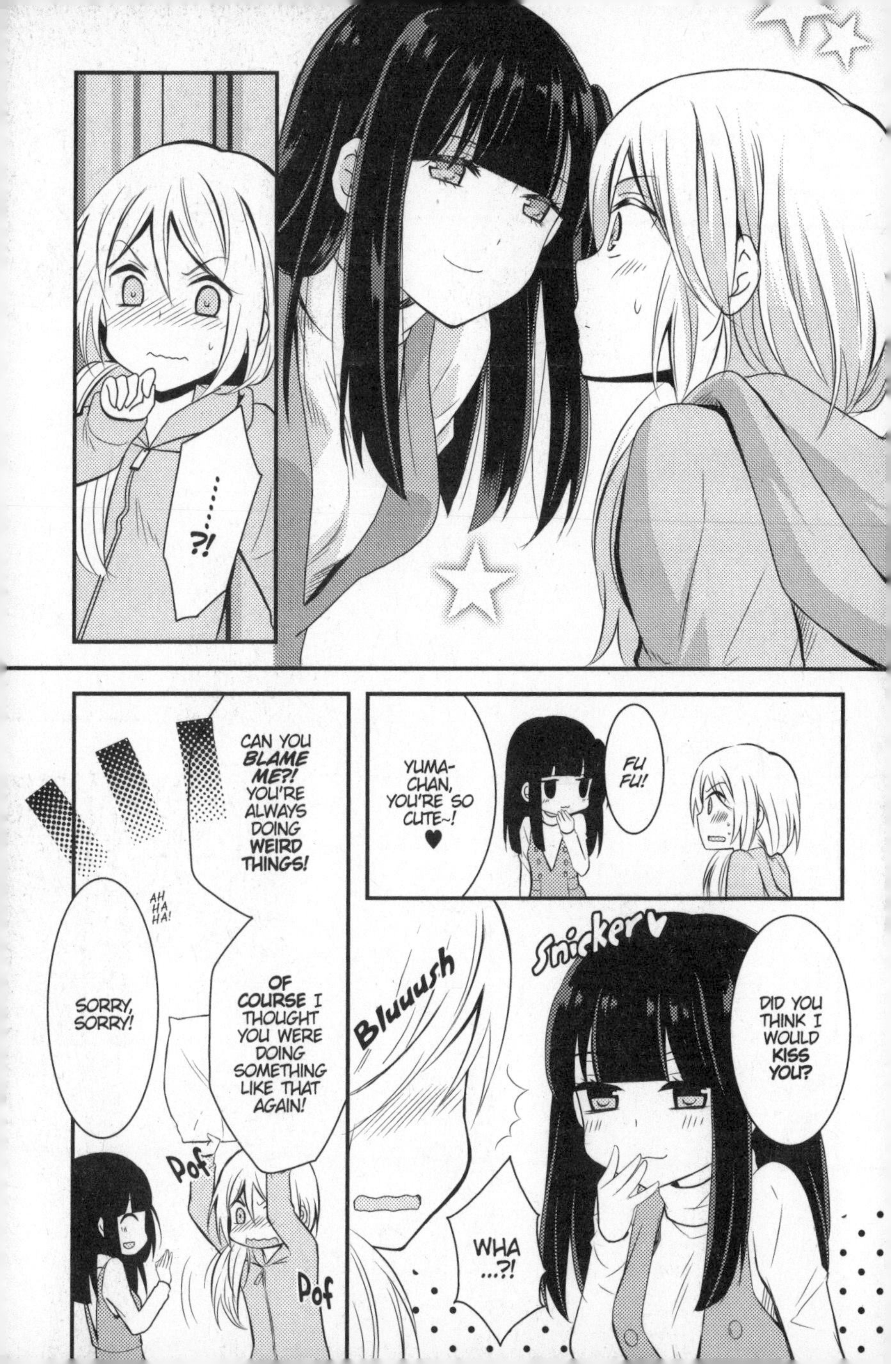
?!......
FU FU!
YUMA-CHAN, YOU'RE SO CUTE~! ♥
Snicker♥
DID YOU THINK I WOULD KISS YOU?
Bluuush
WHA ...?!
CAN YOU BLAME ME?! YOU'RE ALWAYS DOING WEIRD THINGS!
OF COURSE I THOUGHT YOU WERE DOING SOMETHING LIKE THAT AGAIN!
AH HA HA!
SORRY, SORRY!
Pof
Pof

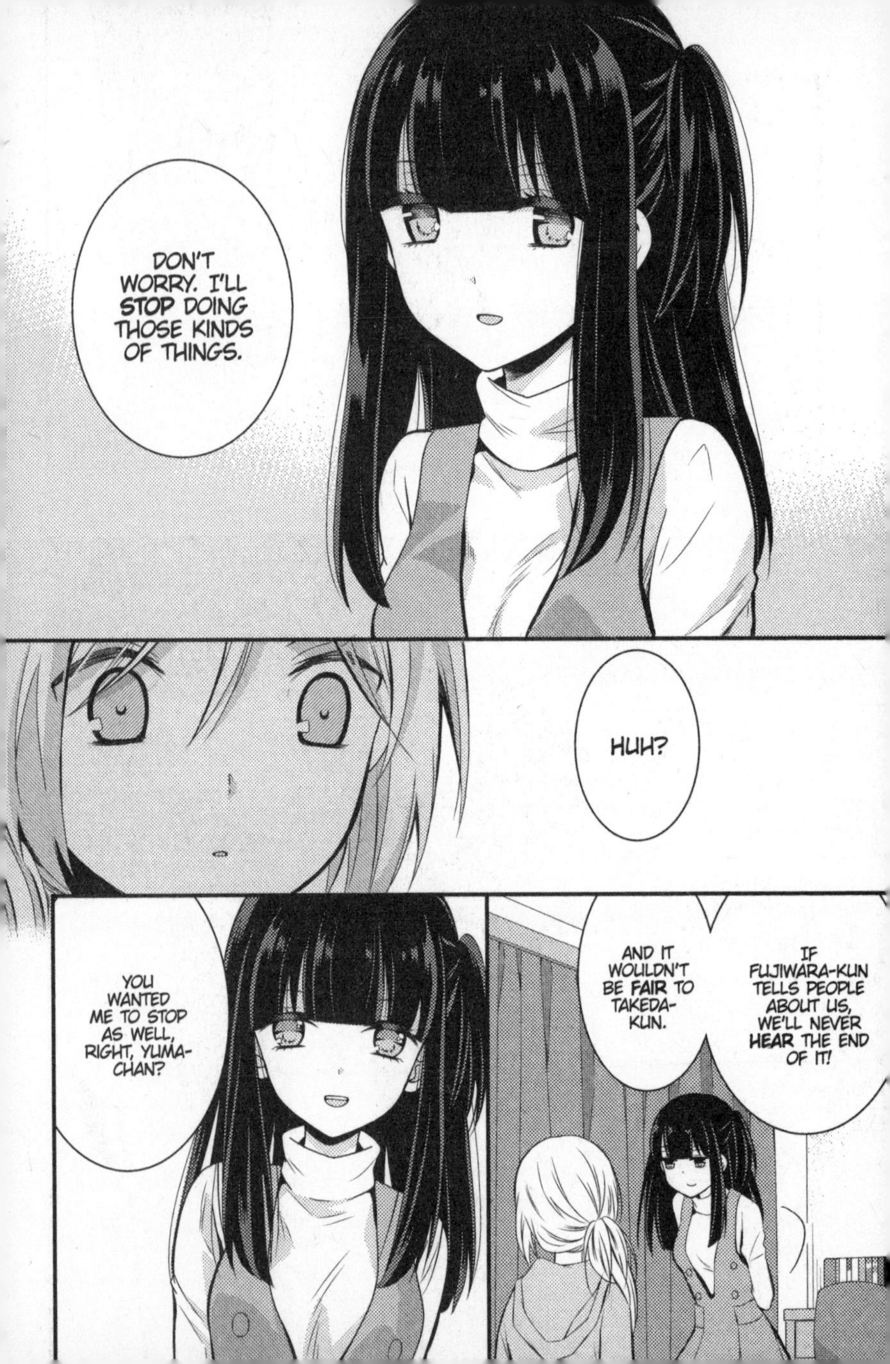
DON'T WORRY. I'LL STOP DOING THOSE KINDS OF THINGS.
HUH?
IF FUJIWARA-KUN TELLS PEOPLE ABOUT US, WE'LL NEVER HEAR THE END OF IT!
AND IT WOULDN'T BE FAIR TO TAKEDA-KUN.
YOU WANTED ME TO STOP AS WELL, RIGHT, YUMA-CHAN?

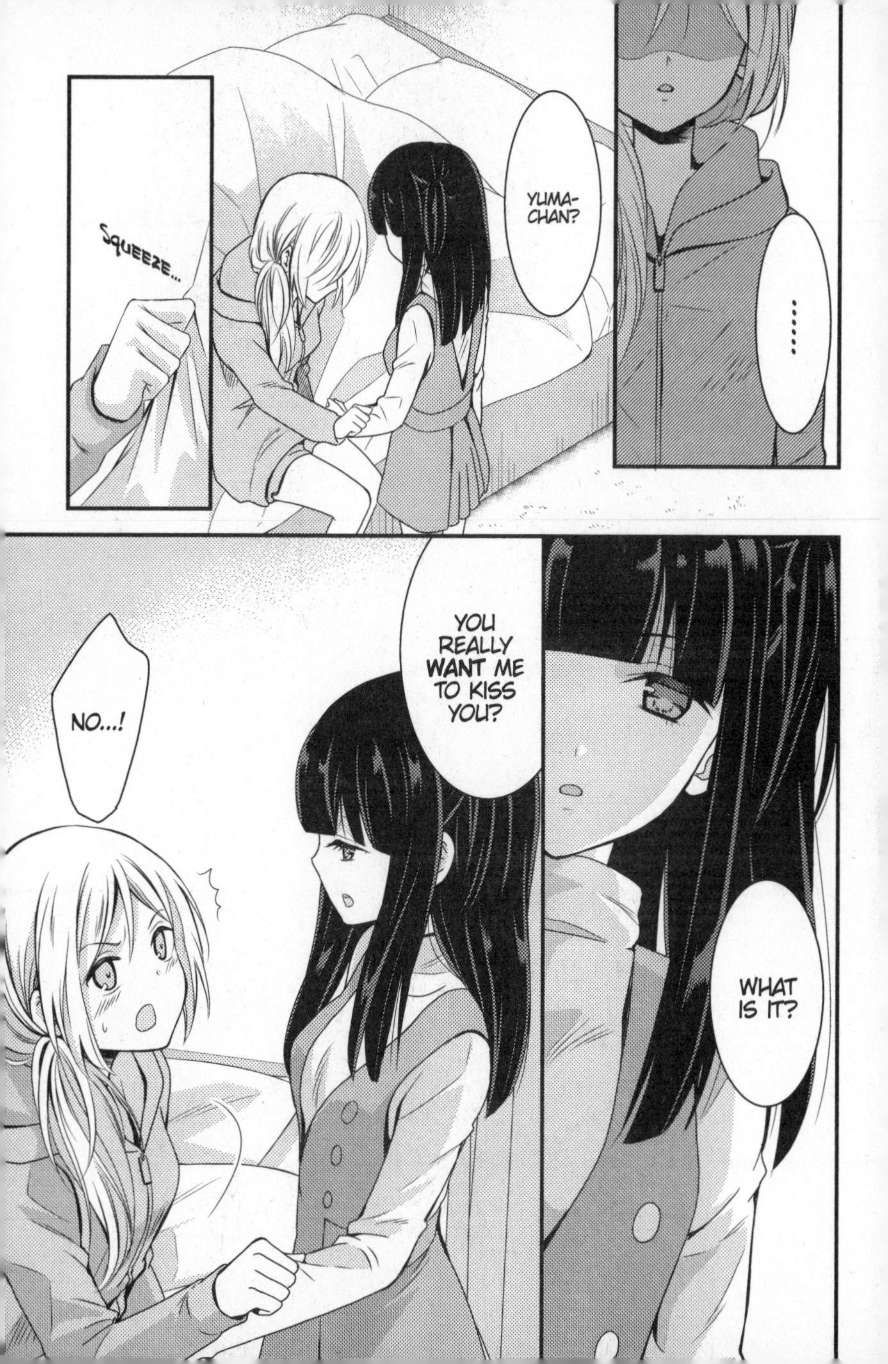
YUMA-CHAN?
......
SQUEEZE...
WHAT IS IT?
YOU REALLY WANT ME TO KISS YOU?
NO...!

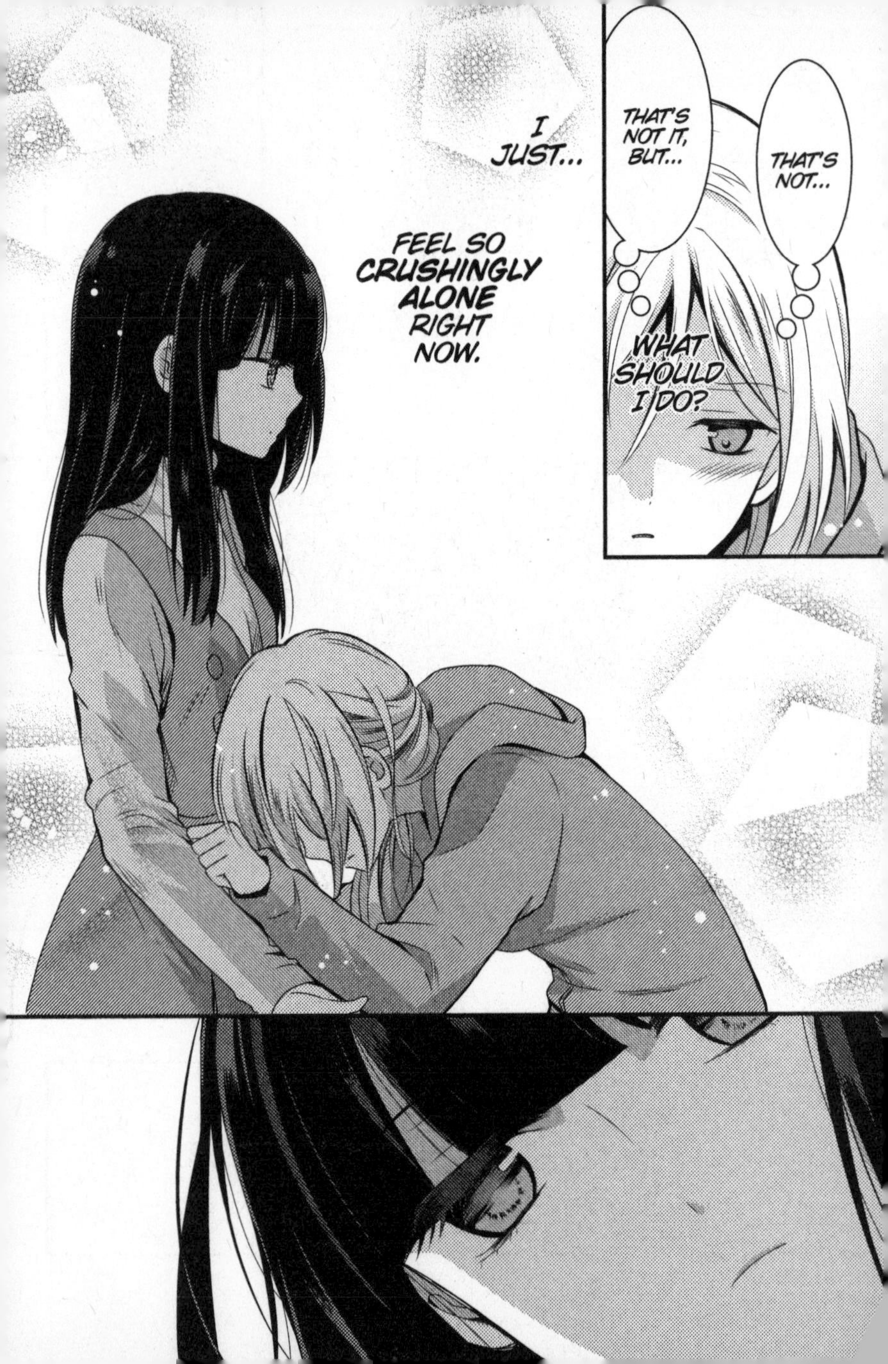
THAT'S NOT...
THAT'S NOT IT, BUT...
WHAT SHOULD I DO?
I JUST...
FEEL SO CRUSHINGLY ALONE RIGHT NOW.

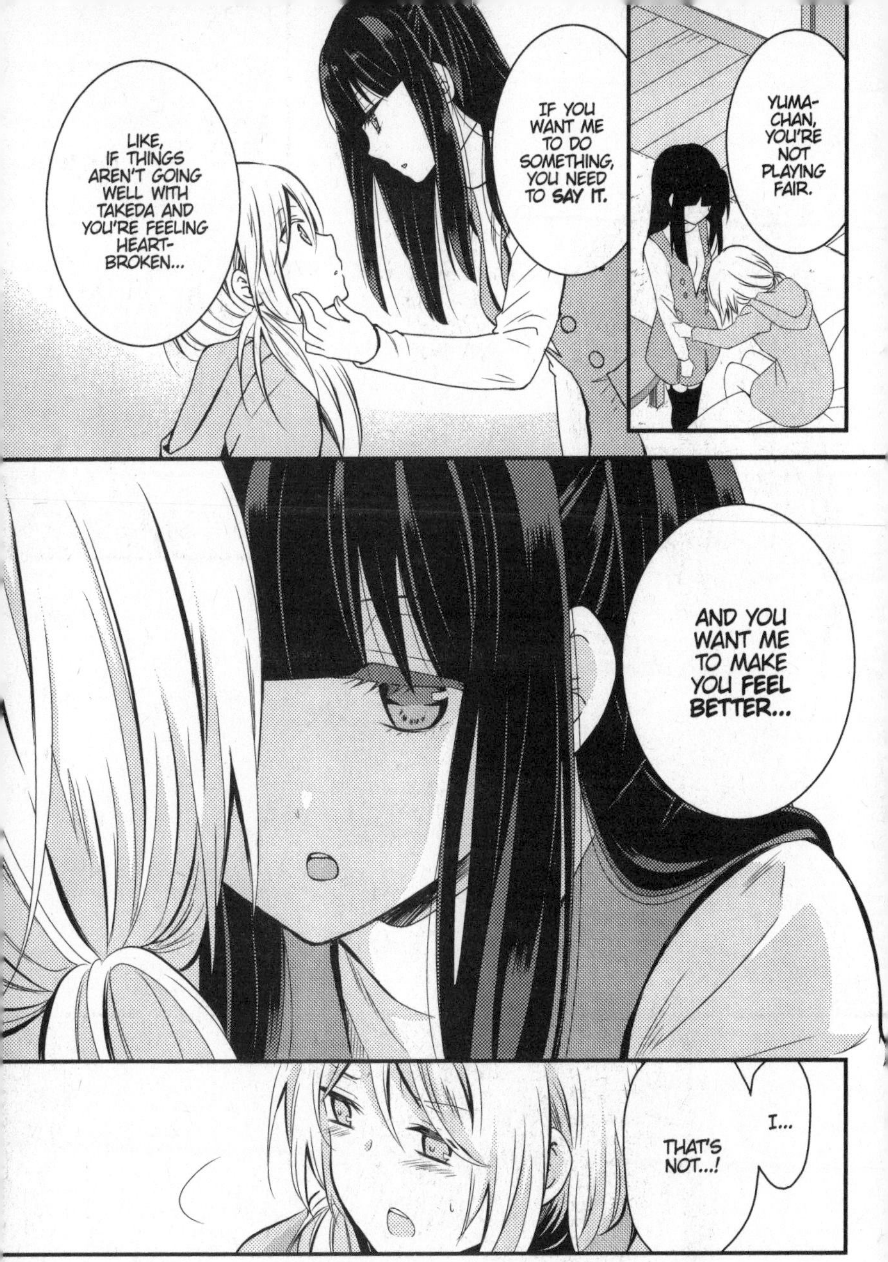
YUMA-CHAN, YOU'RE NOT PLAYING FAIR.
IF YOU WANT ME TO DO SOMETHING, YOU NEED TO **SAY IT.**
LIKE, IF THINGS AREN'T GOING WELL WITH TAKEDA AND YOU'RE FEELING HEART-BROKEN...
AND YOU WANT ME TO MAKE YOU **FEEL BETTER...**
I...
THAT'S NOT...!

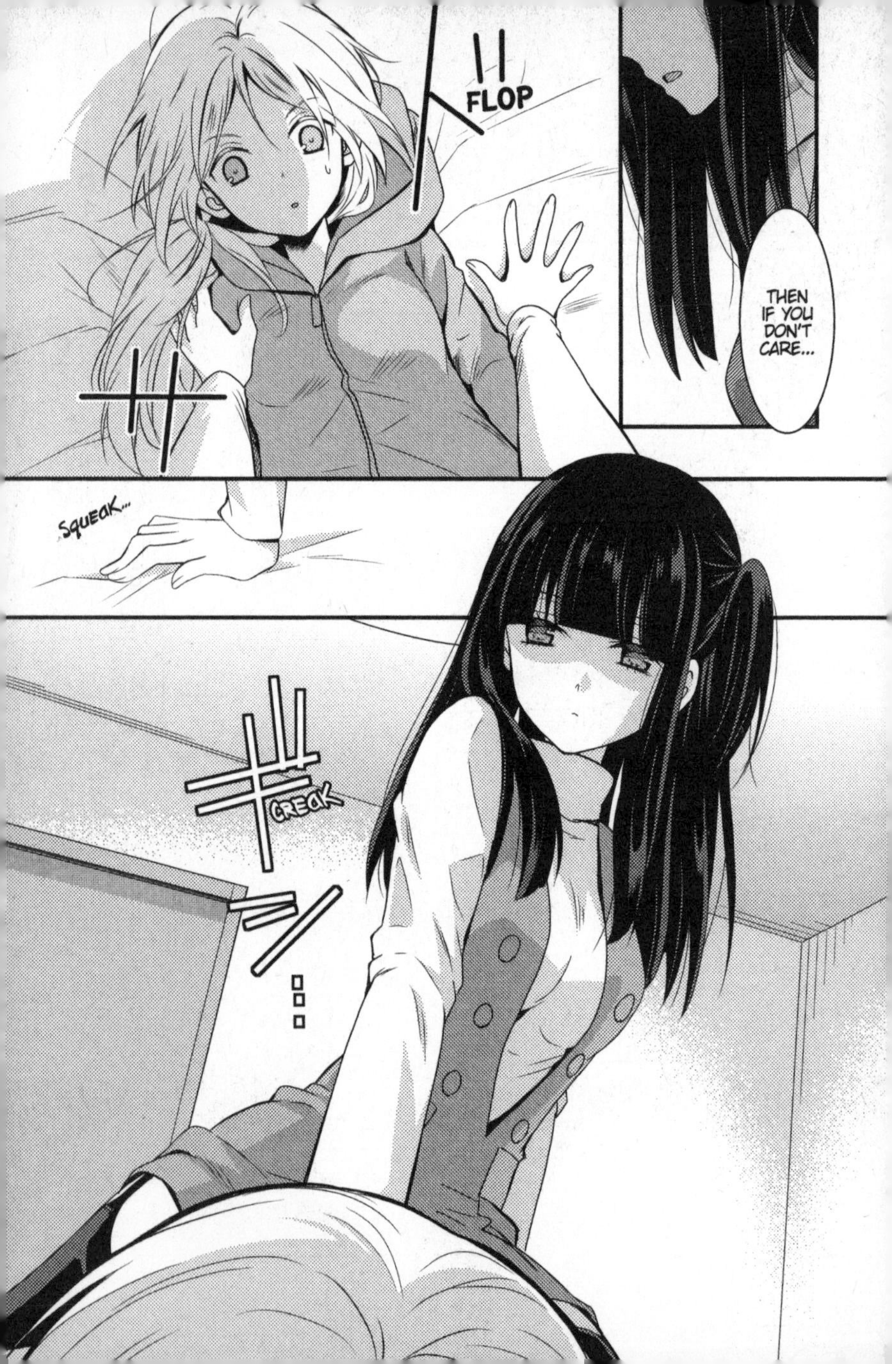
THEN IF YOU DON'T CARE...
FLOP
Squeak...
CREAK
...

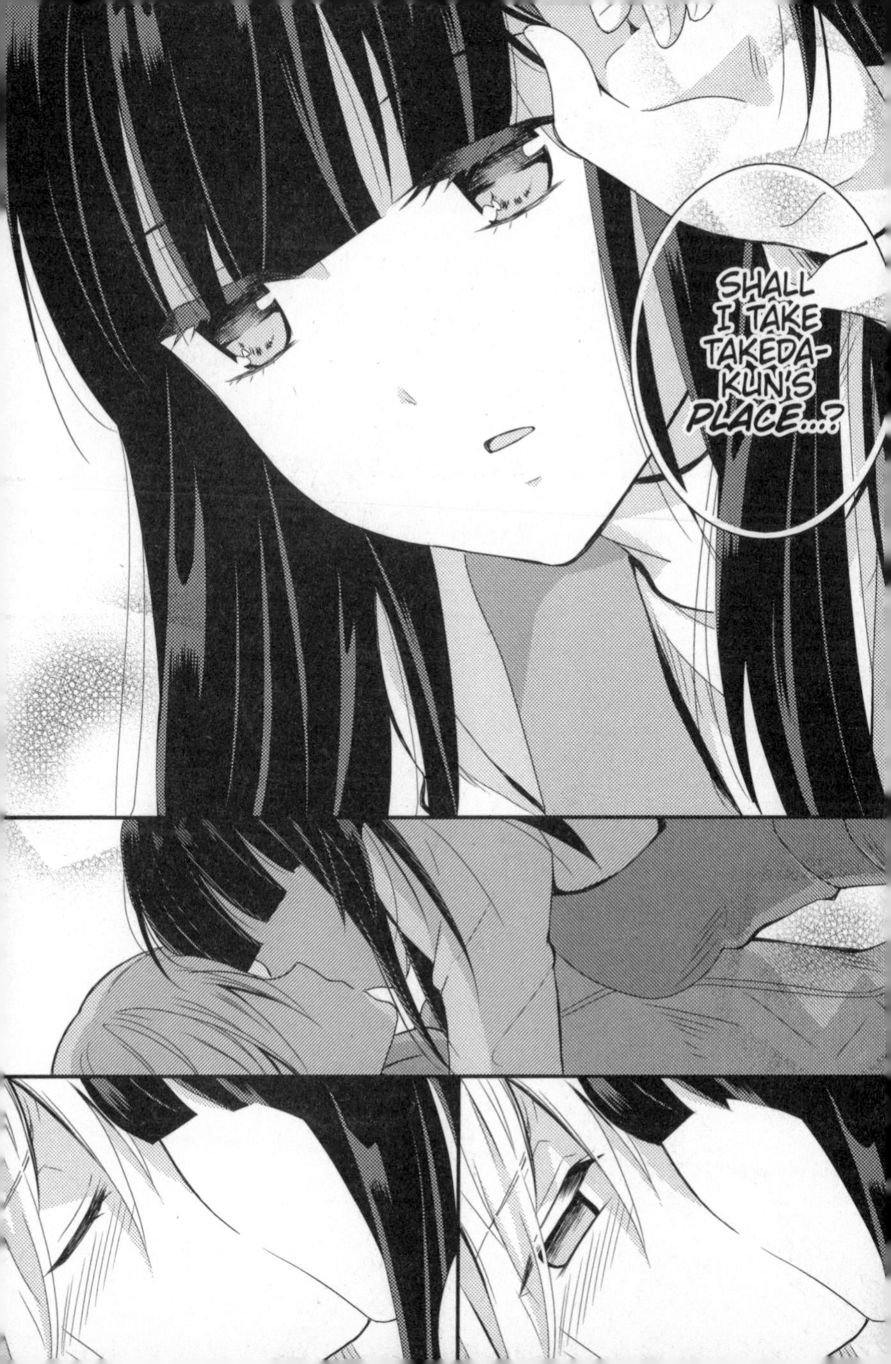
SHALL I TAKE TAKEDA-KUN'S PLACE...?

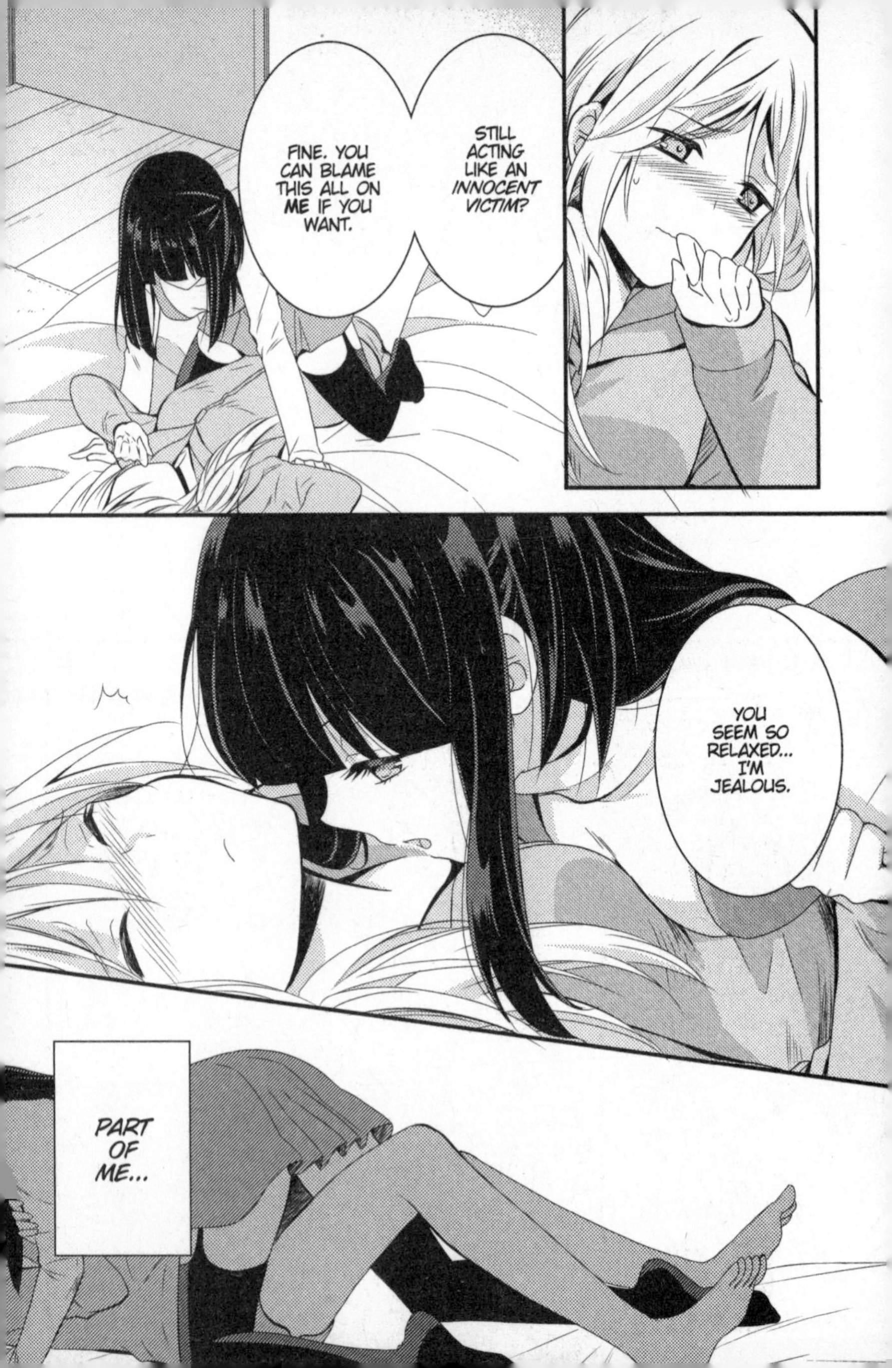
STILL ACTING LIKE AN *INNOCENT* VICTIM?
FINE. YOU CAN BLAME THIS ALL ON ME IF YOU WANT.
YOU SEEM SO RELAXED... I'M JEALOUS.
PART OF ME...

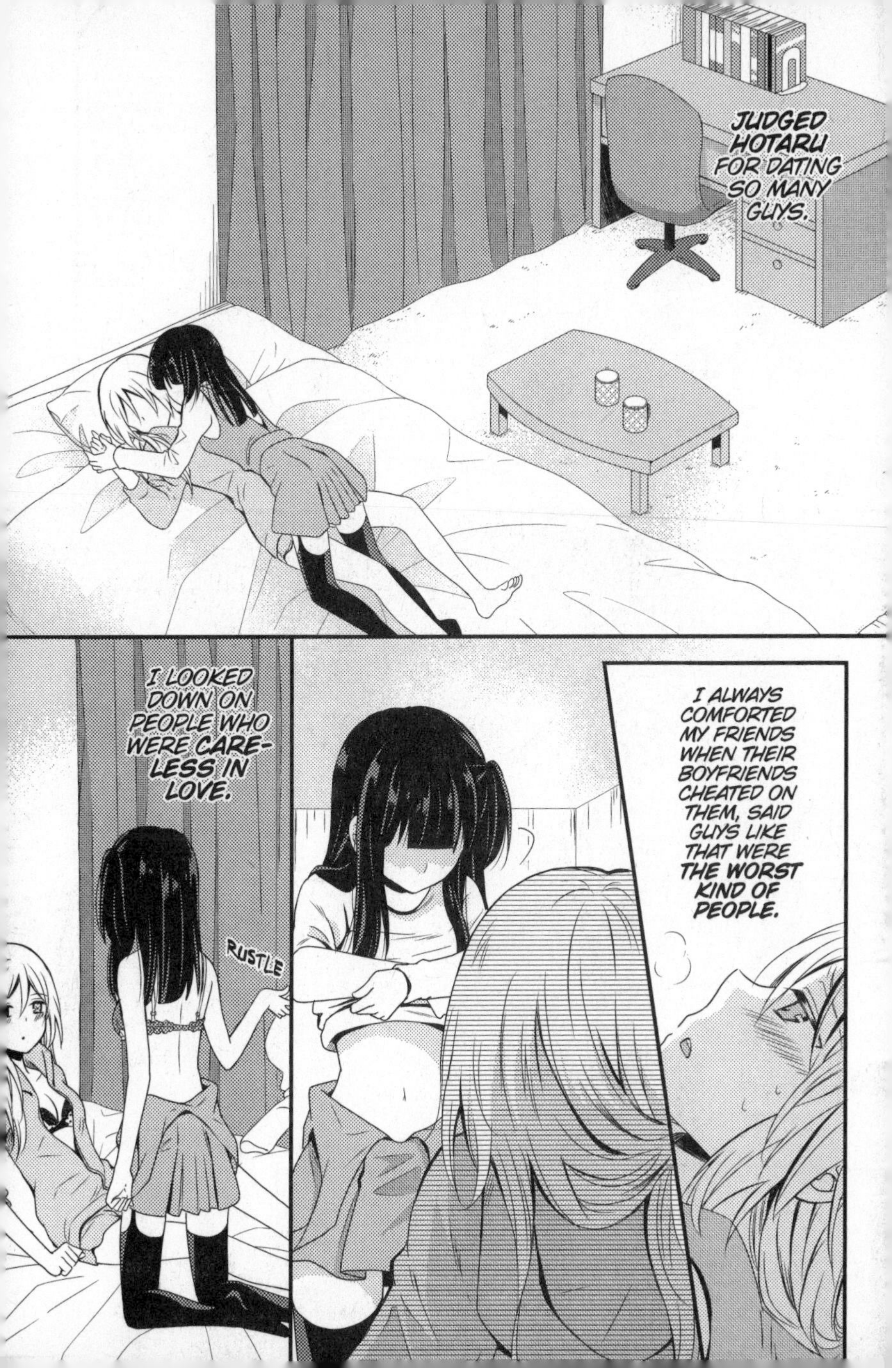
JUDGED HOTARU FOR DATING SO MANY GUYS.
I ALWAYS COMFORTED MY FRIENDS WHEN THEIR BOYFRIENDS CHEATED ON THEM, SAID GUYS LIKE THAT WERE THE WORST KIND OF PEOPLE.
I LOOKED DOWN ON PEOPLE WHO WERE CARELESS IN LOVE.
RUSTLE

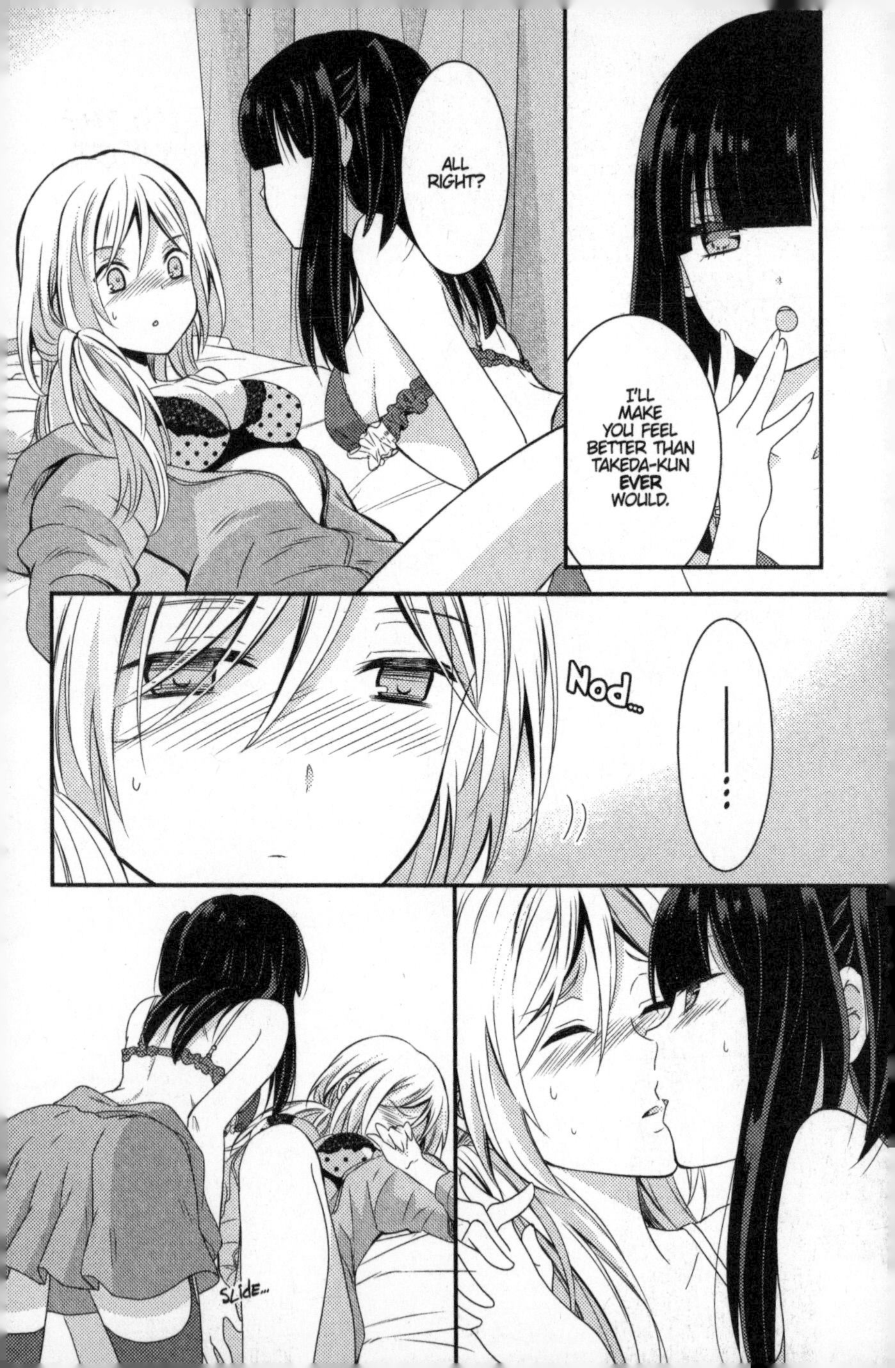

I'LL MAKE YOU FEEL BETTER THAN TAKEDA-KUN EVER WOULD.
ALL RIGHT?
―…
Nod...
SLIDE...

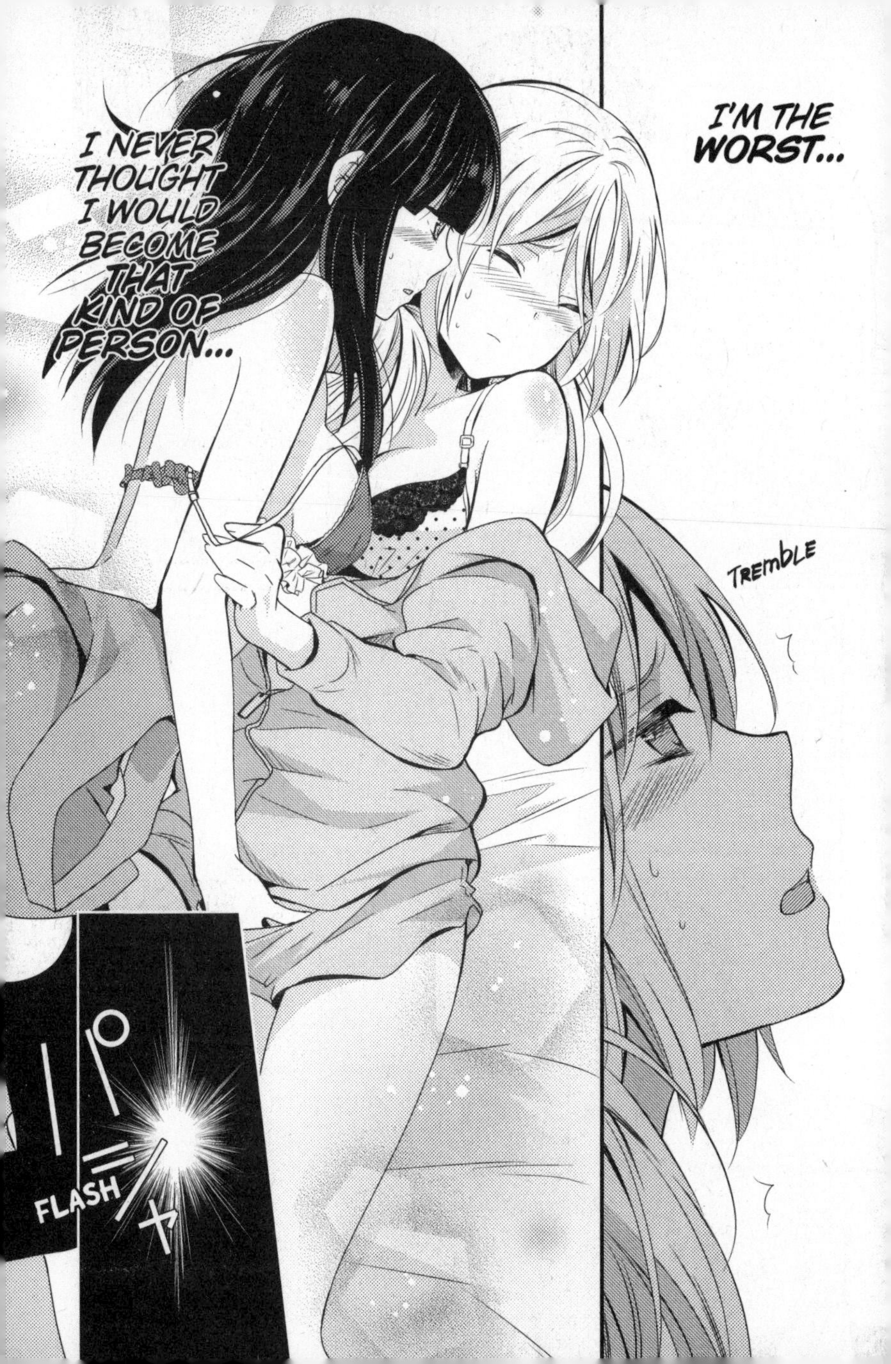
I'M THE WORST...
TREMBLE
I NEVER THOUGHT I WOULD BECOME THAT KIND OF PERSON...
FLASH

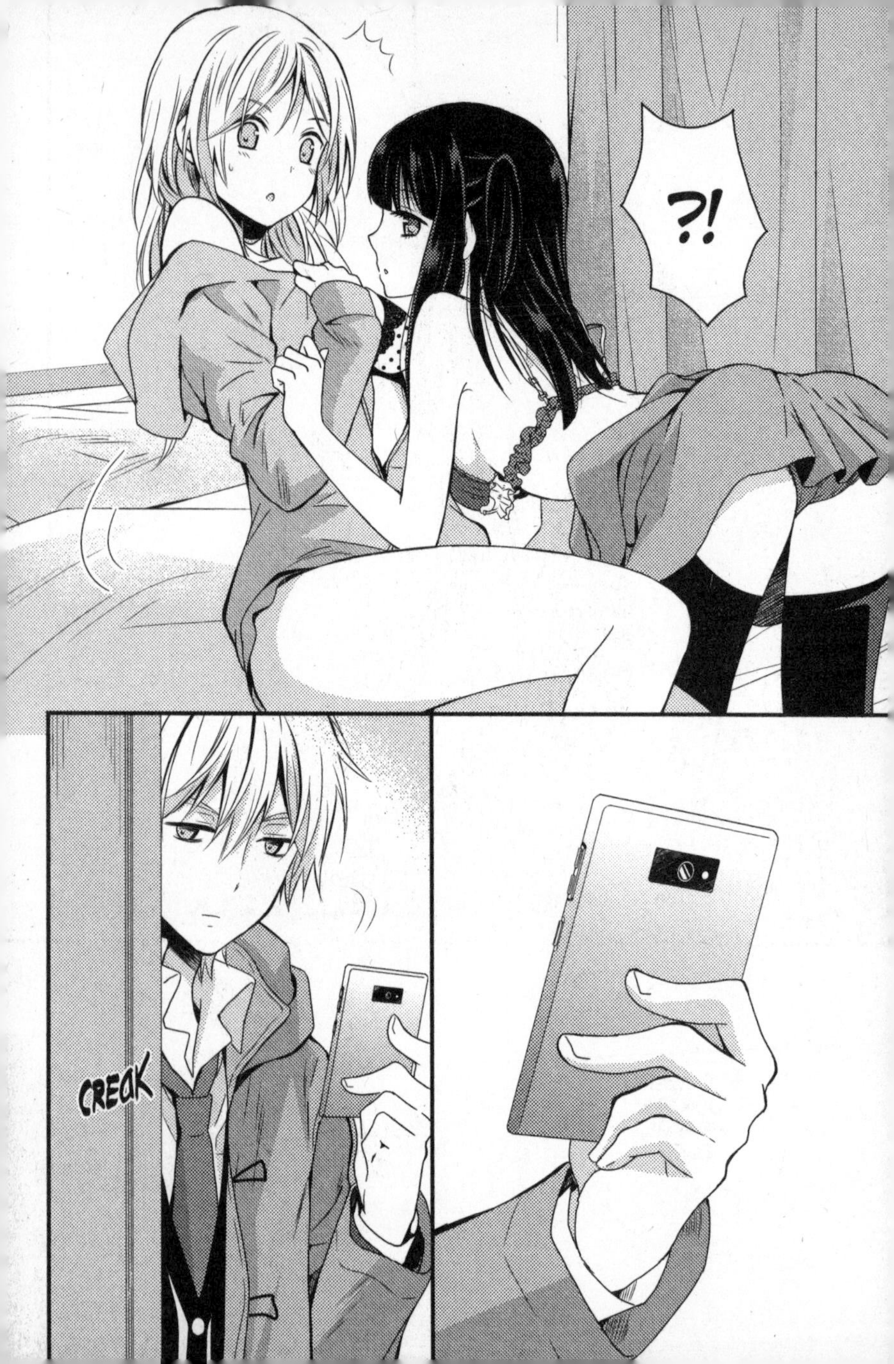
?!
CREAK

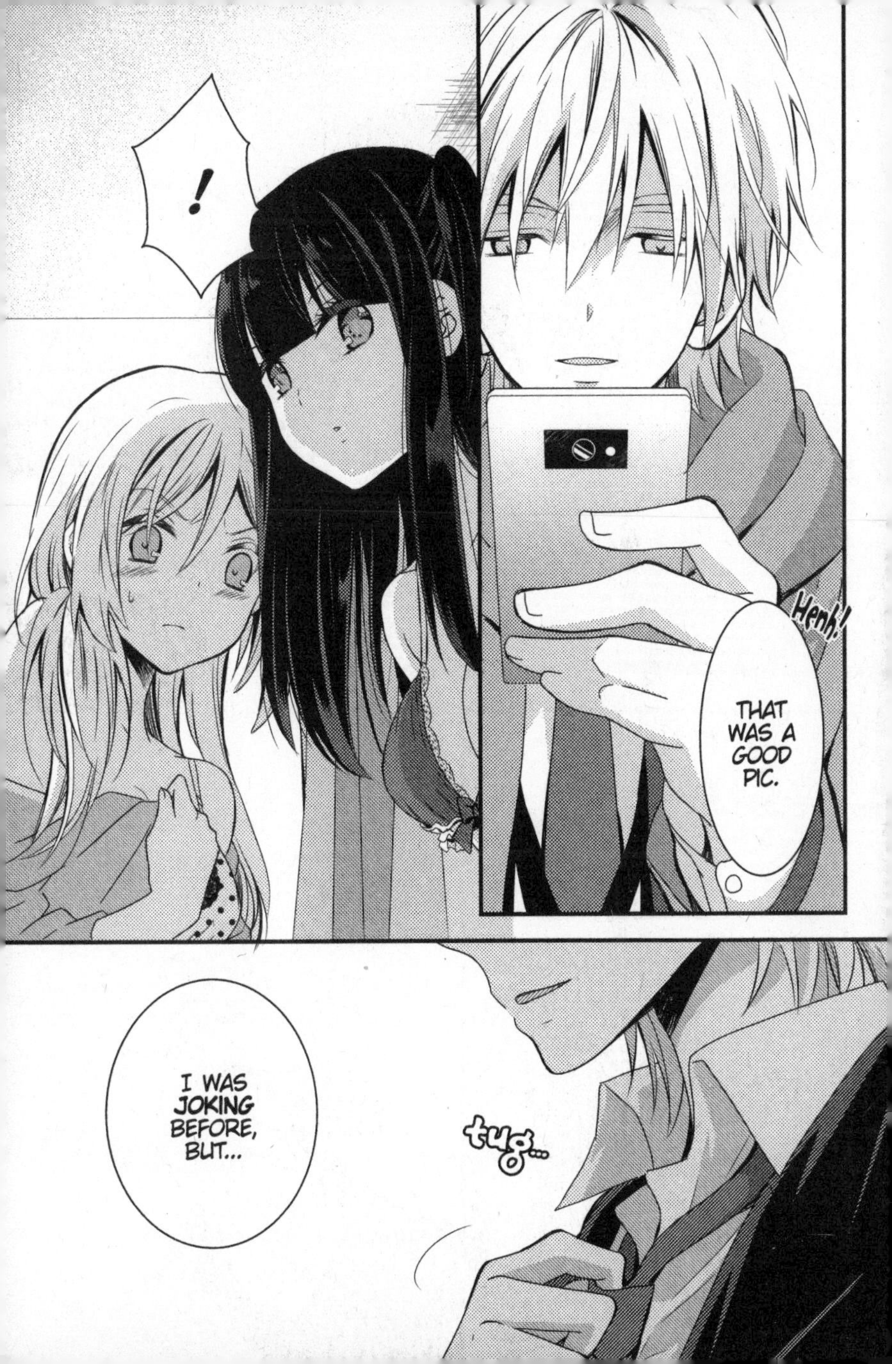
Henh!
THAT WAS A GOOD PIC.
!
I WAS JOKING BEFORE, BUT...
tug...

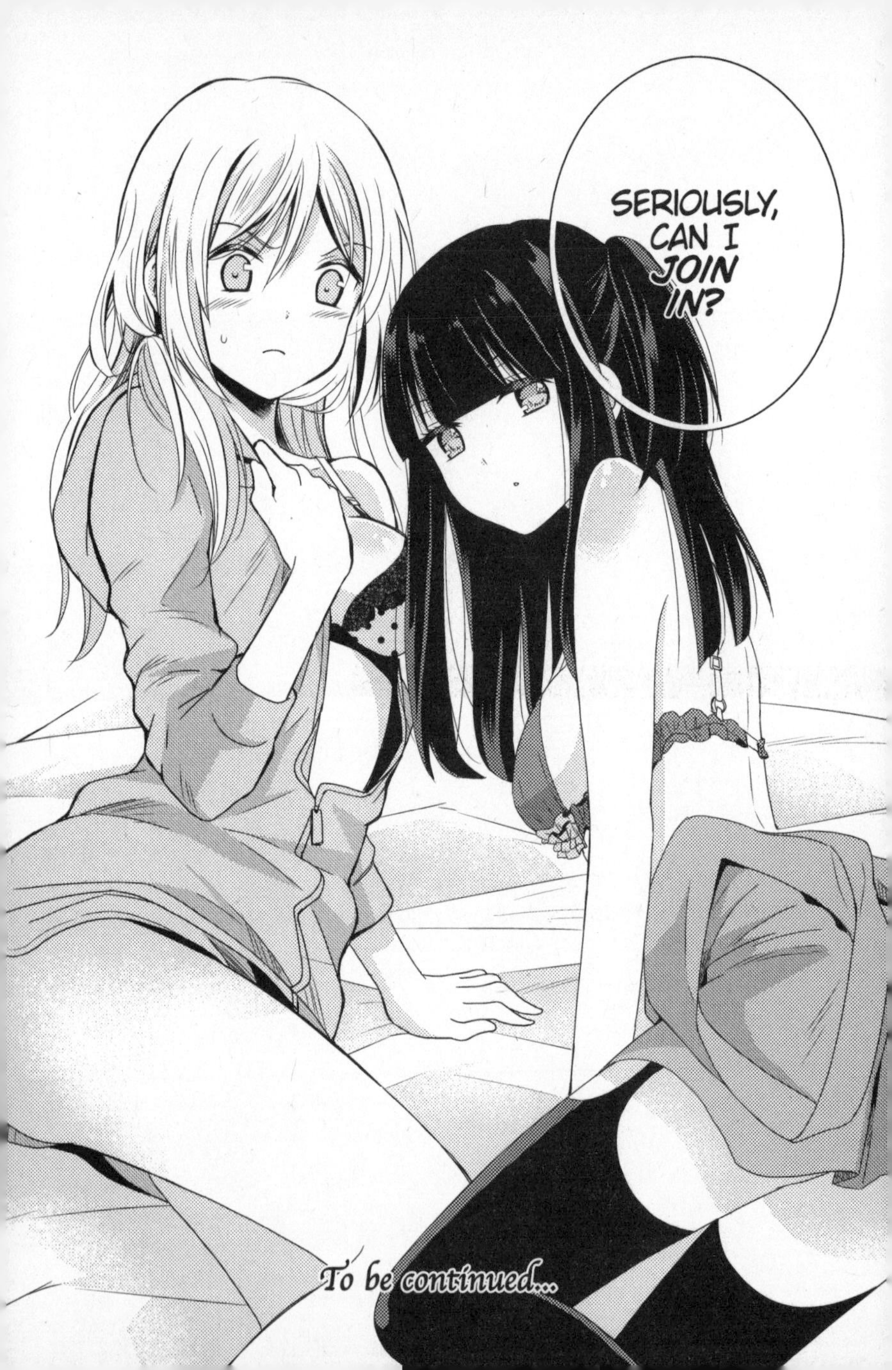
SERIOUSLY, CAN I JOIN IN?
To be continued...

NTR *Netsuzou Trap*

NTR
Netsuzou Trap

NTR★P *Netsuzou Trap* Parallel – Early Afternoon for the Wives

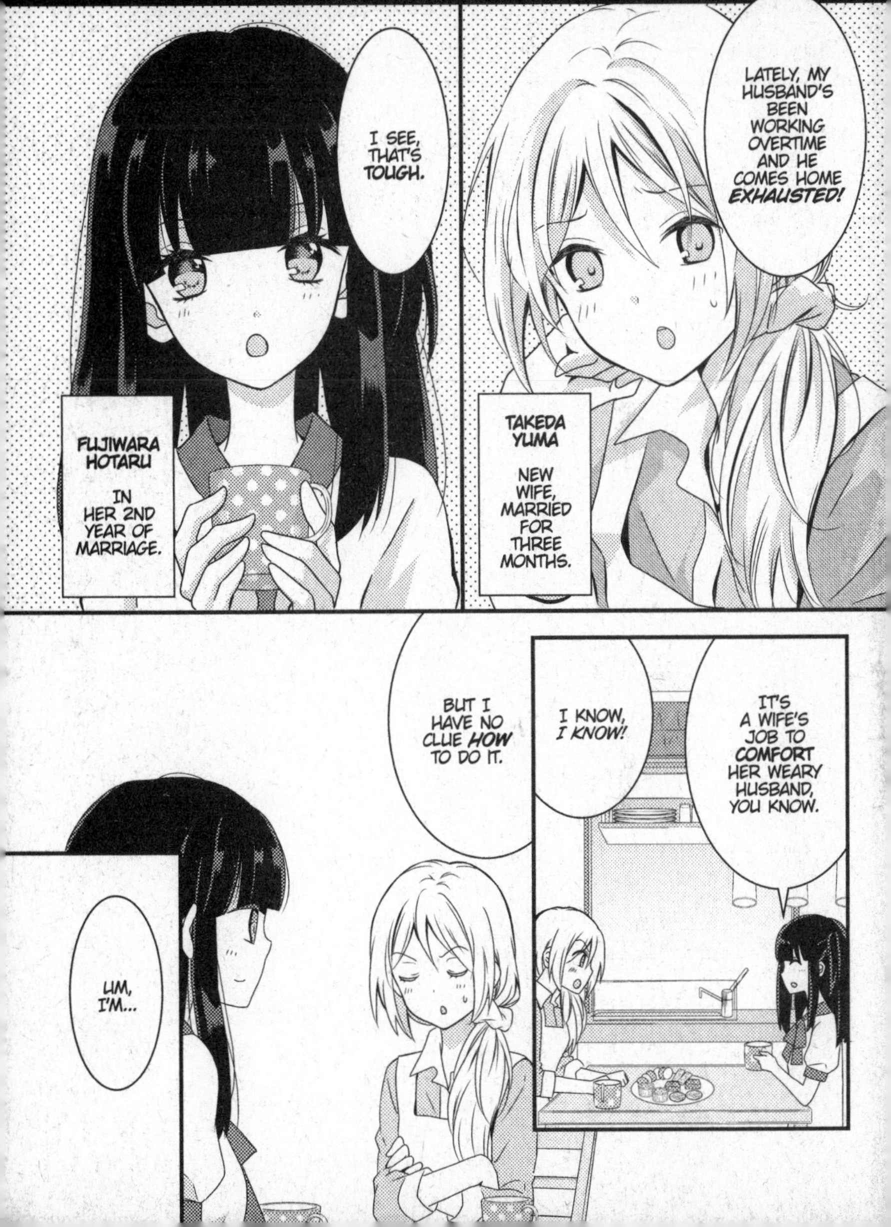
LATELY, MY HUSBAND'S BEEN WORKING OVERTIME AND HE COMES HOME **EXHAUSTED!**
TAKEDA YUMA
NEW WIFE, MARRIED FOR THREE MONTHS.
I SEE, THAT'S TOUGH.
FUJIWARA HOTARU
IN HER 2ND YEAR OF MARRIAGE.
IT'S A WIFE'S JOB TO **COMFORT** HER WEARY HUSBAND, YOU KNOW.
I KNOW, *I KNOW!*
BUT I HAVE NO CLUE ***HOW*** TO DO IT.
UM, I'M...

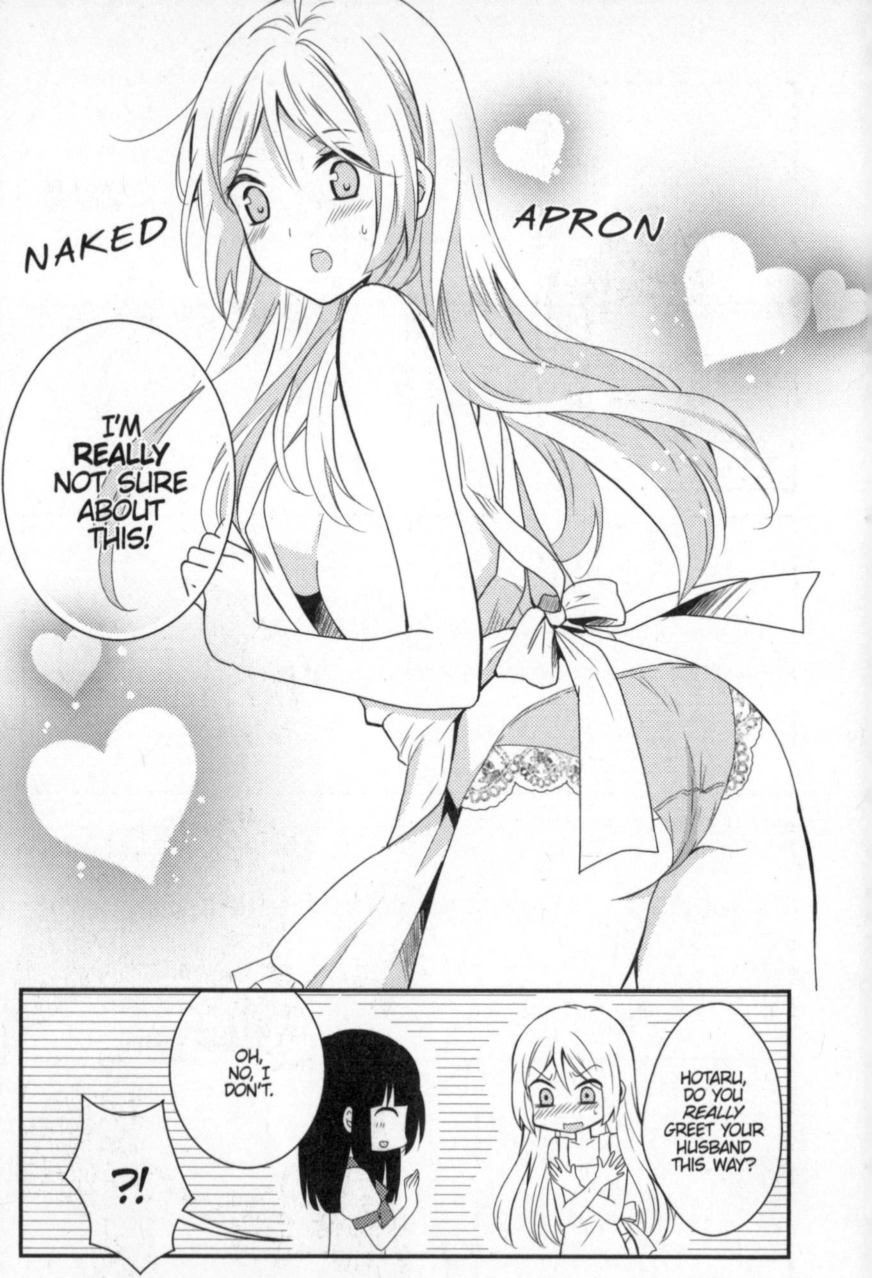
NAKED APRON
I'M REALLY NOT SURE ABOUT THIS!
HOTARU, DO YOU *REALLY* GREET YOUR HUSBAND THIS WAY?
OH, NO, I DON'T.
?!

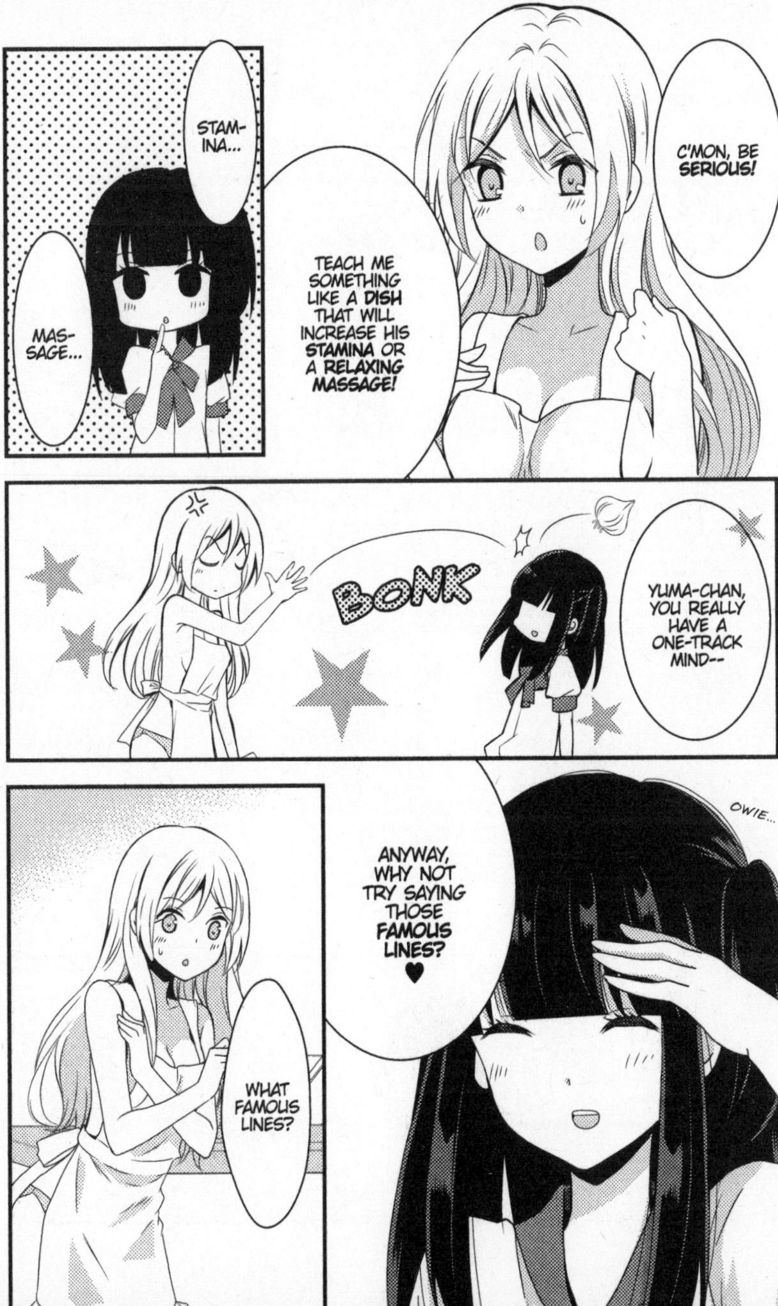
C'MON, BE SERIOUS!
TEACH ME SOMETHING LIKE A DISH THAT WILL INCREASE HIS STAMINA OR A RELAXING MASSAGE!
STAM-INA...
MAS-SAGE...
YUMA-CHAN, YOU REALLY HAVE A ONE-TRACK MIND--
BONK
OWIE...
ANYWAY, WHY NOT TRY SAYING THOSE FAMOUS LINES? ♥
WHAT FAMOUS LINES?

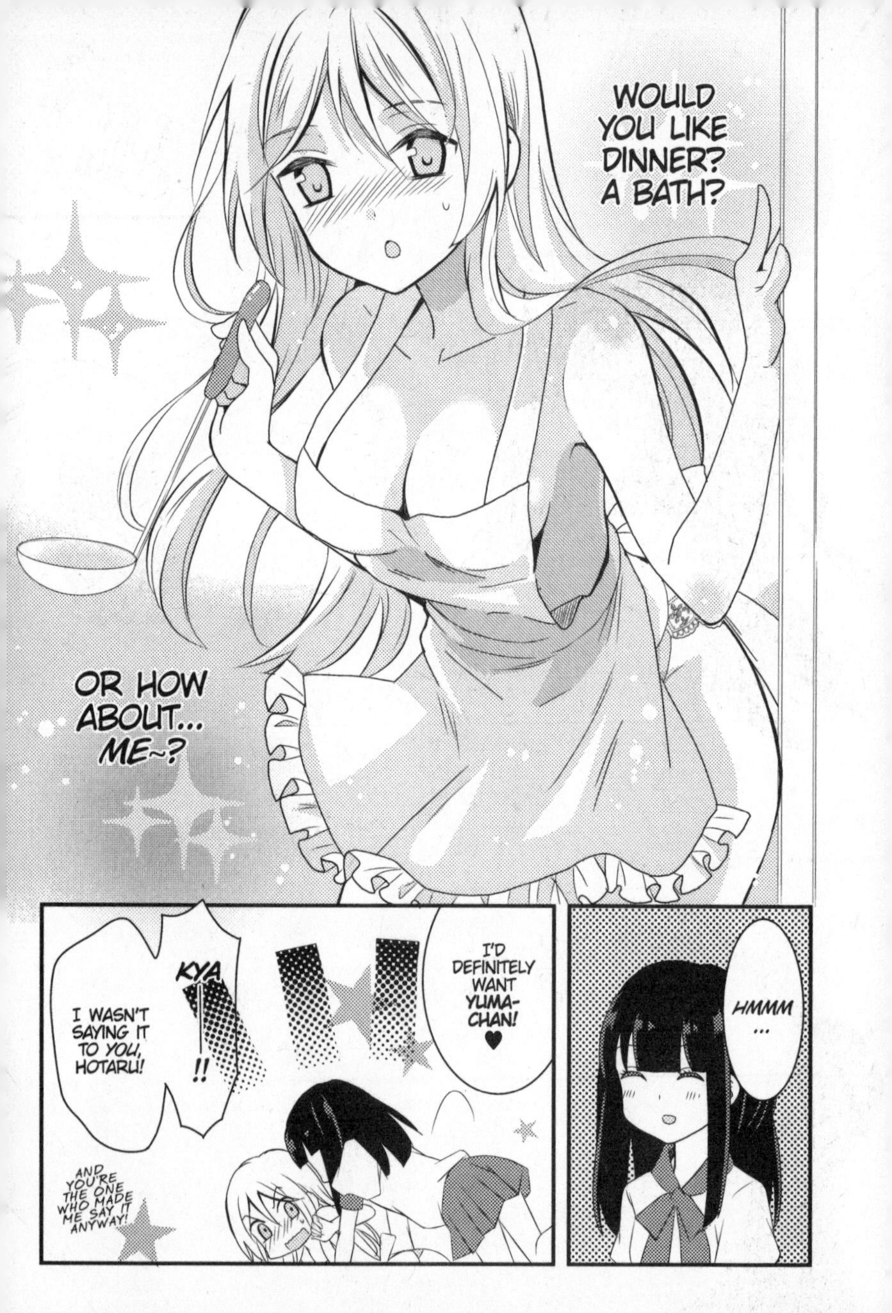
WOULD YOU LIKE DINNER? A BATH?
OR HOW ABOUT... ME~?
HMMM ...
I'D DEFINITELY WANT YUMA-CHAN! ♥
KYA !!
I WASN'T SAYING IT TO YOU, HOTARU!
AND YOU'RE THE ONE WHO MADE ME SAY IT ANYWAY!

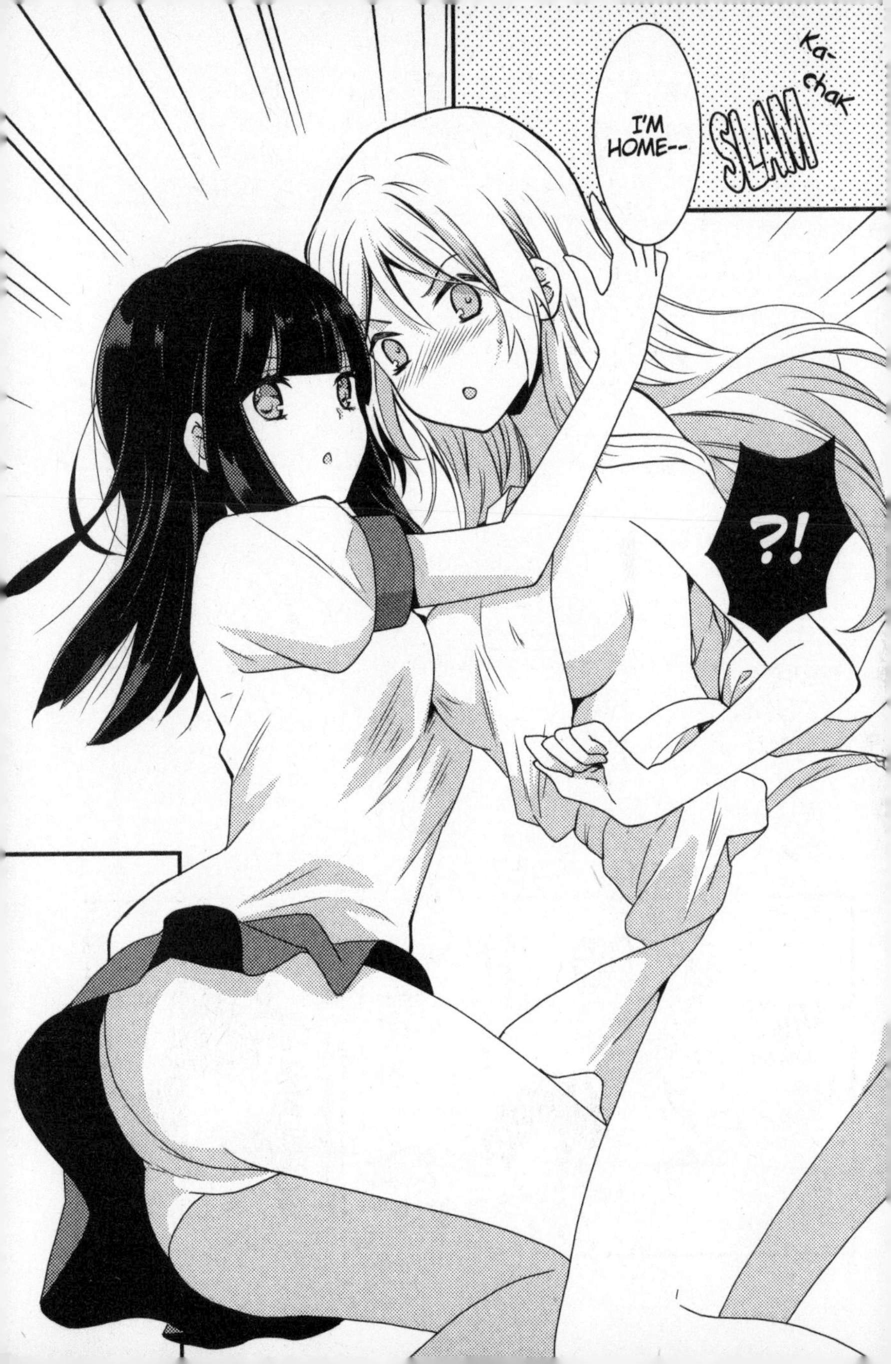
KA-CHAK
SLAM
I'M HOME--
?!

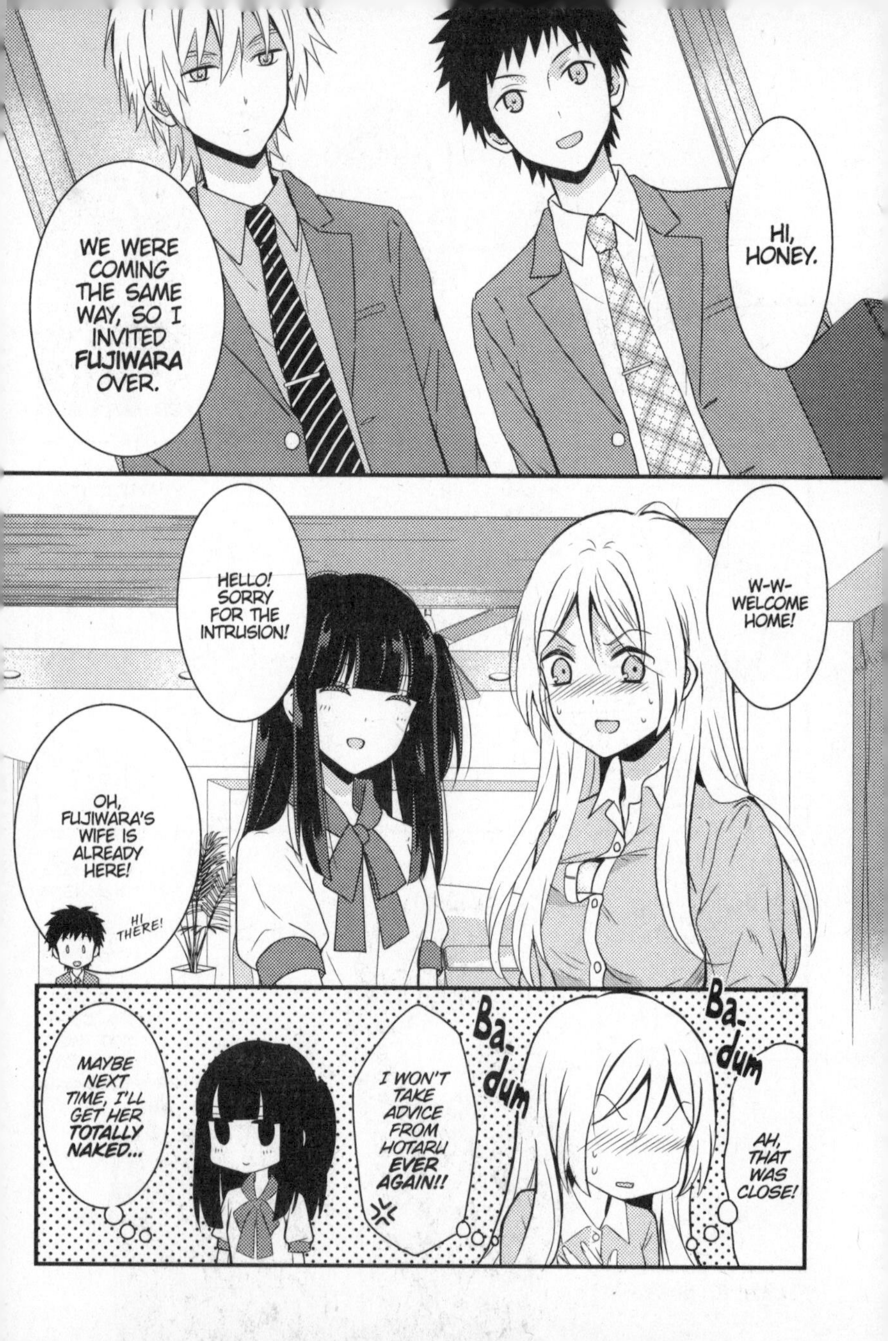
HI, HONEY.
WE WERE COMING THE SAME WAY, SO I INVITED FUJIWARA OVER.
W-W-WELCOME HOME!
HELLO! SORRY FOR THE INTRUSION!
OH, FUJIWARA'S WIFE IS ALREADY HERE!
HI THERE!
Ba-dum
Ba-dum
AH, THAT WAS CLOSE!
I WON'T TAKE ADVICE FROM HOTARU EVER AGAIN!!
MAYBE NEXT TIME, I'LL GET HER TOTALLY NAKED...

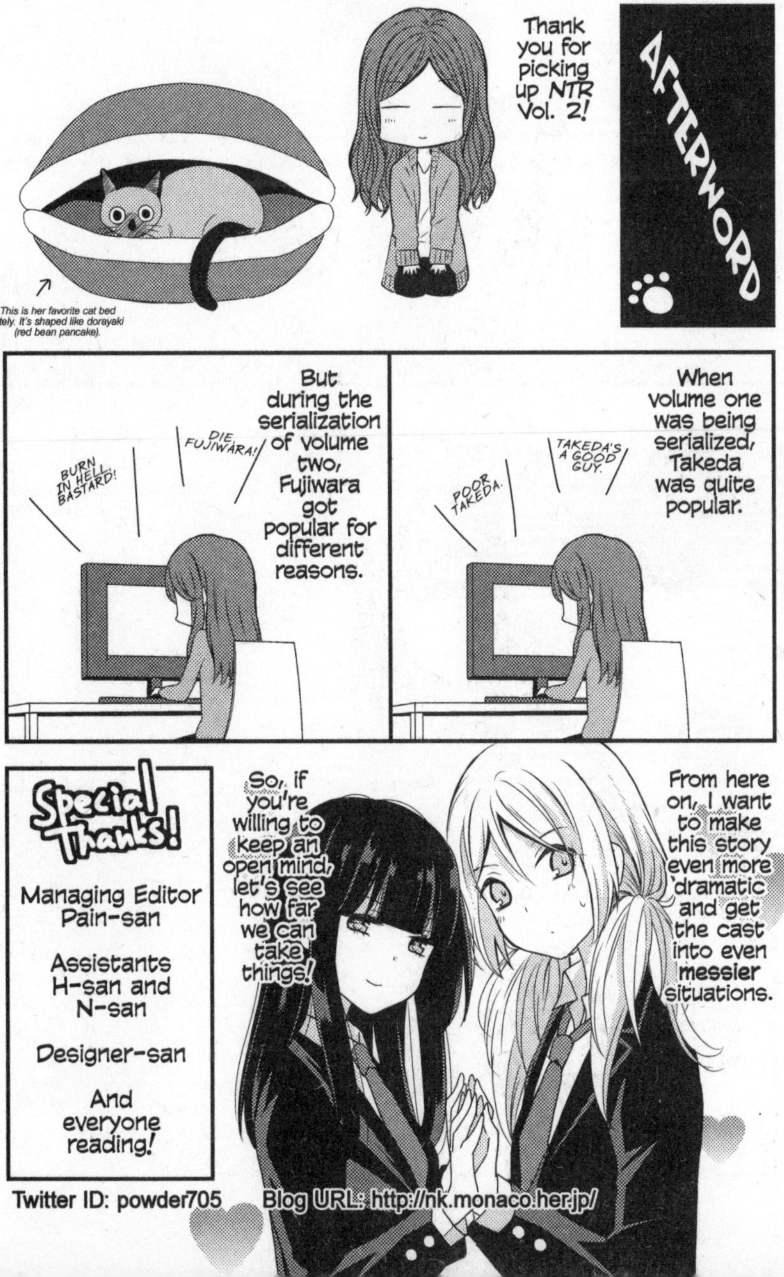
AFTERWORD
Thank you for picking up NTR Vol. 2!
This is her favorite cat bed lately. It's shaped like dorayaki (red bean pancake).
When volume one was being serialized, Takeda was quite popular.
TAKEDA'S A GOOD GUY.
POOR TAKEDA.
But during the serialization of volume two, Fujiwara got popular for different reasons.
DIE, FUJIWARA!
BURN IN HELL, BASTARD!
From here on, I want to make this story even more dramatic and get the cast into even messier situations.
So, if you're willing to keep an open mind, let's see how far we can take things!
Special Thanks!
Managing Editor Pain-san
Assistants H-san and N-san
Designer-san
And everyone reading!
Twitter ID: powder705
Blog URL: http://nk.monaco.her.jp/

SEVEN SEAS ENTERTAINMENT PRESENTS

NTR
Netsuzou Trap
vol.2

Feb 7

story and art by **KODAMA NAOKO**

TRANSLATION
Catherine Ross

ADAPTATION
Shannon Fay

LETTERING
CK Russell

LOGO DESIGN
KC Fabellon

COVER DESIGN
Nicky Lim

PROOFREADER
Shanti Whitesides

PRODUCTION MANAGER
Lissa Pattillo

EDITOR-IN-CHIEF
Adam Arnold

PUBLISHER
Jason DeAngelis

NTR - NETSUZOU TRAP VOL. 2

First published in Japan in 2016 by ICHIJINSHA Inc., Tokyo.
English translation rights arranged with ICHIJINSHA Inc., Tokyo, Japan.

Seven Seas books may be purchased in bulk for promotional, educational, or business use. Please contact your local bookseller or the Macmillan Corporate and Premium Sales Department at 1-800-221-7945, extension 5442, or by e-mail at MacmillanSpecialMarkets@macmillan.com.

ISBN: 978-1-626923-75-1

Printed in Canada

First Printing: December 2016

10 9 8 7 6 5 4 3 2 1

FOLLOW US ONLINE: ***www.gomanga.com***

READING DIRECTIONS

This book reads from ***right to left***, Japanese style. If this is your first time reading manga, you start reading from the top right panel on each page and take it from there. If you get lost, just follow the numbered diagram here. It may seem backwards at first, but you'll get the hang of it! Have fun!!

1
2
3
4
5
6
7
8
9

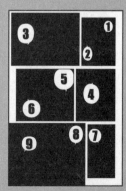